ONE LAST SCREAM

Special Agent Ricki James Thriller

Book 2

C.R. CHANDLER

Created with Vellum

For Mom and David. Thank you for being great beta readers, for all your help and suggestions, and mostly for your support. I appreciate it very much— and appreciate both of you!

Also By C.R. Chandler

SPECIAL AGENT RICKI JAMES

(Mystery/Thriller)

One Final Breath October 2020

One Last Scream January 2021

One Life Lost May 2021

Under the **Pen Name: Cat Chandler**

FOOD AND WINE CLUB MYSTERIES

(Cozy Mysteries)

A Special Blend of Murder 2017

Dinner, Drinks, and Murder 2017

A Burger, Fries, and Murder 2017

Champagne, Cupcakes, and Murder 2018

Tea, Dessert, and Murder 2018

Prologue

A soft rain fell on the deserted stretch of pavement, the broken white lines running down its center shimmering under the wet reflection from thin shafts of moonlight. Rain, gray light from overcast skies during the day, and pitch-black nights were a way of life on the upper peninsula of northwest Washington and its land that was home to miles of national forest. Running up its length was a highway, deserted most of the night during this time of the year, as it waited patiently for the tourists to return. But that was still a month off. Right now, when winter and spring overlapped into cool days and colder nights, the empty highway disappeared into a wall of darkness no matter which way you looked.

A lone figure stepped out of the trees and onto the dirt track leading off from the main road. His hands were buried in the pockets of his jacket and his shoulders were hunched against the cold. He looked at the highway, leading toward something he couldn't see in the dark, something just beyond his reach. Something he'd never get to, he thought bitterly. Not now. Not ever.

He was trapped by the forest on one side that ran for seventy-five miles before it was stopped by the Pacific Ocean.

The other side was just as unforgiving with the deep, cold waters of the Hood Canal. There was nowhere for him to go. If he ran, and somehow miraculously escaped capture, the forest would kill him. If he tried to swim away, he'd drown before he was halfway across the canal. No. The man he'd come to confront had trapped him with his smug smile and superior attitude. Trapped him here in this place where it all had come crashing down on both of them.

Resignation latched itself firmly on to his shoulders, weighing them down as he slowly walked back toward the trees where his truck was parked, where the man had been waiting for him to make up his mind.

"Fight or run, Jimmy," the man had said, the lazy sneer in his voice leaving no doubt which option he thought would win out. But Jimmy didn't run, although he had walked away. Eventually.

The man was still there, but he wasn't waiting for anything. Jimmy had given his answer, and now it was done.

When he finally found the courage to look up, the first thing Jimmy saw was the flashy sports car, its white paint and silver chrome gleaming even in the dark. The man had come from money. More money than he'd ever see in his lifetime.

The first bubble of anger rose in Jimmy's gut and began a slow march deep into his chest. It wasn't his fault he was poor. He'd never minded before, but now it was different. Now that man's money would be used to make sure his life was over. Anger swamped what was left of the crushing regret, and with it came clarity. He needed a way out. He had to find a way out. He deserved to keep everything he wanted, everything that was important to him.

His hands left the safety and warmth of their cocoon and hung down by his side, slowly curling into tight fists as he stared at that sports car. Through its window, he could see the jacket of a park ranger draped over the back of the seat. It was a symbol of authority, but he didn't care. It didn't make any difference. He turned his head and spat into the ground. He'd sure never owned any shirt made from silk, and his boots weren't ever polished to a high shine. But even though they were caked with a good inch of mud, he wasn't going to run.

Driven by a potent combination of anger and hope, he strode to the back of his truck and stood for a long moment, his breath coming in fast bursts. His jaw hardened as he bent over the body of the man who had pushed him past the limits of his temper. The man he had shot.

Jimmy slid his arms beneath the shoulders of the body lying on the ground, staring with sightless eyes up into the night sky. The once-pristine white shirt was now stained red. The blood still dripped out of the bullet hole, mixing with the rain falling from above and the mud on the ground.

Shedding the last of his remorse like a snake shed its skin, Jimmy shifted his hands to get a firmer grip on the body and slowly dragged it the rest of the way to his truck.

Chapter 1

"BE QUIET. We have to be quiet."

The short and stocky teenager added a wave of his hand to give more weight to his warning as he scanned the overgrown path in front of him. His face beamed a bright red as he leaned over and braced his hands against his knees, trying to catch his breath. Dragging a loaded-up wagon to the top of the hill was harder than it had looked.

He swiped a sleeve across his forehead to keep the beads of perspiration from dripping down into his eyes before taking a firmer grip on the rope pulled tight over his shoulder. His taller, leaner companion, who was holding on to an identical rope attached to the other side of the wagon, glanced over and laughed.

"Why, Anson? Who's going to hear us? There's nothing around except that old lighthouse, and no one's been inside it in, like . . ." The lanky boy paused for a brief moment and scrunched his face up as he thought it over. "Well, like forever."

"Forever is a long time, Nate." The third member of their small band was stationed at the back of the wagon. His job was to push from behind, lift the wagon and its forty-pound cargo over any protruding rocks that brought their slow progress to a jarring stop, and keep the carefully wrapped contraption inside it steady.

The last thing any of them wanted was for the wagon to tip over, catapulting their joint creation down the hill, destroying months of hard work with every bounce it took. Their intricate robot, or "bot" as they usually called it, was not made to survive that kind of punishment.

Tall, with the solid build of a linebacker that he'd inherited from his former high school football star father, Eddie James had been assigned his job in the back because he'd been deemed their only chance to save the bot should disaster strike. Having celebrated his fourteenth birthday just two days before, he was the youngest in the group. Both Anson and Nate had already passed their fifteenth birthdays, with Nate frequently exercising the bragging rights that came from obtaining an instruction permit to drive. Eddie didn't mind. It was a milestone in a guy's life, so he figured Nate was entitled to wave it around every opportunity he got.

Eddie cast a quick look to the side of the narrow path to be sure they weren't too close to the edge as his friends began pulling on the ropes again, both of them grunting as the trio slowly wound their way up the hill. The drop-off was steep. If their precious cargo took a tumble that would mean the end of the bot, not to mention inflicting serious injury on the guy unlucky enough to follow it down the slope.

Which would most likely be him. He didn't welcome the prospect of being plastered against one of the trees or tall boulders standing between the narrow path and the small town below.

The early-afternoon sun filtered through the forest, and for once the air was clear without a rain cloud in sight. Unusual for June, especially in the northwest corner of the state of Washington. The regular showers fed the only rain forest within five thousand miles. Olympic National Park, with its rugged mountain range and unique ecosystem, was sprawled across the upper peninsula cut off from the main body of the state by a tangled set of canals, bays, and inlets. Hood Canal flanked the eastern border of the park, slicing its way through the land and gradually narrowing from four miles at its widest point to one mile at its northern tip, where it settled into Dabob Bay.

The calm, attractive bay drew tourists and fishermen from late spring into the fall. They came to try their luck at catching salmon or trout, and to enjoy the beauty of the primitive forest surrounding the entire length of this spectacular piece of nature's paradise. The three towns of Brewer, Edington, and Massey hugged the shores sandwiched between the waters of the bay and the national park. Most of the residents made their living from the thousands who flocked to the park during the sunny months. During the winter, the year-round inhabitants were left in peace to enjoy the majestic scenery surrounding them—along with the cold, snow, and rain that fell in a continual drizzle.

Massey was the northernmost of the three towns, and the smallest, with a population of just over four hundred permanent residents. It swelled to twice that number on summer weekends as the refugees from the much larger city of Seattle fled to their vacation homes that dotted the shoreline all along the bay.

The rustic retreats were a far cry from the mansions that nestled gracefully in the Hamptons three thousand miles and a whole universe away and catered to the insanely rich. Dabob Bay was an everyman's place, where a cozy house was still affordable, if you weren't overly picky about the size and condition, and dock space for an open boat with an outboard motor could be had without needing to take out another mortgage in return.

The compact town was more comfortable thinking of itself as a village, and thrived mostly on tackle and bait shops, with an equal number of fast-food stands that were only open during the "good weather" months. All in all, there was a hearty, strangely appealing air about the small cluster of stores and eateries that hugged the gentle curve of the shoreline.

"How much farther?" Anson demanded, breathing heavily between each word. "I thought you said it wasn't that far."

Eddie looked away from his study of the town below and sent his friend a sympathetic look. Anson had crimson streaks running along his cheeks, and his shirt was covered in sweat.

"Obviously you hadn't factored in pulling a forty-pound robot up the hill," Nate chimed in. "And it's just around that next bend."

"Automated crawler," Eddie corrected. He glanced down at the blanket covering the round object with its long arms that were neatly folded into the sides. "That's how we entered it into the contest, so we need to get used to calling it that."

Over the last year, the threesome had forged a bond over their mutual love of designing and building all kinds of mechanical contraptions, especially remotely powered ones. So when the state science fair had announced the categories for several types of automated machines, they had immediately gone to work assembling their vision of a mechanical crawler designed to retrieve whatever was entered into its programming, from wherever it needed to retrieve it. Which, according to the rules of the category, had to include maneuvering up and down curved stairs.

The problem was that the three towns along the Bay had a combined population of 2,300, which meant most of the businesses were small, with a noticeable absence of any kind of structure that was more than one story tall, much less one with a curved set of stairs.

Of course, there was the St. Armand. It was the only resort hotel in the area and had a wide, curving staircase that led from the floor of its grand ballroom up to the surrounding balcony. But after thoroughly discussing it, the boys agreed that the powers that be at the St. Armand would not be keen on subjecting the impressive focal point of their expensive wedding venue to the maneuverings of forty-pound robot. Not to mention the high possibility of it taking a potentially damaging tumble down their set of very expensive stairs.

Which had left them stumped, until Nate had remembered the old lighthouse. It had occupied the hill overlooking Massey for as long as anyone could remember, and after a few discreet inquiries to their parents and a teacher or two, the teenagers had discovered that no one knew exactly who owned it, or even why it had been built at all for that matter. The far end of the bay didn't host any big ships or have a lot of dangerous shoals and rocks. But for whatever reason, the lighthouse had been standing sentry, unoccupied, for all of this century, and probably a good chunk of the last one as well. And it was very possible that no one had even stepped foot inside it in decades.

Until Nate had gone up there exploring two days ago.

"You're sure we can get in?" Anson asked.

"Yep." Nate pushed his wire-rimmed glasses farther up his nose. "There's an old lock on the door, but the boards on the windows in the back are really loose. I could probably pull them off with my bare hands. That's why I brought the hammer and the crate. The window's pretty big, so once we pry the boards off, we can stand on the crate and lift our crawler through it."

"If the lock is that old, we can use the hammer to break it off and just open the door. That way we won't have to lift the crawler at all," Anson pointed out. "We're already hauling it up there, and we'll have to carry it up the stairs, so why do any more work than we have to?"

Eddie frowned. He straightened up and pushed a thick strand of dark hair hanging over the top edge of his black-framed glasses to one side. "We can put the boards back when we're done, but we can't fix a broken lock. We don't want to damage anything."

Anson huffed out a long breath. "You're just saying that because your mom is a cop."

"Mom is a special investigative agent with the National Park Service," Eddie said. For some reason Anson always referred to his mom as if she worked for the local police department, when everyone in the Bay knew that Clay Thomas was the chief, and Jules was his deputy, and they were the only two people in the department. "She's not a cop."

"Same diff," Anson said. "She carries a gun and hunts down murderers."

"Not most of the time," Eddie muttered, but not loud enough that the other two could hear him over their labored breathing. He wished his mom only chased down guys who were trying to grow marijuana on park land or had destroyed park property in some way or another. But it never seemed to work out that way. Instead, she always ended up in the middle of something a lot more dangerous. Something like a serial killer operating inside the park. That was what had drawn her back into law enforcement after she'd sworn off it for more than a year. A year he hadn't had to worry every night about her making it home still breathing.

"I don't want to damage any property either," Nate declared, turning his head to grin at Eddie. "With our luck, the old lighthouse is sitting on park land and your mom will have to arrest us if we destroy anything."

"Yeah, that would be cool. She's a badass," Anson put in.

Before Eddie could decide if he should be defending his mom, Anson let out an excited yelp. "Hey! There it is."

Made of stone, with a wide wooden door, the old structure wasn't particularly large for a lighthouse, but it still stood a good thirty feet high, which meant it would have plenty of stairs to test the crawler out on. The window that Nate had found was on the far side, not visible from the path leading up to the abandoned lighthouse. Eddie's gaze tracked up the length of the building to the top, where sheets of plywood had taken the place of the glass that used to surround the powerful light that he assumed had disappeared long ago, along with anyone who used to take care of it.

The boys pushed and pulled the wagon, finally coming to a stop several feet from the old wooden door. Eddie was rolling his shoulders to work out the kinks from bending over all the way up the hill, when Anson startled him by letting out another yelp.

"Hey! I thought you said the door had a lock on it."

Nate adjusted his wire-rimmed glasses and took a step forward, leaning over to peer closer at the rusty latch hanging from the doorframe by a single corner. "There *was* a lock." He scuffed his feet in the dirt and looked down, swiveling his head from right to left until he bent at the knees and scooped up a brown piece of metal. "Here it is." He held it up so both his friends could see it. "Looks like it's been busted up. Or maybe it just fell off."

Eddie gazed at the mangled lock and then over at the broken latch. "I think someone's been here," he said slowly.

Nate shrugged and dropped the lock back to the ground. "Weird, huh?" He reached out and pushed against the old door. It let out a loud creak of protest as it swung inward, its slow momentum coming to a complete halt at the halfway point.

Anson quickly lifted a hand and covered his nose. "What's that smell?"

"I don't smell anything," Nate said.

"Well, I do." Anson's face scrunched up. "It stinks."

Eddie walked forward, catching a faint whiff of something that he didn't recognize but that did indeed stink. Lifting a hand to cover his mouth and nose, he took another tentative step, stopping in the middle of the doorway. "Probably some animal that found its way in and then couldn't get out."

Nate pursed his lips and gave a sage nod of his head. "Then it probably leaned against the door and broke the lock off. It was already rusted through, so it wouldn't have taken much."

Anson immediately brightened at the thought. "Yeah. Then the door just shut behind it and it couldn't get out. Now it's lying dead in there, stinking the place up." He gave Nate a friendly slap on the back. "Good thinking. Let's take a look at those stairs."

Eddie thought it was an idiotic explanation, but since his two friends had crowded in behind him, he had no choice but to walk inside the dark space. From what he managed to see through the deep shadows, it looked to be about twenty feet in diameter, and was a good ten degrees cooler than the outside air. He grinned at the spiral staircase, rising out of the pitch-black shadows on the opposite side of the room. Pointing at it, he looked over his shoulder and wiggled his eyebrows. "Get a load of that. We hit the jackpot."

"That should work great," Nate declared.

Anson turned his head enough to look behind them, his nose wrinkled in disgust. "First, we need to get rid of that sme—" He sputtered to a halt and whipped his head back around, turning eyes that had grown as wide as saucers on Eddie. "What is that?" His breathing audibly spiked as he reached out and dug his fingers into Eddie's arm. "What *is* that?"

Eddie squinted into the gloom over Anson's head. He froze for a moment, then fumbled for his phone, quickly tapping on the flashlight feature. He almost dropped it when the beam of light landed on a grotesque face, its bulging eyes staring right back at him.

Anson shrieked and immediately jumped back, landing squarely on Nate, coming close to knocking them both over. Arms and legs flailed as the two boys scrambled to keep their balance and flee outside all at the same time. Rapidly blinking behind the heavy frame of his glasses, Eddie barely breathed as he slowly backed away, not taking his flashlight off the body lying on the ground. He half expected the man to jump up and chase after them like something out of a zombie movie. Once he'd passed through the open doorway, Eddie sprinted to the top of the path, where Nate and Anson were huddled together.

"What was that?" Anson repeated, his voice a full octave higher than its normal pitch.

"You already asked that, you jerk. It's a body," Nate choked out. "That was a dead body, wasn't it?"

Both boys turned questioning eyes on Eddie, who gaped back at them. "How should I know?"

"Well, your mom has seen dead bodies. Probably plenty of them," Anson said.

"That doesn't mean I have," Eddie snapped back. "It's not like she takes me out on tours of crime scenes or anything."

"Okay, okay. It doesn't matter," Nate shouted, then bit his lower lip and took in a deep breath. "It doesn't matter," he repeated in a much softer voice. He pointed to the phone Eddie still held in his hand. "You need to call your mom."

Eddie stared at him for a moment before shifting his gaze to his phone. Yeah. He should do that. He didn't want to, but he should. He lifted his arm and looked at the upper edge of the screen. One bar. Probably just enough to get through to her. Great. He desperately wanted his mom there, but sure didn't want to face the crap load of trouble he was going to be in.

Resigned, he tapped on the call icon and raised the phone to his ear.

Chapter 2

RICKI JAMES STOOD over the dead body, her legs braced apart and her hands on her hips. Whoever this guy was, she was certain he was the only murder victim in the Bay at the moment, and didn't it just figure that her son would be the one to find him. She shook her head in disbelief, sending a long fall of dark hair pulled back into a low ponytail sliding across her back.

Tall and slender, with high cheekbones and an arresting face dominated by dark-blue eyes, she impatiently tapped one foot encased in a heavy hiking boot against the hard-packed earth that served as a floor in the old lighthouse. There was just enough sunshine coming through the single wide-open door to see the body lying ten feet away, right at the edge of where the shadows began to deepen. The rest of the space was swallowed up by the dark, with only the outline of a boarded-up window and a curved staircase barely visible on the far side of the circular room.

Clad in faded jeans and a plaid wool jacket hanging open over an olive-green T-shirt sporting the park service logo, Ricki grimaced at finding another dead person this close to home, with a bullet wound in his chest. She and her son lived in Brewer, the southernmost of the three towns in the Bay, and a twenty-minute drive up the two-lane highway that was the only road spanning the entire length of their small community. At least this time she wasn't looking at a murder victim dumped inside Olympic Park. It was also helpful that the hike up to the old lighthouse was a lot easier than almost any trail the park had to offer.

It had only been six weeks since she'd taken back her old job as a special agent with the Investigative Services Branch of the park system. The ISB was a mix of the FBI and NCIS that focused on major crimes committed within the country's more than four hundred national parks, three of which were in her home state of Washington. Always short on funding, the bureau's agents had usually had to haul their low-tech equipment into remote locations. Since there were only thirty-three of them in the entire country, they all had literally a lot of ground to cover. But she didn't mind any of that. She'd grown up in the Bay and loved the rugged beauty of the Olympic Mountains, so working here was no hardship.

Except when a dead body turned up.

Wondering how she got to be so lucky, Ricki glanced over her shoulder when a shouted greeting came from outside. She moved to the doorway and leaned against it, folding her arms across her chest as Chief Clayton Thomas walked into view at the top of the trail.

He crossed the distance between them with the easy stride of a natural athlete. His solid, muscular build topped six feet, and he had a face that could have easily earned him a good living as a movie star if he hadn't chosen to be a cop. Gray eyes, rimmed with green around the iris, crinkled in silent amusement when he spotted the three boys sitting in a row on a fallen log, their heads down and shoulders slumped over as if the overgrown grass beneath their feet was absolutely fascinating.

The chief stopped in front of Ricki and inclined his head toward her son and his two friends. "Are they under arrest?"

"I'm thinking about it," Ricki said, just loud enough to earn her an annoyed look from her son. She raised one eyebrow, which had Eddie immediately shifting his gaze back to the ground.

Clay chuckled softly at the silent exchange between mother and son. "Thanks for the call." His grin widened. "Before you punished my only witnesses."

"That will be coming," Ricki said, forcing herself not to return his grin. It wasn't funny. Not really. Although the three boys did look completely pathetic, huddled together on their log like a bad caricature of see no evil, hear no evil, speak no evil. "Is there anyone else with you?"

Clay nodded as he slid his backpack off his shoulders and set it on the ground. "Jules will be along. He's tracking down our new medical examiner, and I put in a call to Captain Davis for a forensics team. They're on their way." He glanced at his wristwatch. "They should be here in an hour."

Frank Davis was with the Tacoma Police Department, and a good friend, not to mention her uncle Cy's favorite fishing partner. The three towns in the Bay banded together to share the two-man police department, relying on the bigger cities on the other side of Hood Canal, as well as the state police, for additional help. Usually Clay didn't need any, but there were exceptions to that. A murder was one of them.

"You're sure it wasn't an accident?" Clay asked.

Ricki nodded. "I'm sure. Bullet to the heart, or very close to it." She let out a long, slow breath of air. "I doubt if it was suicide. I didn't see a gun lying around but didn't make a thorough search of the place. Thought I'd wait for you." Her gaze cut over to the three boys. "The crime scene was already disturbed when I got here. From what they told me, all three of them walked over it." She switched her attention back to Clay. "What new ME?"

"The one we hired last week and who is currently out fishing somewhere on the bay."

Her frown quickly turned into a wide grin. "You aren't telling me that TK took the job, are you?"

TK was the local nickname for one of the only two physicians in the Bay, having been bestowed on the doctor many years ago. Known all over town as the Trout King, and proud of it, Dr. Richard Evans was an avid fisherman, and so was his much younger partner in their small medical practice. The two of them generally worked different office hours, spending all their extra time out on the water, indulging in their favorite pastime. Ricki had recently heard through the usual small-town grapevine that after forty years of tending to everyone's cuts, bruises, and more serious ailments, TK had decided to retire.

So the report that the sixty-something doctor was taking on the job of the local ME was something new. The very efficient gossip mill that usually ran like wildfire between the three towns had failed to pick up that juicy tidbit.

"I gave him a standing offer last year, and he let me know a week ago that he was ready to accept it." Clay shrugged. "His thinking was that he wouldn't have to do much to earn the monthly stipend to be on call."

"Then he's going to be really pissed off to have his fishing interrupted," Ricki mused. The old doctor wasn't exactly known for keeping his opinions to himself, and she was certain his complaint over having to deal with a murder victim so soon after accepting the ME job would be immediate and very loud.

"Maybe not. But I think he's looking forward to it more than he's willing to admit. He told me he's been taking some online classes from the University of Washington ever since I brought the job up, and even went out and bought an old station wagon."

"What for?"

"To transport bodies in," Clay said with a straight face before looking around her to peer into the dark interior of the lighthouse. "Ready?"

Transport bodies? Was TK kidding? Ricki rolled her eyes. Trust the crusty old man to come up with something like that. She pushed away from the doorframe and with a stern "Don't move a muscle" warning called out to the boys, turned to head inside when she was stopped by a voice yelling out from across the small clearing.

"Hey, Chief!" Deputy Jules Tucker's thin, spidery form loped into view. His eyes squinted as he gave the boys a curious look before coming to a gangly stop in front of Ricki and Clay. "TK should be here in about thirty minutes. He has to row in, but he put out this morning close by, so his car is right here in Massey." The deputy held up a hand-sized instant camera. "I brought this in case that cell phone of yours runs out of juice before we get all the shots you want."

Ricki looked away to hide her grin at the sight of the plastic lens wrapped in yellow cardboard, with the name Kodak splashed across the front. It had probably sat forgotten on a shelf somewhere for at least a decade. Clay reached out and gave his deputy a hard slap on the back.

"That's good forward thinking, Jules. And great timing. We were just about to go inside."

The deputy nodded and then drew back a little as he wrinkled his nose. "Kind of smells."

"Not as much as it will in a few hours once the air heats up," Clay said. "So we better get to it."

Ricki gave the deputy, who was suddenly looking a little green, an encouraging smile. She was all too familiar with the man's weak stomach when it came to odd smells and the sight of blood. Word had it that he'd upchucked all over her last crime scene, and that was after the forensic team had processed it. "It's not as bad as it could be, Jules."

The deputy sucked in a deep breath through his mouth. "Okay. Okay."

Leaving it at that, Ricki turned and walked inside, with Clay following right behind. The body lay sprawled out, with one hand over its head, the other arm bent to one side, and the legs almost straight. She and the chief stood side by side, studying the lifeless form.

"Looks like he fell over backwards after being shot," Clay said.

Ricki nodded her agreement. "From the impact of the bullet to the chest." She tilted her head to the side. "The blood pooled out from his chest and not underneath him, so the bullet didn't go all the way through."

"Probably still in the body," Clay agreed. "Lucky break for us."

"If you can find the matching gun," Ricki said as she slowly walked around the body and squatted next to it. The head was turned to the side so the wide-open eyes were staring toward the open door. The bloat had already started to set in but wasn't as bad as it was going to get. "Eddie said that Nate was up here two days ago, and the door was locked. When they got here today, the lock was broken, so that puts the likely time of death at twenty-four to forty-eight hours ago."

Clay grunted his agreement, then sank down to match her position, balancing his weight on the balls of his feet. He pulled on a pair of latex gloves, then leaned over and pushed the man's jacket away. The gaping wound on the left side of his chest was surrounded by a large circle of dried blood soaked into his light-blue shirt. A wide path of dark red spilled down to the dirt floor. As Ricki silently looked on, Clay gently and slowly searched through the shirt, jacket, and pants pockets, coming up empty.

He raised his gaze to hers. "Nothing. No ID."

"And I don't see any jewelry either," Ricki said. "No

wedding ring, but it doesn't look like there's a tan mark showing he'd been wearing one either."

"Since there's no wallet or money, it might be a robbery gone wrong." Clay rose to his feet and glanced over at his deputy, who was using two fingers to pinch the end of his nose closed. "I'll take the photos, Jules, if you'll go out and keep an eye on those boys. Maybe take their official statements."

"Sure thing, Chief." Jules didn't waste any time heading for the door, still holding the disposable camera in one hand.

Shaking his head, Clay pulled his cell phone out of his shirt pocket. "This one is better anyway."

Ricki watched as Jules walked away, leaving his footprints behind to mingle with the ones the boys had made. If there had been any left by the killer, the teenagers had managed to trample all over them before she'd arrived.

Clay took several pictures then glanced her way. "Did Eddie tell you how they happened to come across the vic?"

"Uh-huh." It had taken a good ten minutes to make sense out of the half-excited, half-terrified slew of words thrown at her as the boys had stumbled to talk over each other, but in the end, she had a pretty good idea of what had happened.

"Apparently they came up here to test out their latest bot."

Clay lowered his phone and stared at her. "Up here? Why up here?"

She tilted her head toward the far side of the room. "Because they needed a curved set of stairs, and those are what they came up with." She shrugged at his puzzled look. "Not important. So they drove up here, in a car that I'm sure Nate's dad had no idea the kid had borrowed, and hauled the bot up the trail in a wagon."

"Is that what's under that blanket I saw?"

Ricki nodded. "Yep. Nate came up here two days ago, probably sneaking out in his dad's car again, and checked the place out. He thought they could get in through the window since the door was locked. But when they got here today, there was no lock on the outside, and a dead body on the inside. That's when Eddie called me." She put her hands on her hips and nodded again. "That's about it."

The chief's forehead wrinkled as he glanced over at the old wooden door. "Nate is sure there was a lock on the door the first time he came up here?"

"He's sure," Ricki said. "Just like he's sure his dad is going to, and I quote, 'blow a circuit' when he finds out Nate took the car."

"Not once, but twice," Clay put in. "Nate's still in high school, isn't he?"

"Uh huh. Not quite sixteen, and the proud owner of an instruction permit." Ricki dismissed Nate's impending problem with his father, which the kid had definitely earned, and focused on the bigger one in front of them. Since Clay had only been living in the Bay for just over three years, a very short time by the local reckoning, she started with the obvious. "I don't recognize him, Clay. And Jules would have said something if he knew who this guy was. The boys would have too."

"Then the odds are good that he's not from around here," Clay concluded.

"No." She raised an eyebrow. "Do you really think this was a robbery gone bad?" She took a slow look around. "Strange place for a robbery."

Clay sighed. "There's an outside chance, I suppose, but that would be a new one, in my experience."

Since the chief had spent a decade as a homicide cop in the Los Angeles Police Department, his experience level was pretty high. And her gut was telling her the same thing. It wasn't a robbery gone bad. Whoever had killed this John Doe had done it deliberately.

As Ricki stepped back and quietly looked on, Clay took a continual string of pictures as he moved around the body. When he was finally finished, the chief tucked his phone away and glanced over at her. "If you wouldn't mind staying, I could use an extra set of trained eyes to walk the perimeter. I can have Jules take Nate's car and drive the boys and their bot home. I think they've probably had enough for one day."

In complete agreement, Ricki nodded. "Can you ask him to drop Eddie off at the Sunny Side Up? And tell Anchorman to sit on my kid until I get there?" The Sunny Side up was the small local diner in Brewer that Ricki owned, and Anchorman was the ex-Marine sniper who was now her cook, and who sometimes doubled as Eddie's babysitter and protector whenever her ex-husband was out of town. Like he was today—which at the moment was a good thing. She needed to get everything sorted out with their son, then she would deal with his father. Who was probably going to blow the same circuit as Nate's dad. Her ex had a very sour opinion of anything to do with her job in law enforcement, especially murder investigations.

"Sure." Clay glanced over at the body with a quick shrug. "At least this guy wasn't left in Olympic Park, so you don't have to deal with it. This one is all mine."

As a general rule, she didn't like to disagree with the local chief of police, but in this case she didn't have much choice.

"Yeah. This one is yours." She jerked a finger over her shoulder toward the wall farthest from the open doorway. "But that one over there is mine."

Chapter 3

TK POSITIONED the small stool and lantern he'd brought with him next to the skeleton and sat down. Placing both hands on his knees, he leaned over and peered through the thick lenses of his glasses. He used a long finger with hair growing out close to the knuckles, to trace along the edge of an exposed rib bone. When he finally straightened up, he pushed his glasses back up his nose before nodding his head and silently moving his lips, talking to himself.

"What do you think, TK?" Ricki asked, used to the doctor's way of thinking things through. She shook her head when Clay opened his mouth. His eyes narrowed at her silent warning, but he crossed his arms over his chest and pressed his lips into a thin line.

"I think these bodies have at least one thing in common," TK said, his loud voice bouncing against the stone walls around them. "They were both shot."

"You're sure about that?" Clay's dry question earned him a stern look from the doctor.

"Well, you can see plainly enough that's what happened to that one over there." TK half turned on his stool and gestured toward the body lying closest to the doorway before looking back down at the bones laid out at his feet. "And this one has a good nick along one of his ribs, not to mention the bullet is lying in the dirt just to the right of the spine. It also looks like there's a serious break in one of the leg bones."

"So the bullet went through him?" Clay asked.

TK twisted around so he could look directly up at the chief. "No, son. It most likely fell there after all the flesh and organs had rotted away." He took off his glasses and started to clean them with a pure-white handkerchief that he'd pulled out of his shirt pocket. Once he was done, he handed the square of cloth to Ricki. "Here. You throw that away for me."

Ricki gingerly took the cloth with the tips of two fingers. TK had always been a stickler for cleanliness. Ever since she could remember, he'd always carried a white handkerchief with him and had never used any of them more than once.

Clay sank down on his haunches and leaned over to get a better look. "Is there anything else you can tell us?"

"They died at different times," TK said blandly. "And judging by the shape of the pelvis, I'd say you were correct in referring to this one as a 'he,' even if it was a lucky guess."

While the two men stared at each other in a silent tug-of-war for the upper hand, Ricki ignored them to carefully look over the skeleton neatly laid out on the dirt floor. The arms and legs were perfectly straight, almost as if the victim had simply fallen asleep and failed to wake up. Her eyes narrowed on the few small scraps of cloth still clinging to one rib and a hip bone before she shifted her gaze off to the side. A set of clothes was neatly folded and placed in a stack, with the jacket on top. The badly tarnished badge of a national park ranger was still pinned to its front. Whoever this skeleton had once been, he'd been one of theirs, and in her mind that made him her responsibility, no matter where he'd been found.

"How different?" Ricki asked into the silence, drawing the gazes of both men. "I mean, how far apart did these two die?"

Clay frowned. "It has to be at least a few years."

TK gave a grunt to go with the exaggerated roll of his eyes. "More like a few decades." He shrugged. "I'll have to study the bones a bit more to figure out how many, but this one stopped breathing at least ten years ago, and probably closer to twenty, maybe even more." He stood up and snapped his portable seat shut before grabbing the handle of the lantern. "Someone's going to have to carry this body down to the hearse."

Clay blinked, then cleared his throat. "Hearse?"

"Since I'm on a case, I taped the ME sign to the side of the station wagon. As long as it's on there, that makes my car an official hearse." TK nodded to put an emphasis on his words. "And I'm too old to be hauling anything other than this chair and lantern up any hills, so you just be sure to get these bodies down to the hearse."

"I'll do that," Clay said through gritted teeth. "The forensic team should be here soon. They'll get the bodies into your car."

"Hearse," TK corrected with a touch of smug in his voice. "And before it starts to rain. It was beginning to cloud up when I was rowing in."

"Great," Clay muttered.

"It's the Northwest, Chief Thomas. There's always rain on the way." TK started a slow walk toward the open door. "I'll be waiting in the hearse, where it's dry."

As the doctor disappeared through the doorway, Clay turned an exasperated look on Ricki. "This might have been a big mistake."

She grinned back at him. "Oh, I don't know. I think he's going to make a great ME and the two of you are made for each other."

"Ha, ha." Clay ran a distracted hand through his dark-blond hair. It was neatly cut with the edges barely curling over the back of his shirt collar. "Two kills, left in the same place, decades apart. Isn't that a bitch of a thing?"

"One civilian, one park ranger," Ricki added. "Which makes it even more of a bitch to deal with. And strange to boot."

"What part? The fact they were both shot out here in the middle of nowhere, or that they might've died in different centuries?"

"Well, there is that," Ricki agreed. But neither of those puzzles was what bothered her the most. "I've never heard of a ranger going missing, much less shot."

"Could be it happened so long ago it's buried in a report sitting in a box somewhere in the storage room."

Ricki shook her head. In a big city, that might be true, but in small towns that kind of thing was usually burned into the collective memory forever, often turning from bare fact into full-blown legend, or a bedtime tale whispered in the dark. But however it might evolve over time, a story like this one would never have died. Not in a small town.

"I'd know about it," she said quietly. "No matter how long ago it happened."

"Okay." Clay looked around. "Since the older vic was shot, I guess that rules out this being some sort of bizarre tomb erected by the family."

Ricki glanced up at the spiral staircase, its curves suspended over their heads. It was a weird place to put what was basically an undersized lighthouse, and since the man had been carefully laid out and his clothes neatly folded beside him, Clay's thought that the structure was built for some other purpose besides guiding ships in the Bay wasn't such a far-fetched theory. Since whoever he was had indeed been shot, just like his contemporary companion lying on the other side of the enclosed space, it wasn't very likely the old lighthouse was built as a tomb by some eccentric family member. But there was some reason it was built on this piece of land.

"It could be he was stationed at another park and transported here," she mused out loud. As a possibility, that held some weight, but her instincts told her no. Mount Rainier, the park closest to Olympic, was over a hundred miles away. Why go to the bother of transporting a park ranger from there, and then not even dump the body in the park?

Clay's gaze rose from the skeleton to center on her face. "Sounds like it needs to be checked out."

"Yeah. I'll get on it." Or rather she'd call Hamilton and see who he could get on it. Since he was the special agent in charge at the Seattle office of the ISB, and her boss, hopefully he could pull some strings and get her help with the legwork. Something told her she'd have to dig deep to uncover just who the mysterious ranger was, and why he'd ended up shot and left in the lighthouse. But resources in the bureau were scarce, so if Hamilton came up empty, maybe she could talk her uncle, who was the supervisor over the law enforcement unit inside Olympic Park, into loaning her one of his rangers. And she had a specific one in mind.

Tucking that away to follow up on later, she looked over at the first body they'd found. "It could be that the latest vic was a tourist who saw the lighthouse, wandered up here, and happened to get shot."

"Why?" Clay asked bluntly. "Why shoot the guy? It's not like there's anything in here to steal."

"It could have been a personal argument with a companion that got out of hand." She gave the bones a thoughtful look. "Or maybe to keep him from telling anyone about the other murder."

Clay scoffed at the idea. "When it happened more than a decade ago?"

Hard to argue with that. Before she could form another theory, a man with bright-red hair and a mustache to match appeared in the doorway. He was dressed in a paper-thin white jumpsuit and held a large black case at his side.

"Hey. We're looking for Chief Thomas?"

Clay nodded and stepped forward, his hand held out.

"That would be me. You must be with the forensic team from Tacoma."

"Yeah, I'm Rob." He looked to be in his mid-twenties, an image only enhanced when he snapped a piece of gum in his mouth. "We're supposed to process a scene with a dead body?" He jerked his head backwards. "And some old guy where we parked the rig told us we should put the body into the back of his car to transport."

Clay turned his head to give Ricki an exasperated glare but managed to keep his tone even when he looked back at Rob. "When you're through here, go ahead and load the body into your rig. I'll talk to the old guy. He's our ME." He pointed over his shoulder to where Ricki was standing. "She's Special Agent Ricki James with the National Park Service. She also has a body that needs to be transported."

Rob straightened up to his full height and stretched his neck to look past Clay. "We weren't told about any second body, Chief."

"I'll clear it with Captain Davis," Ricki said, already reaching for her cell phone. "And there are clothes over here that will need to be bagged, but I want to take photos of them first. There's also a bullet underneath the body that will need to be preserved."

"Okay." Rob turned and blew out a short, piercing whistle. "Hey, Danny? We've got two in here."

When Rob disappeared from the doorway, Clay turned to Ricki and smiled. "Well, what do you say, Special Agent James? It looks like you've got a murder to solve. At least this case is cold enough it shouldn't come with someone shooting back at you."

"Yeah, there is that," Ricki agreed with a quiet sigh.

Chapter 4

Three hours after she'd received the call from her son about a dead body up at the old lighthouse, Ricki walked into the Sunny Side Up, her small, slightly run-down diner just off the center of town. Since she'd rejoined the elite investigative unit for the National Park Service, she had a regular paycheck again, and had used the boost in her income to spruce up the place with a new awning. The building still needed its wooden shingle siding replaced, but that would have to wait.

Anchorman, the Marine-turned-cook, was manning the stove, attacking the stack of order slips on the adjoining counter that were being held down by a coffee mug, with his usual fierce efficiency. Tall, standing a good six inches over her five-foot-eight-inch frame, her cook still sported the close-cropped haircut favored by the military, and was built like a solid block of granite.

He looked like a warrior as he wielded a spatula to flip the burgers in one hand, and a spoon to stir a bubbling pot of beans in the other. Ricki grinned as she slipped out of her windbreaker and turned to hang it on a hook by the back door. Anchorman always seemed to treat every task as if he were in the middle of a battle. Most of the time she appreciated his single-minded intensity. But when he used that same bullheadedness to dig in his heels about something, she could argue with him until she was blue in the face and he still wouldn't budge an inch. She should know. That usually happened about once a week. Which was also how often she threatened to fire him.

"Deputy Jules dropped Eddie off an hour ago," Anchorman said, his voice raised to carry over the sound of meat sizzling on the grill. "He said the kid is in a shitload of trouble."

Ricki looked over her shoulder and nodded. "That's right. He was up at the old lighthouse without permission."

Her cook instantly scowled. "So? It's Wednesday, boss, in case you've lost track of what day of the week it is. A faculty day, if you don't remember the schedule, so no school. Which means he wasn't skipping classes just to hang out with his buddies." He quickly flipped a burger before returning his attention and his scowl to Ricki. "Although that's a necessary thing sometimes."

She crossed her arms and watched him with a gleam of amusement in her gaze. Since Anchorman felt particularly protective of her son, she wasn't surprised that he'd immediately jumped to Eddie's defense. "Uh-huh. Well, he did your idea of a necessary thing by riding along with Nate, who, I'd like to point out, does not have a driver's license, and had taken his father's car without permission." Her mouth thinned into a straight line when Anchorman's stubborn scowl remained firmly in place. It looked like they were headed for one of those arguments.

"Okay. That might be worth a lecture, but not much more than that. All teenage boys borrow the car on occasion." He shrugged. "It's a guy thing."

"Is that so? How about trespassing? Is that a guy thing too?"

"When it's on an old, abandoned property, yep,"

Anchorman said without missing a beat. "And since that lighthouse isn't on federal land, you can't arrest him for it either."

"How about coming across a dead body while he was riding in a borrowed car, driven by an unlicensed driver, to go trespass on private land?" Ricki nodded in satisfaction when Anchorman's mouth dropped open but no sound came out. It was always satisfying to have the last word.

When he started to sputter, she gave him a smug "gotcha" grin, then breezed through the swinging door that separated the kitchen from the main dining room. Several of the booths lining the walls were occupied, as were all the tables crowded together in the center of the room. Ricki recognized most of the customers and raised a hand in greeting when a number of heads turned her way.

Marcie, her waitress, friend, and the first employee Ricki had hired for the diner, smiled at her from across the room. The stocky woman was in her early fifties, which made her twenty years Ricki's senior. She'd also successfully raised six kids of her own, so gave her boss an experienced, knowing look when she tilted her head to the far corner of the room.

Ricki turned in that direction, immediately spotting her son at the end of the counter that stretched along the back wall, sitting on one of the high stools with a faded red-vinyl seat. He was hunched over a book, his dark hair doing its perpetual flop over the top rim of his glasses. She walked between the counter and the back wall with its food and service stations, until she stood in front of him, her arms crossed over her chest. Tapping a heavily booted foot against the linoleum floor, she patiently waited until he lifted his gaze to meet hers.

When Eddie stayed silent, she lifted one eyebrow. "Well?"

"I'm sorry, Mom. But like I already told you, we needed some curved stairs to test out our bot, and there wasn't anywhere else to do it," he blurted out.

Her tall, broad-shouldered son might be built like his

father, but the blue eyes staring back at her were an exact mirror of her own.

"Uh-huh. What about the St. Armand? There's a very impressive curved staircase in the main ballroom."

Eddie added an exaggerated roll of his eyes to his dismissive snort. "They never would have let us test out the bot there."

"Oh? Who did you ask? The hotel manager?"

Her son's gaze cut away as he squirmed in his seat. "Not exactly."

"Meaning not at all." Ricki held up a hand when he started to protest. "You're too smart not to know that what you, Nate, and Anson did was wrong, so let's skip over the debate, bud, and get right to the consequences." She paused and waited for him to look at her. "You're grounded. For a month." When his lower lip jutted out, she waved a finger back and forth. "A whole month, bud, and it's not up for negotiation. You'll come straight here after school, do your homework, and then bus the tables for Marcie until your dad comes to pick you up." When he looked relieved, she shook her head. "And I'll be talking to him before you leave the diner today, to make sure he doesn't cave in and let you slide by on this one."

Eddie deflated into a slump, his expression mutinous, but he did manage a grumbled "Okay."

Hoping she'd made her point since that was never a sure thing with a teenager, she decided that about now her son likely needed another guy to commiserate with. She leaned her elbows on the counter and gave him a half-smile to let him know the worst part of their talk was over. "Since you don't have any homework with you, why don't you go and ask Anchorman to make you something to eat."

He nodded as he closed the technical manual he was reading, replacing it in his backpack before sliding off the stool. He started to walk off and then stopped and gave her a worried look. "Mom? Who was that guy?"

"I don't know, Eddie," Ricki said. "There wasn't any identification on him."

"Someone killed him." Eddie made it more of a statement than a question.

"Yes." There wasn't any point in denying it. Eddie would have seen the hole in the victim's chest, just like she had. She hoped the image wouldn't stay with him, but it was something she'd have to keep an eye on and warn his dad to do the same. Unfortunately.

Her ex-husband had been adamantly against her going into law enforcement in the first place, and even more vocal in his opinion since she'd taken the badge for a second time. Her son was still confused about the whole thing. She could see it in his eyes every time his gaze landed on the badge attached to her belt.

The last time she'd carried it, she'd ended up with a bullet in her side and her partner had been killed. But if she hadn't rejoined her old agency, Eddie's dad would be dead at the hands of a serial killer.

Tough choice for a kid, she mused as she watched him disappear through the swinging doors into the kitchen.

Marcie strolled up, carrying a coffeepot and two empty mugs. She set the cups down on the counter and efficiently filled them both to the brim before pushing one toward Ricki. The waitress took the seat Eddie had vacated and sighed.

"Feels good to get off my feet." She lifted her coffee cup to her lips and watched Ricki over its rim as she took a slow sip.

Wrapping long, slender fingers around the second mug, Ricki stared down into the steaming brew, thinking about the bodies they'd found in the lighthouse. They were on their way to the ME in Tacoma, Clay was probably headed back to his office by now, and she needed to call all this in to ASAC Hamilton. Aside from the fact he was her boss, meaning she was obligated to report it to him, she also wanted his take on a guy who'd been shot decades ago and might have been a ranger.

"Penny for your thoughts, if they aren't all centered around a dead man," Marcie said.

Ricki looked up and over her friend's head, to glare at the group of five older men occupying the table in the very center of the room. Pete was well past seventy and the biggest conduit of gossip in town. Every morning that the Sunny Side Up was open, he was outside, waiting for the door to be unlocked so he could lay claim to that center table. Once his group of like-minded cronies joined him, they spent several hours hashing out the latest rumors swirling about town—or any of the three towns that made up the Bay—before leaving a generous tip and strolling out to take their daily walk.

The group wasn't particular about who had the juiciest story, as long as they got to hear it first. She liked Pete and his charming gang of friends with their refreshingly old-fashioned manners, but seriously, one of these days she was going to have to haul them all in and grill them on just how they always managed to find out her official business almost before she did.

"Well, are they?" Marcie repeated.

Ricki sighed and took a sip of her coffee before answering. "Not exactly. I mean, there wasn't just one dead man."

Marcie let out a soft groan, propped her elbows on the counter, and held her head between her hands. "Not again. How many this time?"

"Two," Ricki said. "The one Eddie and his friends found, and another one they didn't see because it was in the shadows and had been there a while."

"Oh." Marcie's brow furrowed as she lowered her voice. "That explains why Pete only knew about the one."

"How so?" Ricki asked.

"Well, Pete heard it from Brad, who's married to Alice.

Now of course you know Alice. She's Susan's sister, who is Nate's mom, so she . . ."

Ricki raised her eyes to the ceiling in a silent prayer for patience. "Yeah. I get it. Small-town gossip and greased lightning. All the same thing."

Marcie smiled. "That's right. But this bit about a second body, now that's—"

"Going to stay between us," Ricki cut in. "Isn't it?"

The older woman raised a hand and drew an *X* over her left breast. "I promise. Not a word."

Satisfied with that, Ricki nodded. She knew Marcie's lips would be sealed. The waitress considered everyone in the diner her family, and anything they discussed there was strictly "family business." If anyone knew how to keep the gossips in check, it was Marcie. She was born in the Bay and had lived here her entire life. The thought made another idea pop into Ricki's head.

She leaned forward, casting a glance down the counter to be sure the customer sitting four place settings down wasn't paying any attention to them. "Have you ever heard of a park ranger going missing?"

Her friend blinked. "Missing? As in, disappeared?" She blinked again, then lifted a hand to cover her mouth as her eyes popped wide open. "That second body you found was a park ranger? Who?"

"That's just it," Ricki kept her voice low and her gaze on the rest of the customers. "I don't know. According to TK, he's been dead at least a decade. Probably longer."

"What?" Marcie's expression went from surprised to skeptical in less than a second. "That would have been all over town if a park ranger had gone missing. I never heard anything like that."

Ricki wasn't surprised. She'd thought exactly the same thing. If a ranger had simply upped and disappeared, it would still be the talk of the town. Or at least part of the collective memory. Something here wasn't adding up. "What about the old lighthouse? Do you know who owns it?"

"Owns it?" Marcie shrugged. "No one owns it. It's just always been there."

"Well, someone owns the land," Ricki pointed out. When Marcie gave her a blank stare, Ricki let out another sigh. It looks like she'd be paying a visit to the occasionally open office that served as a combined city hall for the towns in the Bay. "How far back do you think city hall has kept land records?"

Marcie took another sip of her coffee then waved at Anchorman, who was pointing to a heaping plate of food he'd just slid onto the wall cutout that served as a food pickup window. She shoved off the stool then glanced over at Ricki. "Well, there're records for at least seventy-five years, according to Lissy. She's been the clerk there since before I was born, so she should know. But after seven years, she ships the records off to the county courthouse." She smoothed out her apron and picked up the coffeepot she'd set down on the counter. Her mouth drooped at the corners and the gaze she settled on Ricki was filled with worry. "Two dead bodies and one of them was killed ten years ago and no one even noticed? What's going on up at that old lighthouse?"

Not waiting for an answer that Ricki didn't have, Marcie moved off, giving every patron at the counter a gentle pat on the shoulder as she passed by them. Ricki watched her for a moment and then turned to stare out the large window at the front of the diner. Like it or not, Clay was right. She had another murder on her hands.

Chapter 5

IT WAS JUST shy of eight in the morning when Ricki climbed out of her ten-year-old jeep while the engine was still doing its usual dance of sputtering a protest before completely shutting off. She gave the front tire a hard kick as payback for the temperamental vehicle taking five minutes to start that morning. It wasn't much of a payback, but it was the best she could do before stalking across the parking lot toward the low, sprawled-out building that served as headquarters for the local police department.

The two-man department was owned by all three of the towns the local residents simply referred to as "the Bay." To save money, they shared not only a police department but most city services. That included the single-story, six-room, all-purpose municipal building that served as the monthly meeting location for the combined city council. Both the police and municipal buildings were located in Edington, the largest of the three towns, and a short ten-to-fifteen-minute drive from Ricki's cabin, depending on what speed her jeep decided to go.

Since Clay and his one deputy didn't need all the space in the large building they occupied, the city council leased most of it out to the National Park Service. Which was why the parking lot was full of vehicles from the law enforcement unit assigned to Olympic National Park. It was also Ricki's home base as the only agent from the Investigative Services Bureau in the state. Well, if you didn't count ASAC Hamilton, and Ricki didn't since her boss had taken on an administrative role and rarely did fieldwork anymore.

While the headquarters was listed as her official office address, she didn't have any assigned space in the building and only used it when she needed a conference room, or somewhere to interview a witness. She usually worked from the small desk set up in her living room, only shedding her favored attire of faded jeans and a T-shirt, for pressed slacks and a tailored blouse on the rare occasions she had to meet ASAC Hamilton at his office in downtown Seattle.

Fortunately for Ricki, that didn't occur too often. She and Eddie had moved back to Brewer just over a year ago, and she'd quickly adopted the local habit of actively avoiding any attire that couldn't stand up to a hike along the wilderness trails in the park.

So far her morning had gone much better than yesterday's had. No new dead bodies to report, and Hamilton had given the go-ahead for her to ask for the services of the park law enforcement officer who had helped her on her last case. *The Mountain Killer,* Ricki thought with a roll of her eyes. That was what the press had dubbed him. At least her current victim wouldn't draw the horde of reporters a serial killer did. Too many murders happened every day for one that went down a decade ago to draw much attention.

She pushed through the glass double doors that opened into the lobby of the joint headquarters for the two agencies. An extra-long desk spanned most of the back, with a line of fencing and a small swinging gate attached to one side. Ray sat in his usual place behind the desk, guarding the entrance to the hallway leading to the offices inside. His eyes squinted against the sunlight that outlined the figure coming through the door, but as soon as he realized who she was, his mouth stretched out in a wide smile.

"Hello there, Special Agent Ricki James."

Ricki smiled back at him. The elderly man was proud to have an eight in front of his age. Still active, with only a slight bend in his posture, he volunteered his services at the front desk seven days a week. She wasn't even sure exactly when Ray Dunning arrived to take up his duties, or when he left. Whenever she came into the building, he was there. At least that had been the case since his nephew, John, had left for college. Until then, Ray had spent his time working as a plumber and raising his sister's only child. She had died shortly after the birth of her son, and Ray had stepped into the role of parent. John was almost eighteen years her senior, so Ricki hadn't known him very well, and what she did know had mostly come from his very proud uncle.

"How's John doing?" she asked, smiling at the pleased look on Ray's face.

"Oh fine, fine. I talked to him last night, and he said he's coming down for an extended visit." Ray beamed as he delivered that news. "He wants to do a little fishing. Said he'd like to visit our secret spot on the Dosewallips River. I found it years ago—a pretty piece of calm water, surrounded by trees growing right to the edge of the bank and a couple of big boulders so it's hidden away pretty good." Ray gave her a broad wink. "Now don't you go asking me where it is, because I won't tell you."

Ricki, who'd grown up playing in Olympic Park, was sure she knew exactly where Ray and his nephew's "secret spot" was, but she held up her hands and laughed. "I wouldn't dream of it."

It was too bad his nephew couldn't spare more time away from his business in Seattle so he and his uncle could be together at their favorite fishing spot along the river. But barring that, Ray had always seemed to prefer hanging out at the police headquarters.

Whenever Clay had suggested he spend more time with his family and friends, doing something he enjoyed, Ray always waved it aside, loudly declaring that he liked what he was doing just fine. Clay was stubborn enough to bring it up on a regular basis, but he always got the same answer. Ricki could have told the chief it was a waste of time, but she figured it was something he needed to find out for himself.

Ricki leaned over to get a look at the desk Ray always kept neat as a pin. There was never so much as a paper clip out of place, even though Jules had a habit of dumping all his traffic tickets onto the desk at the end of the day for Ray to sort through. And the deputy wrote a mountain of traffic tickets, especially once the tourist season got underway.

"I wish I had your knack for keeping everything organized," Ricki said. "You can't tell me you've already processed Tucker's traffic citations?"

Ray's watery hazel eyes took on a sparkle of amusement. "There weren't many to process since he spent most of the day traveling between here and that old lighthouse." His expression grew serious as he stared up at her. "I hear we have another murder to deal with."

Remembering that Jules had left to take the boys home before she'd pointed out the skeleton in the corner to Clay, Ricki didn't correct him on the body count. "It seems so. I thought I'd stop in and see if the chief needed any help."

"I don't know. He got a call just before you came in. Might still be on the phone with the lady. At least his line is still lit up." Ray pointed to the phone on his desk. It had a long row of buttons on one side, all dark except one that was glowing red. "She said she was calling from Chicago. Had a hard time understanding her, though. She sounded like she was crying and didn't even stop for one second." Ray lifted a finger that was permanently bent at one joint from arthritis. "Not even a second. I was glad to pass her on to the chief."

"I'll bet," Ricki murmured. Odds were the distraught caller had been in a rental car and had received a ticket from Jules. According to Clay, that made up the bulk of upset callers.

"You go on back." Ray waved his arm toward the hallway. "He'll be glad to see you." He peered up at her as she opened the small gate next to his desk. "He might even get a chance to ask you out on another date."

Ricki shut her eyes on a silent groan. She'd managed to have one date with Clay, and of course everyone in the Bay knew about it. It wouldn't surprise her if all her neighbors could recite what the two of them had had for dinner and how long they'd been at the restaurant. Which was all the gossips had to chew on because so far, their first and only date had been a few weeks ago.

Between their jobs, and her son and his activities, plus keeping things going smoothly at the diner, they simply hadn't managed to work a follow-up date into their schedules. But it wasn't as if they didn't spend any time together. They saw each other practically every day, and usually managed to grab a quick bite together, either here in the break room or at her place.

Okay, so maybe they mostly talked over cases instead of trading stories about personal stuff, and the setting wasn't exactly conducive to romance. But she still preferred that to going out just for the sake of sitting in a restaurant so they could hash over a relationship that had the possibility of transitioning from friendship to something more intimate.

Since she'd married her high school sweetheart, she'd never had much practice at dating. When their nine-year marriage had fallen apart, it had been hard on everyone, which was why she'd sworn off relationships of the romantic kind and had successfully managed to avoid them ever since.

Until Clay.

And she found herself happy at the thought of having him around. And not just as a friend. A big step for her, and one she was still trying to get used to. Which was why she wasn't ready for any deep discussions about it. She still needed time to let it sink in.

She paused outside his office. The door, which had a paper sign stating "Chief" taped to it, was partially open. She stuck her head around its edge, taking a step inside when Clay waved for her to come in. The office had bare-bones furnishings, with just a desk, two folding chairs for visitors, and a single filing cabinet in the far corner.

A big man was seated in one of the chairs in front of Clay's desk. He turned his head and smiled at Ricki, his blue eyes crinkling at the corners. Cyrus McCormick had high cheekbones and dark hair liberally shot through with several shades of gray. He was the well-respected supervising officer of the Olympic Park's law enforcement unit. He was also Ricki's uncle.

She smiled back as she walked across the small space, taking a seat in the vacant chair next to him before grinning at Clay.

"I hear you had an upset caller already this morning."

Clay shook his head before leaning back in his chair. "Of course you did. Any police business is the worst-kept secret in the Bay."

"Amen to that," Cyrus replied before looking over at his niece. "The chief was about to fill me in on his murder victim, and then I thought you could fill me in on yours."

"Sounds good." Ricki turned an expectant gaze on Clay. "Anything new since we talked last night?"

"As a matter of fact, there is. It seems I have a pretty good ID on the vic."

Caught off guard, Ricki immediately straightened in her seat. "What?"

The chief pushed away from his desk and crossed his legs, settling one ankle on top of the opposite knee. "That upset caller? It was a woman named Demi Lansanger, from the offices of Maxwell Hardy, Private Investigator. I gathered Miss Lansanger is his assistant."

When he paused, Ricki leaned forward. "And? Is the vic someone this PI is looking for?"

"I don't think so. From his assistant's description, it sounds like Maxwell Hardy *is* our vic."

Ricki stared at him for a long moment before sliding her gaze over to her uncle, who lifted his wide shoulders in a shrug.

"Don't ask me," Cyrus said. "I'm hearing all this for the first time too."

She turned her attention back to Clay. A private investigator? Her lips pressed together and her eyes narrowed as she thought it over. It could be Mr. Hardy was looking for someone who didn't want to be found and had the extreme bad luck of finding him. Or her.

"Where's he from?" Ricki asked.

"Chicago," Clay said. "Miss Lansanger is going to email me his picture so we can make a positive ID, but like I said, her description was close to our vic. I'm pretty sure it's going to be a match."

"That'd make TK's job easier," Cyrus observed, then raised both eyebrows when Clay shot him an exasperated look. "What? I heard TK took the ME job you floated in his direction."

"Faster than greased lightning," Ricki declared, grinning when Clay turned his glare on her. "Did Miss Lansanger happen to mention what her boss was doing out here?"

Clay settled back into his chair and rubbed one hand against the side of his cheek. "She said it was definitely business, because he had her book his ticket on the business credit card. Apparently he was always very careful not to put any personal expenses on it. He was a stickler about mixing the two up. But she didn't know what case he was working on. She said she never knows until she's asked to write up a report for the client, and she hadn't done anything lately that involved coming to Washington."

"Lately?" Ricki immediately picked up on the single word. "That's what she said? Lately?"

"Exactly what she said," Clay stated, his knowing glance meeting hers.

"Can we call her back?"

"I intended to just as soon as I got his picture. You're welcome to hang around for it."

"Good. Because I—"

"Ricki." Her uncle's voice cut her off. "This one isn't your case. You have the other body to worry about."

"They might be connected, Uncle Cy." When he looked skeptical, she added a nod.

"I haven't heard much about the other victim, but Clay did mention there's a really wide time gap between the murders," Cy stated. "He said that gap is at least ten years? I don't see how one can have anything to do with the other."

"It's a big gap," Ricki conceded. "But the odds of both murders happening in the same place, which isn't exactly on any sightseeing map, are off the charts. There's a connection. We just don't know what it is yet."

Clay made a neutral sound deep in his throat. "Maybe the autopsy will give us more."

"I hope so." Cy turned to face Ricki. "You're going to need more dots to connect than both bodies ending up in the same place." He stood up and glanced down at her. "Can I talk to you for a minute? In private?"

"Sure." Judging by the slight clenching of her uncle's jaw, Ricki knew he had something to say that she wasn't going to like. Getting to her feet, she sent a pointed look at Clay. "I'd like to be here when you call this assistant from Chicago back," she reminded him.

Clay nodded. "Understood." His mouth twitched at the corners as he tried and failed to suppress a smile. "Don't let your uncle bully you."

Ricki telegraphed a "Don't even try" stare aimed at Cy before heading out the door.

"Ha," Cy muttered under his breath. "I'll be lucky if she settles for a jab or two instead of carving me up into pieces."

Chapter 6

HER MIND still occupied with the dead victim, Ricki plopped into a wooden chair at the small conference table in her uncle's office and drummed her fingers against its wooden top, staring at a web of scratches running along its surface. A PI. What was he doing so far from Chicago? If he *was* looking for someone, then who? There were a couple thousand people who lived in the Bay year-round. Granted, she didn't know all of them since she'd only been back a year, but the majority were lifelong residents. Which meant she knew most of them. But she couldn't think of even one who would be at the center of a search by a PI based halfway across the country.

She gave a mental shrug. Then again, people had secrets. And some of them were ugly enough to keep hidden for a long time. Her years as an investigator had taught her that.

The seemingly random thought had her eyes narrowing in speculation. Secrets hidden for a long time. Like maybe a decade or more?

"Ricki? Hello?"

Startled by the loud intrusion into her thoughts, Ricki blinked and looked up, meeting her uncle's gaze. He'd taken a seat opposite hers, and his arms were crossed over his chest as he stared back at her.

"Do you think you can put murder aside for a few minutes while we talk?"

She gave him an easy smile and relaxed back in her chair. Her father had liked the outdoors well enough, but he'd been a brilliant engineer, and had preferred tinkering away at his projects to camping out in the park. So it had been her uncle who had shown her how to hunt, fish.

Cy had given her a love for the majestic beauty of the Olympic Mountains, along with the skills to survive in the surrounding wilderness. He'd also taught her how to shoot a gun with expert accuracy. And when she'd gotten older, it was her uncle who'd talked her into trying a career in law enforcement, although he'd complained many times since then that he'd intended for her to stay with the park enforcement unit, not to get involved in chasing down killers.

Of course she loved her uncle. He looked so much like the father she missed every day, but on top of that, she'd always be grateful for all the life lessons and good advice that Cy had given her over the years. Which meant it wouldn't hurt her to sit through a lecture or two from him. Studying the expression in his eyes and the set line of his mouth, Ricki belatedly realized that her uncle he looked like he was about to give one of his lectures right now, and she had no idea what she'd done to deserve it.

"Okay," she said slowly, unconsciously bracing herself for a dressing down. "What's up?"

"We need to touch base. We haven't had much time to talk since . . ." He frowned as his voice trailed off.

"Taking down a serial killer?" Ricki offered helpfully, trying not to grin when her uncle shot her an annoyed look.

"Yes. That." When she started to talk, he held up one hand to keep her quiet. "I'm not going to say anything more about you taking off after that bastard without any backup."

Relieved that she wouldn't have to sit through another one of her uncle's rants on that particular subject, Ricki leaned back in her chair and stretched her long legs out in front of her, crossing them at the ankles. "Then what's on your mind?"

"It's about your mom."

Ricki frowned. Her mom? When Miriam McCormick had been diagnosed with Alzheimer's, Ricki had been left with little choice but to place her in a tranquil, highly rated facility in Tacoma, with staff who specialized in the disease. Her mom's monthly income wasn't enough to cover the expense, so Ricki paid a good chunk of money each month to be sure Miriam was comfortable and safe. She also made the hour-and-a-half trip every week to visit her mom, and in fact had seen her just two days ago. As far as she knew, everything was going as well as it could for her mom. At least that was what Liddy Stoltz, the battle-ax nurse with the kind heart who looked after Miriam, had said.

Not sure what her uncle was getting at, Ricki's frown grew deeper. "What about Mom?"

"I went over to see her yesterday." He sighed and ran a big hand down the side of his face. "I should go more often. I know that. But it's hard. She didn't know who I was."

"I know," Ricki said softly. "She doesn't recognize me anymore either."

"She thought I was your dad. Kept calling me Einstein and asking me where I've been."

That didn't surprise her. The two brothers had borne a striking resemblance to each other. She smiled. "Yeah. She talks to me quite a bit about Einstein." That had been Miriam McCormick's pet name for her brilliant husband. "And about Eddie." Which also didn't surprise her. Her son looked a great deal like her dad had when he'd been a teenager, with the same dark hair and blue eyes.

"Well, that's what I wanted to talk to you about," her uncle said. "I think we should take Eddie to see his grandma more often. It might help keep . . . well, keep her in touch with us."

Ricki didn't say anything for a long moment as she studied her uncle's face. There was something bothering him, and since it was the same thing about visiting her mom that bothered her, she was sure she knew what had such a big man squirming in his seat.

"Did Mom say something about seeing Dad? Maybe having a conversation with him?"

A tinge of red crept along her uncle's cheek. "Yeah. She did. And not just your dad. She talked about having a nice chat with Marie, too."

"Marie?" Ricki went perfectly still. Marie had been her college roommate and had gone into law enforcement at the same time she had. The two had been more like sisters than friends, so much so that Ricki had left the park service to join Marie as a deputy with the US Marshals. Their partnership had ended the day they had escorted a prisoner and were caught in an ambush. Ricki had taken a bullet in her side, and Marie had ended up in the morgue. During one of her visits, her mom had claimed she'd seen Marie, but much to Ricki's relief, she hadn't said a word about her dead friend and partner since then. So it came as a complete surprise to hear her mom had brought it up with her brother-in-law.

"What did she say?" Ricki asked cautiously.

"Something about how she'll be sending someone here soon." Cy grimaced. "Nothing that made any sense. I'm just saying that I think seeing Eddie would help remind her of Tom." He shifted his gaze until it met hers. "And you. Which is all she needs to be thinking about now."

Ricki had her doubts about her mom having any thoughts about her or Eddie. It was more likely that her mom would think she was seeing her husband. But her uncle was right about that being better than listening to her mom talk to someone who she had no reason to be seeing at all. At least her dead husband had been family. In the last dozen years, her mom had only seen Marie once or twice. "That sounds like a good idea. Eddie will be home next weekend. I'll take him then."

"How's that going?" Cy asked. "Eddie staying with his father all week and with you on the weekends?"

She didn't like it, and wasn't going to pretend that she did, but after she'd taken up the badge again and gotten tangled up with a serial killer, Eddie had needed some time and space to get used to the idea of her being a special agent again. She had to give him a lot of credit. The idea scared him, but he had supported her decision and was working his way around to believing it had been the right one. She sent up a prayer and a wish every night that he would come around soon, and then want to move back home and see his father on the long weekends and everything would go back to the way it used to be.

Her ex had claimed this new arrangement would be easier for her, now that she had another full-time job that might require her to jump on a plane without notice and head to another park. She didn't really care what he thought. She would have made it work. But Eddie had wanted to try reversing their arrangement, so he was with his dad full-time rather than her. Since her son was old enough to have a say in where he spent his time, and his dad had a townhouse less than five miles away, she'd reluctantly agreed. But she still didn't like it.

"It's going," she finally said with a small shrug. "After the Fourth of July, when the tourist season really gets going, he'll be staying more with me since Bear will be taking out more tours." Job opportunities hadn't been falling off trees in the Bay when she'd moved back, so besides the diner, Ricki was also a partner with her ex-husband in an adventure tour business that took large and small groups on overnight trips in the park. Although recently she'd been thinking it might be time to bring an end to that particular side venture. Bear was a great guy, generally speaking, but he was still her ex. And there was a reason for that.

Her uncle smiled. "That's good. I like Bear. He was a damn good linebacker in high school, but I think after yesterday, it's obvious Eddie is getting to that age where he needs to have a closer eye kept on him. Bear likes the role of buddy more than the disciplinarian part of parenting."

She'd thought the same thing herself but was glad to have an excuse to talk about her son's little escapade up at the lighthouse rather than Bear's idea of parenting. No matter what she thought of it, she absolutely did not want to fall into the trap of bashing the ex-husband.

Bear was a good father, for the most part, and hadn't been a bad husband, but he'd hated her being in law enforcement, and she'd never been able to accept the idea of living off his inheritance from his grandparents. Bear hadn't seen the problem with that. He'd been happy to enjoy the outdoor life and not worry about much else, while she'd wanted something more. "A purpose" was the only way she'd been able to describe it to him, and his reply had always been the same. In the world according to Bear, being happy was purpose enough.

"Yeah. About what earned my son a month of being grounded. Like you said, there were two bodies in that lighthouse, and one of them belongs to us." She tilted her head to one side. "You wouldn't happen to know about any missing rangers that you've never mentioned, by any chance?"

Cy shook his head. "No. Clay asked me the same thing, and I gave him the same answer. He also said something about a uniform?"

"Folded neatly beside the remains, which looked like they had been laid out," Ricki said. "I didn't notice any darker soil underneath the body, so whoever the vic was, he might not have been killed there. But it wasn't very well lit in there even with our flashlights, so I'll have to wait and hear what the forensic guys found."

"You're sure it was a park ranger's uniform?"

Ricki lifted a hand and touched one finger to the side of her chest. "There was a badge pinned to the jacket."

"Huh." Cy leaned forward and rested his lower arms on the table. "If a ranger had gone missing in the last thirty years, I would know about it." His eyes narrowed in thought. "Even if one had gone missing from another park, I'd have heard something. That kind of news tends to get around." He glanced over at his niece. "Think that skeleton could have been up there a lot longer than thirty years?"

That would make this whole thing an even bigger can of worms, Ricki thought, and then shrugged. "Could be. Again, it's up to the ME."

Her uncle sighed. "So TK is going to have to figure it out?"

"He'll have some help from Dr. Naylor at the Tacoma PD."

"That's good. He'll need the help if he's not too stubborn to take it. I don't know if he's ever done an autopsy, outside of maybe in medical school." Cy put his palms down on the table and pushed himself up. "I guess I've had my say about your mom and Eddie. Is there anything else I can help you with when it comes to that skeleton?"

"One thing," Ricki said. "I have a uniform and a pretty cold case that's going to need some expert research."

Cy chuckled. "Like the kind of expert research a former CIA analyst can do?" When she nodded, he grinned. "I thought you didn't like having Dan as a partner."

The idea of having another partner after Marie still made her squirm inside, so she'd come up with another way to characterize her relationship with one of her uncle's officers. "I was thinking more like a part-time assistant. On a temporary basis, of course."

Cy rolled his eyes. "Your murders are never part-time. But if Dan is willing to help out, I'll free up his time." Cy stepped back and pushed his chair up against the table. "You might want to think about giving your son a break on how long he'll be grounded. It's not as if he was cutting school, and testing out one of his bots with his friends isn't exactly a major crime, and he didn't know there were any bodies up there."

She rolled her eyes. "Uh-huh. How about riding in a car with an unlicensed driver and trespassing? Where does that fall in the parenting handbook?"

His eyes crinkled in amusement. "I don't know. But I seem to recall you coloring outside the lines a time or two when you were that age." He shrugged. "And most of what the kid did is almost a rite of passage. It's a guy thing." He gave her a wink and waved her off.

Ricki waited until she was past the office door before muttering to herself, "Yeah. So I've been told."

Chapter 7

RICKI WALKED into Clay's office and used her foot to shove the door closed behind her. When Clay immediately got to his feet and came around the corner of his desk, coming straight at her, she took a small, reflexive step backward, her back slapping into the door. Without saying a word, he put his hands on her shoulders and leaned in to give her a solid kiss on her mouth. When he drew back, he grinned at her wide-eyed stare before dropping his hands back to his sides and returning to his seat behind his desk, leaving her gaping after him.

"When did we start the whole kissing thing?"

He looked over at her, the grin still on his face. "If you thought that was a whole kissing thing, then we need to speed up our timetable on this relationship."

She hadn't minded it, but her eyes automatically narrowed as she made her way to the same folding chair she'd been sitting in before talking with her uncle. She sat down and folded her arms over her chest. "We don't have a timetable, so there's nothing to speed up. And I'm pretty sure that was a kiss, Thomas."

"Uh-huh. But it was one kiss, not a whole 'kissing thing.'"

"Well, whatever it was, it doesn't happen while we're on the clock."

"Okay." His grin grew wider. "Which means we will be doing it when we're off the clock?"

Having just discussed her ex-husband with her uncle, she was in no mood to be dragged into a relationship discussion. There would be no kissing on the job, she was firm on that. As for the rest of it . . . Well, she wouldn't object to it, but given the fact she had a murder on her hands that might have occurred before she was born, she wasn't going to have much free time anytime soon.

Satisfied with that answer to her internal debate, Ricki pointed to Clay's cell phone lying on the desk. "Are we going to call Miss Lansanger?"

Clay kept a steady gaze on her face long enough that she had to fight to keep from grinning. He had been a little high-handed with that kiss and deserved the cool stare she was sending back to him. The look in his eyes silently said he wanted to stick to the topic of their relationship, but after a good five seconds ticked by, he blew out a heavy breath and picked up his phone.

"Yeah. Let's call her." He looked at a scrawled note on his desk and quickly tapped the keys on his screen before setting the phone down between them. "Fair warning, Miss Lansanger is on the emotional side."

"Understood." Ricki leaned forward when the ringing stopped. The first thing she heard was a very loud sniff.

"Hardy Investigations." The female voice on the other end was faint and came with a definite tremor. She also sounded a lot younger than Ricki had envisioned, more like nineteen than the thirtysomething all the assistants on the old investigator TV shows used to be.

"Miss Lansanger?" Clay said. "This is Chief Thomas from Edington, Washington. We spoke earlier?"

"Yeah, yeah, yeah. Did you get my email?"

"Yes. But before—"

He was cut off by a loud squeal erupting from his cell phone.

"OMG. I've been holding my breath ever since I sent it. Is it Max? The dead guy, I mean. Is it him?"

"Before we get to that," Clay began again in a firm, no-nonsense voice. "I want to let you know that you are on speakerphone, and Special Agent Ricki James is here in the office with me." He was forced to pause again when another loud noise filled the room.

"Special agent? Like the FBI or something? Are you looking for Max because he killed that guy you found? I'm telling you, Max would never do something like that. You're chasing the wrong guy, Mister Special Agent Rick James."

Clay pointed a finger at Ricki and mouthed "Your turn."

Great, Ricki thought, but she nodded and shifted her gaze to the phone.

Having had her share of experience in dealing with excitable teenagers, she tried for something to steer the assistant into a calmer discussion. If she opened with *Oh by the way, your boss has been murdered,* the odds were good she'd have to sit through half an hour of hysterics before she could get another question in.

"Actually, Miss Lansanger, I'm Ricki James, and I work with the Investigative Services Bureau of the National Park Service."

"Park service?" The assistant's tone changed from weepy to astonished in the blink of an eye. "You mean like Yellowstone or something?"

"Or something," Ricki said dryly.

"So, what did Max do? Forget to pay for a candy bar in your gift shop?"

OK, Miss Assistant to a PI. Time to rip the Band-Aid off.

"No, Miss Lansanger, that's not why Chief Thomas and I

are calling. The picture you sent has allowed us to make a positive ID on our murder victim. I'm sorry."

There was a drawn-out silence and then came one word. "Murder?"

"I'm sorry," Clay said, echoing Ricki's words. "The picture you sent, of the man you identified as Max Hardy, matches the victim."

"But murder?" Miss Lansanger's voice rose a notch. "When you said a dead guy, I thought you meant a heart attack, or maybe some kind of accident. Not murder. What happened?"

"He was shot," Ricki said baldly, drawing another loud wail through the phone and an exasperated look from Clay.

"Shot?" The assistant was back to screeching. "He doesn't even own a gun. How can he have been shot?"

Clay rubbed two fingers against the center of his forehead. "Well. We're assuming the other person he was with had a gun." After stating the obvious, Clay once again pointed at Ricki.

Sending him a quick "You've got to stop doing that" glare, Ricki turned her concentration back to the disembodied voice.

"Demi—do you mind if I call you Demi?"

"Dem. I'd rather be called Dem. My mom named me after Demi Moore. She loves all her movies." Dem drew in a breath so quickly she made a whistling noise. "Oh God. I have to call my mom. She's not going to believe this. And Max's sister! What am I going to say to his sister?"

"We will notify his sister, Miss Lan . . . uh, Dem," Ricki put in before the woman could work herself into hysterics. "But you could really be a big help if you'd answer a few questions for us."

"Like what? I don't know anything," Dem wailed. "Max never discussed his cases with me. I already told Chief Thomas that I only found out what he was working on when I had to write up his reports, and he hadn't given me any for the last few weeks. He didn't leave me any notes to put into a report. Oh God, oh God! Max owns this place. There isn't anyone else. I'm going to have to find another job."

Tamping down her exasperation, Ricki leaned in a little closer. "Did your boss mention anything at all about who he was working for? Maybe dropped something casual and called his client a he or a she?"

"I don't know, I don't know." There was another brief pause. "We walked over to a food truck that parks over in the next block for lunch the day before he left on his trip. He said something about working with an old client." Dem sniffed. "That's what he said, an old client. But I don't know if he meant the guy was, like, ancient, or if he'd done a case for him before."

"So the client was a guy?" Ricki asked.

"I don't know," Dem wailed. "I just think he probably was. Max talked in that voice he always uses when the client is rich. You know, not just lives in a nice house but in a mansion and has tons of money, that kind of rich. Those are mostly men, right?"

Ricki didn't bother to answer that but zeroed in on what Max Hardy might have left behind. "You said he left you notes for a report. Were they handwritten or printed off a computer?"

"Oh, he never gave me his handwritten notes."

"But he did make handwritten notes?" Ricki persisted.

"Yeah. He had a little notebook he always carried with him, but no one could ever read those scribbles of his. He used some kind of weird code. Like a shorthand that only he knew how to read," Dem said. "He only put them in the computer when the case was done or the client needed an update. He'd print it out and give it to me to polish it up, you know? I'm good at all that grammar and writing stuff."

Her little declaration was a stretch of the imagination, but it was how the PI had kept his case details that was interesting.

Ricki looked over at Clay, who was rolling his eyes in disbelief. She waited until he was finished and then mouthed "Notebook" at him, which had Clay shaking his head.

Taking a breath, Ricki let it out slowly. "So your boss had a notebook that he always had with him. Are you sure about that? Did he sometimes leave it back at his home, or his hotel, or maybe in his car?"

"Never," Dem insisted. "It was like a body part or something. He always had it with him, even when we would go out on double dates, he made sure he had that stupid little book with him."

A double date with her boss? Ricki had to suppress a shudder at the thought. That was almost as bizarre as Dem's claim that she was a wiz at grammar and writing. She rubbed her fingers against her temple and forced her concentration back to the way Max Hardy ran his business. "He always put his notes into a computer?"

"Oh yeah. But like I said, not until the case was finished or he needed to give an update."

As the thread she was tugging on began to crystalize for her, Ricki absently tapped her fingers against the desktop. "I need to go back a step, Dem. I need you to remember your first conversation with Chief Thomas." Ricki heard the chair behind the desk creak as Clay shifted his weight. "Do you remember telling him that you hadn't written up any reports lately that involved a case in Washington?"

"I haven't." Dem was back to sounding like she was on the verge of crying. "I'm not hiding something."

"I know," Ricki hastily assured her. "But you said you hadn't done anything *lately*. Does that mean Mr. Hardy has been to Washington on a case before?"

"Well, yeah," Dem said, her teary voice once again magically disappearing. "He's been there before, and I made all the travel arrangements that time, just like I did this time." She hesitated. "But I didn't write up that report. My mom was having an operation, so I had to take some time off. Max must have done the report himself when I was gone."

Ricki frowned. Dem might not have written up the report, but she'd bet there was a copy of it filed away somewhere. And that report wouldn't have been the only thing to go out to that client. "Do you do the billing, or did Mr. Hardy do that himself?"

"Well, sometimes he delivered the bill to the client, sometimes it was mailed, but I always got the bill ready."

"And what were the travel arrangements?" Ricki asked. "Do you remember those?"

"That's easy," Dem said. "Both times he flew into Seattle and rented a car. I booked him a room at some hotel named the St. Armand. I remember the name because it sounded like some kind of convent. You know, for nuns."

"I know," Ricki said. "In Brewer? It was the St. Armand in Brewer?"

Dem giggled. "Uh-huh. Funny name. Like they make beer there or something. Can't you just see it? A bunch of nuns making beer?"

Ricki ignored the ridiculous comment and the giggles that went with it. "Both times? Your boss stayed at the St. Armand both times?"

"Uh-huh. In Brewer." Dem giggled again.

Ricki smiled. *Bingo.* "Dem. This is very important. Can you get into your boss's computer?"

"Nope."

Okay. Dead end there.

"Did he keep hard copies of all his reports? Maybe put them in a file cabinet somewhere?"

"Nope," Dem repeated. "The office is kind of small, so we keep everything on the computers. Max had me back up all my stuff into a cloud server he paid for. He copied all his stuff there too."

Ricki sighed. *And another dead end.* Trying to narrow down

the pool of people who would know who Max had come out to Brewer to see, she backtracked to an earlier part of the call. "Are most of your clients men?"

"What? No. I mean, I don't know, really. It's not like I keep track of that. We do a lot of cheating spouse work, and those are usually women." She gave a watery-sounding laugh that ended on a sob. "I mean, I mean the clients are usually women. Their husbands are the ones cheating." She stopped to draw in a breath. "But we do some company kind of work. You know fraud, embezzlement, skimming off the top. Stuff like that. Those clients are usually men. And the missing persons gigs can be either. Wait. Hang on, hang on."

Ricki kept silent and waited as the only sound coming from the phone was Dem's choppy breathing.

"He was going to Washington to look for someone. Yeah. He told me that while we were waiting for our lunch order to be cooked. He was looking for someone."

"Looking for someone," Ricki repeated. "Did your boss ever try to find someone who'd broken the law? Maybe some of those company clients you were talking about?"

"I don't think it was a company client. We don't get much of that kind of work, and I've never seen a repeat. Maybe it was a cheating husband that he didn't catch in the act the first time around," Dem said slowly. "That's happened. Max couldn't find anything, and the wife is so sure that she hires him to go looking again."

Or a missing person he didn't find the first time around, Ricki thought.

Now, who in the Bay wanted to stay hidden badly enough to kill for it?

Chapter 8

As Clay went over a few details with Dem, Ricki leaned against the hard metal back of the folding chair and stretched her legs out in front of her. She stared down at her hands, folded in her lap, and mulled over the murder. Maxwell Hardy was technically a local case and fell to Clay, but her instincts were insisting that the mysterious skeleton, with its neatly folded ranger's uniform, and the dead PI were connected somehow.

After Clay hung up the phone, he also leaned back and locked his fingers behind his head to study the ceiling with its original white acoustic tiles. "Do you still think the two murders are linked somehow?" he asked, stating out loud the same thought echoing in her head.

She did, but there was a whole list of other possibilities. "It could be that two killers simply had the same idea a few decades apart. The lighthouse is a good place to hide a body."

Clay glanced over at her. "Maybe. But you aren't giving off that vibe." He went back to studying the ceiling. "You think the two are connected." He was quiet for a moment. "Same killer?"

"Not with that much time between them," Ricki said.

The chief straightened up in his chair and rested his forearms on the desk. "Maybe he left the area and has been operating all this time somewhere else, and now he's worked his way back here. Which would explain why he knew the lighthouse would be a good place to stash something he didn't want found. Like a dead body."

"Lovely thought," Ricki said under her breath before drawing her legs in and getting to her feet. "I need to get over to the diner and check on things. I'll work from there until Eddie gets out of school and then head on home. I'm hoping we'll have some forensics back by then and maybe the autopsy. I don't know how busy Dr. Naylor is, but I'd guess your ME could bully him into doing the autopsy right away."

"I wouldn't put it past TK." He studied her with those smoky-gray eyes that could look right through her. "Is Hamilton going to send you some help, or did you not bother to ask?"

"I bothered. I told him I was going to ask Cy for some of Dan's time to help with the research."

Clay grinned. "Good idea. Former CIA guys tend to be pretty good at research."

While Ricki had never been too thrilled with Dan's background, she did appreciate the skill set it came with. And as long as none of his former colleagues came snooping around, she didn't have to think about Dan having once worked for the covert agency. After all, he'd made the decision to leave that all behind him, so at least he'd stepped away from the dark side. She could live with that.

"Any other help coming?"

Ricki put her hands on her hips as her eyes narrowed on his very practiced, innocent expression. "Dr. Blake wasn't mentioned."

Jonathan Blake worked for the FBI and was one of the best profilers in the nation. They'd worked together on her last case, and even though they'd only talked on the phone or over the internet, for some reason, Clay, who hadn't spoken to the man at all, had taken a disliking to the doctor.

"But you might mention the good doctor at some point?"

"We don't even know who the second vic is." Ricki moved her hands from her hips and crossed them over her chest. "I thought I'd work on that first."

"Where are you going to start on that?"

"With Dan and his much-discussed research skills," Ricki said. "Which brings us back to where this whole conversation started." She took several steps toward the door before turning around to look at him. "Want to come over for dinner tonight?"

Clay's whole face instantly lit up with a smile. "Does that mean I should bring the pizza?"

Ricki nodded. "I'll stop and get beer." Feeling like they'd had a spat and then made up, Ricki returned his smile. "Around seven?"

"Sounds good," Clay said. "Maybe we'll have some evidence to look at." He sighed as he swiveled his chair around to face the computer. "We could use some."

Hoping he was right and something would pop up this afternoon, Ricki strode down the hallway, stopping at Ray's desk out front just long enough to ask him to let Ranger Dan Wilkes know where she could be reached, if Ray happened to see him.

Two minutes later she was climbing into her jeep with its faded yellow paint job and patched-up seats. Silently repeating her usual prayer, she turned the key, nodding when the engine came to life. Satisfied that her prayer had worked this time, she maneuvered her way out of the parking lot and onto the two-lane road that connected the three towns along the Bay.

It only took her fifteen minutes to reach the outer edge of Brewer, and one minute more to pull into the alley behind the diner. She hopped out of the jeep, sparing it her usual kick to the tires since it had started up on the first try, and walked over to the back steps that led into the diner's kitchen.

Her eyes widened in surprise when she spotted Eddie standing at the stove, a huge spatula in one hand as he stared intently at the burger sizzling away in front of him. He had the same look of concentration that he did whenever he was building one of his bots. She smiled at the great picture her tall, gangly son made with his dark glasses sliding down his nose and a snow-white apron wrapped around his narrow waist. Anchorman stood behind him, leaning against the long prep table. When she started to shrug out of her jean jacket, intent on putting her gun into the small safe bolted to the floor in the closet, Anchorman reached out and wagged a finger back and forth at her.

"You might want to keep that on for a bit." He jerked his head backwards. "You have company."

Eddie looked up, his glasses covered in steam. He took them off and wiped them against the sleeve of his shirt. "He means Dad is here. He's out front talking to Marcie."

She lifted an eyebrow as she made a show of looking at her watch. "Did your dad pick you up early from school?"

Her son shook his head. "No. I forgot to tell him the seniors were having a ditch day today," Eddie said, referring to the annual ritual that happened every June as the end of the school year drew near. "So the rest of us got out early." His mouth pulled down as he gave her a long-suffering look. "I came straight here, didn't even stop to talk with anyone."

Ricki would have been impressed by that if it weren't for the hamburger cooking away on the grill. The odds were Eddie had hightailed it to the diner because he was hungry. Lately, no amount of food seemed to fill him up.

She walked over and laid a hand on her son's shoulder. "Want to clue me on why your dad is here?"

"He's taking a tour out this weekend. Those people from Portland."

Surprised, Ricki cocked her head to the side. "I thought he passed that one up."

"He did. But some lady called him last night and asked if he would take it as a favor to her."

Eddie grabbed the plate Anchorman was holding out to him. A toasted bun was already laid out on it, waiting for a burger. When he turned to finish putting together his sandwich, Ricki glanced toward her cook.

"Lady?"

Anchorman lifted his heavy shoulders, then let them down again. "Don't ask me. It's not my job to keep track of your ex's love life."

Ricki frowned. She didn't care one iota about Bear's love life. She'd given up that right the minute she'd signed their final divorce papers, but she did care about who was referring people to their business. They'd both worked to build up a solid reputation for Adventure Tours, and had managed to carve out a boutique, exclusive niche in wilderness camping.

Their website and questionnaire made it clear their trips were only for experienced hikers and campers. The last thing they needed was for Bear to find himself miles from any amenities and stuck with a group of amateur outdoor wannabes. Knowing him the way she did, she was sure he'd get fed up and abandon the group and might not even bother to send anyone else into Olympic Park to guide them back.

It was fine for Bear to take that attitude. He had that comfortable inheritance, and the truth was he didn't need to work at all. But she needed the summer boost to her income that their little joint enterprise provided. The diner brought in good money during the tourist season but barely broke even in the winter, and while her government paycheck covered her and Eddie's expenses, there was still the bill for the nursing home taking care of her mom. Taking on a steady paycheck again had been a huge help. But she still needed her side gigs to keep all her balls juggling in the air.

Since there wasn't much she could do to avoid having a talk with her former husband, Ricki quietly left Eddie to enjoy his hamburger and pushed through the swinging doors leading into the dining room. Bear was sitting at the counter, a mug of coffee in his large hands. He was smiling as he listened to whatever Marcie was saying to him. When he spotted Ricki, his smile stayed firmly in place, but his eyes took on a wary look.

She nodded a greeting before heading to the coffee machine with a full pot sitting on the warming plate. Ricki picked up an empty mug and slowly filled it to the brim before carrying it and the pot of coffee over to the counter. She set her mug down and lifted the pot up, refilling Bear's cup to the brim as well.

"I hear you took on a tour for the weekend," she said casually, keeping her tone friendly and her gaze on his face.

Bear topped out at six foot four and had a trim waist, wide shoulders, and massive arms left over from his high school football days. It was his prowess on the field that had earned him his nickname, and the admiration of every teenage girl in town. But it was Ricki who'd been his girl from their first year in high school, and no matter what had gone on between then and now, she'd always have a soft spot for Bear. It was just buried much deeper on some days than others.

Marcie took the coffeepot out of her hands. "I'll take this and make the rounds while you two talk." She poked a sturdy finger into Ricki's shoulder. "Have you eaten anything today?"

Used to her waitress always trying to feed her, Ricki gave a quick bob of her head. "I had a muffin with butter and cinnamon sugar at home, and a rice cake on the way to headquarters."

"To balance out the sugar, which I'm sure does no such thing," Marcie said. "And a puny little muffin isn't enough to keep a bird alive, even if it is paired up with a rice cake. I'll bring you a PB&J special."

Bear instantly made a face. "You still eat those things?"

She mimicked his facial expression right back at him. A fried peanut butter and jelly sandwich was one of her favorite foods, and he'd known that when he married her. "Yes, it is. And don't change the subject."

"What subject?" Bear asked. "We haven't said anything yet."

Ricki's booted foot began to tap against the tile floor. "The tour. I asked you about the weekend tour."

"Oh, yeah. Sure. That's what I came to tell you. I booked a four-day tour to go over the weekend." He peered at her over the rim of his coffee cup. "I thought you'd be happy about it. You're always saying we need to grow the business."

"Not quite, Bear," she said evenly. "I always say we need to grow the right kind of business. Did you check out this group? Are they up for a four-day hike? Where are you going?"

"Up to the glacier. I already called for the permits and got them approved. I can pick them up tomorrow."

No surprise there, Ricki thought. Bear considered every ranger who worked in the park a drinking buddy.

"This group is a hiking club out of Portland. When they first called, I'd never heard of them, but a good friend of mine vouched for them. Said they could make the glacier hike without a problem."

Noticing he hadn't used any word that would indicate the gender of this new friend of his, Ricki's eyebrows winged up. "A friend of yours?" As Bear's cheeks took on an even redder hue, the devil inside her had Ricki's mouth curling into a knowing grin. "Is this a 'she' by any chance?"

"Just a friend, babe." His jaw was set into a stubborn line. "You're a woman and we're friends, aren't we? That's what you keep telling me, anyway."

Touché. There was no way she was going to get sucked into that old argument, so she only nodded. "Fine. If you think the group will hold up, then it's okay with me."

"The thing is, I'll be leaving Friday, so I have to go into Tacoma tomorrow to pick up some gear for the trip."

Gear? The man had to be kidding. He had two sheds full of gear, not to mention the huge pile under a tarp on his patio. When she continued to stare silently at him, he doggedly plowed on.

"Anyway, Eddie will need to stay with you tomorrow, and Monday night. If that doesn't work for you, he can stay with my mom."

As much as she still liked her former mother-in-law, who lived right outside of town, Ricki wasn't going to give up spending a few extra days with her son.

"Of course Eddie will stay with me." She waited until Bear started to relax. "What kind of gear?"

She watched in satisfaction as he immediately tensed up. "Just some little stuff." His cheeks started to heat up again. "I get a good deal at Mountain Outfitters." The red spread faster across his face.

Interesting. Bear used to swear by another store. She didn't know when he'd started going to Mountain Outfitters instead. He hopped off his stool and took a hasty step backward under Ricki's steady gaze.

"I gotta go, babe. I'll see you Tuesday."

"Oh, no rush," Ricki said sweetly. "Take your time."

As he practically ran for the front door, Ricki barely managed to keep herself from laughing out loud. Marcie strolled up, carrying a plate with a fried PB&J sitting next to a small mound of salad greens.

"That boy's up to something. It was all over his face the minute he walked in the door."

"Yeah, he is. And I'd say it has something to do with a good friend that works at Mountain Outfitters."

Correctly hearing what Ricki hadn't said, Marcie's mouth dropped in surprise. "Is that right?" She set the plate down and faced Ricki from across the counter. "How do you feel about that? After all, the man was your first love."

Ricki shrugged, but silently admitted to herself she really didn't know. In all their years together, Bear had hardly even looked at another woman. She turned her head and stared at the empty stool where he'd been sitting a few minutes ago. It would definitely take some getting used to.

"Your first love, but maybe not your only one," Marcie said. "A man's been standing at the front for a while now, staring in your direction." She winked at Ricki. "Do you have another admirer besides the chief?"

Ricki looked over to the front of the diner, then grinned and pointed at a nearby booth.

"Not an admirer," she told Marcie. "A kind of assistant partner."

As she walked away, she heard Marcie say under her breath, "What in the world is an assistant partner?"

Chapter 9

RICKI SET her plate down and slid into the booth opposite Dan. The wooden framework attached to the wall creaked as she scooted across the cloth seat to reach for the pepper shaker kept in a small metal carrier next to the wall along with the salt, ketchup, and Tabasco sauce. Looking over the booth was a framed photograph of Mount Olympus in its full winter glory. She watched Dan studying the place while she dumped a fair amount of pepper onto her salad, enough to make him wince when he glanced over at her.

"Are you going to eat that?"

She smiled, unwrapped her fork from the paper towel the Sunny Side Up used in place of a napkin, and stabbed at a piece of lettuce covered in brown speckles.

"Uh-huh," she said just before popping the greenery into her mouth. "Do you want anything?"

He stared at her plate of food before pointing at her sandwich. "What is that?"

"A peanut butter and jelly sandwich fried in butter."

"You're kidding."

"Nope." Ricki picked up the sweet and salty mix, cushioned between two slices of crispy bread, and took a large bite. "Are you hungry? Anchorman will make one for you."

"I thought the chief was kidding when he said that was your favorite meal." He looked at her plate again and shook his head. "A fried sandwich and a salad drowning in pepper. Really?"

"We all like to eat different things, that's why there are restaurants and grocery stores with aisles filled with food," Ricki said dryly. She liked Dan, although she was hard-pressed to admit it. After all, she might have accepted his prior life working for the CIA, but he still should have told her about it up front when they'd started working together on her first case back as an agent. But no. All he'd said was that he'd transferred to Olympic Park after working at Independence Hall for a year. He hadn't breathed a word about what he'd done before that, and she'd just assumed he'd been assigned to another park, not mucking around with covert operations.

"How's your shoulder?"

The ranger had been shot a month and a half ago, and she still felt responsible for his injury. He'd been working on her case.

In response to her question, Dan rolled it back and forth several times. "Good as new."

An awkward silence fell between them. Dan had once said that they didn't know much about each other, and that was true. He was in his early fifties, with a comfortable face and a quiet, unassuming manner. Aside from his stints at Independence Hall and with the CIA, Ricki didn't know much about him, which wasn't a great basis to have any kind of conversation. It didn't help that she was uncomfortable that he knew a great deal more about her than where she'd been working for the last few years. It seemed the entire law enforcement community knew that her last partner had died in an ambush, that she had an uncle with the park service, and she was divorced. At this point, she was sure all the rangers based at Olympic, including Dan Wilkes, knew she'd gone on a date with the local police chief.

Finally, Dan sat up a little straighter and cleared his throat. "Um. Thanks for letting me help out."

"Sure," Ricki said. "I appreciate the help. I'm just sorry that we don't have much to go on."

Dan pulled his cell phone out of the pocket of the jacket he'd laid across the seat. "The pictures were interesting."

She raised an eyebrow. "What pictures?"

"The ones from the Tacoma PD forensic guys." He looked down at his phone. "Chief Thomas forwarded them to me."

She frowned at the unspoken "because you didn't" in his voice. "I didn't know they'd sent anything. I had to deal with Bear, so I haven't had a chance to look at my phone." She pulled her phone out of its case clipped to her belt and set it on the table beside her plate.

"Bear?" Dan glanced over at the counter where she and Bear had been talking. "That was Bear? That walking mountain was your husband?"

Resigned to everyone knowing her business, she took another stab at a piece of lettuce and nodded. "My ex-husband and yeah." When she glanced up, he had an almost comical look on his face. "Who did you think he was?"

"Um. Another agent." Dan looked down and fiddled with the buttons on his phone. "I thought maybe the ISB had hired another agent with a lot of muscle to work with you."

"So you think I need a lot of muscle to tag along on my investigations?" Ricki asked, her words carrying no heat as she studied him. Puzzled by his reaction, she put her fork down and leaned back against the cushioned padding of the booth. "No. The only other agent in the office is on medical leave from an automobile accident, and I took the place of the one who retired. There aren't any openings in the Seattle office at the moment." She'd added that last bit to see if he'd take the bait and tell her what was bothering him about the idea of another agent, big muscles and all, paying her a visit.

"Oh. So there are only two agents in Seattle?"

Her curiosity piqued even more, Ricki slowly nodded, keeping her gaze on his face. "There aren't that many agents to begin with, so yeah, there's only two and an agent in charge assigned to Seattle." She paused for a moment. "But if you're interested in openings, I can ask if there are any in one of the other offices."

"No, no," Dan quickly protested. "I like the park service." She counted off a full three seconds before he added, "Do you think the guy on medical leave will be coming back?" When she smiled, he shrugged. "I just thought you might like some help."

Thinking this day was full of surprises, Ricki shrugged. Since Dan clearly didn't want to admit to her that he was interested in the ISB, she reached for her phone and started a one-handed search through her email. "Let's look at the pictures. Did you see anything interesting?" She opened the email from Captain Davis that had several attachments. One looked like a file folder, and the second one was labeled *Preliminary Autopsy Report: John Doe Number 15.* Ignoring the report for the moment, she opened up the file, and a long series of pictures began to populate her screen.

"The first group of photos are from your cold case." Dan looked up. "I'm assuming since all that's left is a skeleton that you consider this a cold case?"

"Doesn't get much colder," Ricki agreed. She pulled up the fifth photo and studied it, using two fingers to enlarge it on her screen. From what she could see, it looked like the same uniform the rangers wore today. "Looks the same as the one you have on, so not much help there."

"It's a help," Dan contradicted. "Believe it or not, the uniforms have changed over the years, so if it is the same one

I'm wearing, then at least we'll know the upper age of the corpse."

"As in, he can't be older than this date because that's when the uniforms changed?"

He nodded. "Exactly. I'll study the uniform, but it's really picture number twelve that's the key."

"Twelve?" Ricki scrolled through the files, stopping at number twelve. Again she enlarged the photograph on her screen. "It's the park service badge."

"Uh-huh. It's a little different from yours, since you have the shield with the eagle on top."

She raised her gaze from her phone and frowned at her assistant partner. "Okay. That's the ranger badge. So you're saying the victim was a ranger?" Something she already knew just from the uniform.

"Well yeah, that too," Dan said. "But over the years the badges have changed. I'm not really sure when, I just know they have because I saw a display once at the Northeast's regional office back in Philadelphia. I don't remember the dates exactly, but I do know the badge has been redesigned more than a couple of times, and each new design was released in a specific year."

"Then you're looking to see the maximum number of years back the vic could have been a ranger," Ricki said, following his train of thought.

"And if we're lucky, maybe there's a number. I didn't see any photos of the back."

She immediately shook her head. "I don't think an employee number of some sort has ever been put on the badges." At least she'd never noticed one.

"I'm thinking more like a batch number from the company that made them," Dan said. "But I need to do some research first to determine if the badge makers, whoever they were, did that kind of thing way back when."

Ricki made a sound of agreement and opened the second

attachment on her phone. She scanned the autopsy report. Dr. Naylor was as thorough as usual, and she could easily imagine TK standing over his shoulder, prodding him on. "Did Clay forward you the autopsy report along with the picture?"

"No. Just the pictures."

She sent him the report, then continued eating her now cold sandwich while he read through it.

"'Male. Estimated at twenty-five to forty years of age at time of death,'" Dan read out loud. "'Probable cause was a gunshot wound to the heart.'"

"Hmm." Ricki added a nod as she chewed and swallowed the last bite of her food. She looked around and caught Marcie's eye. She pointed at herself and then Dan before making a drinking motion with one hand. When the waitress nodded, Ricki turned her attention back to the ranger. "There are a couple of things that are more interesting. Dr. Naylor's best guess at how long our unknown ranger has been dead is over twenty-five years, and he stated it could easily be double that."

"Big window to work with," Dan said.

Yeah, it is. She tapped a finger against the tabletop. "Rob was the forensic guy. His contact number is on the report. Give him a call and have him take a more thorough look at that badge. Maybe he'll see a number on it."

Marcie bustled up to the table, carrying the mugs in one hand and a coffeepot in the other. "Here you go, boss." She set the drinks down and smiled at Dan. "And who might you be?"

"Ranger Dan Wilkes," Ricki supplied. "Dan, this is Marcie."

Marcie laughed. "Long introductions aren't something we usually need in the Bay. Most of us have been here a while, and they never were one of Ricki's strong points." She held out a hand. "I work here, along with Anchorman, who I know you've met."

Dan tried to get up, belatedly realized he was trapped by the table, and sank back down in his seat with a mumbled apology.

"Stay right where you are, Ranger Wilkes," Marcie said. "Just tell me how you like your coffee."

He stared at the pot she was holding up. "My coffee?"

"Black," Ricki said. "He drinks his coffee black." She scowled and considered giving him a swift kick beneath the table. He seemed fascinated by the coffeepot. He briefly looked up at Marcie before returning his gaze to the pot in her hand. The man had lost his marbles.

"Black it is," Marcie declared cheerfully, completely ignoring the ranger's strange behavior. "I'll just leave the pot right here for you and let you both get back to work."

Dan's eyes followed her as she walked across the room, forcing Ricki to lean over the table and snap her fingers in front of his face. "Hello? Badges? Autopsy reports? A dead body?"

He kept his gaze on Marcie but nodded absently. "Yeah. Good. I'll call the forensic tech." He finally sighed and shifted his gaze to Ricki. "A couple of things. You said there were a couple of things more interesting in the report besides the victim being shot. How long he's been in that lighthouse is one thing. What else?"

Satisfied he was finally focusing back on the case, Ricki picked up her phone and scrolled to the entry on the report that had caught her eye. "There were still some cloth fragments around and underneath the bones."

"So?" Dan prompted. "Does that mean he wasn't wearing his uniform when he died?" He shook his head. "That doesn't make any sense. The picture shows a bullet hole in the front jacket and the shirt underneath. So he had to be wearing it."

"I'd say someone took it off him after he died," Ricki said slowly. "His uniform but not his underwear." She turned her screen around. "See here? The report states the cloth fragments are a light cotton, the kind that undershirts and boxers are made from."

Dan paled a little. "Do you think he was sexually assaulted and then shot?" He stared off into the distance for a long moment, before rubbing a hand across his forehead. "No. He had the uniform on when he was shot, so he would have had to have been shot and then undressed and assaulted?" The ranger's lip curled up in distaste. "That's some sick bastard who would do something like that."

The world is full of sick bastards, Ricki thought, but stayed silent as she read through the rest of the report. It could have happened the way Dan said, but something about it seemed off to her. The body was posed as if someone had cared about the way it had appeared, but then left it in a place where it wouldn't be found. She frowned as she turned that little oddity over in her mind. A show of respect from his killer? Or maybe remorse?

"Anything else you need me to dig into?"

Ricki slowly lifted her gaze from her phone. "Once we get the timeline narrowed down as much as we can, you can start going through the personnel records."

"Back in DC? Those would be kept there, wouldn't they? Old computer disks maybe, or an electronic archive somewhere?"

"Maybe," Ricki said. "If our vic went missing in the last twenty years. But if Dr. Naylor is right and we're talking about more than twenty-five years ago? Then we're talking paper records."

"I'm sure they've digitized a lot of that old stuff."

"Digitized could mean microfiche." Ricki raised an eyebrow when Dan grimaced. "And they might have done that back in DC, but the records here were just stored away in boxes." When his eyes widened, she nodded. "Stored in the basement right there in Edington."

"How many years are down there?" Dan asked.

"I haven't been to the basement in a while, but there are a lot of boxes." When he propped his elbows on the table and dropped his head into his hands, Ricki grinned. "Luckily it stays pretty cold and dry down there, so you shouldn't run into much of a mold problem."

His head immediately shot up. "Mold?"

She went back to studying the report on her phone. "Uh-huh. But you might want to take a mask with you, just in case."

Chapter 10

Ricki pulled into the parking lot of the headquarters shared by the park service and the Bay's police department an hour later than her usual time to check in. While Eddie had been getting ready for school, she'd completed and sent a report to ASAC Hamilton on the progress of her assigned cases. Most of it involved finishing off the details of investigations in other parks in the Pacific-West region the Seattle office covered, and there was the one close to home that hadn't technically happened in the park.

The one with a dead ranger who no one remembered had gone missing.

She sighed and got out of the car, slamming the jeep door twice before it finally stayed shut. She glared at the offending piece of metal that had lost most of its paint. Clay was always trying to float her a loan so she'd get something more reliable. She had to admit she was running out of patience with simply being aggravated by it, not to mention with wearing out a good pair of hiking boots from kicking the tires every time the touchy thing gave her grief. Deciding she had enough things looming to ruin her morning without adding the jeep to it, she turned her back on her four-wheel problem and strode across the gravel lot.

Working from home had its upsides, but she made a point of coming in every morning. She enjoyed having a cup of coffee with Clay, or any of the park's law enforcement guys who were hanging around before their patrols. It gave her a feeling of being connected and put off the start of the nagging daily aggravations that dogged anyone trying to juggle three jobs, a kid, and an ex-husband. And oh yeah. There was still the matter of the dead guy.

Two cars away, a lone figure emerged from a mid-sized SUV. Ricki smiled at the slightly bent man wrapped in a thick wool jacket, with a scarf draped over his head.

"Ray," she called out, picking up her pace when he turned around and waved at her. "You're getting in later than usual."

He smiled and gave her a broad wink. "So are you, Special Agent James. My nephew came in last night and we were up late catching up." His smile widened. "I left him setting up his temporary office in my dining room. It should work out fine since we prefer to eat at the kitchen table."

"I'm glad you can spend some time with him," Ricki said. "Maybe even take a few days off so you can enjoy that fishing you were talking about."

Ray's head bobbed up and down underneath the scarf. "In our special spot. I'm looking forward to it, but lots depends on John's schedule since he'll still be working." He pushed his hands into the pocket of his coat and started walking toward the building's entrance. "Not sure who you'll be having your coffee with this morning. I don't see Clay's car."

Ricki adjusted her quick, long-legged stride to match his much slower one, and gave him a sideways, speculative glance. "That's too bad, I wanted to ask him something, but maybe you could help me?"

"Be happy to. Ask away."

"It's about the lighthouse." Ricki looked over when Ray didn't say anything. "The one up near Massey?"

"Oh. That one."

"Uh-huh," she said slowly. "That one where the dead body was found."

Ray huddled deeper into his coat. "Yep. Yep. What about it?"

"Do you know who owns it?"

The elderly man lifted one hand from his pocket and lightly rubbed the end of his nose. "No one, as far as I know," he finally said. "It's always been there, so I figured some fool government agency built it and has been ignoring it ever since." He turned his whole body so he could look at her from beneath the edge of the scarf hanging down to his scraggly eyebrows. "I seem to recall someone mentioning it might have been one of those projects the government did to help people get work right after the Great Depression. That would have been what, almost ninety years ago?"

Ricki considered it. It was possible, but those projects had been commissioned by the federal government, and if that were federal land, she thought she'd probably have heard that by now. Or at least would have when she was a park ranger right out of college.

"Why is that important?" Ray asked. "Something to do with the chief's murder victim?"

"More for me," Ricki said easily. "My son was trespassing on that land, and I was wondering who he should apologize to."

Ray laughed. "Well, if that's what you're thinking, every kid in the Bay will need to do some apologizing. I figure most of them have been up there one time or another."

She nodded as they started up the five steps together. "True enough. It was just a thought."

Ray paused at the top and drew in a couple of quick breaths. "Not as young as I used to be." He slowly unwound the scarf and tucked it into one of his coat pockets. "If it's really that important, you can always make the trip over to Port Jefferson. The land records would be in the county offices there." He put a hand on her arm when she started to open the door into the building. "But I imagine there's been more than a couple of fires in the last hundred years, so you might be disappointed at making the trip for nothing."

Ricki pulled open the door and held it for Ray. She could put Dan Wilkes on the problem of tracking down the owners, letting him make the trip over to Port Jefferson. But in a small town like the Bay, the county offices weren't the only source of information. Deciding she would pay a visit to one of her neighbors, Ricki walked inside.

Ray was already behind the lobby desk, waving a small piece of paper in the air. "Got a note here from the chief. Says he'll be out most of the morning, but he can be reached on the radio. Want me to let him know you're here?"

Disappointed at missing their morning coffee together, she shook her head and did an about-face. Now that she had a plan in mind, there was no time like the present to stop by and say hi to that neighbor.

"He might be out patrolling," Ray called after her. "I can give him a ring on his cell phone."

"No, thanks. I'll find him." Ricki waved her hand and headed back to her jeep. Fifteen minutes later she turned onto a small lane leading off the main highway, about a mile from Brewer.

She passed a few cabins, and more than a few sheds, before coming to the narrow dirt driveway leading up to a white clapboard house set back from the road. More in the cottage style than the log cabins that were more popular in the Bay, the small house had a tidy postage-stamp-sized yard and a wide front porch with two rocking chairs.

Ricki brought the jeep to a stop and grinned at the pair of chairs. Wanda Simms had made it very clear to the entire population of the Bay that she only entertained one visitor at a time. And for a very good reason. Wanda was the keeper of all knowledge about the Bay, its history, and all its residents, both past and present. In other words, she was the grand lady of the local gossip. Pete paid her regular visits, and so did anyone else in Dabob Bay who had a juicy tidbit or two. If Wanda didn't know about it, then it never happened.

She'd barely shoved the door shut when Wanda herself appeared on the porch, carrying two of the largest ceramic mugs Ricki had ever seen. They were a good size for serving beer, but it was definitely steam coiling off the tops as she made her way across the porch and set the mugs down on a small table strategically placed between the two rocking chairs. She then turned, walked over to the porch railing and leaned over it, adjusting the tiny wire-rimmed glasses she always wore on the tip of her nose.

"Well. If it isn't Richelle McCormick James."

Ricki laughed. Wanda was one of the few people on earth who ever called her by her full name. The only other two were her uncle and her mom, when Miriam McCormick had been able to remember who her daughter was.

She lifted a hand in greeting. "Hey, Wanda. How are you?"

"Doing well, doing well. You come right up here and have a sit. I already have some coffee for you. If you're hungry, you best bring some of those rice cakes you keep in your car. The biscuit dough is still rising." She slanted her head to one side and straightened away from the rail. "I don't usually have visitors this early in the morning."

Ricki doubted that, but she gave an amicable nod before crossing the short distance to the porch steps. Wanda was still settling into her favorite chair when Ricki took the seat next to her.

"I'm just going to mention it's a pretty day," Wanda said,

"to get it out of the way. I know you aren't here to talk about the weather."

"No. I'm not." Ricki smiled. She appreciated the fact that Wanda had never required a lot of small talk before getting down to business. "Do you know who owns the old lighthouse on the hill above Massey?"

"Where those two bodies were found?" When Ricki scowled, Wanda laughed. "How long were you thinking to keep that second one a secret, Agent James?"

"Longer than this," Ricki mumbled.

"It isn't out much yet. Just found out about it myself this morning."

"I don't suppose you'd care to tell me how you found out about it?"

Wanda laughed, setting the layers of wrinkles on her cheeks and neck into motion. Her steel-gray hair was pulled back from her face and fixed into a small, tight bun at the nape of her neck, and age spots covered most of the skin on her hands. But her brown eyes were as sharp as they'd ever been as she stared at Ricki over the rim of her glasses. "No. And I wouldn't tell you that if we were sitting in front of a jury and you were trying to get it out of me." She leaned forward and dropped her voice to a whisper. "I also heard that second body was only bones, and a ranger's uniform was folded up next to it."

"I don't suppose you know how long those bones have been up there?" Ricki asked dryly.

"No, I don't." Wanda settled back into her chair and stared at Ricki. "Do you?"

Fully aware that Wanda worked strictly on a "you scratch my back and I'll scratch yours" basis, Ricki had already decided on the one piece of information she was willing to part with. "We aren't sure yet, but it looks to be at least twenty-five years."

For the first time in Ricki's memory, Wanda looked

completely taken aback. One frail hand came up and covered her mouth. "Who is he?"

"No idea." Ricki reached for the coffee mug nearest to her and carefully lifted it to her mouth. "Know of any rangers who have gone missing?"

"There's never been one," Wanda declared. "So whoever he was, he must not have been from around here."

"Maybe not." Knowing that might be the plain truth, Ricki focused on the information she'd come for. "I was hoping you'd know who owns that land."

"I know, but I can't tell you," Wanda said. She chuckled at Ricki's sudden frown. "What I mean is that I can't tell you right this instant. I wrote a book a while back on Massey's history." She waved a hand in the air. "It's still sitting on a few shelves in a couple of the shops up there."

"So it's in the book?" Ricki asked, already making plans to track a copy down if that was what it would take to save her or Dan a trip to Port Jefferson.

Wanda shook her head. "Oh, no, no. The original owners are listed, of course. As I recall, they built that old lighthouse as a guide for lost hunters, not for ships, and to be honest, I'm not sure they ever did get around to putting a light in it." She paused as her forehead wrinkled in thought. "But they sold the land to someone else right after World War II. Those people still own that whole section above Massey as far as I know, but they've never done a thing with it. So of course, I didn't include that in the book."

Ricki's hopes sank. So much for getting a small break on the case.

"But I do have the information in my notes."

Ricki set the mug down and braced both hands against her knees. "Do you still have those notes?"

"Of course, Richelle. It's an insult that you would think I didn't." Wanda braced one foot against the floor of the porch and set her chair into motion. "I'll look it up. You give me a ring tomorrow and I promise I'll have it for you. But not too early, mind you. I've been sleeping in a little later these days." She smiled. "Now, with that out of the way, how's your mother?"

Ricki spent another ten minutes answering Wanda's questions about her mom, Eddie, how the divorce was going with Bear, and of course her relationship with "that handsome chief." She blurted out an excuse at her first opportunity and made her escape, feeling she'd gotten off lightly for the information Wanda had promised her. Hopefully by tomorrow.

She'd just made the turn out of Wanda's driveway when her cell phone rang. It was her habit to put it on the seat next to her so she could see the caller ID easily. The name that flashed on her screen had her sucking in a startled breath and then letting it out in one rapid whoosh.

She gingerly picked it up and put the receiver to her ear. "Hi."

"Hi, yourself. I'm here in town. At the hotel. I need to see you."

"Okay," Ricki said slowly. "When?"

"Now is good."

"Okay." Ricki winced. She sounded like a parrot with a one-word vocabulary.

"I'll wait for you in the bar."

Telling herself she couldn't duck out on repaying a favor forever, and it would be better to get it over with sooner rather than later, she resigned herself to making the extra stop at the St. Armand.

It only took her a few minutes to reach the winding road leading up to the luxury hotel. As she made the turn, her uncle's words flashed through her mind. Her mom had said that Marie was going to send her someone.

It seemed like her mom had been right.

Chapter 11

Ricki walked into the St. Armand, pausing just a few feet in to take a look around. She nodded at the desk clerk, a bubbly twenty-year-old who occasionally dropped by the Sunny Side Up for breakfast before starting her workday at the grand hotel. The young woman returned a cheery smile and a wave before scurrying to the far end of the counter to help a waiting customer.

The lobby boasted wide panels of antique oak and brass accents that gleamed in the soft light of crystal chandeliers. At the far end of the spacious room was a twenty-foot wall of glass that provided a perfect frame for the serene bay stretching out beyond the treetops.

"Ricki."

She turned her head to the familiar voice, smiling as Clay paid for his coffee at the small cart against one wall, then walked over to join her.

"Looking for me?"

"Check the ego, Thomas. I'm here to meet a friend." She glanced at the disposable cup in his hand. "Did you decide you liked the coffee here better than Anchorman's? He'll be crushed."

He grinned. "Unlike my ego, Anchorman's is safe enough." He gestured to the bank of elevators. "I've been up checking out Maxwell Hardy's room."

Her mind happily shifted off her impending meeting and back to their case. Or cases. "Did you find anything interesting?"

"Mostly it's what I didn't find," he said. "No laptop. No little notebook."

"No leads," Ricki said, correctly interpreting the frustrated look on his face. "I might have something." When the chief quirked an eyebrow, she shrugged. "A small something. I paid a visit to Wanda Simms. She might know who owns that land and the lighthouse. She's going to look through some notes she made and get back to me tomorrow."

Clay's forehead wrinkled and his eyes narrowed. "Wanda Simms? The local . . ." He paused, obviously struggling to come up with the right description for Wanda.

"Historian?" Ricki supplied with a grin. "And keeper of all gossip." She nodded. "Yeah. That Wanda."

"And she has notes?" Clay asked.

Now Ricki laughed. "In Wanda's case, that wouldn't be hard to believe, but it turns out she was writing a book about the history of Massey. She said the same people have owned that land since World War II."

"Good to know," Clay said. "I hope your skeleton doesn't go back that far, because that wouldn't be a cold case. It would be a frozen-solid one."

And most likely the end of my investigation, Ricki thought. Hamilton wouldn't let her put much time into it if it were that old, especially since there was no record of a missing ranger.

"What friend are you meeting here?"

Ricki quickly adjusted to the abrupt change in topics and wiggled her eyebrows at him. "Why the interest?"

Clay chuckled. "Check your own ego there, James. Just a

natural curiosity. But now that you brought it up, is it another guy?"

"As a matter of fact, it is." When Clay gave her an expectant look, she sighed and pushed her hands into her jacket pockets. "Josh Crawford."

Clay's eyes opened wider. "Marie's fiancé?"

"The one and only."

"The guy whose calls you avoided for almost a year until you asked him for profiling help to catch Tatum Quinn?"

Getting irritated, she shoved her hands even deeper into her pockets. "Yeah. Him."

"What does he want?"

"I don't know," Ricki admitted. "I haven't talked to him yet. He's waiting in the bar."

He glanced in that direction. "Want some company?"

She felt a small warmth in the pit of her stomach, calming some of the jitters dancing around there. It was nice to have someone watch your back. It was even better if that someone was Clay Thomas. But she shook her head. This was something she needed to do herself. "No, thanks. I'm good."

He put his free hand on her shoulder and gave it a gentle squeeze. "I'll be back at headquarters if you need to stop by."

"Thanks," she repeated before taking a small step back and breaking the contact. "You have work, and I need to get this over with."

Despite the public setting, Clay leaned forward and placed a soft kiss on her mouth. It was over and done before she could manage a protest. "I'll see you later." He straightened up and gave her a nod before walking off toward the front doors.

She watched him for a moment before turning in the opposite direction, not sure what she felt about this one-sided shift in their relationship. Although she wasn't doing much to stop it either. Sighing in annoyance at herself, she silently ordered her feet to get moving.

The bar was off to the right of the front desk. Without breaking stride, Ricki turned in that direction and walked through the wrought-iron archway. The same bank of tall windows offering a slightly different, still spectacular view dominated the space with its comfortable chairs and mixture of square and round tables. She'd always thought the atmosphere wasn't a hotel bar as much as a lounge for the leisurely rich, with drink prices to match. On her current tight budget, she never spent any time up at the St. Armand, much less indulged in its tourist-priced drinks, although she could certainly appreciate the views.

She spotted Josh among the scattered tables of patrons, and he'd clearly been watching out for her because he immediately got to his feet. They stared at each other for a long moment before she finally moved forward.

Josh Crawford. Medium height, handsome face with chiseled, masculine features, and dark-brown hair with eyes the same color. She remembered how they used to sparkle with laughter, especially at his own jokes. She hadn't heard any laughter from him in a long time. Josh. An FBI agent with a bright future, a good athlete, and an all-around nice guy. And Marie's fiancé. Or he used to be. When her former partner was alive.

Once she crossed the room, Ricki halted next to the table, looking at him, not sure what to say. She hadn't seen Josh since the funeral and had only talked to him a handful of times since then. Not from his lack of trying, but hers. Which had seemed like a good idea at the time, but with him standing right in front of her, made her feel petty and small.

She opened her mouth and then closed it again, at a complete loss for words. And could only stand helplessly when Josh stepped around the edge of the table to engulf her in a hug. After a small hesitation, she raised her arms and hugged him back, accepting the comfort he was offering and giving some of it in return. When he stepped back, he held her at arm's length and studied her face.

"You look good, James. Better than when I last saw you. I could hear it in your voice, too, when you called."

Feeling a spurt of guilt, Ricki stiffened. "Look. I'm really sorry it took me so long."

He shook his head, a smile playing on his lips. "Not a problem. I could wait. And I was happy to help. Thanks for the follow-up and letting me know that you got the guy." He frowned. "Although I heard through a back door that he almost got you." Josh's brown eyes grew a shade darker. "You left out that little detail."

"Since he didn't get me, it wasn't relevant," Ricki said.

His gaze took on a resigned look. "Uh-huh. Rushing in without backup is what I heard."

"I didn't have much choice."

"And I wasn't surprised, James. That's so you."

"It is not." Ricki glared at him, and then couldn't help grinning when he broke into a laugh. A hint of that familiar sparkle was back in his eyes.

"Thirty seconds before we start arguing." Josh shook his head. "That might be a record."

"Not even close," she declared before pointing at the table. "Want to sit down? Or we can keep arguing. Either way works for me."

He laughed again. "Let's sit. I have something to give you."

She glanced at the table and for the first time noticed a thick manila envelope lying on it. She pulled out a chair while he settled into his seat. When she lifted her gaze from the envelope, he was staring at her.

"You do look good, Ricki."

"So do you, Josh."

He turned his head and looked out the large bank of windows. "I was nervous about seeing you." He sighed and shifted his attention back to her. "The two of you were always together. I see you. I see her."

"It's been over a year," Ricki said softly. "I'm told it will get better."

"Has it gotten better for you?" Since his tone was more curious than anything else, she relaxed a little.

"In some ways, yes. In others, not so much. What about for you?"

Josh ignored her question as he leaned in a little closer. "What do you mean, 'in others not so much'?"

Knowing he probably needed to talk it out with someone who'd known Marie, Ricki braced herself for an uncomfortable discussion. She'd avoided this for over a year, but it was the least she could do after all the help he'd given her.

"I still have nightmares, Josh," Ricki admitted. "About that night. For a few months I even saw a shrink about them. Now I take a hard run after I have one."

"It helps with the depression?" Josh asked.

She hesitated. Depression was what the shrink had assumed, probably because she'd never been completely honest with him. But it wasn't depression.

"Anger," she finally said. "I feel anger. It all plays out again, then I'm looking at Marie lying on the ground, and then I wake up angry." She reached out across the table and laid a hand gently over his. "I'm sorry. I don't mean to bring up all that pain again."

"No, no," he quickly denied, flipping his hand over and curling his fingers around hers. "Anger is good. I understand that perfectly. I'm no shrink, but I think I can help."

"Help?"

"I brought something I want you to read."

She withdrew her hand from his, her eyes narrowing in suspicion. "What is it?"

"You read it. And then you tell me." He pushed the envelope toward her. "It isn't a lot to ask, Ricki. Just read it."

When she reluctantly reached for the envelope, he looked past her and nodded. "There's someone who wants to meet you. I promised him an introduction."

"What?" Ricki swiveled around, spotting the tall, lean man with heavy-rimmed glasses who stood just inside the archway leading into the bar. She blinked once, and then twice. The last time she'd seen him had been on a Skype call.

She turned back around. "Is that Dr. Blake?"

Josh nodded. "Your personal profiler. When he heard you had another case, he wanted to come out and meet you in person." Josh leaned back in his seat and studied the ceiling. "I'm sure it was the case that had him jumping on a plane from DC."

"I see that back door where you always got all your inside information is still fully functional," Ricki said. "And my case might not be mine for very long. Right now it's an unknown vic, who was shot, not on park land. If I don't find a connection soon, I'll be turning it over to the local police chief. So Dr. Blake made the trip for nothing."

"Uh-huh. Like I said, it's probably the case." Josh's gaze turned troubled as he lowered his voice. "I'm hoping this isn't a mistake." When Ricki frowned, he shook his head. "Keep an open mind, and remember, you don't have to agree to anything."

Her internal defenses snapped into place as Josh's sudden intensity disappeared in the blink of an eye, watching silently as he got to his feet. "Jonathan. Perfect timing. We were just finishing up." He clapped a hand onto his friend's shoulder while he smiled at Ricki. "This is Dr. Jonathan Blake, FBI profiler." He looked at Jonathan. "And this is none other than Special Agent Ricki James, expert investigator for the park service."

When Josh insisted that the doctor take his seat, Ricki sent a pointed look to the FBI agent. "Where are you going?"

"To make some phone calls," he said. His tone was bland, but he gave her a quick, hard stare before walking off.

Left alone with the profiler, Ricki cast a sideways look at the bartender, who was openly watching them. Wondering how long it would be before Clay heard that she had met not one but two strange men in the bar, she inwardly groaned and settled back in her chair. She had a murder to solve, and a son and a diner to take care of. She didn't need all these other complications, and especially not those cryptic comments from Josh. And what did he mean she didn't have to do anything?

The doctor glanced at the envelope lying in front of her. "I guess you agreed to look that over and get back to Josh?"

Ricki lifted the envelope and tucked it into her lap underneath the table and out of sight. "More or less."

He pushed a lock of hair off his forehead. It was the same gesture that Eddie always made.

"I guess since we've had a formal introduction, it's time for me to explain why I'm here."

Ricki leaned back in her chair. The doctor didn't look nervous or the least bit contrite for ambushing her this way, but once again, like Josh, he'd been a huge help on her last case. She at least owed him a few minutes to listen to what he'd come to say. "That would be nice."

"I wanted to meet you." He shrugged. "Sometimes it's just that simple. I'd heard during your first stint with the park service how good you were at solving puzzles and pinpointing killers, which is why I jumped at the chance to watch you in action. You didn't disappoint, Ricki."

She smiled. As compliments went, that one was pretty good. So why did she feel like there was more to it than one professional acknowledging another? "Neither did you, Jonathan. The body count would have been a lot higher without your help."

"Then we made a good team."

Wondering where this was going, she kept her smile in place. "It would seem so."

He let out a big breath, as if he'd been holding it, waiting for her answer. "I hear you have another case?"

"Are you keeping tabs on me, Dr. Blake?"

"I'm a fan," he said easily. "I understand there's a couple of odd twists in this one?"

Ricki relented. She'd rather talk about the case than wander into some other strange territory, which is where the good doctor seemed to have been heading. "I'm not sure it's the park service's case. What we have is an old skeleton with a bullet wound along a rib, lying next to a neatly folded ranger's uniform."

Jonathan folded his hands and rested them on the table. "Interesting. Anything else? I hear there was another body, and the location where they were both found was rather unique."

She quickly gave him the bare facts, which didn't take long because there weren't many, ending with Dan Wilkes's thoughts about the badge.

His eyes widened behind the oversized lenses of his glasses. "And the ME thinks the skeleton is at least twenty-five years old?" Jonathan asked.

"At least," Ricki confirmed.

"This killer went to great lengths to conceal the body. From the way you describe it, it couldn't have been easy to get it up there. Unless he met his victim there?" He kept his gaze locked on hers while she shrugged.

"I don't know. He might have, but the lab guys tested the dirt under the body. They didn't find any traces of blood, so I'm thinking he was transported up there somehow after he bled out," Ricki said.

"It's not unheard of, but still unusual to be that respectful." Jonathan said, abruptly changing directions. "Thc body was laid out, the uniform neatly folded. I'd say you're looking for someone who knew the victim quite well. Maybe a family member, or a friend, or coworker? Doesn't sound like the actions of a jilted lover, but that can't be ruled out either." Jonathan leaned back, his lips pursed, his eyes half-closed behind the lenses of his glasses. "I'd be leaning more toward one of the closer relationships, like family, friend, or maybe a lover, which would explain why the uniform was neatly folded. Your victim might have taken off his own clothes in anticipation of a sexual encounter."

"He undressed himself in a meeting with a lover?" *Not unless he took them off after he was shot,* Ricki thought, but she kept that tidbit to herself. She really didn't want to prolong this meeting with the doctor, not even to talk over a case. There was something off about the way he was watching her so closely. She felt like a bug under a microscope.

Keeping her body still and her expression neutral, Ricki nodded. "Meeting a lover makes sense."

Jonathan smiled, his eyes crinkling at the corners in amusement. "Yes. Perfect sense."

He glanced at his watch before standing and holding out a hand in a clear signal that the meeting was over. Still wary, Ricki also stood and reached across the table to shake his hand.

He nodded at her and stepped back. "Thank you for talking with me. I think you'll do just fine." When her gaze narrowed on his, he blandly added, "with your case, Ricki. I'm sure you'll have it solved in no time."

Chapter 12

A NIGHT of tossing and turning didn't bring her any more answers than she'd had before. What it did bring was the same nightmare that had plagued her since she and Marie had been ambushed on a Seattle dock during a prisoner transport. Each time the dream was the same. Hernandez, their prisoner, was dead, and she lay wounded on the dock, staring into her partner's lifeless eyes. And just like always, she woke up engulfed in a cocoon of anger.

The psychiatrist she'd seen after she'd been released from the hospital had kept telling her she was confusing anger with grief, but she'd had enough of both in her life to recognize the difference. But this time the anger was so intense, she'd come awake all at once, radiating fury. Clutching handfuls of the blanket, she'd stared at the ceiling as she concentrated on slowing down her breathing, willing each part of her body to relax. By the time she let go of the blanket, her hand muscles had painful cramps in them.

Shaking them out, she waited until the pain had faded to a dull ache before sitting up. Drawing her knees in, she hugged them to her chest and stared out the window at a sky that was just beginning to lighten over the treetops.

There was only one way she'd found to deal with the nightmare.

She sat quietly for several more minutes before throwing the covers aside. She made a face when her bare feet hit the cold wooden floor. Staying on her tiptoes, she half walked, half hopped to her dresser and pulled out drawers, tossing her favorite sweatpants over her shoulder where they landed in a heap on the floor. She grabbed a long-sleeved running shirt and some underwear and dumped them on the bed next to her sweatpants before heading to the compact shower in the tiny bathroom attached to what passed as the master bedroom in the cabin she'd rented over a year ago as a temporary home for herself and Eddie.

It had all the necessary rooms, but every one of them was on the small side, and storage was pretty much nonexistent, which was why there were still a lot of unpacked cartons stacked against any available wall.

It was the last day of school, and Nate was coming to pick Eddie up an hour earlier than usual. Since Nate's parents had banned him from driving for at least a month, his mom would be chauffeuring the boys, and had offered to pick them up from school as well. With Eddie going straight from school to help out at the diner, Ricki figured that whole part of her day was taken care of, so she could concentrate on the rest of her very long to-do list.

Which was going to start with a five-mile jog to clear the nightmare out of her head.

Ninety minutes later she was dressed in her sweats and waving goodbye as the boys headed off in Susan's sturdy little compact. Ricki looked down at Corby, the boxer mix who had simply shown up on their doorstep one day and never left. Fortunately, Corby had turned out to be house-trained and well mannered, which had earned him the right to become part of the family. He was also her running companion.

"Well. Are you ready?"

Corby didn't nod, but he did start off, looking back at her before he broke into a quick lope down the gravel driveway. Ricki laughed before taking off after him, catching the dog with her long-legged stride just as he turned onto the road heading into town. When she stopped, so did Corby. He plopped his butt on the ground and looked up at her with liquid-brown eyes, his head cocked to one side.

"I don't feel like running down to the St. Armand today. You never know who you might meet." It bothered her that Jonathan Blake had made the trip all the way to Washington just to ask her a few questions about a case he had no part in. And right behind that was a feeling that hadn't been his motive for meeting her at all. She shook her head in silent denial. No. Not a feeling, a certainty. The profiler had been interviewing her. At least that's the vibe she'd gotten. The only problem was, she had no idea why.

"I'm thinking we'll go the other way this time." When Corby continued to stare up at her, she stuck her hands in the pockets of her windbreaker and shrugged. It was more than enough explanation for a dog, and all he was going to get.

She started out in the opposite direction, with Corby taking up his usual place by her side. She glanced at him and smiled. That was the great thing about dogs. They were happy to go along with whatever you wanted without demanding long, involved explanations.

She was finally beginning to loosen up as she approached the halfway point in her morning run and was about to turn around when a lone black SUV appeared on the road. When she slowed down, so did the car. Clay pulled over to the side of the road and rolled down his window.

"Trying out a different route?" he called out as Ricki made her way across the deserted road.

She leaned against the doorframe. "Corby wanted a change of scenery."

"Corby, huh?" Clay rested his arms on top of the steering

wheel, leaning forward enough so his gaze could meet hers. "I was hoping you'd call last night. Let me know how the meeting with Josh went."

"It went."

He stayed silent, waiting her out until Ricki gave in and relaxed the stiffness in her shoulders.

"He gave me something he wants me to read."

"Something?" Clay frowned. "What something?" He sat up and reached across the seat and opened the passenger side door. "Why don't you and Corby climb in. It's warmer in here."

Ricki thought it over for a moment, then rolled her eyes at the pleading look in Corby's eyes. "Okay, I get it. Your fur coat isn't made for cold mornings unless you're moving." She walked around the front of the SUV then pointed to the open door. "Go on."

Corby wagged his stump of a tail, then practically bounced off the ground and into the front seat of the car, half landing on Clay's lap. The chief wrapped an arm around the muscular body and pulled the dog upright to give Ricki enough space to slide in next to him.

She gave the wiggling Corby an exasperated look. "You just sit here and behave yourself."

"So, what something?" Clay repeated after she'd closed the door and settled back into the seat.

"Feels like a report. I'm not sure because it's in a sealed envelope."

He tapped a finger against the steering wheel. "Is that all he wanted?"

Ricki nodded. "Uh-huh. Read the report and get back to him." She gazed out the front windshield. "We talked a few minutes. It was good." She looked over at Clay. It would be better if she told him about Jonathan Blake before he heard it through the ever-churning gossip mill. "Actually, I spent more time talking to Dr. Blake then I did with Josh."

Clay's eyes narrowed, exactly the way she knew they would at hearing that the profiler was in town.

"As in the persistent Dr. Blake? He came all the way from Quantico just to see that you got that report?"

Despite her own leeriness concerning Jonathan Blake, Ricki raised an eyebrow. "As in the guy you called the best profiler in the country when he helped out on the last case in Olympic Park. Yeah. That guy. He wasn't interested in the report so much as the unidentified body in the old lighthouse, who was possibly a ranger." She hesitated before meeting Clay's watchful gaze. "And in sizing me up." Ricki shrugged. "At least that's the impression I got."

"Why would he do that?"

"Because he's a profiler, and that's the kind of thing they're interested in." She smiled at Clay's irritated look.

"Why would he need to profile you?" Clay shot back.

Ricki opened her mouth and then shut it again. She'd asked herself that same question yesterday even before she'd pulled out of the St. Armand's parking lot. But when no answer presented itself, she dismissed it as something she was blowing out of proportion and switched her mental efforts organizing the long list of things for her evening routine, which had included picking up Eddie at the diner along with the daily receipts to deposit in the bank. Then there had been dinner to prepare, the diner's books to balance, and a call to ASAC Hamilton, which she hadn't gotten to until after her son had headed to bed.

Having finished with the top priorities on her list, she'd turned her attention to what was now her third job—running the adventure tour business she owned with Bear. After taking a quick look at the scheduled bookings, and making a note that they were a little sparse for June, she'd started to shut down her laptop when she'd noticed a new email from the Tacoma ME. Dr. Naylor had sent her the forensic report, and despite the fatigue demanding she get some sleep, she hadn't been able to resist pulling up the report and giving it a brief once-over before finishing up for the night.

By that time she'd been too tired to do much else, and none of it had completely banished the conversation with the famous profiler from her head. She was hoping some sleep would. But it had felt like she'd barely climbed into bed when the nightmare had jolted her awake again.

The run had helped clear out the cobwebs, but she still had a lot to do today, and did not want to start it out by getting into a debate with Clay. "I don't know. Since I haven't killed anyone, he doesn't have any reason to profile me. Maybe it's just the way he is, and he can't help himself." Ricki shrugged and once again forced the whole thing to the back of her mind. "He did mention that he thought my dead vic was probably meeting a lover."

Clay was quiet for a long moment before his shoulders relaxed. He nodded as if agreeing with her change in subject. "And what do you think of that explanation?"

Now she gave a short laugh. "I think he should stick to profiling people rather than analyzing crime scenes. But he had a point. It's possible it happened that way. Blake's fictional lover could have shot the vic, then taken off his uniform and put it and the mostly naked dead body in a car, driven up to the lighthouse, and then dragged the body up that last hill." She gave Corby an absentminded pat. "Even if the vic had arranged to meet a lover up at the lighthouse, he still wasn't killed inside. Since he was shot while still wearing most of his uniform, he didn't get naked and then parade around outside in the brush where his lover shot him before dragging him back inside, which was what Blake was envisioning. So I'm thinking another crime scene."

She glanced over at Clay. "There's enough loose dirt on that floor that any drag marks would have shown up, and there weren't any near what was left of the body. Just those footprints we found. Whoever put him there didn't drag him in, so the body was carried. According to the forensics report I got last night, the two shoe prints were from a size ten shoe, provided the killer was male, or a size twelve for a female." She gave him an apologetic look. "I was pretty tired last night, and the report came in late. I just gave it a quick look-through before crawling into bed. I was going to forward it to you as soon as I finished my run."

"I know you would have." Clay pursed his lips into a thin line. "So we're dealing with a smaller guy or a tall woman."

"And a strong one," Ricki said. "If he or she carried that body up a hill. The ME put the vic at about five feet, eleven inches. Even at a lean weight, that's still a lot of mass to cart up a steep hill." She turned toward Clay and rested one knee on the wide seat. "I also had a talk with Hamilton last night. He said his contacts back in DC couldn't find any record of a ranger going missing at any of the parks for the last twenty-five years, so he wants me to hand the case over to you."

"What about the uniform?" Clay asked.

Ricki squinted her eyes and changed her voice into a fairly good imitation of Hamilton's tony, slightly southern drawl. "An anomaly." When Clay frowned, Ricki shrugged. "His words. He said it could be a ranger wannabe, or maybe the guy had retired or left the service. Either way, it makes him your problem, not ours. Especially since he wasn't found in the park."

Clay was silent for a long moment. "Is that what you want? To hand the case over?"

"No." And that was the truth. Her gut told her this guy was a ranger, and he'd been wearing his uniform just before he was shot. So whether or not he was found in the park, he was one of theirs. But it was frustrating that there wasn't a record anywhere of him going missing.

"Are you supposed to let me know the case is coming my way, or is Hamilton going to make that call?"

"He didn't say."

"Okay. Can you get a few days off?"

She blinked at the odd question. "Now?" Then immediately shook her head. "Not until Tuesday. That's when Bear gets back. But why? I'm not in the mood for a vacation."

Clay grinned. "Can you stall Hamilton until then, so we can make a quick trip to Chicago?"

She went still. Chicago. Where Max Hardy was from, and where there might be a clue to his secret client, and from there to her victim. Her first instinct was to agree, but she hesitated. Even if she didn't like it, Hamilton had a good point. Unless Dan came up with something to identify the man as a park ranger, there wasn't anywhere else she could go. She hated the thought that his murder would fade away into the archives, neatly labeled as a cold case that was never solved.

Frustrated over the whole situation, Ricki opened the passenger door and stepped out onto the side of the roadway. Corby immediately scrambled across the seat and jumped down beside her. She waited until he was out of the car before leaning over and peering back inside at Clay.

"Let me talk it over with Hamilton, see if he'll go for it just so we can tie off any loose ends."

Clay smiled. "I still have to talk to the head of the town councils to approve the expense. We can hash it out on Monday." He pointed a finger at the road stretching out in front of the SUV. "Enjoy the rest of your run. I'll see you back at headquarters."

Ricki stepped away as Clay pulled the big car out onto the road. She watched him drive away until the SUV disappeared around a distant curve.

Whether she liked it or not, she might not have any case at all.

Chapter 13

JUST OVER AN HOUR LATER, Ricki shut the cabin door behind her. Crossing the very small porch, she took the two steps to the driveway, then walked across the gravel, her head down, one thought scrolling through her mind on an endless loop. Who was the dead guy? How could someone be dead for a quarter of a century or more, and no one even noticed he was gone?

It didn't make sense to her. She knew it happened. Every day there were runaways, and people who simply walked off the grid by choice. But it always baffled her. Somewhere, someone must care at least enough to file a report. Especially in an area as small as the Bay. Maybe someone from Seattle, or even Tacoma, had known about the remote lighthouse and carted the guy all the way out here along with his uniform, but her instincts were telling her whoever he was, at some time in the past, he'd lived in the Bay. Or somewhere nearby.

Still thinking it over, Ricki switched on the jeep's engine and was surprised when it immediately turned over and purred like it was brand new, which made a change from the nightmarish behavior its ten years and two hundred thousand miles usually favored.

"Good omen for the rest of the day," she said under her breath, putting the car into gear and making her way toward the two-lane highway one hundred feet away. Since the hour was later, there was a little more traffic, but not much, as she turned toward Brewer. She planned on stopping at the Sunny Side Up to check up on things before heading farther down the road to Edington and the headquarters the park service shared with Clay and his deputy.

Just under a mile from town, she was rounding a curve when a sharp crack split the air. The jeep immediately lurched to the left, crossing the painted lines on the road and heading straight for the thick stand of trees on the far side. From the corner of her eye she caught a flash of red, rocketing straight for her. She yanked the steering wheel to one side and stomped on the accelerator. The jeep shot forward, but not quickly enough to avoid the oncoming sedan. It hit the jeep on the back fender, the crunch of metal on metal splitting the air as the jeep went spinning in one direction and the sedan in another.

"Shit," Ricki yelled, throwing her arms around the steering wheel and hugging it tightly to her chest as the jeep reared onto two wheels and rolled over several times, stopping when it hit a large tree five yards back from the road.

Her eyes slit open. She was lying on her side, pain radiating up the one arm still locked around the steering wheel. All she could see was the weathered bark of a large tree trunk.

She barely heard the muffled voices calling for help before the world went completely black.

Chapter 14

"Come on, Ricki. Time to wake up."

She heard the command, given in a low, gravelly voice, but she kept her eyes tightly shut. Everything hurt. She didn't have to move to know that. Even her eyelids ached.

"If you don't open those eyes, I'm going to have to keep you in the hospital tonight. Probably for more than one night."

Now that was a serious threat. She'd had her fill of hospitals after the ambush. Just the thought of the constant poking and prodding, accompanied by hours of staring at stark white ceilings and breathing in the antiseptic smell, was enough to have her lids slitting open.

TK's large nose and watery blue eyes were only a few inches away. Her instinctive jerk to put some distance between them had those aches jumping out all over her body. Letting out a gasp, she took short, quick breaths to cope with the pain as she glared up at the doctor.

"Move back," she croaked out.

With a satisfied look, TK straightened up. "Good of you to join us."

Us? When the doctor took a small step back, her uncle

Cy's face appeared over one of his shoulders and Clay's over the other. When her gaze shifted back to TK, he shrugged.

"I tried to keep them out, but small towns being what they are, just the two of them in here was the best I could do. The rest of your fan club is out in the lobby."

She shifted a tiny bit, trying out the movement, grimacing at the pain that shot up one arm. She gingerly turned her head and stared at her right wrist, lying on a raised small table nestled beside the narrow bed. It was almost invisible between a metal splint and thick bandages.

Following the direction of her gaze, TK slanted his head toward the small table. "You'll need to have that elevated as much as possible to help keep the swelling down. You're lucky. It was a clean break. Should be healed up in five or six weeks." His shaggy eyebrows drew together. "As I recall, you're right-handed, so I guess you won't be shooting anyone for a while."

Ricki's glare returned to the doctor. "I can shoot with my left. In case you have any ideas about keeping me here." She worked through several more shallow breaths as she tried moving her legs. That brought on more of a dull ache than a sharp pain, but that was almost a blessing considering her back was on fire and her chest hurt every time she breathed.

"We'll have to talk about it in a bit," TK said mildly, not looking at all put off by her threat. "Do you remember what happened?"

"Jeep rolled." She closed her eyes and saw a red car coming at her. "I was hit by another car." Her face scrunched up as she slowly brought back the scenes imprinted on her memory. "A tire blew out. I heard the noise. The jeep went sideways, and then it was hit by a car in the other lane." She looked at Clay for confirmation. He nodded, his mouth pulled into a grim line.

"That's right." His voice was low and calm.

She frowned. His tone was the kind a cop used when he

expected a witness to have more to say. She thought back, but that's all she had. The loud noise. Then the tire blew out, sending the jeep across the road. The red car had suddenly appeared from around the corner, coming straight at her. That's all she remembered.

"What am I missing?" she asked.

"Nothing," Clay said. He stepped around TK and laid a hand gently against her shoulder. "I didn't have time to get much of a look, but that's what I thought had gone down from the skid marks and what's left of the jeep. Your front left tire blew out." He paused for a moment. "You heard it blow?"

"I heard a loud noise and then the car skidded left," Ricki said. She briefly closed her eyes. "What time is it? Eddie gets out of school early today." She started to sit up, not able to suppress a loud groan from even that small movement. "I need to get to the diner before he hears about this."

"He's already heard," her uncle put in. His voice was hoarse, and deep lines of worry were etched down his cheeks. "I picked him up from school. He's out in the lobby with Marcie and Anchorman."

With some effort she managed to pull herself up against the pillows before giving her uncle an exasperated look. "Well, go get him so he can see for himself that I'm fine."

"I'll get him," TK volunteered. "The bruising is starting to show, so I want to warn him not to run out of here screaming. Then we'll talk about concussions."

"I don't have a concussion, TK," Ricki said to the doctor's back as he disappeared through the doorway to what Ricki knew was the short hallway leading to the front lobby of the tiny hospital.

Down the hall in the opposite direction was a large alcove with a nurses' station, and beyond that were several rooms with X-ray and ultrasound equipment, as well as five patient rooms for any overnight guests. Which would not include her.

"Mom."

The sight of her son's frightened face immediately pulled her away from the unacceptable prospect of spending the night in the hospital. She smiled and managed to reach out her good hand without grimacing.

"Hey, bud. I'm fine."

Eddie ran over to the bed, forcefully pushing his great-uncle aside to wrap his arms around his mother's bruised shoulders. She pursed her lips against the sudden spurt of pain, but didn't utter a sound as she returned a one-armed hug before Cy put his hands on the tall teenager's shoulders and gently pulled him back.

"She's good, son. But she got banged up a bit. You'll need to treat her like a piece of china for a few days."

"China. Right." Ricki met Eddie's gaze and rolled her eyes, relieved when his body relaxed and he grinned back at her.

Eddie adjusted his glasses and leaned in a little closer again. "Your face is turning kind of purple."

"Not pretty, but not life-threatening," Clay said. "We were about to discuss getting her home and who should be staying with her."

Ricki lifted an eyebrow. "We were?"

Eddie turned and faced Clay. "I'm staying with her. There's no more school, so I can take care of my mom."

"I'd feel better if I was there too, son," Cy said. He reached out and patted Eddie's shoulder. "That way we can take turns listening to her complain."

Ricki took immediate offense to that. "I don't complain."

"Remember what she was like the last time she came home from a hospital?" Cy asked, addressing Eddie and completely ignoring his niece. "All she did was complain."

"After our last case, she was kind of whiny about the bruise from the bullet she took to the vest she was wearing, too," Clay put in.

"I was not," Ricki said, her glare bouncing between the two men.

Eddie gave her a pitying look. "You kind of were, Mom. I figured it's just your way of dealing with pain. Dad's a lot quieter about that kind of thing."

Macho man strikes again, Ricki thought sourly, then felt a niggle of guilt. Bear really wasn't a complainer, and considering how much he'd been banged up over the years between playing football and then running groups out on their wilderness tours, she should be happy he wasn't a whiner, rather than annoyed about it. Still, getting tossed around in a rolled car was worthy of a small complaint or two.

"Hey." Marcie's cheerful voice floated across the room. "TK said we could come in and see how you're doing." She walked over to the bed, her short, sturdy build bouncing on the toes of her feet. She leaned over and gave Ricki a kiss on the cheek. "Honey, you sure do have a knack for finding trouble." She leaned back and studied Ricki's face. "How are you doing?"

"Looking forward to going home," Ricki said loud enough to carry out into the hallway where TK was standing, looking over the papers attached to the clipboard he was holding.

"Okay," Marcie said. "We can arrange that." She turned her head and looked at Anchorman. "Can't we? Maybe get her into your car since it's bigger than mine? I'm sure Clay and Cy have official kind of things to take care of."

"Sure," Anchorman said easily. "No problem."

"Yeah, Mom. We should get out of here."

Ricki's eyes narrowed on her son's face. Rather than meet her gaze, he dropped his head and looked at the floor, but not before she saw the flash of anxiety in his eyes. Something was bothering him. And not just her getting hurt in an accident.

She looked at Cy, then at Marcie and Anchorman. Now that she could focus on them, it was easy to spot the identical fixed smile on their faces, and the same guilty look in their eyes. Since she didn't have any major injuries, and they could all see that for themselves, there was obviously something else going on. She looked over at Clay and frowned.

"Want to tell me what's up?" She gestured toward the group standing beside him. "Whatever it is they're trying really hard not to tell me?"

Clay reached out a long arm and herded the others away from the bed. "Why don't you all give us a few minutes. Go check with TK on what we have to do to spring her out of here."

"I really don't think . . ." Marcie began.

"I want to talk to the chief, Marcie," Ricki said quietly. "Please."

Cy shepherded the other three out, giving his niece a long worried look before pulling the door shut behind him.

Ricki waited half a beat before looking over at Clay. "Well?"

"You said that you remember skidding across the road, and seeing another car?"

"Yeah." Ricki frowned. Despite the headache clawing its way up from the base of her skull, she clearly remembered the flash of red. "A car just appeared from around the corner. I put the pedal down, trying to get out of its way, but it still clipped me. I heard the metal hit my rear fender, but nothing after that . . ." She trailed off. She didn't remember hearing the other car crash, but she did hear someone calling for help. She thought it had been for her, but now she wasn't so sure. "What happened?"

"That car had five people in it, two in front and three in back. University students. They were staying at the resort to celebrate the end of the semester."

All the color drained from Ricki's face. She could tell from Clay's expression that it was bad. "Are they all right?"

"From the skid marks it looks like their car took a spin or two then hit a tree broadside. On the driver's side."

She felt dizzy and put her hand to her forehead to keep it from flopping over onto her chest. She couldn't get any words out, but her eyes widened, waiting for the floor to drop out from under her and swallow her whole, hospital bed and all.

He took in a deep breath and laid a large hand over her limp one, lying across her stomach. "Two were airlifted to Tacoma. Two were brought here with minor injuries." His hand tightened around hers. "The driver didn't make it. TK says she died instantly from the impact."

"She?" Ricki closed her eyes and didn't fight the mist welling up beneath her lids. "How old was she?" When he didn't answer, she opened her eyes and stared at him, ignoring the tears that were slowly dripping down her cheeks. "How old, Clay?"

He sighed and ran his free hand through his dark-blond hair. "Amanda Cannady. Twenty years old."

"Oh God." Ricki collapsed onto the pillows. She'd lost control of the jeep, hit another car, and now a twenty-year-old woman was dead. If there had been enough room on the bed, she would have curled up into a small ball. Instead, a weight settled next to her and Clay's arms pulled her close, drawing her up against his chest.

"It wasn't your fault. I'm going to have a look at the jeep and find out what happened, I promise. But I know it wasn't your fault."

She didn't nod her agreement, but slowly straightened up, pushing away from him.

"You can say that, but you weren't the one behind the wheel of the jeep. I was." She pulled away even farther, rolling to her side so her back was to him as the tears came more rapidly. She was the one who hadn't reacted in time, hadn't hit that gas pedal fast enough. And now Amanda Cannady was dead.

Chapter 15

RICKI WINCED as she shifted her position on the small couch in her compact living room. The aches and pains had made themselves known from the minute her uncle had driven her home from the hospital, and had kept reminding her they weren't going anywhere all through the next day. They were still putting up a protest, but only a half-hearted one compared to the day before, although the bruises had certainly added an interesting dimension of color to her face, chest, and arms.

The more they had bloomed and become visible, the more anxious Eddie had grown, which led him to take his job as head nurse and keeper to a degree that would have bordered on the comical if he weren't checking on her every five minutes. She had to admit that he was persistent.

Her son continually tried to get her to drink a glass of milk, making sure one was always available on the table next to the couch, and every meal he expected her to consume plates of raw vegetables that he had painstakingly cut into mismatched pieces. Seeing the stubborn determination on Eddie's face, she didn't think it would do her any good to remind him that she preferred water, or tomato juice with a bit of Tabasco in it, or would have liked the comfort of a fried PB&J.

Purely to keep him from nagging, and to get a little peace and quiet for herself, she'd drunk the milk and eaten the vegetables until she'd finally decided that two days of nonstop milk and healthy food was about all she could handle. Fully invoking her mom prerogative, she sent him outside with the excuse that Corby needed some exercise, and then slowly walked into the kitchen and made herself a cup of coffee.

It was bitter, and nowhere near the level of Anchorman's superb blend, but it was still better than a glass of milk.

She took small sips from the steaming mug and watched as boy and dog played a game of tug-of-war with four old socks tied together. It was one of Corby's favorite games, and judging by the smile on her son's face, one of Eddie's favorites too. Normally she'd be itching to go out and join them, but a heavy tiredness seemed to have settled permanently on her shoulders, so she returned to the couch. The second-hand piece of furniture wasn't quite long enough for her to sprawl out, forcing her to keep her knees bent.

Settled back into the same spot she'd occupied for three days, she tugged a light blanket up to cover her from feet to waist and stared at the blank TV screen on a small stand across the room, only because there wasn't much else to look at.

The cabin had a single large space downstairs. The kitchen ran across the back, separated from the rest of the living space by an island with just enough room for three barstools. Taking up the rest of the space was the couch she was curled up on, along with a crude coffee table made from two boards held up by stacks of bricks under each corner, two straight-backed chairs, the TV stand, and a small desk in the corner. Upstairs were two bedrooms and the sole bathroom that she had to share with her teenage son.

The cabin was cramped, and two corners of her

bedroom were stacked high with boxes she still hadn't unpacked since moving back to Brewer, so she'd always preferred to spend her time outside—whenever the fickle weather of northwestern Washington allowed it—whereas Eddie liked to hide away in the detached garage he'd commandeered to build his bots. But as crowded as her small home was, over the last few days she'd stuck to the inside.

The cluttered space had become her sanctuary—a place to retreat from the rest of the world and brood in peace. It was hard not to think about Amanda Cannady. The twenty-year-old hadn't been doing anything except driving down a public road with her friends, enjoying a break from school. And now she was dead.

A split second, Ricki thought for the hundredth time since Clay had told her about the crash. Another second and she might have avoided the other car and Amanda would still be alive. Just another second, maybe two.

On the coffee table's rough surface, her cell phone began the peculiar wobble-and-jiggle dance of a device switched to vibrate mode. When it continued to rattle, she gave it a disinterested look. It had done that all day yesterday, and most of this morning, although it had slowed down considerably in the last hour. Hopefully her voicemail was finally full and that would be the end of the calls for a while. She was grateful for the reprieve from the noise. Up until now, she hadn't realized how annoying the sound was.

She hadn't picked her phone up since she'd left the hospital the day a day and a half ago, and had no plans to answer it the rest of today either. Or play any of the twenty-two messages left by well-meaning people. Or maybe her boss. She shrugged. She really didn't care. It was the same with opening her laptop and going through what she was sure were a gazillion new emails.

She shifted her gaze back to the front window. Too bad.

The rest of the world could wait. It was Sunday, and still the weekend. She was off the clock.

Satisfied with that rationalization, she settled back into watching her son and their dog. Several minutes went by in peace before Corby suddenly dropped the sock and started barking, making Eddie turn and look down the driveway. Ricki tensed when a white Ford truck with tinted windows came into view, and then relaxed again as Clay's official SUV pulled in behind it.

Her forehead wrinkled when Clay stepped out of the truck, and his deputy out of the SUV. What? Had he given up being chief? She let the thought slide off when Eddie called out a loud greeting while Corby continued barking as if he were being attacked by a pack of wolves. When Clay strode toward the cabin, Ricki sighed and plucked at a stray thread sticking out from the edge of the blanket. It seemed she was going to get company whether she wanted it or not.

Her cheeks reddened as she remembered the last time she'd seen him. Good Lord, first she'd wept all over his shirt, and then she'd turned her back on him. She'd never done anything like that. It was downright humiliating. She always did her crying in private, when no one else was around. Not her son, not her uncle, not even Bear when they'd been married. Hell, she hadn't cried all over anyone during Marie's funeral, much less at the news of a complete stranger dying in a car crash. Of course, Marie had signed up for a dangerous job, and Amanda hadn't . . .

Ricki forced herself not to finish the thought. It was just a variation on the same one that kept replaying over and over in her head. She couldn't seem to shake it off, or even put it into what her head knew was a proper perspective. To distract herself, she silently called up the apology to Clay that she'd already mentally practiced a half dozen times.

She looked over when the cabin door opened, managing

to work up a half-smile as Clay stepped in and shut the door behind himself.

Now is as good as any time, she thought. "Hi." She looked out the window where Jules was following Eddie toward the garage. Corby was bringing up the rear as the three of them disappeared from view. "Jules isn't coming in?"

"Hi, yourself." He walked over to the kitchen and opened a cupboard, retrieving a clean coffee mug. "No. I told him we needed a few minutes."

He walked over and set a large thermos next to her phone. The minute he unscrewed the top, the heavenly scent of freshly brewed coffee filled the air. She inhaled slowly, savoring the smell, thinking it was possibly the best aroma on earth. "You stopped at the diner?"

Clay nodded and filled the mug up to the brim, holding it out as Ricki quickly set the cup she had in her hands down on the floor. "I thought I should bring something you couldn't refuse in case you had barricaded yourself in here." He smiled when she took a long sip and closed her eyes and made a soft humming noise of approval. "Anchorman says hello, and that you have until three this afternoon to pick up your phone or he's coming over here." He watched as she made a face. "And Marcie said she's coming with him. They'll shut the diner down and sit on your porch until you talk to them."

Ricki tucked a stray piece of dark hair behind one ear. "There's nothing to talk about. I'll send them a text and let them know I'm fine."

He turned and sat in one of the straight chairs facing the couch. Propping a booted foot on top of the opposite knee, he quirked an eyebrow at her. "Does that mean there's also nothing to talk about with your uncle, or your boss, or your doctor?" He paused for a brief second. "Or me?"

"Uncle, boss, doctor, no. You, yes," Ricki said. "I need to apologize."

Clay's eyebrow lifted higher. "For . . . ?"

Her back stiffened, but it had to be said. "For falling apart on you. I know you drew the short straw to tell me about Amanda Cannady, and I should have held it together. None of it was your fault, and I shouldn't have taken it out on you."

"I don't recall you taking anything out on me, Ricki," Clay said evenly. "You were upset, and that's okay. No one likes to hear they were involved in a car crash where a life was lost." When she looked away, he snorted loudly enough to draw her attention back to him.

His bland look annoyed her enough to give him a good glare. "I'm trying to apologize here."

"And I'm trying to tell you that the accident was no accident, and it wasn't your fault."

"Look, I can't help feeling—" She abruptly stopped talking, her mouth still open as she stared at him. "What do you mean it wasn't an accident?"

"I talked to the two kids who spent the night at the hospital. They both gave statements that they were late meeting some friends for a hike in the park and were driving too fast."

"Maybe. But they were in their own lane," Ricki interrupted, then fell silent when Clay lifted a hand.

"Let me finish, Agent James." He was all cop now, staring at her until her mouth snapped shut before lowering his hand again. "They were well over the speed limit coming around that curve, so there was no way in bloody hell you could have reacted fast enough to avoid hitting them. They also said they thought you were going to hit them head-on, but you suddenly turned and headed straight for the tree line." Clay let out a long breath. "If you hadn't flipped over, you would have ended up wrapped around a tree." He leaned forward. "And you wouldn't have been in their lane if it hadn't been for the shots fired at you."

All the irritation drained out of her in one single moment. Shots? "What shots?" she demanded.

"At least two," Clay said. "There's a bullet hole in the left front fender, and another one in the tire."

Ricki slowly shook her head. "I don't remember hearing a gunshot. Are you sure?"

"Unless there was already a bullet hole in the jeep's fender, I'm sure," Clay stated flatly. "And so is Charlie. I had the jeep towed to his shop. He found both bullet holes." Clay leaned back again and met her gaze. "Right now, he thinks you were the victim of some stray hunting accident because that's what I told him, although I'm not sure how long that explanation is going to hold up."

Ricki's eyes narrowed. "Someone hunting that close to the highway, who fired two shots, and both happened to hit the jeep?" Charlie wasn't the brightest crayon in the box, but once he had a chance to think it over, he wasn't going to buy the "stray bullet from a hunter" story.

"Yeah. Like I said, it probably won't hold up for long." He slid his foot off his knee. It made a solid thump as it dropped onto the floor. "Cy sure didn't buy it, and he wanted me to tell you that Hamilton expects a call."

"It's the weekend. I'm not on the clock," Ricki said absently, her mind still on her tire being deliberately shot out. Why would someone do that? She'd been in town more than a year, and she was pretty sure that Quinn, whom she'd recently tossed into jail for murdering half a dozen people, didn't have any other relatives in town who might want revenge. So why her, and why now? A picture of the skeleton lying in the old lighthouse, a uniform folded neatly at its side, popped up in her mind, but she couldn't catch hold of her thought as it faded away.

"Well, maybe this will get you to communicate with someone," Clay said. "Ranger Wilkes also sent along a message. He says he's found out something about the badge that you'll be interested to hear."

Her attention caught, Ricki set her coffee mug on the table and waited expectantly. "What did he find out?"

Clay grinned. "I don't know. You'll have to ask him. Tomorrow is Monday. You'll be on the clock."

"With other things to do," Ricki said. "So I'll need to take a few days."

"What things?" Clay looked around. "You can work from home. You know, internet, virtual meetings, all that stuff your son can help you with if you can't manage it."

"Funny, Thomas. But I have a diner I should look in on and a mom I was supposed to visit this weekend. Not to mention I don't have a car, so I need to make some transportation arrangements, and I look like something out of a horror movie."

He stood up and stuck his hands in his pockets. "I have to admit, it's a different look for you, but I've never known you to be vain."

"Says the man who looks like he stepped off a movie screen," Ricki muttered.

"And," Clay went on as if he hadn't heard her, "I've never heard you dig around for so many excuses to hide out. The diner is fine. I was just there, remember? Anchorman and Marcie have everything under control. I know you should visit your mom, but maybe Cy can take you later this week, since you shouldn't be driving that far on your own yet."

She rolled her eyes at that. "I can't drive anywhere at all. The jeep is sitting in Charlie's shop, totaled, and I don't happen to have a spare one sitting around."

"Uh-huh." Clay drew his hand out of his pocket and tossed a set of keys onto the low table. "I brought you these."

Ricki looked at them and then back up at Clay. "What are those?"

"The keys to my truck," Clay said. "I have the official chief of police SUV, so I never use my truck anymore. Keep it as long as you like." Seeing her dumbfounded expression, he grinned. "You're welcome."

She knew she should be thrilled to have one immediate problem solved, but the heaviness from the last few days settled in around her again, like a dense fog that only receded a little before coming right back. "I can't take your truck."

Clay crossed his arms over his chest and stared at her. "Well then, it's going to sit there and block your driveway because I'm not moving it. You need to ditch the guilt and get back to work, Ricki."

Turning her head to stare out the window, she lifted her shoulders in a small shrug. Maybe. But it wasn't that easy. "I need a few days." She'd call Dan to hear what he'd found out about the badge, but that could wait until tomorrow.

"We all have something, Ricki." When she glanced back at him, Clay nodded. "Something we do to get our head screwed back on straight." He walked over to the couch, leaned down, and placed a quick kiss on her forehead before she could get out a protest. "Whatever that something is for you, do it, and soon. There's someone out there shooting at people, not to mention two dead bodies who have already been shot. This needs to be figured out, and you owe it to a ranger that everyone's forgotten about to get it done."

Clay captured her hand and gently tugged until she was forced to get to her feet. Annoyed, Ricki glared at him. "What are you doing?"

"You need to get dressed. There's something you have to do down at headquarters." Clay shrugged. "You can go like that if you want, it's up to you. But either way, you're coming."

Chapter 16

When the SUV rolled to a stop, Ricki made no move to open the door. All through the ordeal of tugging on a pair of jeans with her one good hand, and sitting through the minor bumps along the highway which had seemed more like mountains as they jarred against her bruised body, she'd maintained a stoic silence. She didn't know what was so important that Clay had insisted she make an appearance at headquarters, on a Sunday, no less, but she was sure it wasn't something she was going to enjoy. And until he fessed up to that, she wasn't going to do anything except sit in the SUV, her gaze steadfastly glued to the view out the side window. She didn't glance over even when Clay let out a heavy sigh.

"Okay. We might as well go in. They've been waiting long enough," he said quietly.

Ricki's head slowly turned until she was looking right at him. "Who is waiting?"

Clay's mouth turned down at the corners, but his gaze never wavered from hers. "Richard and Lisa Cannady." He hesitated before adding, "Amanda Cannady's parents."

All the color drained from Ricki's face and her hands went ice cold. Amanda's parents? God only knew what they would have to say to the person who killed their daughter. Ricki closed her eyes in sheer self-defense against the tidal wave of dread and sorrow crashing over her.

"Now?" was all she could get out. "You brought them here and they're waiting for me now?"

"TK called me. Talking to you is the only request they've made," Clay said. "They deserve to be heard. You know that."

She did know it. The only problem was, could she hold up under the recrimination and onslaught of guilt that was about to be heaped on her? She winced when Clay reached over and took her hand, gently rubbing his thumb over the top of her knuckles.

"I wouldn't have brought you here if I thought they were going to blame you."

She looked down at their joined hands. "Why wouldn't they? They lost a child. It's someone's fault, and I'm the one that was behind the wheel of the other car. Why shouldn't they blame me?"

"They shouldn't because you weren't to blame."

Clay's gentle patience had her eyes misting up. She didn't believe him. At least not completely. But he was right that Amanda's parents deserved to be heard, and if talking with her was all they wanted, then the least she could do was give them that chance. No matter how much it might hurt.

She gave an abrupt nod of her head and withdrew her hand from Clay's. "Let's go."

Enveloped in a fog of dread, Ricki walked stiffly through the double front doors. Ray's usual spot was empty. Even on a Sunday he would normally be manning his post, but not today. Maybe Clay had warned him who was coming in this morning, and he was back in Clay's office, keeping the mourning parents company as they waited for her. Or maybe the elderly volunteer hadn't wanted to face that kind of grief at all and had simply stayed home.

The walk down the long hallway seemed endless, the echo

of their combined bootsteps bouncing off the walls. Clay opened the door to his office and then stepped back, giving Ricki's shoulder a reassuring squeeze as she passed by him. She walked halfway across the room and then stopped, slowly taking in a quiet breath as she nodded at the couple, sitting in the visitor chairs in front of Clay's desk, staring at her with wide, haunted eyes.

"Why don't you take my chair, Ricki?" Clay said.

Grateful to have even that small barrier between herself and the pool of grief surrounding Amanda Cannady's parents, Ricki nodded and stepped round the desk before slowly lowering herself into the utilitarian chair reserved for the police chief.

"Mr. And Mrs. Cannady," Clay began. "This is Special Agent Ricki James. She was driving the other car involved in your daughter's accident."

Even with her dark-brown eyes glistening with moisture, Lisa Cannady managed a watery smile. "Yes. We know, Chief." Her chin quivered slightly as she laid a hand on her husband's arm. "I'm Lisa, and this is Richard." She paused and took a quick breath. "As the chief said, we're Amanda's parents."

Ricki simply nodded, not trusting her voice. Lisa Cannady had brown hair, pulled back from a pretty face with even features and a generous mouth. Her husband had lighter hair, liberally streaked with a darker gray. He wore glasses with plain, no-nonsense frames and even sitting down, clearly towered over his wife. When Ricki met his gaze, he nodded back at her, like a fellow combatant in a war where they were barely hanging on.

He started to say something, then stopped when his voice cracked on the first word. Clearing his throat, he took a deep breath and tried again. "Special Agent James, we're grateful you agreed to meet with us today." He stopped for a moment and studied her face. "It looks like you're still recovering."

"Ricki. Please call me Ricki. And I hope you'll accept my deepest sympathy." Ricki chewed on her lower lip as her gaze shifted to Lisa. "And my apology, although I know it isn't enough. But I'm sorry. So sorry for not being quick enough to keep the accident from happening. I want you to know that I. . ."

"Agent James," Lisa cut in. "Ricki. We didn't come to hear an apology."

Her husband laid a hand on top of the one Lisa still had resting on his arm. "No, we didn't. We know the accident wasn't your fault."

Ricki blinked, struggling to process their words. "Not my fault?"

"No," Richard said, a clear conviction in his voice. "And with our own apologies to your police chief, we didn't just take his word for it. He explained about someone deliberately shooting your tire out, but we also talked to the other girls riding with Amanda, and they all told us the same thing. They were driving too fast when they came on that curve, and neither you nor our daughter had time to get out of the way." His shoulders slumped as he looked over at his wife.

Lisa nodded in response to his silent plea. "They also said you deliberately turned your car toward the trees, and if your vehicle hadn't rolled over, you would have hit them head on."

Not comfortable with how she was beginning to sound like some kind of hero, Ricki shook her head. "There wasn't anything else to do, Mrs. Cannady. It was turn toward the trees or hit Amanda head on. The trees were the lesser evil of the two options." She bit her lower lip. "Although not lesser enough."

"The other girls lived because you did that," Lisa said. "We're going to keep thinking of that as a blessing, even though we lost our Amanda."

"Lost her to someone who had no regard for someone

else's life," Richard said. "He's the one I can't forgive. I'll never forgive."

The fury and anguish of a father who hadn't been able to protect his child spilled into the room. This was something Ricki understood, and wholeheartedly agreed with. She'd never forgive anyone who took Eddie from her, who took anyone she loved from her. She cut a swift glance over to Clay who nodded back at her. This was something they both understood.

Feeling like she was standing on ground that had shifted back into place beneath her feet, Ricki felt a great weight slide off her shoulders. "I can't either," she said softly. "And thank you." The words came from her heart and brought tears to Lisa's eyes as well as her own, as a look of understanding passed between the two mothers.

"We came to ask a favor," Lisa said. "For your help."

"For ourselves and for Aiden," Richard said. "He's our son, and Amanda's brother."

"I'll do my best," Ricki said, then folded her hands and waited.

"Catch him." At Ricki's startled look, both husband and wife nodded in unison.

"Catch him," Richard repeated. "Like our son said to us, and we're passing along to you, we want this man who killed our daughter to look out at the world from behind a set of iron bars for the rest of his life. It won't bring our daughter back, but it will bring her justice."

Ricki stood up, her back straight and her mouth set into a determined line. "I intend to do just that."

Chapter 17

Ricki tightened the shoulder straps of her backpack, then did the same to the ones around her waist. It had taken some contortions to slip the pack on with an unforgiving splint holding her broken wrist in place, but she'd managed. After she'd exchanged goodbyes, and a long hug with Lisa Cannady, Clay had dropped her off at her cabin. Her uncle was there with Eddie, and had plans to keep the teenager busy all day. Later that afternoon, Anchorman was going to stop by and spend the night so the two of them could play video games until who knew when.

It was just past noon by the time she'd pulled into the small clearing just above where the Dosewallips River had washed out the road that had once led across the state land and into the national park. She'd have to travel the last six miles on foot to reach the primitive campground that was one of her favorites in Olympic Park, and the one she'd always gone to for her "alone time" campouts.

Ricki took one last look at the truck, which sat all alone in the small clearing that served as a parking lot. She hoped it would still be there and in one piece whenever she got back. Explaining away a vandalized truck to her insurance company would be awkward since it wasn't her truck. Not to mention telling Clay. Because she couldn't do anything about it, she turned around and started off down the trail toward the washout.

She hiked completely alone all the way in, which was no surprise given the empty parking lot. It wasn't long before she caught the distant sound of the river, which rapidly grew louder until it settled into the steady roar of the spring runoff tumbling its way down from the mountains to the west. A good piece of the tension in her shoulders and back eased away at the familiar sound as she took the lower trail to the left. It skirted around the massive slide of rock and debris that had taken out the old road leading into the forest a good twenty years ago.

As she passed through the state land, the sun rose in the sky, filtering through the green canopy over her head and shining brightly on patches of trail as it wound its way in and out of the shelter of the trees. About halfway to her destination, the aches and pains of the accident faded into the background, and her mind began to empty of the constant flow of troubling thoughts about the accident as her body fell into the natural rhythm of hiking, something that she'd done all her life.

The deep smell of pine mixed with clean air that still held a hint of the bite of winter, despite it being the middle of June, was both familiar and relaxing. The corners of her mouth curled up. The longer she strolled along the trail, the more the feel of the forest settled into her. She wasn't in any hurry. The place she was headed to wasn't going anywhere, and since she still hadn't seen a soul, the area was most likely deserted. Which would suit her just fine.

She passed through a burnt-out area that still showed signs of the fire that had swept through it over a decade ago. She picked up her pace, and in less than a mile she stopped by the old range gate, still hanging on to its worn-out sign marking the boundary between state land and the national park. She stood still for a long moment, a shadow of a smile growing into a full grin as she pulled her ball cap with the National Park Service logo on it out of her back pocket and firmly set it into place on her head. After pulling her long ponytail through the opening in the back, she settled her good hand onto one of the straps of her backpack that curled across her shoulder blades and over her chest.

Clay was right. She needed to go to her place, where she could clear her head. During her childhood and all through the years she'd been married, this was what she'd done whenever life had closed around her. She'd taken off on her own and come right to the park for a day or two. It was hard to believe that it had been almost six years since she'd gone on one of her campouts.

Staring down the trail that disappeared into the trees, it hit her just how much she had missed this. Her grin widened as she stepped to the side, kissed the tips of her fingers, then slapped them against the Olympic Park welcome sign before heading to the primitive walk-in campground located another mile in.

The official Dosewallips campsites offered a small cleared-off space and a picnic table, although most who hiked in this far usually preferred to simply pick a nice spot by the river to pitch their tents. Which was exactly what Ricki did. She found her favorite spot, with its postage-stamp-sized clearing and the fire ring she and her uncle had built together when Ricki was nine.

Despite its lack of a table, it was deemed an official campsite, and the small firepit still sported the grate her uncle had installed so long ago. Over time it had needed some repair work, and a bit of shoring up here and there, but the site's location on the outer edge of the campground was still as beautiful as ever.

She slid her backpack off her shoulders and dropped it

into the grass before walking around the small circle hemmed in with stones. She'd have to collect a few rocks and reinforce one of the sides that was caved in. She'd get to that as soon as she set up her small dome tent and laid out her sleeping bag, which was all she needed in order to complete her camp.

It was late in the afternoon when Ricki sat down next to a fallen tree six feet from the fire she'd built. Leaning against it, she lifted the mug she'd filled with instant cocoa and topped off with a small mountain of mini marshmallows. She'd raided the food supplies and refrigerators at the diner, swiping a bag of freshly cut vegetables along with a bottle of ranch dressing, while Anchorman had made her two fried PB&J sandwiches. She pretended not to notice her balance-out-the-bad-stuff rice cakes on the shelf. This wasn't a time for watching her diet.

She'd also brought along a small bag of ground coffee since that was pretty much a requirement to kick off any morning no matter where she woke up.

Ricki sipped at her cocoa and crunched on vegetables as she stared into the crackling flames of the fire, letting time drift by.

The voices of Amanda's parents floated in the air, telling her she wasn't at fault, telling her to catch the person who treated the lives of others so callously, telling her they believed in her. She closed her eyes and let the sound drift through her mind, letting it take root until a familiar purpose pushed its way forward. Justice. For Amanda. That was what her parents were asking for. She couldn't bring back their child, but she could give them that.

It wasn't until she felt an involuntary shiver ripple down her arms that she realized most of the light had faded away and a thin mist was wafting through the early-evening air.

With a new energy, she gathered up her food and cup into a neat stack then picked up the small electric lantern she'd set next to the log before walking over to put the fire out. She carefully smothered it with dirt, leaving a bucket filled with river water next to it. If any hidden sparks showed themselves, they would get a good dousing.

Her small tent was just big enough for her sleeping bag, with her backpack squeezed in by shoving it up against one side of the small nylon dome. Because of the tent's round shape, she could sit up inside, but even then, her head brushed against the top poles. Ricki crawled in, set the lantern down, and reached for her backpack. She stowed the remnants of the vegetables in a small tin box, then reached deeper into the top pocket of her backpack and pulled out a manila envelope with an official US Marshals stamp on the side.

She'd picked up the report Josh had given her on a last-minute whim, telling herself she probably wouldn't read it, but ought to bring it along. Now she fingered the clasp holding it closed, her brow furrowed in thought as she stared at it.

"Might as well face everything today," she murmured to herself, not making a move to open the envelope. Just then the distinct call of a spotted owl rose above the rustling of the trees as the creature went about its nightly hunt for food. Even though she couldn't see it through the walls of the tent, Ricki smiled. The message from the forest to its inhabitants was always the same: get on with it. Letting out an easy laugh, she pulled her backpack around, laying it on its side so she could lean against it. Squiggling to find a comfortable spot, she picked up the envelope and opened the clasp.

"RICKI? ARE YOU OUT HERE?"

Ricki shook her head and rolled her eyes before taking another sip of coffee. She'd heard her uncle coming through the trees a full two minutes before. Or more likely whoever he had with him. And judging by the heavy wheezing that was undoubtedly due to not being used to the altitude or the exercise, she guessed it was Dan Wilkes.

Well, at least she'd gotten one full day and night of peace. A night during which she'd slept like a log, in spite of what she'd read in the US Marshals report. Which was strange. Usually anything that reminded her of the last assignment she'd had with Marie triggered one of her nightmares. She wasn't left any time to puzzle over that odd fact because her uncle called out again, this time with a definite edge of annoyance in his tone.

"Ricki! Where the hell are you?"

"I'm here," she yelled back. "You know where."

It was another minute before her uncle and Dan appeared between the trees. Even from where she was standing, Ricki could see the newest ranger's chest heaving up and down.

"I was pretty sure this was where you'd disappeared to," Cy said as he drew closer. He eyed the mug in her hand. "I don't suppose you brought an extra one of those?"

Ricki handed over her cup. "No, since I wasn't expecting any company." She looked around her uncle and nodded at Dan. "I hear you found out something about the badge?"

Dan sank to his haunches and waved a hand at her. "Hi. Nice to see you too. I'm fine, thanks, and yeah. I found out something about the badge." He drew in another long breath before looking up at her. "But I wasn't expecting to have to climb up and down a couple of mountains to give you a report."

"Winter's over, Ranger Wilkes," Cy said. "You need to get out and do more hiking and get into shape unless you plan on transferring back to Philadelphia."

The former agent shook his head as he slowly rose to his feet. "No. I like it here just fine. I'll be sure to get some hikes in on my days off."

"You do that." Cy swung his gaze and the coffee mug in his niece's direction. "He can tell you about that badge you found up at the old lighthouse right after I tell you that Hamilton will be at headquarters in about an hour. But first, you can explain to me what you're doing out here."

Ricki frowned and quickly calculated the amount of time it would take to break camp and get back to headquarters. She figured ASAC Hamilton would be cooling his heels for at least another hour before she showed up. And that was if she didn't stop at home and get cleaned up first. Her boss was not going to be a happy person, which meant after their talk, she wouldn't be either.

"Same reason I've always come out here," she finally said. She reached over and lifted the coffee mug out of her uncle's hands. "It's not as if I'm hiding out somewhere since you obviously knew where to find me."

Cy braced his legs apart and crossed his arms over his chest. "What I meant was, what are you doing out here alone? Or don't you remember that someone took a shot at you?"

She drank the last of the coffee, then tilted her head to one side as she stared at her uncle. "I don't know if someone was shooting at me, or just shooting at anyone who came along and it just happened to be me. Either way, whoever it was, he wasn't much of a shot, and I doubt he would have followed me all the way back here, even if he had known to be on the lookout for Clay's truck."

Dan gave her a genuinely puzzled look. "How do you know the guy wasn't much of a shot? He hit your tire."

She walked over to the water bucket and picked it up. "Yeah, he did." She started sprinkling water onto the low-burning fire, drawing loud hisses from the smoldering wood and sending a small cloud of steam into the air. "But he fired two shots. If he was aiming at the tire, he missed once, and if he was aiming at me, he missed twice."

"Now you sound like your cook," Dan said, returning her grin.

Since Anchorman had been a sniper during his army

career, she took that as a compliment. Setting the bucket aside, she walked over and propped one foot on top of the fallen log, resting an elbow on her raised knee. "Now, what about that badge?"

"We aren't done talking about this poorly timed campout of yours," Cy warned.

Ricki thought it was perfectly timed but kept her gaze on Dan while she answered her uncle. "Great. We can get into it later when there's more coffee available. Now, about that badge?"

"Well, it's a design that was adopted by the service in 1969 and is still pretty much the same today."

Since that was a long span of time, and well over the twenty-five years or more the ME had said the vic had been dead, she didn't think that was much help. "Okay. So, the badge design is fifty years old and could have been issued to that ranger any time after that."

"Yeah, but here's the thing. There were four thousand badges made up in that first order of the new design, and they were all numbered," Dan explained. "The number on the back of this badge was two hundred and eighty-six."

Ricki straightened away from the log. "Two hundred and eighty-six? When did they start distributing those badges?"

Dan grinned. "At the end of 1970, so I figured whoever owned that badge got it in 1970, or 1971 at the latest."

She whistled softly under her breath. Fifty years ago. She still had no proof that the skeleton in the lighthouse had actually owned the badge, or even if he had, that he'd been killed right after it had been issued to him. He could have gone on to serve as an active ranger for years. But still, it gave them a solid place to start.

"That's good." She slowly drew her cell phone out of her pocket. "I have something too." There was barely one signal bar on the front screen, but it was enough for her to get into her voice mail. "I waded through all my messages this morning and came across this one." When she held the phone up, Wanda Simms's voice came out of the speaker.

"Hello, Ricki. I heard about your accident and wanted to call to be sure you're going to be all right. I've been told you will be, but I wanted to hear it for myself. I'm going out of town to visit my sister for a few days, but if you want to talk about what happened, you just give me a call back and leave all the details. Oh, I also found my notes on that land the old lighthouse sits on. It seems that I sent a letter off to what I wrote down as 'the foundation.' I didn't write down the exact name, but that little note shook something loose in the old noggin because I remembered it was named after a man, and it was the full thing, like 'the John Doe Foundation' instead of just 'the Doe Foundation,' if you follow my meaning. Anyway, back then I asked them if they had any plans to build out there, like putting up a bunch of condominiums or something. Of course they never answered me, but it didn't make any difference because no one from that foundation ever showed up in the Bay. But it was a concern because they weren't from around here, and I remember thinking, now what would some foundation in Chicago want with a bunch of land in Washington?"

Chapter 18

"CHICAGO?" ASAC Steven Hamilton ran a hand down his silk tie, subtly striped in different shades of blue. His suit was a perfect fit for his five-foot-six-inch frame, which he ruthlessly kept in good shape even with his sixtieth birthday looming large in front of him. His deep-brown eyes gave away nothing of what he was thinking as he kept a steady gaze on Ricki. "You believe there's a connection between the dead PI and a foundation that might own the land where his body was found?"

"Might?" Ricki asked.

Since there were five of them crammed into Cy's office, she was leaning up against the back wall. Hamilton had commandeered the chair behind the desk, and at her insistence, Cy and Dan sat in the only two visitor chairs. Clay was standing next to her, his gaze fixed on the man behind the desk. From his slightly rigid posture, Ricki knew the chief of police was simmering away at something, and since he'd barely given her a nod when he'd walked into the room, it wasn't hard to figure out who had set his temper off. Or why.

Probably should have called him, she thought, along with Hamilton, who'd given her the same cool look as he'd politely asked how she was feeling. At this rate, she'd end up talking to herself for the entire investigation.

"Might, Agent James, because according to your source, this alleged foundation bought the land after World War II. Which means there's a good chance they sold it to someone else decades ago." The leather chair creaked as Hamilton leaned back. "Which would make its Chicago connection to Mr. Hardy tenuous at best."

"They haven't sold it," Ricki flatly stated. "If they had, Wanda would have known about it."

"That's true," Cy concurred. "Not one thing in the last forty years has gone on in the Bay that Wanda Simms hasn't known about."

Hamilton didn't look convinced. "Maybe so, but the last World War ended seventy-five years ago, well before she was born, according to the background you gave me on Ms. Simms, so it's not too far-fetched to assume she missed it." He looked over at Ricki. "At any rate, do a cross-check with county records. If this foundation did sell that land, the tax records will tell you who owns it now, and establish if that Chicago connection still exists."

Even though she felt there was a better-than-even chance that a Chicago-based foundation still owned that land, Ricki nodded. Hamilton was right. It needed to be checked out.

"Good." Her boss nodded his approval. "And there still isn't any confirmed direct connection between Maxwell Hardy and the other unknown victim." The senior agent quickly held up a hand before Ricki could put up an argument. "Although finding them both in the same remote place is one hell of a coincidence, and I'm definitely not going to ignore one of my agents being shot at, let's hear everything else you've got and we'll go from there."

Satisfied with that for the moment, Ricki suggested they all move to the small conference room that had a little more space and a large whiteboard.

Once the others were each settled in a chair, she stood in front of the board, a black marker held awkwardly in her left hand. She managed to write down the two victims' names. They were barely legible, but at least she got them on the board. "Okay. We have no identity, and our only evidence is an old bullet and a ranger's uniform. So we start there." She glanced over at Dan. "What did you find out about the badge?"

He repeated what he had told her before, while Ricki literally scrawled a pared-down version on the board.

"So whoever owned that badge would have been on the staff list in 1970 or 1971?" Hamilton asked. "Might not be so easy to find. I don't know when we started automating those records. That information could be buried in a box, or on a roll of microfiche stored somewhere unknown to anyone on earth."

"Or it might be right here in the basement," Cy stated, drawing every eye in the room to him. "All the files for the park, including the old staff files, are stored in the basement. And they go back a long way, as I recall. But I haven't been down there in at least a decade." He looked over at the closed door. "Ray would know. He goes to the basement to poke around from time to time."

"I'll ask him about it," Clay said.

"And I can spare some time looking too," Dan volunteered, then hastily looked over at Cy. "If that's okay with you, of course."

When Cy's gaze narrowed on his ranger, Hamilton spoke up. "We'd appreciate the help, Supervisor McCormick."

Cy aimed a polite smile at the man who looked entirely too comfortable leaning back in his chair with one foot propped up on the opposite knee. "It's no problem, Special Agent Hamilton."

To head off any pissing contest between the two senior

men in the room, Ricki quickly went over the rest of the mounting coincidences, ending with the car crash.

"Then you think those shots were aimed at you because you're investigating the John Doe victim found in the lighthouse?" Hamilton frowned as he drummed one finger against the surface of the conference table.

Her uncle crossed his arms over his chest and gave her an exasperated glare. "Yes, Ricki. Why do you think that? The shooter could have been aiming at anyone who happened to drive by."

Since she'd said the same thing to her uncle just a few hours before, Ricki ignored the sarcasm in his tone and kept her attention on her boss. "My jeep is pretty well known, and no one was taking shots at anyone until we found that body."

Hamilton didn't look impressed. "You're assuming it was a local who took those shots, and there were two bodies found up there. Maybe it has to do with the PI and not the John Doe."

"The dead PI is my case," Clay put in. "My car is also well known around here, and would be to someone who isn't a local since it's well marked as a police vehicle, and no one took any shots at me."

Hamilton frowned again. "Your point is well taken, Chief." He looked from Clay to Ricki and then folded his hands and leaned forward. "It's Tuesday. Keep this at the top of your pile, Agent James, at least for the rest of the week. But if you can't establish more connection to the park service than an abandoned uniform and badge by the end of the week, move it down the pile and focus on the rest of your work."

Knowing a five-day window, if she counted the weekend, was the best she was going to get, Ricki dutifully nodded. As the men got to their feet, she looked over at Clay and caught his eye. "Can I have a moment of your time, Chief?"

Clay's expression wasn't exactly friendly, but at least he

nodded and sat down again. Ricki waited until the room had emptied out, then walked over and closed the door before skirting around the table and taking the vacated seat next to Clay.

"Look. I'm sorry." She smiled sheepishly. "Again."

He leaned back and stretched out his long legs beneath the table. "This time you have something to apologize for. Why did you take off like that without telling me where you were going? I thought after you met the Cannadys, and talked with them, everything was fine."

"I took off like that because you suggested it," she said, nodding when he gave her an incredulous look. "Yes, you did. You said I should do whatever it took to clear my head, and spending time alone in the park is that thing." When he remained silent, she went on. "Even when I was married I used to make regular trips alone into the park. It's always helped me see things more clearly." Her lips curved up into a rueful smile. "It's where I decided to get married in the first place. And where I decided to get a divorce, for that matter."

Clay sighed and scrubbed a hand along the side of his face. "Yeah. Okay. I get that. But I tried calling, and you weren't home. I stopped by the diner and Marcie told me about this campout habit of yours."

"Which is what I'm apologizing for," Ricki said. "Not for going on the campout, but for not calling and letting you know about it."

He drew in another deep breath then slowly let it out, keeping his gaze on hers. "All right. Apology accepted." His shoulders relaxed as he continued to study her face. "Make any decisions while you were out there?"

"A couple." When he lifted an eyebrow, she grimaced. "I'll always think I should have reacted a little quicker and maybe have stopped the accident from happening, but you and Amanda's parents are right. I didn't fire that bullet, and did the best that I could to get out of the way of that car, so I can live with it." Her expression softened at the look of relief in his eyes. It gave her a warm feeling inside to know that he'd been worried about her, even when he was mad. Warm enough that she broke her new rule of no touching while on the job and reached over and squeezed his hand before leaning back in her chair again. "I also took along that report Josh gave me."

His eyes widened slightly over lifted brows, but he didn't show any other reaction to that announcement. "Did you read it?"

Ricki nodded. "I read it. I thought it was something the FBI had put together, but it was the official report from the US Marshals Service."

When she frowned, so did Clay.

"Was something wrong with it?" he asked.

"Let's just say it had my name on it, but it wasn't my interview."

Clay's jaw hardened along with his gaze. "Someone doctored the interview?"

"Or can't listen very well." She had been stunned when she'd read what the interviewing agent had stated were her words, transcribed from the taped interview she'd given from her hospital bed. Maybe the recording had been garbled somehow, so he hadn't understood what she'd said. But she didn't think so.

"What was different?"

She slowly shook her head. "I need to talk to Josh first. Find out what he's thinking." She chewed on her lower lip, still thinking it through. "And I'm not sure you want to get tangled up in this."

"Hey. I'm already tangled up in it, so read me in, James."

Her face lit up with a grateful smile. She wanted to tell him, bounce her thoughts off him and hear his, but it had to be his choice. "Okay. I still want to talk to Josh first, I owe that to him, and I need to get Dan started on that search in the basement. How about we meet at the Sunny Side Up? Say around six?"

Clay nodded. "Sounds good." When Ricki got to her feet, he did the same. "I'll talk to Ray and ask him to help Dan out. If anyone knows where those records are in that mess in the basement, it would be Ray." He smiled. "How's the truck working out for you?"

Since she was now more comfortable accepting his help, another conclusion she'd come to during her campout, Ricki returned his smile. "It's working out great, thanks. I appreciate the loan."

"No problem." He gave her arm a light pat. "I still think we need to make that trip to Chicago, but the two council members I've talked to aren't in agreement. They think it's a lot of money to spend without any assurances it would solve the murder. They want me to turn everything over to the Chicago PD, even though I've explained to them Hardy wasn't murdered in Chicago." He blew out an exasperated breath. "I've gotten all the information I can out of Demi Lansanger, so I'd sure like to get a look at Hardy's desk. There might be a note or something there to connect him with a foundation in Chicago."

Ricki grabbed his arm and stopped him before he could head toward the door. "Do you think that's who Hardy's client was? Someone in that foundation?"

"Could be," Clay said. "Maybe he came out to check up on the place for them, since his assistant said Hardy had been out here before. Might be a regular, every-few-years kind of job for him."

She wasn't buying that. "Why hire a PI? Why not just send some lower-level minion from the foundation, or hire someone from here to run up and check on the place?"

The chief shrugged. "I don't know. Which is why I'd like to establish that connection and then pay the foundation a visit."

Satisfied that they were on the same page and would run into the same roadblock on going to Chicago—him from his bosses on the town council, and her from Hamilton—Ricki nodded. "Yeah. I know what you mean."

When her phone rang she glanced at the caller ID and frowned. "Hang on a minute. It's Captain Davis."

Chapter 19

"They're a match," Ricki said softly, staring at the phone she was still holding in her hand, disbelief written all over her face. "The forensic guys are saying that the rifling on the bullets match up."

Clay lifted both eyebrows. "A match to what?"

Still a bit stunned, Ricki pulled out the chair again and sat down. "To each other." She waited, watching Clay as her little bombshell of information sank in.

"The two . . . ? You aren't talking about . . ." He stuttered to a halt and ran a hand over the top of his head when she nodded.

"I *am* talking about that," Ricki said. "The rifling on the bullet that killed Hardy matches the one that killed the John Doe."

Clay's eyes widened and now he was shaking his head in denial. "But that would mean they came from the same gun."

Ricki threw up her hands in a helpless gesture. "Yeah. That's exactly what it means. Same gun, fired at least twenty-five years apart. Maybe longer. Who knows at this point?"

"Well, shit." Clay's mouth flattened into a thin line. "I don't even know what to do with that."

She didn't either, but Captain Davis had said the forensic tech who had looked over the two bullets was positive. Same marks, same gun. "A Smith & Wesson .22."

"What?"

"A Smith & Wesson .22," Ricki repeated. "That was in the original forensic report as the most likely weapon for both murders. But it was a popular gun back in the sixties and seventies, so I didn't zero in on it."

"I didn't either," Clay said. "All that told me was that the killer wasn't a hitman." When Ricki frowned, he shrugged. "Not the gun of choice for a professional."

So, does someone who kills over a time span of twenty-five years, or maybe even more, count as a professional? Ricki wondered. She stood and headed for the hallway. "We need to let Cy know, and then I'll call Hamilton," she said over her shoulder.

Clay followed her out the door and down the hall to the supervisor's office. When Ricki reached her uncle's door, she gave a quick rap, not waiting for an invitation before stepping into the room. She stopped short at the sight of her boss sitting in one of the folding chairs in front of Cy's desk. Both men looked over at her and Clay as the chief took a hasty step to the side to avoid plowing into Ricki's back.

Cy's gaze swept over his niece's face before he half rose out of his chair. "What's wrong?"

"Nothing." Ricki looked over at Hamilton. "It's a good thing that you're still here. It saves me a phone call."

"Glad to be of help." Hamilton smiled. "A phone call about what?"

Ricki lifted the phone in her hand and waved it back and forth. "I just heard from Captain Davis." She paused and took a breath, wanting to select her words carefully so she wouldn't be misunderstood as she repeated what she'd told Clay about the bullets that killed both victims coming from a single weapon.

A stunned silence settled in the room, lasting a full minute before Hamilton cleared his throat. "Let me understand this. A couple of forensic techs in the Tacoma Police Department are saying that the same gun was used to kill both men?"

She nodded. "That's right."

Hamilton leaned back in his chair and steepled his fingers together in front of him. "Now why would they have compared the two bullets since we don't have a gun to go with them?"

"Curiosity, according to Captain Davis. The techs saw the bullets were the same caliber, and after they did the standard analysis, they both got curious."

"Hmm." The senior agent made the sound deep in his throat, his direct gaze holding Ricki's for a long moment before he let out a sigh. "No mistake, then?"

"No, sir," Ricki said. "No mistake. The same gun killed both our vics."

Hamilton looked over at Clay. "And what do you have to say about this, Chief?"

"What is there to say?" Clay asked in return. "Two dead bodies, same place, same gun."

"And at least twenty-five years between them." Hamilton shook his head. "More like fifty, actually. Unbelievable."

Cy's gaze bounced between Hamilton and his niece, and then over to Clay. "So you're all saying that the same guy committed both murders, with the same gun, in the same way?"

"Not the same way," Ricki said, drawing three pairs of eyes to her. She shrugged. "They weren't killed in the same way."

"Explain that, Agent James," Hamilton demanded.

"It wasn't the same for the killer," she stated. The firmness in her voice lent weight to her words. "Sure, they were both shot. But the John Doe was laid out almost like he was in a coffin. Very proper, with his arms at his side, his legs straight. And the uniform was neatly folded, with his badge still pinned to it. He meant something to whoever left him in that lighthouse." Since she was getting tired, she walked across the room and sat in the empty chair next to Hamilton. "Hardy's body looked like it was left exactly where it fell. He was shot. The killer went through his pockets, and then just walked off. He didn't know Hardy at all, or if he did, he didn't think much of the PI Where he was shot was probably a simple matter of known convenience."

"Known convenience?" Cy asked.

"Yeah. The killer knew about the lighthouse because he'd used it before. He knew it was remote, that no one was going to hear the shot, and if he used his parking lights and not his headlights to get up the mountain, the trees are thick enough that he wouldn't be seen." Ricki nodded. "Convenient."

"Makes sense," Cy muttered, then leaned back in his chair far enough to make it creak. "So what happens now?"

Clay walked over and propped a hip on the edge of Cy's desk. "Well, it narrows down our suspect pool considerably. Whoever we're looking for is probably at least in his fifties, and maybe in his seventies or older."

"He?" Hamilton asked.

"It's unlikely a woman could have carried a body up that path, or would wear a size twelve shoe," Clay said, repeating what he and Ricki had already concluded.

Hamilton nodded. "Agreed, Chief. But the suspect pool is only narrowed if the suspect is still around here. If he's now living anywhere else, say in Tacoma or Seattle, it's another needle in the haystack."

"He's here," Ricki said flatly. "Hardy came here for a reason that's connected to the Bay. The ranger, or whoever he was, was killed here, and someone knew Hardy had come here looking for something." She glanced up at Clay. "Or someone."

"Or someone connected to something," Hamilton said, finishing the thought. "Because that someone very likely killed

Hardy." He glanced over at the open office door long enough that Clay walked over and closed it before returning to his spot near the desk. "Thank you," the senior agent said. He leaned forward until his elbows rested on his knees. "I want this information kept in this room. If our guy is a local, I've heard enough from Ricki about the gossip machine around here to know that if this connection between the two murders gets out, the killer will hear about it."

"That's the truth," Cy agreed. "And he might get desperate enough to take another potshot at Ricki." He nodded at Clay. "Or you."

"That being the reason for the shooting hasn't been established as a fact yet," Hamilton said.

"Then a coincidence strong enough to make it just short of a fact," Cy retorted.

Hamilton straightened up and immediately gave in on the point. "Most likely." He glanced over Ricki's head, his stare aimed at Clay. "How are you on resources, Chief?"

"I could use some help," Clay flatly stated. "We need to nail down who owns that land to see if we can find a link to Hardy's client. We also have to dig through the files in the basement until we come up with a name for the first vic. Without that, it's going to be damn near impossible to find the connection between him and Hardy."

"The Dabob Bay PD lent us a pretty big hand on that last case in the park," Cy quickly pointed out. "Seems we should return the favor." He smiled. "We like to keep friendly, cooperative relations with the local law enforcement."

"He did more than help," Ricki put in quietly. "He risked his life on my last case."

Hamilton rolled his eyes even as a smile tugged at his mouth. "Fine. Fine. I can see I'm outnumbered and outvoted." He shifted in his chair so he was squarely facing Ricki. "In the name of good interdepartmental relations, you are authorized to help the police chief." When she grinned, he gave her a bland look. "As long as you keep up with your other work."

That had her smile wobbling a bit, but she was still doing a high-five inside. At least until Hamilton added, "I hope you enjoy doing all that research, Agent James. It sounds like you're going to be chained to a desk for a while." Now he smiled at her. "Fitting punishment for not returning any of my calls, and then taking off on your own when you should have been here, on the clock."

Chapter 20

THREE HOURS later Ricki straightened up and stretched her back, letting out a small groan as her muscles protested at the foreign movement. She'd been hunched over a desk, staring at a computer screen for so long, she was sure she'd developed a permanent curve in her spine. The bones in her neck crackled when she did a slow head roll to the right, letting out the same sound when she repeated the movement to the left. If Hamilton were more enthusiastic about this case, she'd demand hazard pay for all this desk work. The only quick break she'd had was when she'd made two phone calls—one to Josh, and the other to someone she knew in the county office located in Port Jefferson.

Why did Wilkes find this research shit so intriguing anyway? All the literally backbreaking work had gained her were three names. She stared down at the notepad next to her uncle's computer. Luckily Cy had left to attend to business in the park, which had allowed her to commandeer his office and his computer, although at the moment she would have gladly traded places with him.

She'd much rather be out in the field than sitting behind a desk, staring at a glowing screen that had grudgingly yielded a small handful of names. Knowing desk work was not her forte was the reason she'd happily turned all the staff scheduling duties at the Sunny Side Up over to Anchorman.

Resigned to having to keep plowing through the endless pages of information, both accurate and otherwise, spewed out by the internet, Ricki looked at the first name on her list and considered it for a moment. The description she'd found on the Jennie Dobbs Foundation's website had touted it as the place where wishes came true, followed by a lengthy request for donations to purchase toys for Christmas for kids in the greater Chicago area. She didn't see any reason the small foundation, which proudly proclaimed reaching its annual twenty-thousand-dollar goal, was a good candidate for buying land out in the wilds of the state of Washington. Unless they were considering starting their own Christmas tree farm.

The second name on her list was more promising. The Edward Tarkard Foundation was into environmental issues, from saving a rare breed of pond frog to stopping climate change. Their donation goals were a lot more ambitious than those of the Christmas gift group, which meant they might be large enough to buy some forest land on the Pacific coast. And with their environmental mission, they'd also have an interest in owning that kind of land. She typed the name into the browser and pulled up the website again, giving it a more thorough look. In the upper left-hand corner was what appeared to be a logo. Ricki doubled-clicked on the image to enlarge it, then made a face at the oversized picture. The year 2002 came right after the words "Founded in."

"Too late. Way too late," she said out loud, her voice bouncing around the room. She rubbed a hand across the back of her neck to ease the growing ache as she ran the possibilities through her mind. It could be this was simply the current version of the foundation. It might have sprung up from another one that had been operating around the Second

World War. But that would take some digging that was beyond her internet research skills. She grinned. Lucky Dan.

After circling the name to remind her to shoot it off to her assistant partner, she typed the third name on her list into the browser. The Lillian M. Young Foundation didn't have a website, and every piece of information she pulled up on it was at least ten years old. But when she came across an article that had been written in the late nineties, proudly proclaiming the foundation's fifty years of service to the community, her instincts came alive. That would have put it in operation around World War II, and at one time, at least, it had accepted project requests from anyone who needed or wanted help. Maybe that extended to purchasing land out west? It was a stretch, but maybe. It was also the only name on her list that had brought all her senses to full alert.

When her phone rang, she absently looked over to where it lay on the desk. Josh's name was on the front display, which had her glancing at her watch. It was almost five, which made it eight o'clock at Quantico. The FBI agent was putting in some long hours.

Reaching over, she pressed the speaker button then picked up the manila envelope she'd retrieved from her backpack before she'd put in the call to Josh several hours ago. "Hi, Josh. You're working late."

"I just got off a plane and made it to the motel. Yours is the first call I'm returning."

Since he didn't sound like he was in the mood for any preliminary chitchat, Ricki got right to the point. "I read the report." She drew it out of the envelope and stared at the US Marshals emblem in the corner. "How did you get a copy?"

"I still have contacts there," Josh said, then fell silent.

Okay. I guess he wants me to start. Ricki flipped over the first page of the report and zeroed in on the section that started with her name. For a moment she struggled between the oath she'd taken for the service she'd once worked for, and loyalty to her best friend. It didn't take long for her to come up with a hands-down winner.

"Like I said, I read the report," she began, keeping her tone low and even. "And either the tape failed somehow at a couple of critical places and the agent relied on a very faulty memory to fill in the blanks, or someone is really lousy at transcription."

"I'm going for door number two on that one," Josh said. "How about you?"

The question came out as a dare, and Ricki took it that way. If she agreed with Josh, she was also agreeing to help him out with whatever he was doing to look into Marie's death.

All in or nothing, Ricki thought, then nodded to herself. Did she really have a choice? Marie had been more than a best friend. She'd been a sister, and Ricki couldn't walk away not knowing the truth about her death. So, all in it was.

"Me too. The report has either been altered, or it was never truthful in the first place." She skimmed down the page, looking for the passages she'd marked up the night before. "The sequence is wrong." She stared down at the words. "Marie was killed first, then the prisoner, and then I was hit."

"That's what you told me when I went to see you in the hospital," Josh said. "Are you still sure that's the way it went down?"

"It was fast, Josh, but I'm sure. I was in front. Marie and the prisoner were slightly behind me. She was shot first, and then Hernandez, and then me."

"I picked that up too," he said softly. "But I needed you to confirm."

"There's something else," Ricki said.

"What else?" Josh's voice took on a sharp edge. "The rest of it looked like it matched what you told me."

"It was something I didn't tell you. It isn't in this report, but I told the deputy who interviewed me. But something he said, insisted on, actually, made me think I was imagining it, but now I don't think so."

"What is it?" Josh asked.

"I got a shot off."

Surprise leaped out of the phone. "You what?"

"I fired my weapon, and I'm a pretty good shot."

Josh let out a crack of laughter. "Good is an understatement, Ricki. You're an expert shot. But that would have been in the report, and your weapon would have been tested."

"Yeah. Well, before I lost consciousness, I got one off. I'm sure of it, and I heard a scream, so I thought I hit the guy."

"You're shitting me." Josh's breathing picked up, and she could hear the anger growing every time he inhaled. "Why didn't you tell me this before?"

Why indeed? Ricki closed her eyes, wishing she *had* told Joshua instead of letting that deputy marshal put doubts into her head. Under her dad and uncle's watchful eye, she'd handled guns most of her life, and Josh was right about her being an expert shot. She damn well knew when she hit a target and should never have believed Olyman's mournful "You're so confused" look when he came to interview her. "The deputy marshal said they checked all over the scene and didn't find any blood anywhere. He had me believing I didn't even draw my gun, much less hit the guy who was shooting at us."

"The guy? You're sure it was a male?" Josh asked.

Ricki nodded again as if Marie's fiancé were right in front of her. "That wasn't a woman's scream I heard. It was high-pitched, but definitely male."

There was a drawn-out silence before Josh finally asked, "Is Olyman the marshal who interviewed you?"

"Yeah. He's also the one I turned my badge in to the day I was released. I ran into him outside the hospital."

"Did you talk to anyone else?"

"No."

"That's it then," Josh said with a finality that echoed the silent message that there was no turning back. "I'll get on tracking down this Olyman and arrange to have a little chat with him. What's his full name?"

"Chad. Chad Olyman, deputy marshal out of Arlington," Ricki said. "And I'd like to be in on that chat."

"Yeah, I'll bet," Josh replied. "I'll see what I can do."

He hung up without saying goodbye, but Ricki understood completely. Josh had been on a mission for over a year now. One that she'd just joined. Despite not knowing what she'd gotten herself into, she felt a satisfaction deep in her bones. Questions about that night had always lurked in the back of her mind, and it was long past the time to get some answers.

Her watch said she needed to get going if she wanted to meet Clay on time. It was a fifteen-minute drive from Edington to Brewer, and that was about all the time she had. She picked up her phone and stuffed it into her back pocket before shutting down Cy's computer. Satisfied that everything on the desk was as neat and tidy as her uncle liked, she picked up the report and slid it into its envelope just as there was a knock on the office door.

She curled her fingers around the manila envelope and stood up. "Come on in, I was just leaving."

Dan Wilkes stuck his head around the edge of the door. "Got a minute? I found something."

"Like what?" Ricki asked, coming around the desk. She waited for Dan to step inside the office and shut the door.

"It took some heavy lifting, and I mean that literally, but I found a couple of boxes with records from 1970 to 1971. I managed to dig out the staff rosters from both years. There were twenty-two rangers on the 1970 list, and twenty-three on the list the following year."

Ricki leaned a hip against the desk and grinned. "That's good. Are those lists dated by any chance?"

He wiggled his eyebrows to go with his own grin. "Oh

yeah. January 1970 on the first list and September 1971 on the second one." He looked down at the paper in his hand. "I compared the names, and it looks like they lost three guys between the two time periods and picked up four more. So that gives us twenty-six guys to look at." He shrugged. "At least for these two years."

"Twenty-six is a big pool," Ricki noted. "But it gives us a place to start."

"We only have three more days," Dan pointed out. "Not a lot of time to narrow the list down to one victim."

"Five days, if you're willing to work the weekend," Ricki said.

The ranger immediately nodded. "I am. But it still isn't a lot of time." He laid a photo the same size as a standard piece of paper on the desk. "I also found a picture in the 1970 file."

Ricki carefully picked it up and held it in front of her, studying the men who were at attention and arranged in two rows. In their uniforms, they looked surprisingly similar, except for differing heights and hair colors. She was quiet for a full minute as she counted out the same number of bodies as there were names on the staff roster.

She was still staring at the photo when her cell phone rang. Thinking it might be Clay wondering where she was, she grinned when she saw the name that flashed on the caller ID. "We might be getting a break. Hang on a minute." She tapped the screen and then held the phone up to her ear. "Hey, Beth. What did you find?" She reached over and grabbed a pencil from a repurposed soup can sitting on Cy's desk. Since the only available paper was the envelope tucked under her arm, she set it down and began scribbling across its back. "Yeah, I got it. And is that also the listed owner?" Ricki frowned as she listened, writing down the name her contact at the county courthouse was spelling out. "Barbara G. Metler. Okay. Thanks. I owe you." She listened for another moment, smiling. "Sure. One of Anchorman's famous burgers is on the house the next time you come to town. I'll leave it up to you about any plans you have for my cook."

She said her goodbyes and hung up before picking up the manila envelope and holding it out for Dan to see. "Hamilton was right. A foundation doesn't own the land. They must have sold it because it belongs to a Barbara Metler."

"Great." Dan sighed. "There goes our only Chicago connection, and we're right back where we started from."

Ricki shook her head. "Not exactly." She pointed at a name she'd written higher up on the envelope. "See that? It's an accounting firm. The annual tax bill is sent to their office, in Chicago, Illinois."

While Dan grinned, she picked up the photo again. "Now. Which of you gentlemen ended up in the old lighthouse?"

Chapter 21

RICKI WAS ONLY twenty minutes late meeting Clay by the time she walked into the diner. She'd left the truck in her usual space in the alley out back. The big Ford was even more of a challenge than her jeep to fit into the tight area, but she managed before heading around the building to the front door.

She'd spotted the chief's SUV out front and figured he was probably sitting at his favorite spot at the end of the counter. She didn't want to keep him waiting even longer by coming in through the back door and being waylaid in the kitchen by Anchorman.

The place was crowded. It looked like half the town was taking advantage of the diner's expanded summer hours and enjoying a casual dinner out. Marcie was flying around the room, a pitcher of iced tea in one hand and her order book in the other. Tonight she had help from Cindy, daughter number two, who was weaving her way between the tables, several plates of food balanced on her arms. With Marcie's cousin was holding down the hostess station up front, the Sunny Side Up had become quite a family affair. And that included her own son, who was toting a large gray tub under one arm as he cleared a table on the far side of the room.

Ricki looked up at the battered clock hanging on the wall behind the back counter. Her eyebrows drew together as she quickly scanned the room, expecting to see Bear. She certainly was always glad to see her son, but she'd expected his father to have picked him up by now. He was due back from the guided tour today, and they'd agreed that Eddie would go home with him tonight. She took out her phone and checked to see if she'd missed a text message, but didn't see one.

Wondering if she should be worried or annoyed by her ex-husband's tardiness, Ricki slowly made her way across the room, stopping to greet customers at the tables she passed, and waving to others who called out to her. When she finally reached Clay, she plopped onto the low-backed swivel stool next to his and made a face.

"It's like running a gauntlet."

"It's like walking into a family reunion," Clay corrected. "That makes you a lucky person, Agent James."

She smiled and nodded her agreement. "I guess it does." She glanced over at the empty space on the counter in front of him. "Not hungry?"

He winced. "Not yet. My last phone call was to Demi Lansanger, and I'm still getting over it." He rubbed a hand across his forehead. "What you're missing here is a liquor license."

Ricki made a sympathetic sound and patted him softly on the back. "Is she still going into hysterics every time you mention her dead boss?"

"Hasn't shown any sign of calming down as far as I can tell." He rolled his eyes to the ceiling. "All I have to do is say 'hello' and the tears start coming. It took me thirty minutes to get her to agree to look back through the records for that report on the previous trip Hardy made out here."

"The one he wrote up himself because she was out helping her mom through some surgery?"

"Yeah, that one." He gave Ricki a sideways glance. "She almost makes me glad I haven't been able to talk the town council into paying for a trip to Chicago. Although I'd still like a chance to go through Maxwell Hardy's desk."

"We might be a step closer to identifying his client." When Clay shifted in his seat to face her, Ricki nodded. "My contact down at county records came through with the name of the landowner."

"The foundation in Chicago?" Clay asked.

"It might have been at one time, but now it's owned by someone named Barbara Metler, and the taxes are paid by an accounting firm in Chicago." She grinned. "I have it on my to-do list to track down the phone numbers for any Barbara Metler in the Chicago area, and I'll give the accountants a call tomorrow."

"They aren't likely to give up the name of a client," Clay said.

"Maybe not to a special agent with the park service, but what if the call came from an upstanding member of the Chicago PD?"

Clay grinned. "Good idea. I'll reach out to them in the morning." He signaled to Cindy for two iced teas. "Did our relentless ranger find out anything else?"

Ricki thanked the young temporary waitress as she set down a glass filled with ice and Anchorman's secret tea blend, then waited until she moved off to help another customer. "Dan found some staff lists." She quickly filled him in, including Dan's plan to start looking for personnel files in the boxes stacked in the basement.

"Another good idea," Clay said. "I'm sorry I can't send Ray down there to help. He wasn't in the front lobby, and when I got back to my office, there was a note on my desk saying he'd had to leave early to go to Olympia with his nephew."

"Doesn't sound like his nephew is getting much work in," Ricki mentioned.

"Probably not. Ray brought John in to meet me last week. Nice guy. The two of them seem pretty devoted to each other."

"They are," Ricki confirmed. "John's mother was Ray's sister. The story around town is that she passed away when John was a baby, and his uncle stepped in to raise him."

"What happened to John's father?" Clay asked.

"Some kind of accident right after they were married, as I recall. I think Ray told me that once." Ricki idly stirred her iced tea. "One of those things small towns don't talk about, I guess."

Abandoning the topic of his longtime volunteer, Clay fixed his gaze on her face. "What about your talk with Josh? Did you manage to get hold of him?"

She inched closer on her stool and lowered her voice. "We talked. He's going to track down the deputy marshal who interviewed me in the hospital."

"Why?" Clay asked bluntly.

"Because he recorded the interview, but somehow what I said didn't make it into the transcribed report."

Clay let out a soft whistle. "Then he's the one who doctored the report?"

"Someone did." Ricki leaned in and gave Clay the short version of the changes in the report. When she was finished, Clay's gaze had gone flat.

"You hit the gunman and the deputy denied it?"

She appreciated the fact that he hadn't questioned her version of events for one second. It was a far cry from the way Deputy Marshal Olyman had insisted she was confused about what had happened that night. "I told Josh I wanted to be there when he questioned Olyman."

"I wouldn't mind being there myself," Clay said. "Something stinks about that whole investigation."

She couldn't argue with that, but there was more to it. She was sure of it. And she'd bet the diner that Josh was too. "The question is, why does it stink, and how high does that stink go?"

Her phone interrupted them with a loud beep, indicating a message had arrived. It was from Bear. She frowned at it. "It seems my ex can't make it back to town tonight and wants to know if my mother-in-law should come pick up Eddie." She quickly tapped in a "No. He can stay at home," and sent it off before looking over at Clay. "Now, why would a man who took a last-minute trip with some clerk over at Mountain Outfitters that he has the hots for suddenly need an extra night away from his own bed?"

Clay immediately held out both hands. "Whoa. That is a loaded question, and I'm not answering it."

Ricki laughed, then caught sight of Ray and his nephew making their way across the diner. She reached over and poked Clay in the arm. "Saved by your volunteer. I thought you said Ray went to Olympia?"

"That's what his note said." Clay glanced over his shoulder. "Looks like it was a short trip."

"Chief!" Ray waved at Clay and then winked at Ricki. "And Special Agent James." He stopped and shifted to the side to let the man following in his wake step forward. "Ricki, do you remember John?"

She smiled and held out a hand. "Sure. How have you been, John?"

John took hold of her hand and gave it a firm shake. "Fine, just fine. Even better now that I've had a chance to spend some time with my uncle." John was close to six feet tall, with thinning brown hair and a friendly smile. There had been quite a gap between them in school since he was close to fifty, so Ricki hadn't seen him much while she was growing up.

John had been gone and on his own when she'd barely been out of diapers.

"I called in to make sure everything was going okay without anyone at the front desk today." Ray smiled at Clay. "Deputy Tucker told me that you were looking for me to give Dan Wilkes a hand in the basement." He turned his attention to Ricki. "And that you wanted me to take a look at some picture Dan found down there."

Surprised that piece of information had gotten back to Ray so fast, Ricki automatically shifted her own smile into neutral when she nodded. "That's right. But I'll catch up with you whenever you're in again."

"What kind of picture?" Ray persisted. "Deputy Tucker didn't know."

Ricki shot a quick look at Clay, clearly conveying the message that he needed to have a talk with his chatty deputy, before giving Ray an easy shrug. "Nothing too exciting. It's a picture of a group of rangers from 1970. I was just wondering if you might recognize any of them."

Behind his wire-rimmed glasses, Ray's eyes widened until they looked like small moons. "Wow. That's a long time ago. Does this have to do with that missing ranger you asked me about?"

"Maybe," Ricki hedged. "I'm not sure."

"I don't know if I can help you much. I didn't hang out with any rangers back then." He wrinkled his nose and squinted up at her. "I might know a couple of people who could help you out. Do you want me to ask them?"

"No," Ricki said. "If you'd write their names down, I'll contact them."

"Sure thing, sure thing, Ricki. I'll get right on that." He let out a mournful sigh. "Not a lot of us left, you know. Pete's only been here forty years, so he doesn't go back that far. No one else in the group does, I guess."

"Well, it was only a thought," Ricki said.

"We need to get something to eat, Uncle Ray." John wrapped a hand around one of his uncle's thin shoulders. "I think we've bothered Ricki and the chief enough."

Ray didn't make any protest as his nephew led him away. Ricki watched them claim a booth on the far side of the room and settle in with menus before looking over at Clay. "What was that all about?"

"Anxiety," Clay said distinctly. "Ray's always calling in and worrying whenever he's not at his post in the lobby."

"Hmm." Ricki let the noncommittal sound stand. Clay was probably right. Ray did consider his presence at the station vital to keeping it running smoothly, which was why he was there seven days a week.

"Anchorman's waving at you," Clay said, tilting his head toward the long cutout window between the dining area and the kitchen.

Sure enough, the cook's long arm was sticking through the opening, his index finger pointing at her. Shaking her head at how ridiculous it looked, Ricki stood and told Clay she'd be back in a few minutes. She walked over to the center of the window, shooing Anchorman off once she came into his line of vision.

"I'm coming," she hissed. "You look like an idiot."

"We need to talk about the schedule," he shot back.

She didn't bother to answer but stalked through the swinging doors. Five minutes later they still hadn't come to any agreement on what time, or even what days, Sam, who had slid into the job of relief cook, would be scheduled to work. She was about to point out that Anchorman had given all the early mornings to Sam and none to himself when the doors to the kitchen swung open and John walked through them.

"Who are you?" Anchorman demanded.

Well aware of Anchorman's small tolerance for anyone invading his space, Ricki stepped in front of him. "Calm down. He's Ray's nephew." She took a step closer to John, who was looking around with wide-eyed fascination. "Did you need something?"

"Believe it or not, I've never been inside a commercial kitchen." John turned a sheepish smile on her. "I'm sorry. I didn't mean to barge in. My uncle said the bathrooms were past the swinging doors."

"He meant to the right of the swinging doors," Ricki said. She pointed behind John. "Back that way."

"Oh. Right. Sorry." His mouth turned down. "My uncle's been getting a little more confused lately."

"I haven't noticed it," Ricki said.

"Well, it's mostly when he's somewhere he hasn't been in a while. I guess he doesn't go out to Mom's grave much, because today when we stopped by the cemetery in Olympia, he couldn't remember where it was."

Ricki's gaze softened. With her own mother in the advanced stages of Alzheimer's, she could certainly sympathize with that. "It's all part of the aging process, John. And Ray does really well. You don't need to worry about him."

"Thanks. I do worry. I was going to try to catch you before we left, but since I seem to have made a wrong turn here, I might as well put it to good use." He reached into his shirt pocket and took out a business card with a number inked onto the back. "I heard what you said to my uncle. You could keep asking around, looking for someone who might remember those rangers back in the seventies, but I thought I'd save you some trouble. Uncle Ray's memory isn't what it used to be, and it isn't likely he'll remember anyone back that far, so I thought I'd let you know that and save you some time."

He held the card out to her. "That's my business card. MMG is my company in Seattle. You can call the number on the front and ask for me or call the number on the back. It's my personal cell phone." His gaze turned apologetic. "My uncle is getting on in years, and, well, if anything happens, or he needs some extra help at home, I'm hoping you'll give me a call." He sighed and his chin drooped a little. "I don't think anyone here in the Bay has my number any longer. I've been gone for almost thirty years."

"Sure. No problem." Ricki tucked the card into her shirt pocket.

"Thank you." John took another look around and smiled. "Well. I'll get out of your way."

Chapter 22

WEDNESDAY MORNING, or as she'd come to think of it, the first full day of her five-day countdown, she'd just sat down at her desk in the corner of the living room when there was a loud knock on the front door, followed by a raised voice.

"Hurry up, Ricki. These are heavy."

Wondering what Dan was doing on her doorstep before 8 a.m., Ricki opened the door just in time to catch a file box that was in danger of tumbling off the stack that Dan was juggling with her one good hand and a forearm.

"Hang on, hang on." Ricki managed to get her arms around the falling box without upending the contents, then quickly set it on the floor. Reaching up, she helped steady the teetering box on top, then eyed the ranger over its top. "What is all this?"

"Personnel files." Dan peered back at her. "Can I come in?"

Ricki answered by stepping aside. She shoved the door shut with one foot while Dan headed straight for the kitchen island.

He dropped the last box onto the laminate top, then wiped the back of his hand across his brow. "That was a close one."

"Why didn't you just make two trips?"

"Too far, and I thought I could do it in one," Dan said. "But those damn boxes somehow got heavier on the drive over here."

She looked out the front window. Dan's SUV was parked right behind the truck, making the walk to the cabin about fifty feet at a stretch. "Too far? You're kidding me." She eyed the small beads of sweat dotting the ranger's forehead. "You really need to get out and get in some of that hiking Cy told you to do."

He grinned. "Too much work."

She walked over and plopped her box onto the counter next to his and then went back for the third one, easily lifting it and carrying it over to the counter. "You picked a weird profession if you think hiking is too much work." She slapped a hand on top of the nearest box. "What are you doing with these, anyway?"

Dan turned and pulled out one of the stools tucked under the overhanging lip of the island. He sat and hooked the heel of one work boot around a lower rung. "I pulled them out of the basement last night and was going to put them in the conference room, but some of the guys were working late on the new safety regs, and they were using it for a pizza break. So I hauled them out to the car to bring over here. I thought you'd want to see them first thing."

"Uh-huh." She should have objected to him taking official files out of the building without permission from his supervisor, which she was sure he didn't have, but he was right about one thing. Her hands were itching to go through them. Inside one of those boxes could be the key to the unidentified ranger, and maybe why he was murdered. Provided he was a ranger at all. The sooner she found that out, the better.

She slid the nearest box off the counter and carted it over to her makeshift coffee table in front of the couch. "Look for anything that seems out of place."

"Yeah. That's specific enough," Dan grumbled as he plopped down onto a stool and pulled one of the file boxes across the counter.

Ignoring him, Ricki began sorting through papers yellowed with age. An hour later she suddenly stood up, her gaze glued to the folder she was holding in her hands.

Dan looked over from his perch next to the island. "Did you find something?"

"Maybe." She stood up without taking her eyes off the paper in her hand. "Maybe."

"I've got a couple of guys here who quit in 1970, and one who died in a climbing accident," Dan said. "But no one who has gone missing." He glanced over at her. "Are you looking at the 1971 box?"

"Yeah." Ricki's eyes narrowed as she reread the short separation note, signed by a supervisor and tucked away in a forgotten file.

When she didn't say anything else, Dan got up and walked over to the couch to look over her shoulder. "That file is stamped 'Resigned.' I didn't think we were looking at anyone who'd left the rangers."

"It seems there were steps to leaving the service, even back then," Ricki said. She tapped a slender finger against a piece of paper yellowed around its edges and clipped to a handwritten letter. "This says he missed a few of them."

"Who did?" Dan asked.

"Mr. Benjamin Graham. As in last name starts with a *G*, Graham." Ricki's gaze gleamed with satisfaction. This was her guy.

"And that's important because . . . ?"

"Same initial used by Barbara G. Metler, the owner of the lighthouse." Ricki flipped over the page and started down the next one.

"That's interesting, but it's still a common initial," Dan argued. "Have you got anything else?"

"He was a ranger for less than two years, and stood five ten, brown on brown," Ricki said, more to herself than to her assistant partner, who had hopped down from his stool and was now breathing down her neck. She didn't know about the eye and hair color, of course, but the height fit the ME's estimate for the skeleton.

"What step did he miss?" Ricki suddenly turned around, almost knocking Dan over, forcing him to take a quick jump backwards before repeating his question. "What step?"

"He put in a resignation letter. It even gave his last day of work as April 10, 1971. But according to his supervisor, he never showed up for his shift that day, and failed to turn in his badge. He wasn't in the enforcement unit, so he didn't have a gun." Ricki's smile held more than a hint of smugness. "The badge is missing, and we also have the approximate date he went missing. The tenth."

"No badge." Dan rubbed his hands together. "Okay. That's better. But it's still a coincidence and not a solid link."

"Oh, it's solid enough." Ricki turned the report around and held it up. "Take a look. Three lines down."

Dan leaned forward and squinted a little. "What is that?"

"Someone recorded the numbers on the new badges that were handed out, and that one was issued to Ranger Benjamin Graham." Ricki pointed to the box on line three. "See what that says? Badge 286. Graham is our guy."

Dan's jaw dropped. He snatched the file out of Ricki's outstretched hand, staring as if he'd never seen anything like it. "There it is, plain as day. Two-eight-six." When he looked up, his eyes were gleaming. "But he resigned, so technically he wasn't a ranger when he was killed."

"Technically, he never finished the process," Ricki countered. "And if he never showed up for his last shift, then the odds are he was killed before that, when he was still a ranger."

Dan stuck his hands into the back pockets of his jeans and nodded. "That might work."

"That's a fact," Ricki said. "Benjamin Graham was still a ranger when he was murdered, so the case is mine."

"And the chief has the dead PI." Dan retreated to his stool and sat down again. "How do the two relate?"

"Don't know," Ricki said, still flipping through the file. She paused on the last page and stared at the name listed under next of kin. It just put a seal on the whole thing. "It seems Ranger Graham wasn't married. He listed his next of kin as his father, Herbert Graham, and put down a second name. Barbara Graham." She looked up and grinned at Dan. "Sister."

"Holy shit, holy shit!" Dan gasped. "The dead guy is related to the woman who owns the lighthouse? Do you think she killed him?"

Ricki had no idea, but those two things definitely put Barbara Graham Metler at the top of the list of suspects.

"You said the accounting firm that pays the tax bill is in Chicago. Do you think this guy's sister is there too?" Dan pointed to the laptop sitting on her desk. "If you don't mind me using that, I can take a look."

"You're welcome to try, but I already did a search when I got home last night," Ricki admitted. "Couldn't find a Barbara Metler in the greater Chicago area."

He gave her a pitying look. "Did you try a Google search of her name?"

Ricki sniffed. "Three hundred and fifty thousand results."

"How about narrowing it down to Chicago?"

Now she rolled her eyes. "Fifty-five results, Mr. Know-It-All." She jerked a thumb toward her desk. "But you're welcome to give it a try."

While he crossed over to the desk, Ricki pulled out her phone and called Clay. The internet wasn't the only way to get information.

When he answered a moment later, she skipped the usual greeting.

"I need Demi Lansanger's number. Do you have it on your phone?"

"Hi to you too." His deep voice sounded amused. "I'll text it to you. Anything else?"

"We got an ID on the dead ranger."

There was a brief pause before he asked, "So the vic was a ranger after all?"

"Yeah. Benjamin Graham. Went missing April 10, 1971."

"That's a story I really want to hear," Clay said. "But I'm tied up right now."

Since she'd clearly caught him at a bad time, Ricki promised they'd exchange notes later, then hung up and waited for his incoming message. She didn't have to wait long. It showed up thirty seconds later. She tapped in the number as Dan opened her laptop. She had a hunch all these pieces were connected somehow, and she was about to find out how.

"Hardy Investigations," the bright voice on the other end chirped out. "Mr. Hardy is out of the office today, but I'd be happy to help you."

"Out of the office" was such an understatement, Ricki rolled her eyes. "Ms. Lansanger? This is Special Agent Ricki James from the National Park Service. Do you remember me?"

"Sure," Demi said. "Sure. You work with that hunky chief from Dimsum Bay, right?"

"Dabob Bay, Ms. Lansanger."

"Is that chief as good-looking as his picture?" Demi blurted out. "I looked him up after he called me about Max."

"I'll arrange an introduction," Ricki said dryly. "I'm hoping you can give me the number for Barbara Metler?"

Half expecting to hear *Barbara who?* her nerves leaped to life when the PI's assistant said, "Mrs. Metler? Sure, sure. I have it right here in my client log. Hang on a minute."

Ricki walked over to the desk and pushed Dan aside as she reached for a pen and a scrap piece of paper. She held her breath and waited for what seemed to be a hell of a lot longer than one minute before Demi finally came back on the phone and slowly read off a phone number.

"Area code 6-3-0. That's in Chicago?" Ricki asked.

"Nearby. Mrs. Metler lives in Oak Brook. Very ritzy area," Demi said. "Can you really get me an introduction to Chief Thomas?"

Oh brother. "Sure," Ricki said easily. "The next time you're out here, you let me know. I'll get it all arranged."

"But—"

That's as far as the young woman got before Ricki cut her off. "Thanks for your help, Ms. Lansanger. I'll be in touch." She hung up before Demi could say another word, only to find Dan staring at her.

"Ms. Lansanger?" He smiled. "I thought the chief said he'd rather live out his life alone in a cave than have to talk to her again."

Ricki waved an airy hand in front of her. "There are a lot of sacrifices you have to make in the line of duty." When Dan laughed, she dialed the number she'd written down and waited. The call went directly to voice mail. Apparently no one in the Metler household, in the very ritzy neighborhood of Oak Brook, was answering the phone today. She listened to the greeting with its lengthy list of instructions, waiting for the beep that indicated she could leave a message. When it finally sounded in her ear, Ricki smiled.

"Hello. This is Special Agent Ricki James with the investigative bureau of the National Park Service. I'm calling for Barbara G. Metler, who owns the land in northwest Washington close to Olympic National Park. I would appreciate a call back at your earliest convenience. We've found your brother."

Chapter 23

"THEN YOU THINK this Metler woman was Maxwell Hardy's client?"

"There's a good chance." Ricki shifted her weight to a more comfortable position in the folding chair in front of Clay's desk. She hadn't been able to catch up with him the night before, so was sure to make his office her first stop that morning.

She was careful to keep her wrist still in her lap, mindful of the small warning throbs it had been sending out since that morning, when she'd rescued the box falling out of Dan's grip. Not the best move for a wrist with a hairline fracture. But she considered it an even trade for everything she'd learned today. "I looked up the neighborhood she lives in. Like Demi said, it's definitely on the ritzy side, so she fits the description of a client Hardy would take care of personally."

Clay swiveled a half-turn in his chair and looked out the window into the thick stand of trees that surrounded three sides of the building. "Maybe she's been looking for her brother all these years."

"If she has, she doesn't seem too anxious to hear about it,"

Ricki said. "I've been waiting to hear back from her, but so far, nothing."

He shifted his gaze back to her. "Which leads to the other possibility."

Easily following his line of thought, Ricki nodded. "Yeah. She could have been sending that PI around every few years to make sure nothing had been disturbed."

"And her secret remains safe?"

She shrugged. "Someone's secret anyway. Unless you think she followed Hardy out here and shot her own PI."

Clay shook his head. "Odds wouldn't be good on that one, but people have done stranger things."

Thinking about her last case, and why all those people had died, Ricki nodded her agreement.

The chief tapped a finger against the screen of his computer. "I put an inquiry in to the Chicago PD. They sent a detective out to interview Ms. Lansanger in person and came up with the same answers I got." He winced. "And the same impression. It seems she cried all over the Chicago detective too, poor bastard. He let me know that I owe him a big one." Clay's casual posture said plainly enough that he wasn't worried about it, which had Ricki fervently hoping the emotional Ms. Lansanger never made it out to the Bay and demanded her promised introduction to the "hunky" chief.

The object of Demi's fascination glanced at his wristwatch. "It's getting late. I was hoping we could . . ." He stopped midsentence and looked past Ricki. "Hey, Bear. Something I can help you with?"

"Sounds like you're already doing that."

Ricki shot to her feet and moved to block her ex-husband's view of the chief. Behind her, she heard the distinct scrape of boots on the floor as Clay got to his feet. "Get a grip, Bear. What do you want?"

"I wanted to let my wife know that I was back in town and picked Eddie up at the diner. He's at Mom's house."

"Ex-wife, and fine. Great." Ricki gave him a pointed look. "You could have called and let me know instead of making the drive up from Brewer."

Bear hadn't moved from his place in the doorway. He stood with his arms crossed over his broad chest, blocking the only exit, as he shifted his glare from Clay to Ricki. "I also need to talk to you about the schedule for our son this week, now that he's out of school."

"Also could have been done over the phone," Ricki said, but she waved toward the hallway. "Since you're here, let's talk. Out in the parking lot."

He sent a smirk over her head, aimed at the man standing behind the desk. "That's fine."

"I'll meet you outside." Having no patience for what she considered a juvenile and purely unjustified show of male ego, Ricki put enough warning into her voice to draw a startled look from her ex.

When Bear disappeared into the hallway, Ricki turned around and found Clay grinning at her. "Need me to come with you?"

She snorted at that. Not likely. "No." She pointed a finger at him. "Stay here."

"Not a dog, Agent James."

"Not in the mood, Chief Thomas." She turned on her heel and stomped out the door. She had a murder to solve. She didn't have time for this crap.

When she pushed through the front doors, Bear was leaning against one of the thick pine posts holding up the roof of the porch.

"I'm sorry," he blurted out before she could open her mouth. "I was out of line. I'm just not used to walking in and hearing guys hitting on you."

Her annoyance quickly deflating, Ricki let out an exasperated sigh. "Not very flattering, but apology accepted. And he wasn't hitting on me." At his dark look, she grinned. "You didn't give him a chance." When he continued to glare at her, she walked over and sat on the railing next to him. "Funny attitude coming from a guy who spent the weekend, and an extra night, with his good friend, the clerk at Mountain Outfitters."

She'd only been guessing, but it must have been an accurate one because Bear's cheeks turned a very bright crimson.

"Ah, come on, Ricki."

Perfectly willing to let him squirm for a bit more, she huffed out another breath. "I thought we came up with a rule about no sleeping with a customer?" The devil on her shoulder had her cocking her head to one side and lifting an eyebrow. "As a matter of fact, I think that was *your* rule, wasn't it?"

"Ah, come on, Ricki," Bear repeated, scuffing one heel against the porch's wooden floorboards. "She wasn't even the customer. Her friends were."

"Oh. Well. Then I guess she was along on the hike as your guest?"

He squinted at her through the fading light. "You aren't going to let this go, are you?"

"Not until you apologize and mean it."

"I'm sorry," he groused. "There. Are you happy?"

"Very." She gave him a sunny smile. "Now what about Eddie's schedule this week?"

Ten minutes later she walked back into Clay's office, the smile still on her face.

"I guess that went pretty well," Clay said.

Ricki nodded and slid back down into the folding chair. "It seems Bear's new girlfriend requires more of his time."

Clay lifted his hands off the keyboard he'd been clicking away at and turned to face her, his gaze wide. "He has a girlfriend?"

She lifted a hand and wiggled it back and forth. "Or

something. I'm not sure what her status is, but they are definitely dancing between the sheets."

Clay laughed. "And you intend to hold that over his head?"

"If it means Eddie spends more time at home? Oh yeah."

His grin grew wide enough to split his face in two. "You're an evil person, James."

"I'll make a note that you think so," Ricki said, then quickly turned around at the knock on the door casing, half expecting to see Bear standing there. But it was Ray, looking bemused as his watery gaze fixed itself on Ricki.

"There's a lady here to see you."

When he stopped and seemed to lose his train of thought, Ricki gave him a gentle prod. "Did she give you her name?"

"She says you called her."

Ricki blinked, then looked over at Clay. "You've got to be kidding me."

"If you're Special Agent James, I can assure you, I am not kidding."

A woman appeared in the doorway as Ray simply melted out of sight. She was tall, with silver hair brushed back from her face to emphasize the large brown eyes staring boldly at Ricki from across the room.

"I'm Barbara Graham Metler, and I believe you left me a message about my brother?"

Quickly gathering herself together, Ricki stood almost at attention and nodded. The woman with her inbred air of superiority had that kind of effect on people. "I'm Special Agent James." She gestured toward Clay. "And this is Police Chief Thomas." She paused for a moment. "Welcome to the Bay, Ms. Metler. I have to admit, I'm surprised to see you here."

"I'm surprised to be here." Barbara Metler marched across the room and set her huge purse down on Clay's desk before gingerly lowering herself onto the edge of the folding chair next to Ricki. "Very functional," she commented politely in what Ricki was sure the woman thought passed for a compliment to someone on a lower level than the exalted one she occupied.

"It's Mrs., not Ms., as a matter of fact, and your message said you'd found Benjamin."

"I believe so. The medical examiner will need to make a positive ID. If you have any . . ." Ricki closed her mouth when Mrs. Metler pulled a large manila envelope from her voluminous purse. "I brought his dental records. Now please tell me why you think you found him, and where?"

Ricki started with the last question, since that was the easier one to explain. "We found him on your land."

"My land?"

"You're the owner on record, Mrs. Metler. Fifty acres, about twenty minutes away, near Massey."

"I've never heard of Massey," their unexpected visitor said. "But I do own land somewhere in Washington. It might be around there."

"You've never seen the land?" Clay asked.

Mrs. Metler turned her head to look at him. "Of course not. I don't have any reason to. The foundation bought the land many years ago for an investment. They had no real interest in it, and Benny had only put in a formal request to purchase it himself just before he went missing. It was another ten years before the board finally decided to sell it, so I bought it." She faced Ricki again. "To hold it for him until he came home."

"Was Benjamin a park ranger, Mrs. Metler?" Ricki asked.

"Please. It would be easier if you called me Barbara, and yes. He was. He signed up as a lark, and to annoy our father, who had expected him to go into the family business."

Becoming a ranger on a whim would explain why he'd resigned after only a couple of years. It didn't sound as if he'd ever had any intentions of making a real career in the park service. "Did you know that he was leaving the rangers?" Ricki asked.

Barbara nodded. "Of course. He said he'd had enough of mucking about the woods and was ready to live back in civilization again."

Must have been a lousy ranger, even for that short of a time, Ricki thought, but she kept her expression neutral. "When was the last time you heard from your brother?"

"On April eighth, Agent James." She paused. "Forty-nine years ago. He was supposed to be driving back for my wedding, which had been planned for over a year to be held at the end of April. He wanted me to be sure that his tuxedo was cleaned." She picked at an imaginary piece of lint on her smartly pressed jacket. "He called me almost every day, mostly to talk about nothing, really. Even though he was ten years my senior, we were very close."

Ricki exchanged a look with Clay before locking her gaze back on Barbara Metler. "Then I'm very sorry to inform you that the body we found is most likely your brother, and he's dead." She softened her voice. "He has been for quite a while."

Mrs. Metler sucked in a quick breath, then went very still. "Why do you think the body you found is Benny?"

"He'd been given a numbered badge and it was still with his body, along with his uniform," Ricki said. "And he was found on your land."

"How long has he been . . ." She stopped and looked at her hands. "How long has he been gone?"

There wasn't any good way to say it, so Ricki kept it as simple as possible. "Since the last time you talked to him. Or within a day or two." When Barbara's head jerked backward as if someone had slapped her, Ricki kept her voice low. "He was supposed to turn his badge in and complete his paperwork after his last shift on the tenth. He never showed up."

"Why didn't they call us?" Barbara's voice had gone from

quiet despair to the edge of anger in nothing flat. "They should have called us when he didn't report for work like that. It wasn't like him at all."

Thinking it sounded very much like a guy who'd taken a job on a lark and then couldn't wait to be rid of it, Ricki only shook her head. "I don't know. Maybe because he'd turned in his resignation." *And his supervisor probably thought the rich boy couldn't be bothered to finish out his shift and turn in his badge.*

"Very lax," Barbara declared indignantly. "When he didn't arrive in Chicago as he'd planned, I called his supervisor, and all that man told me was that Benny had resigned and was no longer employed with the rangers. Then he said my brother had left town." Her back had gone stiff as a board and her hands in her lap were balled into fists. "He lied. If you've found Benjamin on that miserable piece of land, then he never left here."

Ricki let the woman's rant roll right over her. Even though she was sure Barbara Graham Metler had been expecting this news about her brother for literally decades, it didn't lessen the pain to hear it out loud.

"How did you find him?" Benjamin's sister demanded. "After almost fifty years, how did you ever find him now?"

"There's a lighthouse on the land," Ricki said. "We found him in there. Or rather your PI, Maxwell Hardy, found him, and then we found Maxwell Hardy and your brother."

"Max?" Some of the anger in Barbara's gaze was replaced with confusion. "Max found him?" She looked around as if she expected to see the burly PI standing in one of the corners. "Why didn't he call me? I'm the one who hired him."

"He couldn't," Ricki said flatly. "He was shot. Just like your brother."

"What?" Barbara stared at her, the color rapidly draining from her face. "Someone shot Benny?" Ignoring that the same thing had happened to her PI, and a lot more recently too, her stunned gaze slid over to Clay. "Who would shoot Benny?"

"Who would shoot your PI?" Clay countered.

"I don't know." Barbara raised a hand to her cheeks and brushed away the tears that had started to leak from her perfectly made-up eyes, leaving tracks of mascara down her cheeks. "I just don't know."

Chapter 24

"So where did you leave it?"

Hamilton's face filled the screen of the iPad that Cy had propped against the desk lamp. Ricki and Clay sat on chairs in front of the screen while Dan and Cy stood behind them. Ricki thought they looked like they were taking a class picture, but for a last-minute meeting, it did the trick.

"Benjamin Graham's sister is bringing the dental records back in tomorrow," Ricki said. "TK will be taking them to Tacoma so he and the ME can confirm the ID. Dan will be accompanying them as the representative from this office."

Her boss leaned back and scrubbed both hands up the sides of his face, then pressed his fingertips into his temples. "And you feel this is still our case because this Benjamin Graham never officially left the park service?"

"Half your case," Clay put in. "The dead PI, who was hired by Graham's sister, is still mine."

A shadowy smile crossed Hamilton's lips. "My apologies, Chief. Half our case."

"For our half of the double homicide, yes, sir, I'd say it's our case," Ricki said. "Graham never showed up for his shift, so he didn't finish processing out."

"But his supervisor did it for him," Hamilton stated. "An important point because I doubt if the deputy director is going to be too thrilled if Graham's sister sues the service for fifty years of back pay."

Having no desire to get into a debate about a possible pay dispute, Ricki stuck to what she knew was a fact. "Yes, he did. But not until after Graham was killed."

Hamilton's eyebrows immediately winged upward. "Oh? We're now down to an exact date?"

"Close." Ricki consulted her notes. "Barbara Metler last talked to her brother on the eighth, and the shift he didn't report to was the morning shift on the tenth, so he was killed sometime between those two dates." She looked up. "Before the supervisor processed the paperwork."

The senior agent in charge did not look convinced. "He wasn't on park land and was likely on his own time."

She'd already thought of that and had an answer ready for it. "Not on park land," she conceded, "but since no other clothing was found, he was wearing his ranger uniform, so he could have been on park service business when he was killed."

Hamilton made a snorting sound that ended in a chuckle as he leaned farther back in his chair. "Technically, he wasn't wearing anything at all, and you're pushing it, Special Agent James. But I'm going to let it slide for the moment. Once the body is positively identified as that of former park ranger Benjamin Graham, what's our next step?"

Now it was Clay who spoke up. He kept his eyes on the screen as he propped one foot on top of the opposite knee. "We've already arranged for a follow-up interview with your vic's sister, in surroundings that don't look like a version of an interrogation room." He waited for Ricki's quick nod. "Mrs. Metler doesn't want to accompany the dental records to the Tacoma Police Department. Instead, she's asked if she could see the lighthouse where her brother was found."

"Understandable." Hamilton turned his head, looking directly at Ricki. "What questions are you going to ask her?"

"If her brother had ever mentioned any friends. Someone we can track down who might know what he was doing here in the Bay."

"According to your theory, he was doing job," Hamilton put in. "Weren't you the one just making a case that he was on park business when he was killed?"

"Yeah." Ricki chewed on her lower lip. "And it's possible that business, whatever it was, got him killed."

"Or he could have been on his way home? Maybe he rented a house or a room around here?" Dan's voice floated over Ricki's head.

"Maybe," she said. "But in 1970, the park service headquarters was in Port Angeles, just like it is today. And it didn't lease any additional space out here for another twenty years after Graham was murdered. So why would he live out here and take an hour or more to commute to his job?" She tapped a finger against the top of her thigh. No. There was some other reason Graham had been in the Bay the day he was killed. She'd bet on it.

"Fine," Hamilton said. "So what we have is a ranger traveling to the Bay, probably in his uniform, for some unknown reason that might, or might not, have gotten him killed." Hamilton shrugged. "And since he came from money, it could be he had a habit of carrying a good sum around with him. He might have been killed for that."

"Then why take off his uniform and fold it so neatly?" Ricki argued.

"Something you'll need to find out, Agent James," Hamilton concluded. "And fast. We don't have the resources to spend a lot of time on this." He laid his hand on top of several folders stacked neatly on the desk in front of him. "And quickly. There are other parks in our jurisdiction, and other crimes we need to look into, and the word is out you're back on the job. I've already gotten several requests for your help, so you need to wrap this one up."

Ricki and Clay exchanged a quick look before she said, "Yes, sir."

The ASAC's expression softened. "I'm not even sure I can spare you for a whole week on this one, Ricki. I'm going to have to put a hard stop on it sooner rather than later, but we do have some time. The brass back in DC aren't too thrilled at someone taking a potshot at you either."

She shook her head. "I'm still not sure that was specifically aimed at me."

"Maybe you're not. But I am." Hamilton paused and then frowned, tilting his head to look past her.

"Am I interrupting?"

Ricki closed her eyes and gave a silent groan.

"Hey there, Anchorman," Clay called out. "Can I help you with something?"

Anchorman's gaze swept the room, settling on the floating face on the iPad screen before he stepped inside and closed the door behind him. "Yeah. Who's that?"

"I might ask you the same thing," Hamilton snapped out.

Wanting to strangle Anchorman and toss him out the door all at the same time, Ricki kept her gaze on her boss while she jerked a finger over her shoulder. "That's Anchorman. He's my cook."

Hamilton blinked. "At that diner of yours? The same guy who pulled your collective butts out of the fire on that last case?"

"Yeah. That was me. And yeah again. I'm the cook at the diner. Her pay doesn't exactly run to a personal chef," Anchorman said as he strolled across the room. He stopped by Ricki's chair and gave her a short salute. "Hi, boss."

"What are you doing here?" Ricki hissed out.

"I came to talk to the chief." Anchorman rocked back on

his heels as he clasped his hands behind his back. "I pay my taxes, so I'm entitled to talk to him."

She rolled her eyes and pointed at the door. "When we're done, Anchorman. This isn't a public meeting we're having here. That's why the door was closed."

"Agent James." Hamilton's brusque, no-nonsense tone brought Ricki's gaze back to him. "I'll let you and Chief Thomas get back to business. Remember what I said about a hard deadline. We'll talk soon." The senior agent's face abruptly disappeared, leaving all of them staring at a blank screen.

"Nice to meet you too," Anchorman muttered, then smiled at Cy's good-natured clap on his back. "How're you doing, Cy?"

"Good enough to know I don't want to be part of this discussion." Cy grinned. "I don't even want to know what it's about." He reached out and gave Ricki's shoulder a quick squeeze. "I meant to tell you that I need to head over to Port Angeles for a few days. We all have a boss to answer to. I'll leave the office unlocked, so you can use it whenever you want." He nodded at Clay and Dan, then turned around and headed out the door.

Ricki waited until her uncle had pulled the door closed behind him before slowly standing up. She turned to face her cook, resting one hip on the edge of the desk.

"What's so urgent, Anchorman?"

He pulled the chair she'd been sitting in farther away from the desk, turned it around, and straddled it as he sat facing Clay. He glanced over his shoulder at Ricki and gave her a polite smile. "I came to talk to the chief, remember?"

She crossed her arms and stared back at him. "Okay. So talk."

Anchorman rested his thick forearms on the back of the chair and stretched his legs out in front of him. "I want to be put into the rotation to have her back."

Ricki's mouth dropped open as she straightened away from the desk. "Excuse me?"

"I know you aren't buying this whole 'that guy could have been shooting at anyone' bullshit," he went on as if he couldn't hear Ricki sputtering behind him. "And this agency she's joined up with doesn't seem to believe in having backup." He stopped for a moment and then deliberately raised his voice. "Something I would have mentioned to the talking head if he'd stuck around for a moment or two."

"That talking head is my boss." Ricki reached out one long leg and gave his chair a solid kick. "You know. Superior officer? You might vaguely remember one of those?"

"So when do you need me to take a shift?" Ignoring her, Anchorman went right on talking to Clay.

When Clay glanced her way, Ricki shot him a warning glare. "Don't encourage this. He'll only get worse." She took two steps to the side until she was directly in front of her annoying cook. "I don't need a babysitter. And I'd like to point out that you already have a job."

Anchorman snorted. "Which I can cover with a few tweaks to the schedule. Sam has already agreed to work any extra hours necessary until this mess is cleaned up."

Ricki's eyes narrowed, spitting out a blaze of blue fire. "Enough is enough, Anchorman. No tagging along where you don't belong. This mess, as you call it, is a fifty-year-old homicide that needs solving, not some combat mission, and I already have backup."

The former Marine sniper twisted around in his chair to look up at Dan. "Is she talking about you?"

Dan scowled. "Is that so hard to believe?"

"Nope. Except you need more time on the gun range," Anchorman said bluntly. He turned back toward Ricki. "And what the hell is an assistant partner, anyway?"

"I'd like to hear that explanation myself," Dan muttered.

"Oh for . . ." Ricki slapped her good hand against her forehead. "You both give me a headache." She pointed at Dan. "You keep digging in those stored files. See if you can find any duty rosters from April 1971." She then aimed her finger at Anchorman. "And you go back and keep an eye on the Sunny Side Up." She turned a glare on Clay. "And why haven't you told him we don't take civilians along on official investigations?"

Clay shifted his weight in the chair, his gaze going from Ricki to Anchorman and then back again. "He has a point, Ricki." When she shook her head in denial, he shrugged. "Yeah, he does. This isn't the only thing on my plate. I have the towns to see to, along with a department to run. I can't dedicate all my time to the case, and given the short leash Hamilton put you on, that's what it will take." His jaw hardened along with the look in his eyes. "I know your agency can't give you much by the way of backup. There aren't enough of you to go around as it is. But we're talking murder here, and while your case is fifty years old, Maxwell Hardy's murder is not. Someone very much alive today killed him and probably took that shot at you since the two cases are tied together."

Anchorman straightened up. "Tied together? How?"

"Two bullets, two victims, one gun," Clay said before Ricki could stop him.

While Anchorman let out a low whistle, Ricki turned on Clay. "He didn't need to know that. We don't involve civilians."

"I can go with you and Mrs. Metler up to the lighthouse tomorrow, but I'm tied up in a council meeting tomorrow night, and I know you have something on your agenda."

"The VFW," Ricki said reluctantly. If Clay couldn't come along, that left her in a bind to find another military vet to get her in the door. She caught Anchorman's grin from the corner of her eye and groaned.

"I don't suppose you were in the service?" she asked Dan, not surprised when he shook his head.

"Nope. Sorry."

"Guess that leaves me by default," Anchorman declared.

There was just enough smugness in the look he gave her that she growled back at him. "After our visit to the VFW, you're fired."

"Again?" His mouth drew down into an exaggerated pout. "That makes the third time this month already." In a flash, his grin was back. "But then I'll have lots of time to tag along after you."

She closed her eyes and barely kept herself from screaming out in frustration. The last thing she needed was a burly ex-Marine sniper with an overdeveloped protective instinct dogging her every step. But she did need him to get through the doors of the local Veterans of Foreign Wars post. Like it or not, she only had a few days to find out what had happened to Ranger Benjamin Graham, and she couldn't waste any of it waiting for Clay to free up his time. Which didn't sit well with her at all, but right now, she couldn't see a way around it.

Fine," she groused. "You can tag along one night. If you do any more than that and you get hurt, don't expect any sympathy from me."

Anchorman chuckled and then winked at her. "No sympathy from you. Yeah. I got it."

Chapter 25

"Here? My brother died here?" Barbara Metler looked around the small clearing of brush and overgrown grass that surrounded the old lighthouse. She half lowered her large sunglasses, wrinkling her nose in an obvious sign of distaste before turning to stare at Ricki over the rims. The edges of the scarf covering her hair ruffled in the light breeze. "This can't be right. Benny would never have come to a place like this. It's too isolated, too . . ." She waved her hand to include the shabby structure in her assessment. "Too rough."

"Too much nature?" Ricki inquired politely. Fighting not to roll her eyes when the woman solemnly nodded her agreement.

"Exactly." Barbara looked around again and shuddered. "He never would have come here. It's far too primitive for Benny's taste."

Ricki propped a boot on the log Eddie and his friends had occupied barely a week ago. "He was a park ranger, Barbara. They tend to work a lot in primitive areas."

"I told you. It was just a lark on his part. He certainly had no intentions of making a life around this kind of thing." She pulled her cardigan sweater closer and folded her arms in front of her.

Everything she had on, from the slacks, to the shoes, to the sweater, was a perfect color match of soft green. Only the dark-brown blouse offered a contrast, which was a good thing. Otherwise, the woman might have faded away into the foliage. Not a very charitable thought, but Ricki wasn't sorry for it either.

Barbara Metler seemed oblivious to the fact that everyone else in the clearing earned their living in the very place she was curling her lip over. Ricki smiled when Clay shook his head at her. She bit her lip and reminded herself that she wasn't going to insult a possible source of information, although it was a close thing.

Dropping her boot on the ground, Ricki walked slowly over to the door of the lighthouse and released the police tape Clay had draped across the front. She lifted the rusty latch and gave the door a good shove before stepping aside. Taking a flashlight out of the pocket of her windbreaker, she flicked on the switch and pointed the beam of light into the interior. "Let's take a look."

Clay gently guided a hesitant Barbara toward the door, then put conventional manners aside to step in first and light up the interior with the lantern he'd brought along. "It's fine. There's nothing in here now but a staircase and a dirt floor."

With a hand at her throat, Barbara gingerly stepped over the threshold, stopping when she was barely a foot inside. Ricki came up behind her, shining the flashlight over Barbara's shoulder. When Graham's sister didn't move inside any farther, or make a single sound, Clay started talking, his voice soft and calm.

"Mr. Hardy was found first." He pointed to his right. "Over there." He turned and gestured in the opposite direction. "Your brother was found over there, along with his uniform and badge."

Barbara took another short step inside and stared at the spot where Clay was pointing. "Fifty years?" she whispered. "How long did he lie in there all alone in the dirt before he became a pile of bones?"

"That depends on a lot of things," Clay said slowly. "How cold the winters were, and how hot the summers, or if there were any leaks coming in from rain." He shook his head. "There's no way of knowing for sure."

"But years? Wasn't it probably years that he waited for someone to find him?"

Feeling a small bubble of compassion bump up against her guilt for her earlier thoughts about the woman, Ricki let out a long, slow breath. For all her snotty tone and attitudes, Barbara seemed to have genuinely loved her brother. "It could have been years, Barbara. But your brother wouldn't have felt any of that. He was gone."

Barbara pivoted around, her hand still at her throat, her sunglasses in her hand. Her wide brown eyes had taken on a hollow look. "How do you know? Maybe his soul or spirit, or —hell, I don't know—his ghost? Maybe he did hang around, watching his body dissolve away, waiting for someone to come, waiting for someone . . ." Her voice caught on a sob as her bottom lip trembled. "Someone to care."

Since she looked on the verge of collapse, Ricki reached out and curled a hand around Barbara's arm, gently pulling her out of the lighthouse and leading her over to the log. Barbara sat down without even a wince at the rough bark scratching against her very expensive pantsuit. Wishing she'd thought to bring along a canteen, Ricki squatted in front of her, sympathy in her deep-blue gaze.

"Would you like to go back to the station to have a talk? You could have some water. Be more comfortable."

Barbara blinked, then cast a quick look around before her shoulders lifted in a small shrug. "This is fine." She sighed and lifted the purse that she'd dropped onto the ground beside her and set it on top of the log. She kept it from tumbling off its precarious perch by keeping one hand firmly around it. "I knew you'd have more questions, so I brought what I thought would be helpful." She reached into her purse, withdrawing a picture with a single sheet of paper clipped to it. "That's a picture of the house Benny rented. He sent it to me." When Ricki took it, Barbara leaned over and pointed at the smiling figure in front of a modest structure with a wide porch. "That's Benny." A ghost of a smile played along her lips. "He was very handsome."

He was standing so far away in the picture, it was hard to tell what he looked like, but Ricki dutifully nodded. "Yes, he was." She slid the paper out from under the paper clip. "Is this the address?"

Barbara nodded as Clay walked up and stood beside Ricki.

"It's in Port Angeles," he said.

Ricki studied the photo before glancing over at Barbara, who was watching her. "Did he live there alone?"

"I don't know," Barbara said. "He never actually said there was anyone else living there, it was just an impression I got." She paused, her brow furrowed. "I remember him complaining once about someone drinking the last of the coffee and saying he'd better replace it." She drew back a little at Ricki's suddenly fierce look.

"He? Your brother said *he'd* better replace it?" Ricki asked. "Are you sure?"

"Yes." Barbara cleared her throat and pulled a regal demeanor around her like a thick cloak. "I'm sure that's what he said. I didn't give it much thought at the time, but I did feel he was talking about someone else who lived in the house, and Benny definitely used the word 'he.'" She sat up a little straighter. "Oh, and something I told Maxwell. Benny was coming home, but he intended to keep the lease on the house for another few months. He said there was still some business he needed to deal with here, and of course he wanted to finalize the purchase of the land."

"Keep the house for a few months." Ricki exchanged a "Wonder why?" look with Clay before refocusing her attention on the woman in the expensive pantsuit sitting passively on a mossy log in the middle of the forest. "You don't know what that business was, do you?"

Barbara shook her head, then pulled at the knot under her chin holding the scarf down tight. "No. I have no idea. I think it was a personal debt of some sort. He didn't seem overly concerned about it, just said he needed to take care of it."

"How about friends?" Ricki asked. "Did he ever mention any friends, or anyone at all?"

"He didn't like his supervisor very much," Barbara stated. "Called him Mr. SS." She smiled. "For Mr. Starched Shirt. Benny gave everyone a nickname. I was always LH to him." She sighed and looked at the toes of her shoes. "Little Helper. That's what he called me. He was always asking me to check on things for him, or do small favors."

"Like getting his tux pressed?" Ricki asked.

"Yes. Exactly." She looked up again and her eyes grew damp. "I was always happy to help him. I loved Benny so much. I got that tux pressed, but he never showed up for my wedding. Father was so angry."

Ricki couldn't blame the man, but still, it was a line to tug on. "Did your father make any business trips before your wedding? Was he out of town that last night you talked to your brother?"

"No," Barbara said. "He was home. I asked him if he wanted to speak with Benny and he said no, since Benny would be home in a few days." She sighed. "Poor Father. He was so angry with Benny for the two years he was in the park service and not home learning to run the family business. And then he was furious when Benny didn't make it home in time for the wedding. But over the years, he came to believe something had happened to Benny. I was the one who suggested hiring a private investigator to find him. But that wasn't for at least five years. Until then, Father wouldn't hear of it."

"You were married by then," Ricki pointed out. "Why didn't you hire one yourself?"

She pursed her lips and looked off into the distance. "My husband didn't want to spend the money. He said Benny would show up when he wanted to."

Sounds like your husband knew your brother better than you did, Ricki thought. "Okay. Then about the friends. Did your brother mention anyone he knew, or hung out with? Maybe another ranger?"

Barbara's troubled gaze returned to Ricki. "He might have mentioned more, but I only remember two. Catman and someone he called the OG."

"Catman?" Clay frowned. "Did the guy own a lot of cats?"

She choked out a short laugh. "I doubt it. Benny was highly allergic. He wouldn't have spent any time around someone who was covered in cat hair. And he mentioned this Catman several times, so I think they were friends."

"What about the OG?" Ricki asked. "Male or female?"

"Male, I think." She hesitated, then nodded. "Yes. Male. Benny liked women. A bit too much, as father was always telling him. And he never had a good thing to say about this OG person. He usually just said that he'd seen the OG, or run into the OG, but he always had this kind of annoyance in his voice. He talked about him like he was a kind of pest or was bothering him somehow." She sighed. "Benny never thought any woman was bothering him. He liked to take them for rides in that sports car of his."

"What kind of sports car was it?" Clay asked.

"Oh, that Aston Martin that was all the rage because of some movie."

"James Bond?" Clay supplied.

She nodded. "That sounds right." She suddenly frowned and looked around is if searching for something. "Wasn't it up here too? Where is it?"

"We didn't find a sports car," Ricki said. "What color was it, and you wouldn't happen to have the license plate number?"

She gave Ricki a sour look. "No. Of course not. Who has their brother's license plate number? It was new. He bought it just before he came out here. He said he wanted to drive it across the country. But I do remember that it was a beautiful white, with silver trim. Very eye-catching." Her shoulders drooped. "Is there anything else?"

"Just a few more things and then we can get you back to the hotel so you can rest," Ricki assured her. "You said you called your brother's supervisor?"

Her chin came up as she gave a loud sniff. "A Mr. Abbott. Very rude man. It was no wonder Benny didn't like him."

Thinking the feeling was probably mutual, Ricki smiled her encouragement. "Yes. Easy to understand that. But this Supervisor Abbott? He told you that your brother had resigned?" She waited for Barbara's nod. "And he also told you that your brother had left town?"

"Yes, he did." Barbara's back was once more rigid, and anger flashed in her gaze. "He lied to me. He specifically told me that Benny had left town." She gestured toward the lighthouse. "This is hardly leaving town."

"No, it's not," Ricki agreed, fervently hoping Barbara would stay focused for a little while longer. "And as far as you know, your brother wasn't intending to leave town that weekend?"

"He said he was going to keep the house for a few more months," Barbara raced on, growing more agitated with every word. "He said he had more business to take care of." She slashed a hand through the air. "He wouldn't have sneaked out of town the way that Mr. Abbott was implying. Benny never would have done that." She turned her angry gaze on Ricki. "And where are his things? Especially that car? Did it just disappear into thin air?"

"No," Ricki said evenly. "It wouldn't have done that."

"What about his other things? His clothes, his personal possessions? Whatever happened to them?" she demanded.

"I don't know," Ricki said, keeping her answers short and simple. If the woman needed to let off some steam, that was fine with her.

"Maybe whoever his landlord was still has them?" Clay suggested. He leaned over and tapped the note in Ricki's hand. "We might be able to track them down now that we know where he lived."

Barbara stood up and huffed out a breath, rounding on Clay. "The landlord? From fifty years ago? The one who probably stole Benny's watch? Where's the watch our grandfather gave him? It had diamonds encrusted around the dial, and a solid gold band. He never took it off, but you've never mentioned it being found with the body. So where is Benny's watch?"

Chapter 26

Ricki walked into headquarters, intending to wait for Clay in his office. He'd dropped her off before taking Barbara Metler back to the St. Armand. The wooden structure that looked like a modern-day log cabin, with a wide porch flanked by two long wings, was set off perfectly by the surrounding trees, towering silently in the background. She would be glad to get away from the restrained sorrow that had clung to the Metler woman like an invisible cloak. The deep despair for the loss of her brother was made all the more painful by how hard she worked to hide it.

Shaking her head, Ricki walked up the steps. From what she had heard about Benjamin Graham, he hadn't done much to earn his sister's obvious devotion. Other than being born first.

"Hey there, Agent James. I wasn't sure we would be seeing you again today." Ray leaned to the side and looked around her. "Is the chief with you?" He held up a small stack of square notes. "I have some messages here for him. Mostly from council members about the meeting tonight."

Ricki smiled at the elderly man and leaned against the edge of the counter that also served as his desk. "He'll be along pretty soon. I'm going to wait for him in his office. Want me to take those along and put them on his desk?"

Ray handed them over with a broad smile. "That would be fine. Have either of you had lunch? I could order a pizza from Quick Pie."

It was tempting, but Ricki shook her head. Pizza and a fried PB&J had been the mainstays of her diet for the last week, and her stash of rice cakes to balance out all the junk food was still in her jeep—or what was left of it—and she hadn't had a chance to replenish it yet. But even rice cakes wouldn't do her any good at this point. What she really needed was some lean meat and a few vegetables.

"I'll pass on the pizza, Ray. But be sure to ask the chief when he comes in." She glanced at her watch to confirm it was well past lunchtime. "He'll be hungry." She pushed open the gate separating the lobby from the back hallway. "I'm surprised to see you here. I thought you'd be spending time with John."

Ray's features sagged as he let out a huge sigh. "My nephew had to go back to Seattle. Some kind of tangle in the office, and he had to be there in order to get it unsnarled." He sighed again. "I'm not sure when he'll be back."

"Why don't you take a few days and go see him?" Ricki suggested.

"I don't like the city," Ray stated. "People act crazy when you put that many of them together."

She laughed. "People act crazy no matter where you put them." She stepped through the gate and walked down the hall, lifting the phone messages up high when Ray shouted a reminder after her to put them on the chief's desk.

As soon as she reached the office, she pulled out her phone and checked for messages of her own. There was one from Hamilton, reminding her to call him with a report about her interview with Barbara Metler, and another from Dan. She held her phone to her ear and listened to the ranger's voice confirm that the dental records were a match. The skeleton belonged to Benjamin Graham.

Moving over to the notes function on her phone, she tapped out all the information Barbara had given her, then began scrolling through her emails. After discarding a third of them, she gave a quick response to the rest. When she came to the one from Dan saying he'd get started searching for a daily assignment log from 1971 first thing in the morning, she pursed her lips, thinking it over. Making up her mind, she sent him a reply stating to save that for later and to start tracking down who owned the house that Benjamin Graham had leased.

Something Barbara had said stuck out. What had happened to her brother's possessions? Ricki leaned forward in the folding chair in front of Clay's desk and followed the thought. What would a landlord do with a tenant's things when he hadn't paid the rent for a month or two? After keying in an additional note to Dan, she finished off her emails before returning to her case notes.

Twenty minutes later Clay walked in and went straight to his desk. Tossing his hat to one side, he leaned back as far as his chair would allow and closed his eyes. "I told Ray to get the pizza, I'm starving."

"Yeah. I figured. I left your messages on the desk."

"Did you read them?" Clay asked.

"No. There might be some official business in there."

Clay opened one eye and looked over at her. "Like what? The Rinkmens having another one of their weekly fights?" When Ricki grinned, he smiled and reached for the small stack, quickly thumbing through it. "Got one from TK." He pulled it out, read it, and then handed it to Ricki. "He says the dental records match your victim, so he's been positively identified as Benjamin Graham."

Ricki held up her phone. "I got the same message from Dan."

The chief nodded and leaned back in his chair again. "He's your vic, so you can give Barbara Metler the news. I doubt if it's going to break her up more than it already has."

"He doesn't deserve that devotion," Ricki said quietly.

Rolling his shoulders back, Clay stifled a yawn. "Who doesn't?"

"Benjamin Graham," Ricki said. She reached into her pocket and pulled out the picture of him standing in front of his house in Port Angeles. "I'd bet he wasn't much of a ranger."

"No argument there," Clay said.

Ricki frowned. "And even less of a brother." At his questioning look, she shrugged. "It sounded to me like all he ever did was call his sister with a list of things he wanted her to do. She's in the middle of planning a wedding and he wants her to get his tux cleaned, and I'll bet she kept a whole list of busywork crap that he constantly demanded. There was a reason he called her his little helper." She curled her lip up. "It sounded more like little servant." She tucked a stray piece of dark hair back behind her ear. "If I had known what a schmuck this guy was, I would have told Hamilton to give the whole case to you."

Clay yawned again and then grinned. "Naw. You wouldn't have done that. You like chasing bad guys too much."

"I like closing cases," Ricki corrected. "I told Dan to follow up on that address in Port Angeles, and to check the city and county records, if necessary, for any eviction notices on the property. If Graham didn't pay his rent, then the landlord might have filed an eviction to get him out."

"Wouldn't surprise me. On the way back to the hotel, I asked Barbara about the last trip Hardy made out here, and the report he made about it. She said she didn't know where she'd put it, but that there wasn't anything in it worth keeping. He'd come to the Bay to check up on the land. She seemed to think he'd run out of ideas on where to look for her brother.

So he comes back to get a look at the land and ends up in the same place as Benjamin Graham?"

Ricki nodded. "Yeah. What are the odds?"

"Not good," Clay agreed. "I'd say the PI found something he didn't come across on his previous trips. Something he apparently didn't have time to share with his client."

"Or maybe it was in that previous report and she just didn't pick up on it," Ricki said.

"Which is why I asked Demi Lansanger to look for it." His mouth tightened at the corners and a pained expression settled on his handsome features. "Which I've paid for by having her call me every day with her progress. Or lack of it."

Doing her best to look as innocent as a new day, Ricki barely managed to hold back a grin. "Is that so? Well, anything in the name of duty."

"Funny, James," he muttered. "Hasn't the government got something else for you to do? I have to get ready for the council meeting tonight."

Still keeping her grin at bay, Ricki nodded and got to her feet. "Sure. I need to stop in at the Sunny Side Up and confirm with Anchorman that he can still make it to the VFW tonight."

"Okay. That sounds good. You do that," Clay said as he turned to his computer.

He was already tapping away at the keys before she reached the doorway. Leaving him to it, Ricki headed down the hall. Ray wasn't at his post up front, so she made it out of the building without having to make any polite small talk. She reached the end of the porch just as the delivery boy from Quick Pie pulled up.

Thinking she probably owed Clay something for putting him squarely into the target zone of Demi Lansanger, even if he didn't know it, she stopped long enough to give the kid who went to the same high school as her son, a twenty-dollar bill to cover the pizza and a generous tip, telling him to be sure to get the food directly to the chief so it wouldn't be waylaid by any park rangers hanging around. That would ensure it would be gone before Clay could nab a slice for himself.

Fifteen minutes later she turned onto the main street of Brewer and drove past the small waterfront that had a decent crowd strolling along its length. That meant the lunchtime business had probably been pretty good. Smiling at the thought, Ricki pulled the truck into the narrow alley and maneuvered it into the small space behind the Sunny Side Up. Since the truck had reliable locks on the doors, and an alarm as well, she pulled her gun out of her shoulder holster and slipped it into the glove compartment. She didn't like carrying a weapon into the diner, and with Clay's truck, she didn't have to.

Exiting the vehicle, she gave it a thankful pat on the hood before walking up the back steps and into the kitchen. There was a lone burger sizzling on the grill, and Anchorman was watching it from a chair pulled up next to the prep table. He held a steaming mug of coffee and was reading the local paper that came out once a week.

"Keeping up with the local gossip?"

He looked up, then carefully folded the paper in half and set it on the table. "Well, look what the wind blew in. Is it raining out there yet?"

Ricki shook her head. "Not yet, but it won't be long from the feel of it."

"Too bad. Weather's been fairly decent lately."

She looked around at the tidy kitchen. "I guess the lunch rush has come and gone?"

Anchorman stood up and walked over to the double stoves, where he picked up a large spatula and flipped over the burger. "We did pretty good for it being midweek. I think all the tourists will start pouring in this weekend if the weather holds up." He glanced over at her. "Sam's set to come in for the dinner shift if you still want to head over to the VFW. I just have to give him a call."

Ricki shrugged out of her windbreaker and hung it on a peg next to the back door. "Then you'd better call him. I'm on a short clock to get this case wrapped up."

"I'll do that while you go check on things out front."

She turned and frowned at him. "Why do I need to check out front? I thought you said we weren't busy?" She gave a pointed look at the almost-empty grill. "Doesn't look like we're busy, and I have some paperwork that I need to get done."

"Well, there's checking, and then there's checking."

Now, what was that supposed to mean? Scowling at her cook's cryptic answer, she didn't bother arguing with him, but walked across the kitchen and pushed through the double doors leading into the front dining room.

Half a dozen customers were scattered among the tables and booths. A few of them looked over at her and waved. She waved back, then spotted Marcie at the far end of the counter. The waitress was standing with one shoulder forward and a hand on her broad hip in what Ricki knew was her full-on flirt mode. Curious who Marcie had her eye on, Ricki smiled as she took a step forward and then stopped cold in her tracks.

Dan. That was Dan Wilkes sitting on a stool across the counter from Marcie, who was now leaning in, smiling at the man as if he were the only person in the room.

Torn between shock and annoyance, Ricki quietly closed the distance between them until she was standing right next to Marcie, a polite smile plastered on her face as she stared at Dan. The former CIA guy turned out-of-shape park ranger looked at her and blinked as if he couldn't believe what he was seeing.

Marcie turned her head and beamed at Ricki. "Well, hi. What are you doing here?"

"I own the place," Ricki said, still holding that smile in

place and not moving her stare away from Dan. "Were you looking for me?"

"No, he wasn't," Marcie answered for him. "He came in to have something to eat."

Ricki looked down at the empty space in front of her assistant partner. "Really? It looks like you're finished. Aren't you on duty?"

"No, he isn't," Marcie intervened once more, drawing an exasperated look from Ricki. The older woman turned a sunny smile on Dan, whose cheeks had turned bright red, but he still hadn't managed to get a word out. "You sit right there, Ranger Wilkes. I need to have a short talk with my boss."

She stepped around Ricki then latched on to her arm, towing her much taller boss down the length of the counter and into the kitchen. Anchorman looked up from his seat at the table, a hamburger raised halfway to his mouth. He immediately scooted his chair around until his back was to both women.

"I'm not here," he declared.

"That's good," Marcie said with a nod. "Because this is a private conversation."

Ricki stuck a finger out and pointed at the cook. "He's sitting right there, Marcie."

"But he won't listen." Marcie let go of Ricki's arm and crossed her arms over breasts that were pressed tight against her uniform. "And this won't take long. I like that Ranger Wilkes." She glared when Ricki crossed her eyes. "And you can just stop making those faces. You're a far piece from being my mother. The fact is, I'm halfway to being yours, so you have no say in my social life."

"You were flirting with him," Ricki stated flatly. "And don't shake your head at me, I know that pose and smile of yours. It's the one you use when you're after a date."

"I've already had a date with him, Miss Smarty-Pants." When Ricki's mouth dropped open, Marcie gave her a smug grin. "See? You get caught up in chasing down some missing ranger and don't even notice what's going on. There. We've already had a date and the sky didn't fall in. So that's the end of that." Finishing off with a wave of her hand to emphasize her point, Marcie looked over at Anchorman. "Okay. We're finished. You can be present again." When Ricki started to say something, Marcie flashed her a stern warning look. "That's the end of it," she repeated firmly and marched off, letting the double doors swing back and forth behind her.

Ricki walked over and tapped Anchorman on the shoulder. "Hey there, Mr. I-Know-Nothing. How long has this been going on?"

Anchorman set his now-empty plate aside and stood up. He turned to face her, keeping the chair between them. "I still don't know anything, and I'm keeping it that way. I don't ask where you sleep at night, or where Marcie chooses to kick off her shoes. She's right, you know. It's her life. Stay out of it."

Chapter 27

Ricki shut her laptop and pushed back from her compact desk in the corner of her living room. She stretched her back then took a quick look at her watch. Between finishing off reports for Hamilton, transcribing her case notes, and even making her bed for the first time in a week, she'd managed to burn through the rest of the afternoon and early evening since she'd stomped out of the diner.

She had about three-quarters of an hour left to kill before she needed to meet Anchorman at the VFW post. Her stomach sent up another gurgle of protest, joining the others it had made since she'd arrived home. She still hadn't had anything to eat today, so she stood up, intending to give in to her body's insistent reminders that it needed fuel.

She scuffed her feet as she walked to the kitchen, where she pulled open the refrigerator and peered inside, leaning in as she considered her options. Eyeing the jar of peanut butter, appropriately sitting right next to the strawberry jam, she resisted the urge to splurge on comfort food, instead opening the cooler drawer with the vegetables in it. She grabbed the plastic bag containing the rest of the vegetables that Eddie had chopped up for her at the beginning of the week, along with a bottle of dressing, because in her opinion, the best way to eat raw vegetables was with ranch dressing as a quick and easy dipping sauce. She lifted a plate from the drying rack next to the sink and carried her meal over to the counter. Returning to the refrigerator, she found an unopened package of sliced turkey meat and tossed it over to join the rest of her impromptu meal. After dumping the veggies out on the plate and squirting some ranch dressing next to them, she opened the deli package and took out several slices of turkey. The first bite was salty enough to have her jumping up again to get a glass of water, but once she'd settled down and started eating, her thoughts began to wander. Without the distraction of reports and the case details, she couldn't shake off the effects of that last argument with Marcie.

Now that several hours had passed, her temper at seeing Marcie and Dan Wilkes acting so cozy together had completely evaporated, leaving a sheen of guilt, and yeah, more than a little embarrassment, behind. She picked at her dinner as she silently came to the conclusion she'd acted like a snotty junior high girl. And Anchorman was right. She had no business interfering in Marcie's life. But damn it, the woman was like family to Ricki, half mother, half older sister, and the fact was she adored both halves. It wasn't that she didn't want to share Marcie's attention with someone else. *Well, okay, not all of it's that,* she thought on a burst of honesty. But mostly, she just didn't want Marcie to get hurt.

She knew all too well from personal experience that getting involved with anyone in law enforcement never turned out well. Look at her, for God's sake. Or Clay. Or even her uncle Cy, who'd never had enough time to marry anyone at all. She frowned. Or at least that was what he'd always claimed.

Still, it was true. Law enforcement and a happy relationship never had been a good match. Blithely ignoring all the agents she'd met who had rock-solid marriages, Ricki spent another ten minutes justifying her concerns.

Feeling completely vindicated, she managed to stay on that train of thought for exactly the amount of time it took her to put the remaining food away and rinse off her plate. By the time she'd shoved her arms through the sleeves of her heavy coat and walked out to the truck, the guilt was back.

No matter how much she argued with herself, Anchorman was still right. If Marcie wanted to waste her time on a losing relationship and probably getting her heart broken along the way, it was her choice. Her friend knew the risks of getting involved with law enforcement. *We've talked about it often enough,* Ricki reminded herself as she put the truck into gear and slowly backed out of the long driveway.

By the time she'd reached the small cutout where she could turn the truck in the right direction, her attitude had made the same 180-degree turn as the vehicle. Tomorrow she'd apologize to Marcie.

"No point in calling her tonight," Ricki muttered to herself as she turned onto the main road leading into Brewer. "It'll be getting late by the time I'm done at the VFW." That, plus the fact that since they'd had the argument in person, she felt the apology should be delivered the same way.

Feeling better, Ricki smiled for the first time in hours. She'd make it right with Marcie tomorrow, and with any luck, uncover a solid lead tonight.

When she pulled up on the side street where the VFW was located, she spotted Anchorman hanging at the bottom of the steps leading up to the porch of the house that served as a post. There was a good crowd tonight from what she could see, but then there usually was. Most of the men in town, and a fair number of the women, belonged to the VFW, and it was the major source of their social lives.

She found a place to park a block down the street, and by the time she had climbed out of the truck, Anchorman was strolling down the sidewalk toward her, his hands in the pockets of his well-worn leather bomber jacket. She lifted a hand in greeting before locking the truck and adjusting her gun in its holster. Generally, the VFW didn't allow firearms inside the post, but the local chapter made an exception for anyone in law enforcement. Bill Langly, the commander of the chapter as well as the bartender on most nights, had told her that since she'd "re-upped" with the ISB, she qualified as law enforcement. Of course she hadn't been informed of her new exception status until after she'd tracked down and caught a serial killer, but she figured that was fair enough.

The rain she'd predicted had spent most of itself earlier in the afternoon, but a light drizzle still lingered, coating her hair and shoulders with a thin sheet of moisture by the time she joined Anchorman on the sidewalk. Seemingly oblivious to the wet and the increasing bite of cold in the air, he stopped, effectively blocking her path.

"So, I never asked why you wanted to come to the VFW," he said by way of a greeting.

She shoved her hands into her own pockets and gave him a bland look. "Does that mean you figured the role of a babysitter was to go along anywhere without asking for a reason?"

"Not a babysitter, boss lady. Backup," Anchorman stated. He glanced over his shoulder at the house with all its lights blazing. "Do you figure that ranger, or maybe the PI, was a veteran?"

Ricki shrugged. "No idea. But if you want to talk to anyone in town over the age of sixty, the odds are they'll be here."

Anchorman's jaw jutted out. "You know, there are younger vets, too."

"Didn't say there weren't," Ricki said affably. "But the younger vets probably won't remember a park ranger from fifty years ago. We'll have better luck with the older guys." She flipped the collar of her coat up to keep the rain from dripping down her neck. "Can we go in now and get out of the wet stuff that's running down my nose?"

His shoulders relaxed and he grinned. "It's water, that's all. I'd think a special agent wouldn't mind a little rain."

"I don't when it's necessary, but right now it isn't." She pushed him aside and stalked past, hurrying toward the shelter of the porch. She reached it in sixty seconds flat, taking the steps two at a time. She landed in the middle of a group discussion on the porch and apologized as she wound her way into the converted house.

The long front hallway was covered with pictures of the various functions and ceremonies held at the post over the years. She greeted several people on her way toward the main room, with its long bar stretched all the way across the back. The space was comfortably packed with tables, chairs, and enough bodies to make finding a seat a difficult, but not impossible, task.

The post's commandant was pouring tall mugs of beer from his usual place behind the bar. He spotted Ricki almost as soon as she entered the room, lifting one hand in a high wave above his head while placing a foaming glass in front of one of the members who'd staked out a spot at the bar. Ricki waved back and ducked and dodged her way in his direction, sure that Anchorman was right behind her, keeping an eye on her back. While she didn't like the idea of a babysitter, she really didn't mind having the safety net of a backup, no matter how much grief she'd given him about it. If there had been a killer walking among them for the last half century, then the odds were good he was sitting at one of the tables right now, watching her.

When she finally made it to the bar, Bill's face broke into a friendly smile beneath the beard that reached well past his chin. "Happy to see you again, Ricki." He leaned closer, a twinkle of laughter in his eyes. "Or should I call you Special

Agent James?" He looked over her head and his smile broadened even more. "Hey there, Anchorman." He shot his hand up in a quick, sharp salute. "We're honored to have you come in anytime. Not often we get a decorated Marine sniper in here."

Anchorman smiled and reached over to shake Bill's hand. "Since I'm the only one in town, I guess I can believe that."

"You've got me there." The post's commandant tipped his head back and laughed, making the ceiling lights bounce their reflections off his bald head. "What can I get the two of you? Beer or a soft drink?"

"Soft drink," Ricki said. "I'm on duty."

"Same here, same reason," Anchorman replied, drawing a quizzical look from Bill.

"You join up with the park service too?" the barman asked.

"Nope. Unofficial duty," Anchorman said. He lifted the glass of soda Bill placed on the counter and turned around, scanning the room as he took a casual sip.

"Looks like he's on patrol," Bill said to Ricki in a loud stage whisper.

"He is," Ricki whispered back just as loudly. "He's looking for the enemy."

Bill's eyebrows drew together as he glanced over at Anchorman's back. "What enemy?"

Ricki grinned. "I don't know. He didn't tell me." When the former Marine continued to ignore them both, Ricki took the two pictures she'd brought along out from beneath her coat, where she'd stuck them into her belt to keep them dry. "I need to show these around, if that's okay with you, Bill."

He glanced down at the photos on the counter. "They look old." He shifted his gaze back up to hers, his smile gone. "Is this about that ranger you found up at the old lighthouse in Massey?"

"Yeah," Ricki confirmed. "I'm hoping someone remembers him from these pictures."

Bill picked up the group shot of the rangers and studied it. "All those guys look pretty much the same in those park uniforms." He set the first picture down and picked up the second one. "And he's standing too far away to see his face in this one." He handed the photo back to her with a smile. "But you're welcome to give it a try. Depending on how far back these go, you might ask Pete and his group over there." Bill nodded toward a corner on the far side of the room. "And have a chat with Carl Evans. You remember him, don't you? He used to own the hardware store just outside of town. A gas station is there now. That went up after Carl retired and sold the land." When Ricki nodded and looked around the room, Bill pointed to a small table off to the side, near the door. "He's sitting over there reading a book, like usual. Says he likes all the commotion around him while he reads." Bill shook his head. "Dumbest thing I ever heard, or close to it. Anyway, he's got one of those photographic memories, so he might be of some help to you."

She looked toward the door, spotting the rail-thin man with a shock of white hair through the shifting crowd. He was sitting by himself with a book open in front of him. She had a passing acquaintance with Carl Evans, having gone to the hardware store with her dad from time to time. Mr. Evans had always been friendly, and back then he'd had a full head of jet-black hair. But he'd always been just as thin as he was now. She remembered wondering on a couple of occasions if he'd ever been in danger of being blown over by a puff of wind.

Picking up the picture, she thanked Bill for the advice then started threading her way toward the group of six, where Pete was holding court. Anchorman picked up his glass of soda that was now half-empty and fell into step right behind her.

Chapter 28

When Ricki approached the table in the far corner, all six men looked up at once. Pete, the ad hoc leader of the group, lifted a hand, heavy with blue veining, in greeting. His pure-white hair was a sharp contrast to his complexion, permanently bronzed from spending most of his life working in the sun. Now well into his seventies, Pete spent his days reading whatever struck his fancy and chatting with his friends. His specialty was keeping a close ear to the local gossip mill, a practice he excelled at, and at which he was only surpassed by Wanda. While Pete actively pursued any new tidbits with unabashed glee, Wanda usually had the gossip coming to her.

Either way was effective in knowing what was going on around town, which was why Ricki was always careful about what she said around Pete or any of his friends.

"Hi there, Ricki James." Pete pointed to an empty chair at the next table and waved at one of the other men to fetch it for her. He continued to smile through the general shifting of bodies around the table as the men made room for her to sit down and the chair was slid in behind her.

She nodded her thanks and sat while Anchorman took up

a space against the wall at her back. She smiled when Pete didn't waste any time in getting down to the expected grilling.

"I saw you over there talking to Bill. Looks like the two of you were having a serious discussion." He pointed to the photos she'd laid facedown on the table. "What's that you were showing him? Pictures of the crime scene?"

Ricki deliberately paused, slowly tapping her index finger against the pictures as she glanced around the group, measuring their curiosity, wanting them to take a good look and not simply dismiss the images in the photos out of hand. She finally shook her head.

"Not the crime scene, but a person of interest." She leaned forward and added in a dramatic whisper. "A lot of interest."

She sat back again as heads nodded in conspiracy all around the table. Slowly flipping the pictures over, she passed the group shot to Pete. "If you recognize anyone in this photo, or even more than just one individual, it's very important to my case that you let me know."

Pete picked up the photo and squinted at it, pulling it close enough that his nose almost touched the surface. "Pretty hard to tell," he mumbled. "When was this taken?"

"Fifty years ago." Ricki said, as Pete passed the photo along. As it slowly went around the table, she could feel the interest of the group slipping away. "Maybe this one is a little better?" She slid the picture of Graham standing in front of his house over to Pete, who gave it the same close-up scrutiny as the first one.

"Nope. Still hard to see a face, but can't say I recognize him." He looked over at Ricki. "Don't know that house either. This wasn't taken somewhere in the Bay, was it?"

"No. But close by."

Pete rubbed a hand against his chin. "You need someone who's been here longer than I have." He glanced around the table. "Longer than any of us here, for that matter. Have you asked Ray?"

"Yes." Ricki let the single word stand, not wanting to hand out the additional information that Ray hadn't recognized anyone in the pictures either.

The head of the male gossip circle gave a huge, theatrical sigh. "I don't know who else you could ask, then. Not too many are still around who were here fifty years ago."

Not quite ready to admit defeat yet, Ricki's eyes narrowed in thought. The six men might not remember a ranger who passed them in the street, but a car was a whole different ball game.

"He had a car. An Aston Martin. White with silver trim."

"I remember that."

Ricki immediately turned to the man on her right. Mike grinned back at her, showing several wide gaps in his teeth. He made a modest living carving small figurines from wood he scavenged in the forest and had been part of Pete's loyal posse ever since she could remember.

"I remember that car," he repeated, the words creating a whistle through the spaces in between his teeth. "Flashy. Good-looking." He blinked as if an idea had just landed somewhere in his head. He turned wide eyes on Pete. "I used to wonder how that ranger could afford a car like that. Now isn't that something to recall after all these years?"

Something, all right, Ricki thought. But she wasn't sure just what, since she already had it confirmed by his sister that Graham owned the car. "Do you remember the last time you saw that car?"

Mike instantly shook his head, the crack from his neck bones traveling across the table. "Naw. I just remember seeing it driving through town, that's all. Didn't see it come into town, or notice it parked anywhere. Only driving through." He gave her an apologetic smile. "Sometimes it was going one way, sometimes the other."

"Which town?" Ricki asked. When Mike stared at her as if she were speaking a foreign language, she added, "Brewer, Edington, or Massey? Which town did you see it in?"

"Here in Brewer," Mike said. "It was right here. He might have driven it through Edington to get here, but this is where I saw it."

Ricki pondered that for a long moment. According to Mike, Graham would have had to drive past the turnoff for Massey, where his body was found, and through Edington to get to Brewer, which was the town farthest away from Port Angeles. It could mean Graham had come here on business, or regularly visited someone in Brewer, or maybe he'd been headed for the back access road into the park, which was a few miles past the city limits.

The thought had her turning slightly in her chair so she could look around the room. Carl Evans was sitting alone at a table, exactly where she'd passed him on her way to the bar. He was still reading a book and showing no reaction to the jumble of conversations going on around him. The hardware store he used to own had been just past the outskirts of Brewer, and only a mile or so from the access road into the park.

She turned back around and smiled at Pete and then made sure to include the rest of his group. "Thanks for taking a look at the pictures and letting me know about the car. It's a big help."

Mike's wrinkled features lit up, while Pete slid the two pictures back her way. "No problem, Ricki." When she started to rise, he held her back by reaching across the table and clamping bony fingers around her wrist. "I wanted to ask a question." His gaze shifted from her to Anchorman, who was still leaning against the wall. "Or more to your sidekick over there. How's it going, Anchorman?"

"Can't complain," Anchorman said easily. "What can I do for you, Pete?"

"Some reason you're running shotgun tonight instead of the chief?"

Ricki let out an exasperated snort, which both men ignored.

"Nothing exciting. The chief wasn't available tonight, is all." Anchorman grinned. "He's cooling his heels at a council meeting."

"Okay," Pete said. He cocked his head to the side and winked. "Wanted to check before I let you know that Merlin is wandering about here tonight. She asked about you."

Keeping an eye on Carl Evans to be sure he didn't decide to leave before she could talk to him, Ricki sat down again and smiled at Pete. "And who is Merlin? I don't believe I've met her."

Pete chuckled and winked again at the glare from Anchorman. "You probably haven't since you were pretty busy last month when she moved here. Came from somewhere in the Midwest."

"Kansas," Mike chimed in, then reddened slightly at Ricki's raised eyebrow. "She bought one of my carvings, and we got to talking. She's former military. Like Anchorman."

Ricki grinned. "Really? Sounds like the two of them would have a lot to talk about." She looked over at Pete. "And you say she was asking about him?"

Pete nodded, clearly enjoying the spotlight. "She sure was. She was an army ranger, he was a marine sniper, so both of them were part of an elite unit. I'd say the two of them are a good match."

"So would I." Ricki stood up and pushed back from the table before giving Anchorman an angelic smile. "Why don't you sit right down, then one of the guys can let Merlin know you're around." She pointed across the room. "I'll be right over there talking to Carl, so you can see me just fine from here."

While the other men, who had stood up when she had,

pretty much forced Anchorman into her vacated chair, Ricki made her way across the room, a wide grin on her face. Some former female army ranger named Merlin? Like the magician? It would take a magic act to get Anchorman in line, but wasn't that an interesting thought?

When she stopped by his table, Carl looked up, adjusting his glasses as he peered at her from behind their thick lenses. "Richelle James." Ever since she was a little girl accompanying her dad on a weekend run to the only hardware store in town, Carl had never given in and used her nickname. "I haven't seen you in a while. How's your mother doing?"

"Fine," Ricki lied. She knew Carl was asking out of genuine interest since he and her father had been friends, bonding over a variety of do-it-yourself projects, but she didn't want to get into long explanations about her mom. "Do you mind if I sit down?"

Carl politely gestured to the empty chair across from him, setting his book aside as Ricki sat down and set the photos on the table. He gave them a cursory glance before turning his gaze back to her. Rail thin, with blue eyes and plain square-framed glasses perched on a long, pointed nose, Curt folded his hands in front of him and stretched his narrow lips into a smile. "Have you recovered from your injuries?"

She held up her bandaged wrist. "This was the worst of it for me. I wish I could say that about everyone involved in the accident."

"Yes." Carl's features settled into sober lines. "I heard about that. A stray gunshot, wasn't it?" When she only smiled, he stared back at her. "Or was it not a stray shot after all?" He adjusted his glasses on his nose. "Deliberate, perhaps?"

"The jury is still out on that." Ricki pushed the pictures toward him. "I'd like your help in identifying anyone you might recognize in these pictures."

"Certainly," he said without even a glance in their direction. "But I wanted to ask about your injuries when you chased that killer into the mountains. I understand you went after him by yourself?"

Now why does everyone have to harp on that? she wondered. *It isn't as if I had a lot of choices at the time.*

"No serious injuries," Ricki said, ignoring his comment about her not having any backup.

Carl cleared his throat and looked at a point somewhere over her head. "Yes. Well. That's good. I was worried when I heard about it." His eyes cut over to where Pete and his ever-present group were sitting. "Of course, it's hard to tell what's the truth and what isn't sometimes."

"Mostly the stories are way overblown," Ricki said before pushing the photos another inch closer. "I'd appreciate it if you took a look at those."

The former store owner picked up the pictures and carefully studied them. "The quality isn't very good. Is this about the bodies found in the old lighthouse?"

"Persons of interest," Ricki said, sticking to the same explanation she'd given Pete. "I'm looking to see if someone in town remembers one of these guys, or maybe talked to him. Or maybe remembers talking to a ranger driving a white Aston Martin with silver trim."

He set the pictures aside and refolded his hands, looking down at them. "I remember seeing that car a time or two. About fifty years ago now. Haven't seen one like it since then." He looked up and smiled. "At least not around here." He nodded at the pictures. "There was a ranger driving that car, a couple of my customers mentioned it. Seemed like a pretty expensive car on a ranger's pay."

"He came from money," Ricki said. "So he never stopped in at the store?"

"Him?" Carl shook his head. "No. Not him. But the other ranger who was looking for him did. A very nice man. Very polite."

Ricki went still. "Another ranger was looking for him?"

"Yes. I remember because it was a slow day, and I was trying to get my taxes done when he walked in and interrupted me. He asked about the car, and I told him that I had seen it, usually in town. But the Friday before, I'd been locking up when it went past. He was flying pretty good down the highway. It was dark, but he was moving fast and that white car was hard to miss."

"About what time was that, Carl? Do you remember?"

"Around eight, I guess. The store closed at seven sharp, and it always took me about an hour to get everything done." A tiny smile played around his mouth. "Don't know that I can tell you much more than that."

"Did this ranger friend give you his name?" Ricki asked.

Carl's tiny smile disappeared. "Now, Richelle, that was a long time ago, and I'm afraid the car was more memorable than that ranger. If he did, I sure don't remember it."

Ricki hadn't expected him to, but she'd had to ask. "Did he tell you why he was looking for his friend?"

"He didn't show up for work, as I recall, but his friend thought he'd just gotten the schedule mixed up." Carl's thin shoulders lifted in a shrug. "He didn't stay long. Since he didn't look like he was going to buy anything, I told him I needed to finish up my taxes, and he just left." He pushed the pictures back toward her. "I heard your jeep needs a lot of work."

"More like a eulogy," Ricki said, gathering up the pictures and tucking them beneath her jacket. "I haven't been over to see it yet, but Charlie gave me a pretty dismal report."

"Well, that's why I mentioned it. I figured you'd be over to see Charlie, so you should ask him about the pictures."

She knew she owed a visit to the garage where her jeep had been towed but hadn't had the time yet. And as far as Charlie looking at the pictures, she didn't think that would do any good. "I don't think Charlie would even have been in school yet when these were taken."

Now Carl did manage a real smile. "No. No, he surely wouldn't have been. But before he took over his dad's garage, he wanted to be a photographer. Built a kind of darkroom in the back. I bet he could blow those pictures up so you could get a better look at the faces."

Chapter 29

"CALL me as soon as you get this." Ricki ended the message and stuck the phone into her back pocket.

She'd already made her regular morning call to Eddie, to be sure he was up and getting started on his day. With Bear's overnight guest gone, he'd spent the night at his father's place. It wasn't that she didn't trust her ex to roust their now-on-summer-vacation son out of bed at a decent hour, but it was never a bad idea to give them both a reminder to get up and get going after an evening undoubtedly spent playing video games.

Eddie intended to come home and spend the day in his bot garage, doing some minor adjustments on the science fair entry. The final message had been for Clay. She'd called him last night, but he hadn't picked up, or tagged her back with a call. And he hadn't answered when she'd called him just now, either.

Wondering if he was annoyed with her over something she had no idea about, or if the council meeting had not gone well for some reason she couldn't even come up with, she walked over to the kitchen counter and picked up her gun. Since she still couldn't get it into the harness with her broken wrist, she stuck her weapon into the holster clipped to her belt at the small of her back. The gun wasn't loaded, but at least it was close enough she could get at it. She'd already slipped a small tin box of bullets into the pocket of her jacket. Given her current handicap, that was the best she could do.

With nothing else to keep her inside the cabin, and Corby sitting impatiently by the front door, his tail thumping loudly against the wooden floor, she decided to wait outside for her ride. The minute she opened the door, the big dog leaped out and disappeared into the trees, making Ricki grin. Corby was very particular about his bathroom habits, the number-one rule being that no one could watch him go.

She was only halfway across the drive when she heard the distinct crunch of tires on gravel. A few seconds later, the light-colored SUV came into view, rolling to a gentle stop behind Clay's pickup truck.

Ricki walked over to the car and climbed in. She snapped her seat belt into place before looking over at Dan.

"Ready?" He made a show of adjusting the rearview mirror, looking everywhere but at his passenger.

"Not quite," Ricki said. She turned in the seat until she was facing him, while he put his hands back on the steering wheel and stared straight ahead. Seeing the stiffness in his back and shoulders, she felt a small twinge of guilt, balanced out with the same amount of exasperation. Catching him with Marcie at the diner wasn't that big a deal. It wasn't as if she'd walked in and found them in some kind of contorted, compromising position. Now her own shoulders hunched at the mental picture of the two of them in a messy lip-lock—an image she immediately banished from her mind.

"Look, I'm sorry. I don't have a problem with you seeing Marcie. It just took me by surprise, is all."

Dan visibly relaxed and turned his head enough to give her a cautious look. "Really? You're okay with it?"

Thinking "okay" was about all she was, Ricki managed a

nod. "Marcie is family to me. So I tend to be a little overprotective, I guess."

His shoulders dropped another inch. "I can understand that. But she is old enough to decide who she wants to date."

"So she told me," Ricki said dryly. "And if she has to date someone, you're as good as anyone else in town."

"Gee. Thanks." Dan laughed, which drew a reluctant smile from Ricki. "Not the highest compliment I've ever had, but I'll take it."

"That's good," Ricki said. "Because that's all the compliments I'm giving out this morning." She settled herself more comfortably in the seat, finding a spot where her gun didn't dig into her back. "Of course, it goes without saying that if you hurt her, I will shoot you." She held a hand up and pretended to be studying her nails. "So will Anchorman."

"Understood." Dan nodded as he pressed the ignition button and the car's engine roared to life. "Where are we headed this morning?"

"Charlie's garage. Take a right at the main road and I'll give you directions from there." Ricki propped an elbow on the armrest as Dan did a neat three-point turn and headed back down the driveway. "I got a suggestion last night that he might be able to blow up the pictures, so I don't have to make a trip into Olympia to get it done." She lifted a hand to stifle a yawn. Sleep had been in short supply last night. She hadn't finished her report to Hamilton until after midnight and then forced herself out of bed at 6 a.m. to take a quick run before making her daily call to her son. "My jeep is there too, and I need to take a look at it."

He cut her a sideways glance. "Are you sure you're ready to do that? You seemed pretty attached to that thing."

"It was a pain in my ass, but it got the job done. Well, usually." She sighed. "And it didn't come with a car payment, which was its best feature." She pointed at a road up ahead, jutting out from the right. "Take that next turn. Charlie's shop is down that way."

A few minutes later, Dan pulled up in front of a one-bay garage just as Charlie was flipping over the "Open" sign in the office window. Still sporting the handsome features of his younger years, only a little rounder and softer with age, Charlie waved at Ricki through the window, then gestured for her to come inside.

She exited the vehicle and walked over to the door with Dan following behind her. Charlie's only work area, besides the large open bay, was crowded with stacks of paper mixed in with boxes of parts and wadded-up rags. The whole place exuded a pungent odor of oil and gasoline, combined with burnt coffee. Charlie stepped around the counter that held a cash register and an old laptop, holding his hand out to Dan.

"Hi. Glad to see you again." The friendly mechanic turned to Ricki and gave her a gentle pat on her shoulder. "I'd shake your hand too, but it might get a little awkward with that wrist and all. TK was in a few days ago, and he said your injuries from the accident were no big deal."

Ricki made a face so Charlie would know exactly what she thought of that. "Easy for TK to say. He's not the one with the broken wrist."

Charlie stuck his hands in his back pockets, his expression drooping into a mournful look. "I guess you're here to see your jeep. I might as well tell you outright, she's done."

"Yeah. Clay told me." Ricki pulled out the envelope she'd been carrying inside her coat. "But before we get to that, I hear that you're a photographer?"

"I play around with it some." Charlie took the envelope she was holding out and rolled back on his heels. "What's this?"

"Some photos I'd like to have blown up. Carl Evans told me that you have a darkroom."

He drew the pictures out of the envelope and studied

them, making a humming noise as he peered at the smaller of the two. "These are pretty old." He looked up. "And not the best quality, but I'll see what I can do." He glanced back down at them. "Are these the pictures you were showing around at the post last night?"

Ricki smiled even as she made a silent mental sigh. Living in a small town and talking with the biggest gossip around pretty much guaranteed every word they'd exchanged would have been out before she'd even made it home last night. "Yes, those are the ones. They were taken fifty years ago."

Charlie set them down on the counter. He rubbed his hands together, and Ricki could see the red creeping up the back of his neck. The man definitely had something on his mind.

"Do you recognize any of those men in the pictures, Charlie?" she asked.

"No." He added a shake of his head. "I wasn't even out of diapers when those were taken. No. It's something I remembered after that. More like twenty-five years ago, I guess. I was in the army so I wasn't here, but I heard about it from Pop."

She didn't say anything, but stood, waiting, letting him get out whatever he had to say in his own way.

"You were asking about a car?" When Ricki nodded, so did he. "Well, I think I know where it is. Or I mean, I know what happened to it." He lifted an elbow and leaned it against the top of the counter. "When I was in the army, I called home every week that I could. During one of those calls, Pop told me that they'd found an old car in the canal. Down at the far end, close to where it turns into Dabob Bay. That's what Pop said, anyway."

Ricki's eyes narrowed. That was a very sheltered area, and at night wouldn't have been well traveled. A picture began to take shape in her mind. "Go on," she urged softly.

"The car was rusted out and a complete loss. Pop said it had probably been in there at least twenty years, from all the damage." He looked over at her. "There weren't any plates on it. Pop thought someone had deliberately taken off the plates and ditched the car. He said it must have been a pretty nice car at one point and couldn't think why anyone would treat it that way."

"Did he mention the make and model of the car?" Dan asked while Ricki held her breath.

Charlie snorted out a short laugh."Oh yeah. Pop was a car guy down to his bones. He wouldn't miss a chance to talk about an Aston Martin being pulled out of the canal. He thought it had been white with silver trim before it spent twenty years underwater." When Ricki and Dan exchanged a look, Charlie straightened away from the counter. "It sounds like the car you were asking about at the VFW. Pete told me last night. I hadn't thought about that old story from Pop until Pete mentioned the car." He drummed a heavy finger against the countertop. "No one claimed it, so Dad sold it for scrap. I was still in the army, so I never saw it myself."

"That's fine, Charlie," Ricki finally said, her mind still on all the deserted places at night along that stretch of highway. "That helps a lot. Thanks."

The mechanic rested a worried gaze on her face. "Look, Pop didn't know a ranger owned that car. He never would have sold it off that way if he'd known who had owned it."

Ricki reached over and laid a reassuring hand on his arm. "Don't worry about it, Charlie, no one is going to get excited about selling off a rusted-out car for scrap twenty-five years ago. Especially when the owner had been killed twenty-five years before that."

"So it was that ranger you found up at the old lighthouse who owned that Aston Martin?" Dan asked. "Pete sounded pretty sure about that."

Ricki rolled her eyes. "Yeah. I'll bet he did."

Chapter 30

DAN PULLED up in front of the Sunny Side Up and cut the engine, then looked over at Ricki. "You wouldn't actually buy that jeep Charlie showed you, would you?"

"Why not? Jeeps do well out here no matter the weather, and especially on some of those unpaved roads leading into the park." Ricki unfastened her seatbelt and reached for the door handle. "Not to mention on dirt roads going up to abandoned lighthouses."

She stepped out of the SUV and shut the door while Dan did the same. He was still shaking his head as he rounded the hood of his vehicle and joined her on the sidewalk. "I'm sure you can find one that isn't—"

"As expensive?" Ricki cut in. "Not likely. That's a great price, and it's only five years old. Decent mileage, too."

"Okay, but it—"

She cut him off again with a wave of her hand. "It runs great. Charlie's a mechanic, so if he says the engine is good and everything else works fine too, I'm good with taking his word on it."

Still shaking his head, Dan followed her into the diner. Since they'd missed most of the breakfast rush, the dining room was only half-full and the hostess station was deserted. When the door opened, Marcie looked up from her position behind the back counter where she had a dozen sugar dispensers lined up in front of her. Her gaze skipped right over Ricki and latched on to Dan for a moment before bouncing back to her boss. She dropped the large container of sugar she was using to fill up the dispensers onto the counter and put her hands on her hips, a huge smile reaching from ear to ear.

Ricki stuck her hands in her pockets as she made her way to the back, doing her best to look as if walking into the diner with her assistant partner was no big deal.

"Hi, you two." Marcie's eyes fairly sparkled. "It's good to see you made up."

"We aren't dating, Marcie. We work together," Ricki muttered, slightly embarrassed that everyone in the room could hear the older woman.

"She apologized."

Dan's loud announcement had Ricki's shoulders drawing in as she felt every eye in the place center on her back. "Nice of you to let the immediate world know about it."

Marcie only looked amused as she leaned in and dropped her voice to a whisper. "Follow me back to the kitchen. You can apologize to me in there."

"Is that so?" Ricki said, but it only bounced off Marcie's back as the waitress was already headed for the double doors.

Not having a lot of choice, Ricki followed her through the doors, stopping when she spotted Anchorman at the stove. He looked over at the two women who were now facing each other and rolled his eyes to the ceiling. "Great. Am I here or not?"

"Not," Ricki and Marcie said in unison.

Anchorman shrugged. "Fine." He turned his back on them and stood with his arms crossed over his chest, watching the burger sizzling on the grill.

"You start," Marcie said, then stood waiting.

Thinking she might as well get it over with, Ricki nodded. "Okay. I'm sorry. I shouldn't have gone off that way about you dating Dan."

When she stopped, Marcie tapped a sturdy, sensible shoe against the tile floor. "And?"

Ricki sighed. Geez. Her friend wasn't going to let her get off very easy. "And," she started again. "He's a good guy." There. She'd said it. The non-wilderness ranger had grown on her over the past few months, and so far had not uttered one word of complaint about all the grunt work she'd dumped on him. She did appreciate that, even if she'd never told him so.

Marcie grinned. "Now, see? That didn't hurt, did it?" She reached over and gently patted Ricki's arm. "I apologize too. I shouldn't have jumped all over you like that." She jerked a thumb over her shoulder in Anchorman's direction. "Especially not in front of he-who-shall-not-be-named."

"I'm not evil," Anchorman called out without moving from his position by the stove. "And not so old I don't know a Voldemort reference when I hear one."

The waitress let out a boisterous laugh. "Not old. Just completely out of touch."

Seeing an opening to needle her stubborn-to-the-bone cook, and get a little payback for him insisting she needed a babysitter, Ricki clasped her hands behind her back and gave Marcie a conspiratorial wink. "Some women like the old-fashioned type."

Marcie's head whipped around. "Is that so? Like who?"

Ignoring the warning glare from Anchorman, Ricki leaned in a little. "I hear there's a new girl in town, who goes by the name of Merlin."

"Ricki." Anchorman's voice cracked out, which had both women smiling even more.

"Like the magician?" Marcie asked. She glanced over at the glowering cook. "Wasn't he a male magician, like a wizard or something?"

"Marcie." Anchorman's tone had gone up a notch or two. "No. She's not a male and stop with the Harry Potter references already."

The waitress only sniffed and turned back to Ricki, mischief dancing in her eyes. "So. It's confirmed. He does know this Merlin person. Who is she?"

"A former army ranger." When Marcie's eyes widened, Ricki nodded. "Who, according to no lesser authority than Pete, has the hots for Anchorman. She was stalking him at the VFW last night."

"She was not," Anchorman huffed out.

"And was he interested?" Marcie asked as if the target of their conversation had suddenly gone invisible.

"I don't know. He fled the scene before I was done."

Marcie slapped her hands against her cheeks. "No! Our decorated hero and former sniper ran away from a woman?"

"Ha, ha," Anchorman said as the two women broke into laughter. "I want you both to get out of my kitchen."

"Which I pay for, so it's my kitchen too," Ricki retorted, grinning at the bright red splashed across his face. It was the first time she'd ever seen him so embarrassed, and she was rather enjoying it.

"He actually has a good idea," Marcie put in. "I need to get out there and give some attention to Ranger Wilkes, and you need to do the same for your guy."

Ricki turned her head and followed Marcie's gaze. Through the large cutout in the wall separating the kitchen from the dining room, she saw Clay sitting in his usual seat, reading a menu. And he didn't look particularly happy. She swiveled on her heel and pushed through the double doors, walking along the backside of the customer counter until she reached the far end. Clay had put down his menu and was watching her but didn't say a word when she stopped and put her elbows on the counter between them.

She didn't bother with any polite small talk, preferring to

immediately get to the heart of whatever was bothering him. "What's up?"

He kept his gaze on hers as he let out a slow breath. "The city council mostly." His voice was low enough it didn't carry beyond the two of them.

She blinked. The city council? Aside from listening to the amount of money raked in from traffic tickets, the council didn't usually do much at their monthly meetings except drink coffee. But apparently last night they had, because the look on Clay's face was inching beyond annoyance and into angry frustration. She frowned as she looked around the diner and the lingering customers. Not a good place to have a discussion neither one of them wanted to get out into the gossip mill.

"Want to talk about this in my office?"

Clay smiled. He knew she was talking about the back alley and not the small closet in the kitchen that held her desk, a small floor safe, and absolutely nothing else. Because that was all that could fit in the minuscule space. "That would be good." He stood up and nodded toward the back. "Let's go."

They passed through the kitchen, with Ricki leading the way, not stopping until they were standing next to the dumpster that served the two buildings on either side of the alley.

Ricki faced Clay, her feet spread apart with her good hand cradling the splinted one. "So? What happened?"

Clay stuck his hands into the back pockets of his jeans and frowned. "It seems the council members have been talking among themselves and are questioning the budget for the police department."

Of all the things she'd imagined, that had not even made the top ten on her list. Budget? The police department covered most of its expenses through a combination of the rent money for the National Park Services space inside the building that also housed the police, and the mountain of traffic tickets given out to unsuspecting tourists every season.

"I took a look at the tri-city budget when it came out last

year," Ricki said cautiously. "The money the department brought in pretty much covered its expenses."

"Yeah. I pointed that out," Clay said. "Then it was pointed out to me that a good piece of that money, and they were talking about the traffic citations, comes in during the high tourist season over the summer. Not nearly as much comes in during the winter."

"Because there aren't as many tourists." Ricki's forehead wrinkled in thought. "That's perfectly natural, so I'm not seeing their point."

Clay held out both hands in front of him as if they were two sides of a weighted scale. "Summer revenue and cost to run the department." He dropped one hand lower than the other. "Winter revenue and the cost to run the department. It seems the department costs the same no matter what month is on the calendar, but the ticket revenue doesn't cover it in the winter."

"And so?" Ricki prompted, not seeing where this was going.

"Since four of the six council members are convinced most of our work is writing out tickets, and that doesn't happen as much in the winter, they think we could pare down the expenses by cutting our manpower from January to April."

Ricki's mouth formed into an *O* as she watched Clay run an agitated hand through his hair. "They want you to cut your hours?"

He shook his head. "Not mine. My deputy's."

Knowing Jules's paycheck as a deputy was his only source of income, and how responsible Clay felt for him, this wasn't a good situation at all. She knew Clay, and he might try to make up the shortfall out of his own pocket. Or look for other work himself and leave Jules on as full-time. Neither prospect was very appealing. The Bay only had one competent, experienced law enforcement officer, and that was Clay. Which was likely the reason the council wanted to reduce the deputy's hours and not the chief's.

"Then we need to find Jules a side hustle," Ricki declared.

"A what?"

She smiled. "A side hustle. It's like a part-time job, more or less. Something to make a little extra money."

Clay's smile was on the glum side. "Great idea. But most of the businesses in the area cut back in the winter themselves." He stuck his hands back into his pockets and glanced toward the diner's kitchen windows. "Even you have reduced hours in the winter, and all the staff you need."

"Then we invent a side hustle," Ricki repeated. "I just happen to be really good at that." When he looked a little more hopeful, she smiled. "Let me give it some thought. I'll come up with some possibles, and then you can talk it over with Jules."

"Okay. It's definitely worth a shot." He shifted his weight and looked around. "Where's the truck?"

"I hitched a ride in with Dan." When his lips twitched, she gave him a cranky look. "Yes, I apologized to him. And to Marcie. And I gave them my blessing to date, or whatever it is the two of them are doing."

"Yeah?" Clay's mouth formed into an all-out grin. "That was very adult of you, Agent James."

"Uh-huh. Nice of you to notice, Chief."

He took a step forward until he was standing right in front of her. He cupped a large hand around her cheek and leaned in for a soft, lingering kiss. "Thank you for helping out with Jules."

"You're welcome." She looked up into the warmth of his gaze and felt it gently flow between them. It was a little unnerving to have that feeling again after so many years. She reached up and took his hand in hers, keeping it there as she took a small step back, putting some space between them. "Want to hear about the case?"

He seemed to accept her withdrawal, but he held on to her hand as he nodded. "Sure. But there's something I want to talk to you about first." His grip tightened as if he expected her to try to snatch her hand away. "It's about Eddie."

A nerve in her gut twitched, and her voice went a little cooler. "What about Eddie? You aren't going to press trespassing charges on the boys, are you?"

Clay chuckled and gave her hand a reassuring squeeze. "No. As a matter of fact, though, this does involve all three of them."

She relaxed, thinking he was about to suggest community service, which wasn't a bad idea at all now that school was out. "What about them?"

"I know they're still grounded, and that's strictly up to all the parents, but I think the kids should be able to test out that bot of theirs."

"Their bot?" For the second time since they'd stepped into the alley, he'd taken her by surprise. "What about the bot?"

"I talked to the manager at the St. Armand, and he's agreeable to them using the staircase, provided the parents pay for any damage that might happen. He doesn't have any events scheduled during the last week of this month, but they're pretty well booked the rest of the summer, so this would be a good time to give it a test run, and still leave enough time to fix anything if it doesn't go smoothly."

"You've already talked to the manager about this?"

He held firmly on to the hand she'd started to tug at. "Yeah. But not to any of the other parents, or to Eddie. You're his mom, so I'm bringing the idea to you first. If you don't like it, I'll call and let the manager know his staircase is safe."

Ricki sucked in her bottom lip as she considered it. The boys would be finished with being grounded well before the science fair in the fall, so there wasn't any reason they couldn't attend that. And testing out the bot would give them time to work out any kinks over the summer. Of course, she'd have to find out how the other parents would feel about footing the bill for any potential disaster.

That would be tough for her to do all on her own right now since the bill for her mom's nursing home was due in a few weeks, and she had to sock money away so they could all stay afloat over the winter. Still, she did have another pool of money to tap into, at least when it came to Eddie. Bear could more than afford to pick up this tab, and she knew he wouldn't mind doing it. Not since it was all for their son.

"Okay," she finally said. "Okay. I'll talk to the other parents and see what they have to say." She looked up at him. "Thanks for thinking of this. I owe you."

Clay shook his head. "No, you don't. Sooner or later you would have dropped in at the St. Armand and made the same arrangements."

She laughed. "Give yourself some credit here, Thomas. I could have tried, but it would have been a lot easier for that manager to turn me down than the local chief of police."

He smiled and swung their joined hands back and forth. "Okay. I'm happy to take the praise. Has this earned me another real date?"

Oh, what the hell, she thought. All the gossips could just wag their tongues. The fact was that she wanted to go out again with Clay.

"Sure. How does next weekend sound?"

The delight in his eyes had her blushing slightly. "Yeah. Next weekend sounds great." He turned toward the diner and started pulling her along. "Now that we've solved all the immediate personal problems, how about we get something to eat while you tell me what you found out at the VFW? I'm starved."

Chapter 31

RICKI STARED at the index cards laid out on the kitchen counter. Marcie had given her a ride back to the cabin since Dan hadn't yet returned from Port Angeles, where he was looking up eviction notices and Clay had gotten a call about a minor fender bender north of Brewer. Staring at the cards, with a microwaved dinner sitting off to the side, rapidly cooling and still untouched, she had to admit she was disappointed Clay hadn't been able to join her. They could have shared a pizza and beer while they talked over the case. Or maybe talked about his life BB—before the Bay.

She frowned. For some reason it was just dawning on her that he rarely talked about it. She'd known him for a year now, and all that time they'd been dancing around the edges of a relationship that was definitely now in its infancy.

Well, they'd gone on one date anyway, but that counted as a start. And it wasn't until recently that he'd even mentioned he'd been married before. And that was all he'd said about it, promising they'd talk about it later. But so far? Nada. She definitely didn't get the vibe that Clay had some sort of dark, secret past, but still . . . He sure wasn't chatty about it either.

She shuffled the index cards around again and studied the

new grouping. Each card contained one thing she knew for certain about the case. She'd pushed the card stating *Last seen going south at about 8 p.m.* next to the one with *Car found in canal 25 years ago.* Satisfied those two things were related, she moved two more cards around, forming the beginnings of a timeline. Graham was seen driving south at 8 p.m., then the car ended up in the canal. But then how did Graham's body find its way to the lighthouse? She picked up another card and considered it. The ranger's uniform, along with his badge, had been neatly folded next to what remained of him, a skeleton that looked as if it had been carefully laid out.

Tapping the edge of the card on the countertop, she considered different scenarios of what might have happened that night almost fifty years ago. Only one stood out. She set the card down, putting it in front of her timeline, before moving the rest of the cards into place in one continuous row, ending with the shooting of Maxwell Hardy. There were only two gaps, but they were the crucial ones, and in her mind related to each other and the central question: Why had Benjamin Graham been spending time in the Bay?

He'd been seen here by more than one person, or at least his car had been, and on more than one occasion. So he'd definitely been hanging around the area. But what was it that the PI had uncovered that had gotten him killed?

Missing something, she thought. She was sure it was there, but she wasn't seeing it. Her phone beeped with an incoming text message from Dan. He was on his way back to the Bay and he'd sent her an email. Switching over, she opened his email and saw that it had two attachments, which she sent to the small printer on top of her desk. It began to spit out paper before she'd crossed the room. She picked up the three sheets and scanned their headings as she walked back to the counter. One sheet was an application as a renter, and the other was a rental agreement. She'd just settled back onto her stool when her phone rang again.

It was Josh.

She set the papers aside and picked up her phone, a tension already snaking its way up her back and into her arms. "Hey." She winced at the sharp edge in her tone. "How are you?"

"Pissed," Josh said without preamble. "You know that deputy marshal I was tracking down? The one who interviewed you in the hospital?"

"Chad Olyman. Yeah. Did you talk to him?"

"Can't," Josh spit out. "He's conveniently dead. Car accident while he was on a very expensive vacation in the Cayman Islands."

Ricki kept quiet, listening to Josh's choppy, angry breathing through the speaker while she thought that one over. "How expensive?"

"A six-hundred-dollar-a-night-room-at-a-luxury-hotel expensive, and he'd run up additional charges in the thousands."

She softly whistled. "Whoa. He'd either been saving up since he was a kid, or living way beyond the salary of a deputy marshal."

"Oh yeah," Josh confirmed. "And he was on his way to meet a hot date when he had the accident. No one can remember her name, or where she was staying, or even one damn thing about her, except she was a complete knockout with a body built for a wet dream."

"But no name?" Ricki closed her eyes. What were the odds that a woman like that was walking around an island, and absolutely no one remembered her name? Unless she simply appeared out of nowhere, met the marshal, set up a time and place to meet, and then disappeared.

"She probably didn't even show up for that date," Josh said, mirroring Ricki's thoughts.

"Not likely," she slowly agreed. "Sounds like Olyman was enjoying a payoff when he was set up."

"Roger that," Josh said. "A loose end that needed tying up." There was silence for a moment before he blew out a breath. "I wanted to let you know what I found out, and to tell you that I'm not going to let this go. I can't."

"Neither can I," Ricki said.

"I have to go. Oh, before I forget, Jonathan is going to call you sometime soon."

She frowned. The profiler? "Why?"

"He heard about the accident, and he's worried," Josh said.

It was a nice thought, but she wasn't sure what to make of that. She'd only worked with the guy once, had a short conversation with him when he'd shown up at the St. Armand with Josh. Agents got hurt all the time, so it wasn't all that unusual or unexpected, so why the interest? "Look. You can tell him it was minor, nothing more than a broken wrist. It isn't worth a phone call. I'm fine."

"I'll tell him, but knowing Jonathan, he'll call anyway. Hang on a minute, okay?" Before Ricki could respond one way or the other to that request, Josh came back on the phone. "Look, I really do have to go." His voice dropped lower. "I have a feeling that this whole thing with Marie is going to get a lot messier. You watch your back, okay?"

When the phone went dead, Ricki set it aside. "Messier" was an understatement. First she and her partner were ambushed, then the investigating agent doctored the report, after which that same agent just happened to be in a fatal accident? Ticking time bomb would be more accurate.

Her thoughts about that night on the pier were interrupted by a quick series of knocks on the door.

"Ricki? Are you in there? Do you want me to leave this envelope from Clay here on the porch?"

Recognizing the voice, Ricki smiled and slid off the stool. "Coming," she called out, and opened the door to Ray, who was standing several feet away, holding out an envelope.

"Clay asked me to drop this off since you're on my way home."

Ricki took the envelope, then frowned at the pained look on Ray's face. "What's the matter?"

He rubbed a heavily veined hand across his forehead. "Headache. That's why I left a little early." His watery eyes crinkled at the corners. "You wouldn't happen to have a couple of aspirin I could have, would you? It would save me a stop at the grocery store."

"Sure. I can manage that. Come on in and I'll even throw in a glass of water."

He removed his battered baseball cap and followed her over the threshold, stopping next to the counter, still holding his hat in front of his chest. "I surely do appreciate it, Ricki. This thing's been pestering me all afternoon. Probably should have eaten more of my lunch, but I just didn't feel like it."

She reached into her cupboard where she always kept a huge bottle of aspirin on the lower shelf and then grabbed a clean glass. Walking to the sink, she glanced over her shoulder. "Didn't anyone at headquarters have any aspirin?"

He carefully shook his head. "Clay didn't, and there wasn't anyone else around today to ask. I think the rangers are all at Hurricane Ridge doing some kind of training up there."

She walked over and held out the water and the bottle of aspirin. Setting his hat down, Ray smiled his thanks before shaking out two white pills, popping them both into his mouth at the same time. He followed that up with a huge swig of water.

"That's perfect. Thanks." Ray picked up his hat and backed up a step toward the door. "Well, you got the envelope and I don't want to interrupt you anymore." He gave her a rueful smile. "And I'd like to get home and lie down for a bit. I'm not so young anymore."

Seeing the droop in his shoulders, Ricki walked with him to the door. "Are you going to be okay? You don't live far away. Corby and I can drive over with you and walk back." At the sound of his name, the big dog sprawled out on the couch immediately jumped to the floor, his tail wagging.

Ray chuckled. "I'll be fine on my own, Corby. You didn't have to move."

Corby plopped his butt on the floor and stared at Ricki, who shook her head at him. "Not now. We'll go for a walk later." She looked back over at Ray. "You're sure you're okay?"

He walked to the door and opened it up, letting a rush of cooler air inside. "The pain's already easing off. You go back to whatever it was you were doing, and I'll get out of your way." He gave her one last wave before stepping outside, closing the door behind him.

When Corby's tail stopped wagging, Ricki shrugged. "He didn't want our company, so you might as well finish your nap." She grinned when the dog turned and leaped back onto the couch, kneading the cushions with his paws before settling back down again.

Thinking she'd probably need to invest in a new couch in the near future, Ricki picked up the envelope and drew out the contents. Inside were the enlarged photos Charlie had promised her, along with the originals and a short note the mechanic had written, apologizing for the poor quality.

He was right about that. The smaller grainy picture had been blown up into a larger grainy picture that still didn't show a lot of detail in the faces of the assembled rangers. But it was better than what she'd had. Every bit of information helped. Thinking she'd give them a closer study later on, Ricki set the photos aside and picked up the papers Dan had sent her.

The rental lease was for the property at the address Barbara Metler had given them, but the name on the lease wasn't Benjamin Graham. The renter's name was Chris Toner. A single male. She scanned the rest of the paper, her gaze drawn to the filled-in line for tenant's occupation. Park ranger. Feeling that tingle in her gut, she reached over the line of index cards and plucked up the staff roster that listed the rangers assigned to the park in 1971. Running her finger down the page, she stopped at the halfway point.

C. Toner. There you are. She smiled in satisfaction. So it had been Ranger Toner who'd rented that house in Port Angeles where Benjamin Graham had also lived, according to his sister. Wondering if the two men had been sharing the house, or if Toner had turned around and subleased it to a fellow ranger, Ricki picked up the eviction notice. She wasn't surprised that it was Toner who'd been evicted, since it had been his name on the lease. But a moment later her eyes widened. The official paper filed with the county had listed Chris Toner as the renter being evicted, all right, but it had identified him by his full name: Christopher Anthony Toner.

Ricki stared at it, repeating the name to herself several times before she finally nodded in satisfaction. Well, well. Christopher Anthony Toner. The mysterious roommate.

"Looks like we found Benjamin Graham's friend," Ricki said softly. "You're probably the same guy who came to the Bay and asked around about him." She tilted her head to one side and smiled. "Nice to meet you, Catman."

Chapter 32

"C-A-T." Clay kept his eyes on the road as he repeated the initials. "Interesting nicknaming system your vic had."

"Uh-huh." Ricki watched the scenery whisk by as the SUV ground out the miles toward Vancouver, on the border between Washington and Oregon. "Makes me wonder what OG stood for."

"Another guy in his unit?" Clay guessed. "Or maybe someone else he met in Port Angeles? He could be our killer."

"Could be." She knew those were the most likely possibilities, but she'd already checked the staff list for a ranger with the initials of O. G. and had come up blank. And she couldn't recall anyone in the Bay with those initials either, but then her knowledge of the area's residents didn't go back fifty years.

Thinking she might have to pay another visit to the VFW and corner a few of the older vets with a few more questions, she stretched her legs out and crossed them at the ankles. "Want to hear my theory of what went down that night Benjamin Graham was killed?"

Clay grinned. "Yep. That's why I agreed to take this three-hour jaunt to talk to Christopher Toner." He shot her a sideways glance. "By the way, you never told me how you tracked him down so fast."

"I didn't," Ricki said. "Mr. Former-CIA-Spook-and-Master-Researcher-Turned-Ranger, Dan Wilkes, pulled that off. It turns out Toner has what Dan calls 'a reliable presence' on Facebook. If he's the killer, then I'd stake my badge on it being the only unusual thing he's done."

The chief let out a loud groan. "Facebook. Great. What does 'reliable presence' mean anyway?"

"According to Dan, Toner posts on a regular basis," Ricki said. "He's part of a group for retired park rangers."

"There's a group for that?" Clay asked.

She shrugged. "There's a group for everything—trust me, I know. I have a teenager. Not that he frequents Facebook. It's not the social media choice for kids."

"Okay. I'll take your word for it. Now back to how your assistant partner found Toner?"

Ricki laughed. "I did tell you. Toner posts on Facebook. Dan read his posts, and he mentioned he'd retired to Vancouver. According to Dan, Toner even put up a picture of his house. Dan did a quick search, got his address and phone number, then matched a picture of the house with the one he found by putting Toner's address into Google Earth, and got a perfect match."

"Will the wonders of the internet never cease," Clay said dryly. "So, let's hear your theory that you worked out with your little index cards about Graham's murder."

She didn't take issue with the amusement in his voice, since her investigative methods had gone from efficiently searching the internet to using lowly index cards. But hey. Whatever worked. "I don't have a big board in my cabin, so you use what you've got." She wiggled her eyebrows. "And it worked out pretty well."

"All right, I'm listening," Clay said. "Shoot."

"I think someone Graham knew lured him to someplace

off the 101, south of town. Back then, that whole stretch was remote and didn't have a lot of traffic, especially in April, before the season got started."

"Why would Graham meet someone in the middle of nowhere?"

"Unknown," Ricki stated. "But he went and ended up being killed there. Then the killer removed Graham's uniform and stuffed the body into the backseat of the Aston Martin."

Clay's lips pursed as he followed her train of thought. "The killer drives up to the lighthouse, dumps Graham's body there, figuring no one is going to find it, puts on the uniform, then drives back through town, heading south."

Ricki nodded. "Exactly. He's hoping someone will see him in the uniform and assume he's Graham, leaving town. Which is exactly what Carl Evans did, and as the killer's good luck would have it, Carl conveniently told Christopher Toner when he came looking for Graham, tying everything up very nicely." Ricki stared out the window as she painted the scene from fifty years ago in her mind. "He ditched the car in the canal—plenty of places deep enough to do that—and then walked back to his own car."

"So why did he go back later and leave the uniform next to Graham's body?" Clay asked. "Why didn't he just burn it?"

"Remorse," Ricki replied. "I don't think we're looking for a hardened killer. It's shaping up to be a spur-of-the-moment kind of crime. You know, a disagreement heating up and tempers getting out of hand. The killer did the only respectful thing he could, short of making a confession. He laid the body out and left the uniform neatly folded."

Clay's expression went grim. "Then what? Considered that good enough and just walked away?"

"Seems like it."

"But not remorseful enough to keep from stealing the guy's watch, according to what Graham's sister told us, or from killing again." Clay's hands tightened on the steering wheel before slowly relaxing. "He could have played the same scenario again with Hardy, luring him up to the lighthouse and then killing him and leaving him there."

She nodded her agreement. "It would take a lot less energy to leave a body where you killed it instead of dragging it around."

He glanced over at her, a question in his gaze. "You're still thinking we're looking for an eighty-year-old murderer?"

"Not necessarily. That's assuming whoever killed Graham was around his age at the time, in his early thirties. What if he was ten years younger? Twenty-year-olds have been known to kill, and that would put him at seventy today, not eighty, which opens up a whole new pool of suspects." She tapped a finger against one knee. "And he has to be someone around here, or he wouldn't have known about Hardy being in the area, probably asking questions."

"He was asking around," Clay confirmed. "I paid another visit to the hotel and found out Hardy had made some inquiries to several people on the hotel's staff, and at the local bar in Edington."

Surprised, Ricki turned her upper body and faced him. "He did? What was he asking about?"

"The land," Clay stated flatly. "He wanted to know if anyone had shown any interest in buying that land or had been around looking at it since it last changed hands."

The land? It kept popping up, but she couldn't see where it fit in to the whole puzzle. "Did anyone tell Hardy anything?"

"They didn't know anything to tell him. I still need to get up to Massey, though, and see if he was asking around there."

She shifted back around in her seat. "When were you going to let me in on this?"

"When we got a chance to compare notes," Clay said instantly. "Which is now." He glanced over at her. She didn't look at him but continued to stare straight out the window.

"Come on, Ricki. I hadn't finished asking around, and you were off to the VFW. I also had a council to deal with. So I'm telling you now."

Since she was sitting in his car, headed to interview a potential source of information about what had happened to her victim, she decided to talk to him later about not sharing information. Shrugging it off, she simply said, "Okay," then looked over at the GPS when it chirped out the instruction to take the next off-ramp.

It was only a ten-minute drive from the freeway to the quiet, tree-lined street of the subdivision Christopher Toner called home. Clay pulled up to the curb in front of the house and slid the gear into park. "Are you mad at me?"

"Not at the moment," Ricki said as she pushed the passenger side door open. "Maybe later. I'll think about it." She glanced back at him. "But right now we need to find out what Christopher Toner knows."

They were halfway up the walk when the front door opened. A tall man with steel-gray hair and brown eyes stood in the opening. Dan had told her he was in his eighties, but no one would have guessed that. His posture was still ramrod straight, and he looked like he'd kept himself fit. The tan on his face also said he'd kept up with the outdoor lifestyle of a park ranger. When she and Clay stepped up onto the small square that passed for a porch, he held out a hand to Ricki.

"Are you Special Agent Ricki James?" When she nodded, he smiled as he shook her hand. "I got a call from a Ranger Wilkes up at Olympic Park saying you'd be by." He turned to Clay and raised a questioning eyebrow.

"Clay Thomas. I'm the chief police in the Bay."

"Police?" Toner's eyebrow winged up even higher. "So an ISB agent and a police chief? Ranger Wilkes said you wanted to ask me about Ben Graham. What in the hell did he do that a police chief and an ISB agent come calling fifty years later?"

He stepped aside and gestured for them to come in, waiting until they were in the tiny foyer before closing the door behind them. He turned and led the way into a living room barely big enough for a small couch and two armchairs. The three pieces of furniture were clustered around an oval-shaped coffee table with a large vase of artificial flowers in the center.

Waving them over to the couch, Toner took one of the armchairs before leaning to the side and yelling toward the back of the house. "Myrna, that agent is here and she brought a police chief with her, so put another coffee cup on the tray." He sat back and laughed. "My wife put the coffee on as soon as you drove up. It won't take but a minute or two. She's got one of those fancy machines that uses up most of the counter space. I told her it was way too big for just us, but she loves it, so what can a man do?"

"Keep her happy," Clay said. He got to his feet while Ricki kept her expression politely blank. "I'll just go out and help her with carrying in that tray. Benjamin Graham is actually Agent James's case."

Toner's eyes widened as he faced Ricki. "Case? What kind of case?" Before she could answer, he leaned back as if he expected a blow. "I was with the service about five years or so when they started up that special investigative unit. Ben had left before then. He and I joined at the same time." He propped one ankle up on the opposite knee, getting comfortable as he smiled back at her. "You look at major incidents, don't you? Like drug trafficking or bad hiking accidents, that kind of thing?"

Ricki nodded, her gaze remaining steady on his. "Those and homicides."

He looked stunned. "Ben killed someone?" He blinked and then frowned. "No. Wait. I haven't seen him for fifty years. Are you saying he killed someone back then?" He went still as he stared back at her. "Or that he's been dead all this time?" He looked away, drew in a deep breath, and glanced back at her. "I knew your uncle."

Not surprised that he'd abruptly changed the subject, Ricki nodded, more than willing to give him time to adjust to the idea that something bad had happened to his friend all those years ago.

"He arrived just a year or so before I retired. How's Cyrus doing?"

"He's fine. Still with the service, going on twenty-five years now."

Toner nodded. "Big guy, and I can tell that you're related. Same eyes. He was mad about fishing, as I recall. He used to go out all the time with some young cop there in Port Angeles."

"Still does," Ricki said in a conversational tone. "That young cop transferred to Tacoma. He's the chief of police there now."

"Is that so?" He looked over as Clay and a short, wisp-slender woman with gray hair and a friendly face bustled into the room. Clay followed behind, holding a large tray with wooden handles and piled up with coffee cups and a pot with steam rolling out of its top.

The woman swept the vase of flowers off the table and set it down on the floor next to Toner's chair. He smiled and reached up to capture one of her hands.

"This is my wife, Myrna." He looked up at her. "You've already met the police chief. That pretty woman over there is Special Agent Ricki James. I knew her uncle when I was still with the service."

"Yes, dear. You told me that already," Myrna said, her voice holding a note of patient amusement. She sent Ricki a welcoming smile. "I'm very fascinated with your job, Agent James. I wish I had time to talk to you about it, but I know you're here to see Chris, and I have a million errands I need to run." Her gaze took on a happy gleam. "We have family coming tomorrow."

"A lot of family," her husband corrected. "Both daughters, our son, and their respective spouses and kids. Eleven of them will be descending on us." He looked around. "I have no idea where they'll all be sleeping. I leave that up to the general here." He patted his wife's hand.

"Yes, well," Myrna said. "That's enough of talking about us. I'll be on my way, and you can just sit here and tell Agent James whatever it is she wants to know."

Toner gave her a short salute. "Yes, ma'am." When she bent down, he placed a quick kiss on her cheek, then watched with a soft gaze as she made her way back to the kitchen. Once his wife was out of earshot, Toner switched his attention back to Ricki. "Well, I guess I have my marching orders. So, what is it you want to know?"

Chapter 33

RICKI REACHED DOWN and opened the side pocket of her small backpack that she'd set on the floor. Pulling out an iPad, she held it up. "Do you mind if I record this, Mr. Toner?"

"Nope, and it's Chris." He settled back in his chair, resting his hands on top of his thighs. "What can I tell you?"

She handed the iPad to Clay to set up for recording as she consulted the notes she'd made on her phone. Once Clay gave her a nod, she started with the most obvious question. "When was the last time you saw Benjamin Graham?"

"April ninth," Chris said without any hesitation. "Since I was pretty sure you'd ask that, I've given it some thought, and went back and consulted a calendar, to be honest. It was the Friday morning before his last scheduled shift, which I remember was on April tenth. That was a Saturday."

"You didn't see him on that Friday in between?"

"Just for a few minutes in the morning," he said just as quickly as he'd answered her first question. "Just long enough to have an argument. I had to work that day. Ben was scheduled to work too, but he wanted to call in and claim he wasn't feeling well and wouldn't be able to make his shift." Chris frowned. "I thought at the time that maybe the phone call he got the night before was the real reason, because I know he wasn't sick." Chris shifted restlessly in his chair. "Anyway, he asked me to cover for him with the supervisor. You know, sort of confirm that he was sick since the whole unit knew that we were splitting the rent on a house. I told him I wouldn't do that. He needed to show up for the last weekend he was scheduled to work, and not screw up the days off for some other guy by playing possum. He went in, but he didn't like it. And as far as I know he never came home after his shift, and I never saw him again. I got concerned when he didn't show up for his last two shifts on Saturday or Sunday, and talked to Supervisor Abbott about it, but he didn't seem too concerned."

Since that lined up with what Barbara Metler had said, Ricki nodded. "I'm getting the impression that Abbott didn't like Ben."

Chris shifted in his chair, clearly uncomfortable. "Well, no, I guess not. Ben could be charming and fun, especially around women, but he came from money, you understand, so putting in a fair day's work wasn't part of his upbringing. It's fair to say that Abbott wasn't too keen on him.

"Not sure what he was intending to do, but I remember where he went." Chris shifted his gaze from Ricki to Clay. "He said he needed to skip out on that Friday shift because he had to make a trip to your neck of the woods. He didn't say why, and I was on my way out the door to report to work myself, so I didn't ask."

"So you think it had something to do with the phone call from his sister?" Ricki asked.

He shook his head. "Naw. She always called right on the dot at seven, because Ben had told her that was the only time he was ever available. It was the call that came in after hers. It was a man. I remember because I answered the phone."

Ricki slowly scooted to the edge of the couch. "A man

called him Thursday night, and the next morning Ben wanted to call in sick and drive up to the Bay?"

"That's what he said he was going to do. Now mind you, I don't know if he did or not. His car was still at the house when I left for my shift in the morning. I know he put in his time that day, but he never came back to the house that night." Chris looked down at his hands, resting just above his knees. "And us having words that morning was the last time I saw him." When he looked up again, his gaze was troubled. "I think he went to Brewer, because I made the trip down there to look for him and the guy who owned the hardware store told me that he'd seen Ben Friday night, driving south, out of town."

Chris stood up and walked over to the front window, staring out onto the street. The room was silent for a full minute, the only sound was the ticking of the clock on a shelf against the wall separating the living room from the dining room and kitchen.

"I chose to believe Ben had just upped and left because it was the easiest thing to do," Chris said quietly before turning around and making his way slowly back to his chair and sitting down. "But I think I knew something had happened to him. He left all his belongings behind, including that baseball of his."

"Baseball?" Ricki asked.

"Yeah. Signed by Ted Williams, no less. Ben loved that thing. He never would have left it behind." He raised his gaze to hers. "But the guy told me that he'd seen Ben driving out of town. He was so sure of it that I just went along." He drew in a slow breath, and his whole body stiffened as if he were bracing himself. "What happened to him?"

Ricki shifted back against the couch and softened her voice. "I'm sorry to have to tell you this, but Benjamin Graham was murdered. We only found his body a week ago."

She watched Christopher Toner deflate in his chair, his eyes taking on a sheen of moisture.

"Oh my God. All this time." He leaned forward and buried his head in his hands. "I can't believe it."

"He was shot," Ricki said before he could ask. "So was the private investigator who'd been trying to find him for several decades. His name was Maxwell Hardy. Did you ever talk to him?"

With his head still down, Chris's words were slightly muffled. "No. I've never heard of him."

So, it seemed the PI had never uncovered the identity of Catman, because if Barbara Metler had coughed the name up to her, she sure as hell told it to her own investigator too.

"Was it a jealous husband?"

"Excuse me?" Ricki said. "What was that about a jealous husband?"

Chris lifted his head and stared at her. "I was just wondering if it was a jealous husband who shot Ben?"

Clay leaned forward, his gaze hard. "Why would you say that, Chris?"

"I told you," Chris stated. "Ben liked women, and he wasn't particular about their marital status. He'd been seeing someone in Brewer. That's why he was making trips down there."

Ricki briefly closed her eyes. She should have known. Money, a woman, or revenge. One of those was almost always the reason a man killed. "Do you think that's why he made the trip to Brewer on that Friday? A woman?"

"I don't know," Chris said. "Maybe, but it wouldn't be the one he'd been going there to see on a regular basis. A month before he disappeared, he told me that they had broken up. Ben never went chasing after a girl who broke up with him. He always said the sea is too big to only put your line in to catch one fish." He shrugged. "Ben's words, not mine. I've been very happy with my one fish."

Ricki pondered that while she picked up her phone and consulted her notes. "Just a couple more questions, Chris. Did Graham ever mention the land his family owned?"

"You mean that place up above that little fishing hole? What's the name of that town?"

"Massey," Ricki supplied. "Yeah. That would be the one. It has an old lighthouse on it."

Chris frowned. "Sure, I remember. We went up there once and took a look around. Not much to it. He said he was going to tell the family he did an inspection and to dump the holding. He wasn't interested in it. We must have spent all of thirty minutes up there, and most of that was making the hike up to that lighthouse, or whatever it was. Didn't seem tall enough to be one, and what was a lighthouse doing up there anyway?"

"Guiding hunters, not boats, apparently," Ricki said. "Last question. Did Graham ever mention someone he called the OG?"

That drew a short laugh out of Chris. "I haven't thought of that in years. OG. Where did you hear that?"

"From his sister." Ricki watched him slap his knee as a smile crept across his face.

"Really? He told his baby sister about the OG?" He shook his head. "OG is what Ben called the other guy."

Once again Ricki leaned forward. "Other guy? What other guy?"

"That woman he was seeing in Brewer? She had a boyfriend. You know, the other guy." Chris sighed. "Like I said, Ben wasn't too particular about that kind of thing." He pushed himself up from the chair and walked over to a small table tucked next to the hanging shelf. Lifting a cardboard box, he carried it over to the coffee table and set it down. "I'm hoping you know how to get hold of Ben's sister, or whoever is left of his family?"

"We're in contact with his sister." Ricki gave the taped-up box a curious look. "What's this?"

"I told you Ben and I were splitting the rent on a house. When he left, the lease was almost up. I was planning on proposing to Myrna, and getting on with making a family, so I didn't want to keep the lease, but the landlord said that Ben had talked to him about extending it for another three months, but hadn't filled out the paperwork." He walked back to his chair and sat down. "That didn't fit into my plans, so when the original lease was up, I just packed up and left. I figured if Ben didn't want any of his stuff, then the landlord could deal with it." He pointed to the box. "Except for that. The clothes and towels, I didn't care about. But the pictures of his family, and some other personal stuff, well, I couldn't just leave it behind. So I packed it up and have been carting it around with me for the last fifty years. I'm hoping you'll see it gets back to his sister. Maybe it will make up in some way for me not searching for him more than I did."

AN HOUR LATER, Ricki was sitting in the SUV's passenger seat, headed north toward the Bay. She didn't notice much about the passing cars or anything going on outside the window. Her thoughts were centered on what Chris had said.

"He was dating a woman who had a boyfriend," she mused out loud. "Maybe a jealous boyfriend?"

"Most of them are," Clay agreed. "But even so, why would this jealous boyfriend wait a whole month after Graham had stopped coming around to kill him?"

"I don't know," Ricki said. "Why would Graham tell his buddy Catman that he intended to tell the family foundation to sell that land, and then turn around and tell his sister he wanted to buy it himself?"

"I don't know," Clay echoed. He glanced down at the box sitting on the seat between them. "Are you going to go through that before you turn it over to the sister?"

"You bet." Ricki reached for the keys in her pocket. Holding one between her thumb and index finger, she neatly slid it across the top of the box, easily breaking the brittle packing tape holding the flaps down. "So what have we got?" She paused at the sight of a small glass case holding a baseball inside. She gingerly lifted it out of the box and tilted her head to read the signature scrawled across its side. "Ted Williams."

Clay whistled and gave it a quick glance. "Seriously? I know a couple of guys from Boston who would kill for that."

"Maybe someone did," Ricki said, carefully putting the case back into the box. "I'll go through this later. Maybe that watch is somewhere in here, and when I give it all back to Barbara, she'll have a better opinion of the park rangers than what Abbott left her with."

The next two hours went by in a companionable silence, punctuated by a couple of short bouts of conversation. But neither of them was interested in making small talk, and she was glad they were comfortable enough with each other that not talking wasn't an issue between them.

They were five minutes from the outskirts of Brewer, with plans to grab a pizza and beer before heading back to her cabin, when Clay's phone rang. Somehow, the jarring note told Ricki that the pizza and beer would once again be put on hold.

Clay picked up the phone, answering it with a "Chief Thomas." He listened without interrupting, his whole demeanor changing from easy companion into cop in nothing flat.

"I'm on my way." His mouth flattened into a hard line. "Bar fight in Edington. And someone brought their gun."

Ricki immediately sat up and picked up the box. "Drop me off at the road up there. I can cut through the trees and walk the last mile to my cabin. It will save you some time."

He didn't argue with her as he pulled over to the side of the road, spewing gravel into the grass. Ricki didn't wait for a full stop to open the door, just hopped out as soon as the SUV had slowed down enough she could make the jump without falling on her ass.

"Thanks, Ricki. Call you later," he said as she slammed the door. One second later he was back on the tarmac, his lights flashing as the SUV leaped down the road.

Shaking her head at the life of a cop, Ricki crossed the highway and trotted down the back road. Half an hour later, still a good hundred yards from the cabin, Corby appeared through the trees, trotting toward her, his tail wagging. She smiled and gave him a firm head rub before covering the remaining distance to her front porch.

Corby followed her inside and was making a beeline for the couch when she called out a warning. "Oh no you don't. I intend to claim the couch." She pointed to the floor near the window. "Pretend you're a dog and lie down over there." Corby gave her an offended look, then went to stand by his food bowl. Ricki rolled her eyes as she set the box down on the counter. "Fine. Food first, then we can both lie down."

Once her dog was slurping away at his food, Ricki grabbed a bottle of water and a rice cake from her stash and headed for the couch. She'd wait to see if Clay could shake loose before she nuked the pizza.

She set her badge, phone, and gun on the coffee table, undid the laces on her boots, and then, lying back with a throw pillow cradling her head, flipped on the TV. After surfing through all four of the channels they got, she settled on an old *NCIS* rerun.

It felt like she'd barely dropped into sleep when her phone blared out. Prying one eye open, she looked at her watch. 12:15 a.m. Not a good time to get a phone call. Reaching out, she grabbed the phone and pulled it close enough to see Marcie's name shimmering on the screen. Great. The diner had been closed for a good four hours, so it couldn't be a work problem. If the waitress had just had a bounce with Ranger

Wilkes and was calling to tell her about it, she was going to make sure Marcie and her new boyfriend paid for it.

Raising the phone to her ear, she barked out, "What?"

"Ricki? You need to get here right now. Right now, do you hear me?" Marcie's voice was bordering on hysteria.

She sat straight up and plopped her feet onto the floor. "What's wrong? Where are you?"

"At the diner. I'm at the diner. It's on fire!"

Chapter 34

Less than ten minutes later, Ricki skidded the truck to a stop right in front of the Sunny Side Up, giving more than a couple of bystanders a good scare. She left it doubled-parked on the street as she leaped out and immediately found her way blocked by a mountain of a man, who held out a beefy hand attached to a long, thick arm. Trip owned the souvenir shop next door and towered a good six inches over her, but she wasn't going to let that stop her from getting by him.

"Get out of the way." She took a quick step to the side, which he had trouble matching.

"Wait a minute, whoa," Trip shouted over the din of noise around them. "You can't leave your truck there, Ricki. I called the fire department. They'll be here any minute, and they're gonna want to park their rig right where your truck is standing."

Ricki tossed him the key she was still holding in her hand. "Fine. You move it."

Trip caught the keys with one hand then stood staring, his mouth hanging open as she ran off.

"Here. I'm over here."

Marcie's voice raised itself over the crowd gathered near

the front of the alleyway. Ricki headed in that direction, pushing through bodies until she spotted Marcie. The older woman ran toward her and latched on to Ricki's arm.

"I don't know what happened. It just sort of shot up out of nowhere." She wiped a grimy hand across her forehead, leaving a dark streak behind. "Dan's working the water line." She pointed to a scraggly row of people manning a few garden hoses and passing along buckets of water. "We were right in front. I was about to open the door so we could go in and have a slice of pie after the bingo game at the VFW, when a giant flame just shot straight up from behind the diner. I thought maybe it was coming from the alley, but Dan checked while I called 9-1-1. He said it looked like the whole kitchen was on fire."

"Kitchen," Ricki repeated, feeling a little dazed. How could the damn kitchen catch on fire? She'd had all the wiring updated before she'd opened the place a little over a year ago. She could hear the sirens in the distance, growing louder with each second, but their screams barely registered as the enormity of this disaster sank in. Her place was burning. By morning it could be nothing more than a pile of ash.

"I don't know where Anchorman is," Marcie fretted. "Everyone else from that bar he hangs out at is here. He wasn't going to work that late, so he should have been at the bar by now. I sent Sam to check."

With her attention immediately diverted to the more ominous problem, Ricki slapped both her hands on top of Marcie's shoulders. "Late? Anchorman was working late?"

Underneath her hands she could feel Marcie tremble. "He said he was going to work on the schedules, but only for an hour or so. I left about eight thirty, so he shouldn't be in there." She turned her head to look at the building, the orange glow from the flames reflecting off the gathering moisture in her eyes. "He can't be in there."

The sound of sirens grew into a high-pitched wave of

noise as the fire truck raced down the main street, followed closely by Clay's SUV, its blue light bar flashing across the roof of the vehicle. Both police chief and firemen came to a screeching halt right where Trip had said they would. As men jumped off the truck and Clay stepped out of his vehicle, Ricki made a straight line for the front door of the diner. She removed an old key ring from her coat pocket and inserted the largest key into the oversized lock. The head of the volunteer firemen, as well as Clay, sprinted toward her.

"Hey. You can't go in there." Dave, the longtime chief of the volunteer fire department, pushed his large helmet farther back on his head.

"It's my place, Dave," Ricki said, twisting the key with her good hand and then reaching for the doorknob. "I need to get in there. Someone might still be inside."

Clay came up beside her and immediately locked an arm around her shoulders. "Who, Ricki?" His sharp gaze scanned the crowd. "Where's Marcie and Anchorman?"

She pushed against his arm and almost brought a sharp heel down on his instep before she caught herself. "Anchorman is missing."

"Well, shit." Dave put two fingers to his mouth and let out a shrill whistle. "Hey. Two of you, bring some masks over here. We need to do a building search." As more men came running toward them, Clay physically jockeyed Ricki back several steps. "Let them take a look. They have the right equipment and training."

Ricki resisted for another second before giving in. Clay was right. The firemen would do the search a lot faster and more efficiently than she could. They waited together on the sidewalk, with Ricki straining to see anything beyond the front windows except the flickering reflection of fire. Ten minutes later Dave emerged. He removed his face mask. His blond hair was dark from a mixture of soot and smoke.

"Didn't find anyone." He paused and stamped his feet.

"Couldn't get a great look into the kitchen, but I don't think he's in there. I would have seen him on the floor." His gaze met Ricki's stare. "The whole back is going to be a complete loss, but we'll try to save the front for you."

Numb, Ricki nodded her thanks. The volunteer chief looked as if he wanted to say something more, but after a brief hesitation, he headed over to join the other men gathered near the back alley.

Clay's hand tightened around her shoulder. "I need to get started on some crowd control. Are you going to be all right if I leave you here for a few minutes?" He stepped in front of her so he could look into her face. "I mean, you aren't going to do something stupid like sneak inside, are you?"

Ricki shook her head. "No. You go." She didn't watch him walk away, her gaze centered on the brand-new awning over the front door of her diner, lightly fluttering in the breeze as if everything were perfectly normal. Watching it, her mind went weirdly blank.

"He's not there."

Ricki slowly turned around to face Sam, her relief cook and Marcie's brother. His chest was heaving and he was pointing up the street as Marcie came up behind him, wringing her hands. "I checked the bar, and his place next door. His car is there, but he isn't. He didn't answer the door and there weren't any lights on."

"Crap." Ricki looked at her diner and then back up the street where Anchorman lived. He'd rented a place next to his favorite bar, insisting it was environmentally friendly since he didn't have to even turn on his car in order to get a drink.

At the time she'd thought it had been a typical Anchorman move, but now she was grateful they didn't have to go chasing all over the Bay looking for him. The only places Anchorman went at night were his duplex, the diner, the VFW, or the bar. He would have taken his car to go to the VFW, and if he wasn't trapped somewhere in the diner, which she refused to believe, that left his place and the bar. She glanced at her watch and frowned. "It's going on one. It could be he made it to the bottom of a Jack Daniel's bottle and is passed out inside his place for the night."

Sam's chin jutted out, and his normally vague blue gaze took on a fierce look. "No matter how much he drinks, Anchorman doesn't pass out."

Ricki blew out a breath and then chewed on her lower lip. Sam was right. She'd seen the ex-sniper drink enough to put two men under the table and still stay on his feet. And if he were still on his feet, there was no way he wouldn't have noticed the commotion going on and come around to take a look, no matter how much alcohol was flowing through his system.

"He's not in there, is he?" Marcie's voice trembled as she pointed at the front door of the diner.

"Dave and his guys took a good look, and they said no." Ricki carefully scanned the buildings across the street. "He didn't just disappear into thin air. We need to take a better look." She stood in front of Marcie and Sam, her hands on her hips, ignoring the chaos swirling around them as she considered the options. Whenever she moved, she could feel the shape of her gun against the small of her back, reminding her who should be taking the risks here. Which meant it would be better if she took the street between here and Anchorman's place, and had Marcie and Sam go wake up the landlord who lived in the other half of the rental. They needed to get inside and make sure Anchorman wasn't in there, just in case he'd decided not to answer Marcie's knock on his door. Which was something Anchorman might do. *If it weren't for all the noise going on outside,* she acknowledged silently. Still, it had to be checked out.

"Anchorman's landlord lives in the other half of that duplex. I want you both to go back there and get the guy out of bed." She looked at Marcie. "Sweet-talk him, bribe him, make threats, just do whatever it takes to get you into Anchorman's place."

"What are you going to be doing?" Marcie asked.

She took in the growing crowd around them. "Checking around. Like you said, most of the bar emptied out and came to gawk, so someone might know where he is. If I see the landlord hanging out here, I'll send him your way."

She shooed them away, waiting until the pair had moved through the shifting crowd before following slowly behind. Once they were a good half a block up the street, she started to move past the storefronts. She stopped at the entrance to the first dark alley, separating two brick buildings. Angling her body away from the crowd, she kept to the shadows as she stepped just inside the alley and drew her gun. It was awkward holding it in her left hand, but she slowly adjusted the weight, getting used to the feel. It still felt foreign, but it would do.

She took out the small penlight that was always tucked into her jacket pocket and put it between her teeth. Its beam only penetrated a few feet into the darkness, but it was better than nothing.

Moving carefully, Ricki walked around a large dumpster pushed against the wall near the entrance, checking the other side before continuing to make her way through the twenty feet between the opening out to the street and the back wall. She shone her small light into all the empty corners, stirring up nothing except a couple of spiders. Lowering her gun, she walked back toward the entrance, slipping her weapon into one of her jacket pockets and the penlight into the other before emerging from the dark and continuing on down the sidewalk.

Ricki passed several more buildings before approaching another alleyway. It looked pretty much like the first one, and even though it was longer, it was just as narrow, with a dumpster near the front blocking half the width. She turned her head slowly, shining the penlight back and forth, when a pair of boots appeared. They were lying on the other side of the dumpster and were clearly attached to someone's feet. Ricki froze, pointing the light past them so it would penetrate the dark as much as it could. She kept moving forward until the small beam bounced off the back wall and revealed nothing else in the alley except stray bits of trash that had escaped the dumpster. Ricki quickly retraced the short distance back to the boots and the man they belonged to.

Anchorman was lying facedown, his arms and hands splayed out to the side. She dropped to one knee and laid a hand against his back, holding her own breath until she felt the rise and fall of his chest. He was alive, but his breathing was too shallow. She ran the penlight down his body and across the pavement next to him. No blood. At least not that she could see. Pulling out her phone, she called Clay, but there was no answer. She wasn't surprised that he couldn't hear the thing with all the commotion going on, but that left her to find help herself.

"Hang in there, Anchorman. I'll be right back." She jumped to her feet, shoved her gun into her belt, and ran to the opening, startling a group of men who were walking three abreast down the sidewalk toward the diner. She didn't recognize any of them, but that didn't stop her from reaching out and grabbing the upper arm of the guy closest to her, digging her fingers in when he yelped and tried to back away.

"Shut up," she commanded. "I'm a special agent, and there's an injured man in the alley. I need you to get Chief Thomas. He's working the fire down the block." She stuck her face into his and glared. "Have you got that? Chief Thomas. Tell him Agent James has found their man and he's badly injured. Tell him I'm calling for help."

"Okay, lady." The man stopped struggling and sent a half-pleading, half-panicked look to one of his companions. "Can't you take care of this?"

The dark-haired man stepped forward and stared Ricki

right in the eye. "I'm a police officer out of Olympia. Do you have some ID?"

Not wanting to waste any time arguing, she dropped the first man's arm and pulled out her badge. The officer gave it a quick look and then turned around and gave his friend a shove. "Go get that police chief, and make it quick."

Both his buddies took off at a dead run while he pulled out his cell phone. "I'll call 9-1-1. Maybe there's an ambulance down at that fire."

She didn't bother to tell him that Brewer didn't have an ambulance. Just TK with his station wagon. She gave him the doctor's personal cell number, told him to call it and explain the situation, then without any other explanation turned back toward the alley. "If you'll stay here and keep watch for the chief, I'm going to stay with the victim," she called out over her shoulder.

Not waiting for an answer, Ricki ran back to Anchorman. She turned on the penlight and set it on the edge of the dumpster, pointing the beam toward her so Clay would be sure to see her. She knelt beside Anchorman and turned one of his wrists over, holding two fingers against the pulse point. It was thready and weak, and at one point her own heart rate spiked when she couldn't feel it at all. She closed her eyes, held her own breath, and concentrated, finally picking up a faint beat against her fingertips.

"Come on, Anchorman," she half whispered, half prayed. "Stay with me."

Chapter 35

The hospital's lobby boasted four chairs, one side table, and a folding table against one wall, on top of which was a single-cup coffee machine, some paper cups, and a bowl of coffee pods with a small sign asking that you place a quarter in a plastic cup next to the machine. Ricki had stuffed a dollar into the cup and had been drinking coffee on that credit, but the third cup she'd poured was still sitting on the table next to her chair, growing cold. She leaned back, resting her head against the wall, and closed her eyes.

With the help of the young officer from Olympia, she and Clay had managed to get Anchorman into Clay's SUV and to the hospital, where TK was waiting for them. He and Nancy Pritchard, his longtime nurse with a constantly good-natured disposition that made her a perfect match for the testy doctor, had whisked Anchorman into one of the two emergency bays and then banished everyone to the lobby.

Clay had reluctantly returned to the fire, promising to tell Marcie and Sam about Anchorman as soon as he spotted them, leaving Ricki alone to fight a paralyzing fear. All during the ride to the hospital, her cook hadn't moved or made a sound. His face had been pale and his breathing sporadic. She hadn't seen any external wound, and she'd checked, which meant it could be that he'd been brought down by a natural cause, like a stroke or a heart attack. But that didn't explain what he was doing in the alley, and her gut wasn't buying it anyway. Which left the obvious. A drug overdose. But Anchorman taking drugs boggled the mind. Her gut shied away from that, too, as her thoughts continued to churn over possibilities at lightning speed.

"Mom?"

Her eyes snapped open and she sat up as Eddie squatted down in front of her. "Are you okay?"

She reached over and cupped a hand against the side of his face, needing the contact, feeling it settle her feet more firmly on the ground. "What are you doing here, bud?"

"We heard about the diner, and when we went over to check it out, we ran into Chief Thomas. He said we should come here and keep you company." A tear slipped out of the corner of his eye and he impatiently swiped it away. "He wouldn't tell us why. I thought you were hurt, but the chief said you weren't, and you'd tell us what's going on."

"Us?" Ricki looked up when the lobby door swung open, letting in a whoosh of cool night air. Bear stood aside and held the door to let a petite blond sweep past him.

Eddie turned his head and followed her line of sight. "That's Cathi," he said. Looking back at his mom, he rolled his eyes. "Cathi with an *i*. She's, uh, Dad's new friend."

Despite the sick feeling in her stomach from worry over her cook, Ricki's mouth twitched upward. "His new friend, huh? Does she happen to work at Mountain Outfitters?"

Behind the lenses of his glasses, Eddie's eyes blinked in surprise. "Yeah. Do you know her?"

"Hmm." Ricki let the noncommittal sound stand. Right at the moment, she didn't care a fig about Cathi with an *i*. She captured Eddie's hand and pulled, waiting until he was standing up before pointing to the chair next to him as Bear walked up with the blond at his side. "Sit down and I'll fill you in." Her glance included Bear, who stopped and looked toward the empty hall with the swinging doors leading into the emergency room. When he looked back, his gaze was filled with worry as he crossed his arms over his chest and waited silently.

"It's Anchorman. He's in a bad way. I found him unconscious in an alley."

"Someone jumped Anchorman?" Eddie's expression was as incredulous as the tone in his voice. He turned wide eyes up to his dad. "Could someone actually do that?"

"No." Bear's answer was short and direct.

The blond put a hand on his arm and gave him a sweet smile. "Now, babe. Anyone can be attacked these days. The world has gotten so out of control." She switched her gaze and smile to Ricki. "Hi! I'm Cathi. And you must be the park ranger agent?"

"Investigative agent," Eddie cut in. "My mom chases really bad guys. Killers even." He shifted in his chair, centering his attention on his mom as he pointedly ignored Cathi. "Is that what you were doing? Chasing someone who was after Anchorman?"

Thinking she'd have a talk with her son later about his manners, as soon as she was done appreciating how quickly he'd jumped to her defense, Ricki barely managed to shake her head before Cathi piped up again. Her voice still held on to a sweet note, but now carried an underlying bite to it.

"Oh my." She made a slow scan of the lobby. "Did you catch the guy?"

Ricki raised an eyebrow at Bear. She didn't have the time or inclination to exchange words with his new companion, and knew she'd gotten that message across when her ex subtly shifted his body away from Cathi. He didn't look over when the blond frowned at him, but kept his attention on Ricki. "What happened?"

"I don't know." Ricki laid a soothing hand on top of Eddie's when he reached over and grasped her forearm. "When he was a no-show at the fire and Sam couldn't find him at the usual places, we went looking."

Bear's gaze narrowed. "We? Then you didn't go out alone to search for him?"

Ignoring the question, Ricki squeezed Eddie's hand. "He was in an alley. Clay and I brought him here. TK and Nancy are back there with him." She smiled at her son. "He's going to be all right. We just have to wait."

The words were no sooner out of her mouth when TK pushed open the doors at the far end of the hall. He took several quick strides, his hawk-eyed gaze going over the small group in the lobby and settling on Eddie. Abruptly stopping in his tracks, he pointed at Ricki and gestured for her to come to him.

Ricki took in a sharp breath. *Oh God, oh God.* She exchanged a quick, meaningful glance with Bear, before gently extricating her arm from Eddie's grip and standing up. As Bear moved to stand next to their son, Ricki quickly made her way to TK, stopping close enough that their voices wouldn't carry down the hallway.

"Tell me quick," she said, already bracing to hear the worst.

"He's still with us."

TK's quick assurance brought on a wave of relief so intense she felt light-headed. Since TK was the only solid thing around, she closed her eyes and clapped a firm hand on the doctor's shoulder to keep her knees from buckling. When she managed to take another breath, she slowly opened her eyes to find TK watching her intently.

"Are you feeling better now? Standing firm in those boots of yours?" he asked. "Because there's work to be done here. And fast."

Ricki kept her gaze on his as she locked her knees and her spine in place. "What needs to be done?"

"I've got about one minute to get this all in, so pay attention," TK commanded. "Someone put a drug in Anchorman. I can see the needle mark in his arm plain as day. And judging by the bruising already showing up at the injection site, whoever did it wasn't too good at it. Which in my mind is the second reason he didn't do this to himself."

She nodded, following his reasoning without needing any more explanation. Anchorman always mastered whatever he chose to do. He wouldn't have left a bruise. And the first reason didn't need to be said. The decorated sniper would never have taken a drug in the first place. Hell, the man didn't even take aspirin for a headache. She knew that for a fact.

"That minute is ticking away," TK said. "My patient has to be watched like a hawk. I can't take the time to arrange an airlift, but he's got to have one."

Ricki didn't hesitate to reach for her phone. "I'll take care of it." She did a quick calculation in her head. There was a place near Dosewallips Road that could be used as a landing pad, but that was to the south of Brewer. The hospital was on the outskirts of Edington, which meant there was a closer option. "The parking lot of police headquarters? Bear can go over to clear it out."

"You do that. And tell that helicopter to get here quick."

She punched in the number for her uncle. Cy and Captain Davis of the Tacoma PD were close friends. He'd pick up Cy's call and get those arrangements made faster than anyone else she could contact. It only took her thirty seconds to get hold of her uncle, explain the situation, and have him off and running. She hung up the phone and rejoined her family in the lobby just as Marcie and Sam came running through the outside doors.

The waitress flew at Ricki, wrapping her arms around her boss's lean frame. "Clay told us. How is he?" She reared back and searched Ricki's face. "You're not crying so he can't be dead. I would see it on your face if the news was that bad."

"He's not dead," she said quietly, then repeated a little louder for everyone to hear. "He's not dead. But he needs an airlift." She caught Bear's wide-eyed stare. "You to go over to police headquarters and make sure there aren't any cars in the lot."

He frowned. "Geez, Ricki. It's after two in the morning. There isn't going to be anyone in the lot."

"Go and make sure," Ricki stated, her voice flat and her tone hard. "We don't need any last-minute surprises for that helicopter." She pointed at Cathi. "And take her with you. She can help."

Bear looked from his ex-wife to the woman who was plastered to his side and then back again. "Look, Ricki. I can . . ."

Was he kidding? She wasn't about to get into a relationship discussion while Anchorman was lying on a hospital gurney, fighting for his life. "Get going. Time is everything here. Cy is making the arrangements right now for that chopper." When he glanced at Eddie she growled out, "I'll be sure he gets home. You go. Go now."

Without another word Bear whirled around and grabbed Cathi's hand, forcing a squeak of alarm from the blond. He ignored it as he sprinted across the lobby, dragging her behind him. He'd no sooner disappeared into the night beyond the doors when Clay walked through them. He glanced back at the swinging doors as he strode into the lobby.

"Where's he off to?"

Ricki quickly told him what was going on as he listened intently.

"Okay. I'll check with Captain Davis on the airlift, see if I can get an ETA."

She nodded. "TK will want to monitor on the way to the parking lot. Can we use your SUV as transport?"

Sam held out his hand. "If you give me the keys, Chief, I'll put the back seat down and get everything ready inside."

Clay tossed him the keys. "Thanks. The back seat is still down, but I threw some stuff back there that needs to be cleared out."

"What can I do?" Marcie asked. "I need something to do."

Ricki glanced over at her son. "Take Eddie back to the cabin and stay with him until I can get there." When her son opened his mouth in protest, she walked over and knelt in front of him. "We're going to be racing out of here with Anchorman as soon as that helicopter is close. Corby needs some company and we'll all need some food when we're done. Think you can handle that?" She worked up a grin, trying for as much normal as she could. "And maybe you could do me a favor and call and deal with your dad? He won't be happy about you jumping ship to come home a day early."

Eddie shoved his glasses up his nose, then quickly nodded. "I can do that."

Marcie walked over and put an arm around Eddie's shoulders. "We'll head out as soon as you get Anchorman on his way to that helicopter." She smiled at Eddie's upturned face. "That sound good to you?"

It was another fifteen minutes before Ricki's phone rang, with Captain Davis on the other end. Once she'd identified herself, the chief didn't bother with a greeting. "The airlift is on its way, and it's just under twenty minutes out."

"Thanks," Ricki said. "We'll be there. And, Chief? I owe you."

"No, you don't. Now get going." The connection broke off, so Ricki tucked her phone in her pocket. "Twenty minutes," she called out to Clay then sprinted down the hallway.

It was half an hour later that Ricki, Clay, and TK stood in the parking lot of the headquarters shared by the local police and park rangers, and watched the Life Flight lift into the air with Anchorman on board.

"They know what's what," TK said gruffly. "The university's hospital is a good one. They'll take care of him." He turned to his nurse, who'd followed behind the SUV in TK's station wagon, and handed her the white handkerchief in his hand. "Here. Take care of this, would you?" He exchanged it for the brown paper bag she was holding out for him. He thrust the bag at Ricki.

"Those are Anchorman's belongings. Everything he came in with. I know you'll see that he gets them back." He stepped away and cleared his throat. "I don't want him showing up on my doorstep and accusing me of being a thief."

Knowing the doctor didn't mean a word of that, Ricki clutched the bag to her chest before looking back up at the sky, watching the lights of the helicopter fade off into the distance. Clay stood beside her, not saying anything, but he didn't have to. Now that they'd done all they could for Anchorman, she could feel the same anger building in him that was filling her. She finally lowered her gaze and turned around to face TK.

"I'm going to find out who did this."

The doctor held her gaze for a long moment before giving a curt nod. "We're all counting on it."

Chapter 36

Sheer exhaustion had forced Ricki into sleep just as night was giving way to the sun's march over the horizon, but two hours later she sat up from her temporary bed on the couch and looked around with bleary eyes. It took her a moment to remember why she'd crashed downstairs as she stared blindly over at the coffeepot. Marcie was in her bed. That was right. Marcie had brought Eddie home last night and stayed with her son while she'd been making arrangements for Anchorman.

Her eyes blinked wide and immediately she reached for her phone. She quickly searched for the number of the University Medical Center, then waited impatiently to be connected. A polite voice answered and then transferred her to what she said was the correct floor. Ricki's heart dropped when the phone was answered with a brisk "Intensive Care Unit."

Identifying herself, Ricki went through the "Are you family?" routine and—since she had to reluctantly admit that, technically at least, she was not—ended up being told exactly nothing on Anchorman's condition. She even tried pulling the law enforcement card and was met with the same polite refusal. She applauded the privacy laws, but right at that moment she could have dropped them into the nearest toilet.

Sighing, she hung up and tapped out another number, but she only reached TK's answering service, which apparently, he still used despite the fact he was retired. When the woman on the other end asked if it was an emergency, Ricki wrestled with her conscience before finally letting reason win out over emotion and said no. She made a quick glance at her watch. TK would have made it to his bed about the same time she'd hit the couch, which was all of two hours ago. He would still be sound asleep, and he needed to be.

She also needed to stay on his better side since it looked like he was the only source of information she'd have on Anchorman's condition. She was sure that the polite person in the ICU wouldn't decline to tell the doctor what Ricki wanted to know.

She just hoped TK wouldn't retreat into one of his pissier moods and refuse to pass the information along to her. Remembering the interactions between the doctor and Clay, she made a mental note to be sure she was the one doing the asking. And to tell that to the Bay's chief of police the first chance she got.

Despite the fact that Clay didn't get to bed any sooner than the rest of them, she picked up her phone again, intent on calling him. He could sleep later. They needed to get to work. He could sleep later. And the fact was, right now she needed the connection.

Just then her stomach let out a growl loud enough that Corby, who had been asleep in his favorite place under the window, lifted his head and stared at her. The big dog must have taken the sound as a signal that breakfast was to be served, because he got to his feet, did a slow stretch, and then leisurely walked over to his empty food bowl by the kitchen counter.

In spite of the potent mixture of fear and anger roiling

through her system on a constant boil, Ricki's mood lifted. Trust a dog to know that no matter what was going on, a body still needed to see to the basics. Like food.

"Yeah. Okay. Hang on a minute." Tucking the phone into the back pocket of the jeans she'd slept in, Ricki padded her way in stockinged feet to the large bag of dog food tucked into the corner of the kitchen, bending down to swoop up Corby's bowl along the way. She quickly measured out the cup and a half of food he got for his morning meal, then added a few dry treats from the small container on the counter before delivering it back to Corby. He wasted no time attacking the bowl, shoving his nose deep into the food and crunching loud enough to fill the room with noise. Giving him a pat on his large head, Ricki straightened up, intending to make a quick raid of the refrigerator. What she really needed was coffee. Desperately at this point. But there was no way her stomach would tolerate the half-sludge, half-water mixture that was how coffee always came out when she brewed it.

Her gaze fell on the paper bag TK had given her the night before. Anchorman's belongings. A suspicion that had taken hold in a corner of her mind had her forgetting about coffee or food. She stepped around her dog and reached for the paper bag. Dumping the contents onto the counter, she paused when Marcie's voice, thick with sleep, called out.

"What are you doing?" The older woman was wearing an old football jersey of Bear's that Eddie kept hanging in his closet. It hung down to the middle of her thighs, and the high school mascot on the front was only partially concealed by Ricki's bathrobe. The terry-cloth belt was knotted around Marcie's waist, and the sides reached halfway across each breast with the hemline dragging along the floor.

She looked both commanding and ridiculous, standing in her bare feet with her hands on her hips. "You need more sleep." Then she sighed and crossed over to the kitchen as she answered her own command. "But I know you won't bother with that. Did you eat your dinner last night? We left it for you in the fridge."

Since she hadn't even opened the refrigerator before falling facedown on the couch the night before, Ricki shook her head. "No, sorry. And you need more sleep too. You should go back to bed."

"Not happening." Marcie tugged on the refrigerator door and bent at the waist, pulling out a small platter of food. She marched over and set it firmly down, just beyond the arc of clothes, change, and other paraphernalia that was scattered across the countertop. She removed the wrap plastered over the top of the food, then stepped back with an expectant look in her gaze.

Ricki eyed the oversized plate. "How many people were you expecting to come back here last night?"

"I was hoping for two." Marcie glanced over at the couch. "But I can see that didn't happen. Besides, your son said you'd eat more if you had a variety to pick from, and since he went to the trouble to cut up those vegetables and made those little sandwiches for you, you need to eat some of it. You don't want to hurt his feelings." She turned back around. "And if you do that, I'll make a pot of coffee, otherwise you'll have to drink your own tar, or go without."

Ricki had thought she could put off munching on a veggie before eight in the morning since it was unlikely her teenage son would roll out of bed anytime soon, but Marcie's promise of a decent cup of coffee had her reaching out and popping a piece of cauliflower into her mouth. She picked up a sandwich, took a bite, and then chewed thoughtfully as she watched Marcie fill the coffeepot with water.

Despite the unusual fare for that hour of the morning, Ricki's stomach welcomed the food. The jitters that went hand in hand with hunger dissipated like fog penetrated by sunlight, letting the nervous energy that had jolted her awake finally settle down. She took another bite of lunch meat, lettuce, and bread, and chewed and swallowed before putting the sandwich down. "I need to ask you a favor."

From her position at the stove, Marcie waved a hand back and forth. "Shoot."

"Can you stay here and keep Eddie company for the next few days?" Ricki pushed a long lock of stray hair away from her face, tucking it behind one ear. "These are my days, and I'd like him to be home where he has his garage and can work on his bot. Stuff he can do that will keep him distracted from what happened last night. He'll need that, but I'll be in and out, and I don't want to leave him alone." She paused. "And I have an even bigger ask. It would be great if Anson and Nate could come and work on the bot with him."

Ricki's nose wrinkled when Marcie slowly turned her head and looked back over her shoulder. She knew it wasn't just a big ask to ride herd over three teenage boys—it was a gigantic one. Especially since it would include a grocery run because there was no way she had enough food around to feed that many growing boys, who came with appetites that were constantly starving.

Marcie's mouth curved into a smile with more than a hint of smugness in it. "I've been a mom most of my life, honey. So I know the drill." She reached over and started to pull down coffee mugs. "We have you covered."

"We?" Ricki's eyebrows shot up. "Who's 'we'?" She frowned when Marcie started to hum as she kept taking coffee mugs out of the cupboard. "Expecting someone?"

She had her answer when Corby lifted his head away from the bowl he'd been thoroughly licking and trotted over to the front door. A second later she heard the sound of tires crunching on gravel. From her place at the counter, she didn't have the right angle on the front window to see who was coming. But since Corby was on alert, but not barking, he clearly recognized the noise as friendly.

There was the slam of a car door, followed by the sound

of heavy footsteps and then a quick rap against wood before the front door swung open. Her uncle Cy stepped over the threshold, then kicked the door closed with one foot since his arms were loaded down with bags of groceries.

He winked at Ricki before looking over at Marcie. "Got everything on the list, and added a little extra that I think the boys and I would enjoy."

"I assume that's some kind of code for 'nothing healthy'." Marcie walked past an astonished Ricki, whose feet had become stuck to the floor, and took one of the bags from Cy. "You'll have to bring them over here since Ricki has confiscated most of the space on the island." She walked over to the much shorter counter next to the stove. Marcie set the bag down and started to poke through it, raising her voice without lifting her head. "And she needs to eat more before she gets a cup of coffee."

Since it was useless to argue with a crazy person in full mom mode, Ricki grabbed a carrot, took a bite, and then pointed it at her uncle. "What are you doing here?"

"I already told her we've worked it all out," Marcie said.

Cy nodded his agreement as he set the rest of the bags down on the floor next to Marcie, then turned and faced his niece. He stuck his thumbs under his belt and smiled. "Marcie and I are going to take turns staying with Eddie."

Marcie waved a hand at Cy. "He's going to keep an eye on the boys, because we already figured out working on that robot would be the best thing for all of them. And I'm going to do the cooking."

Her uncle cocked his head to the side. "It's a small town, Ricki. What happened last night will affect everyone, especially after word gets out that Anchorman was hurt."

"Which I'm sure is already making the rounds." Marcie's muffled voice floated out from the inside of the grocery bag she was digging through. "Eddie spent time madly texting on his phone in between cutting up vegetables."

Cy rolled his eyes, but his voice was low and calm. "Exactly. I have a duffel out in the truck, so I'll be bunking on the couch for a few nights." He gave her a bland stare. "Or as long as necessary. I've already put in for the time off."

Ricki was floored, not really surprised by their joint offer of help, but overwhelmed with gratitude that it was given without any hesitation. There was nothing like family, friends, and the closeness of a small town. Still, there was someone else who had a say in where her son spent his time. "Bear might have an opinion on all of this."

"Opinions are good," Cy said, then shrugged. "I'll take it into consideration if he expresses any."

Ricki smiled. Her uncle sounded exactly like her father used to. "He's Eddie's father, Uncle Cy."

Her uncle's shoulders lifted in another shrug. "And I'm his uncle. I want to take Eddie out to visit his grandmother. I know you haven't had much time in the last few weeks, and Eddie needs to do that." His mouth formed into a wry smile. "I'm sure Bear won't want to intrude and come along."

Not in this lifetime, Ricki thought. Her ex had a lot of good qualities, as well as some she wasn't so fond of. His refusal to deal with anyone's disability, like her mom's Alzheimer's, fell into the latter category. So no, he wouldn't make the trip to spend time in a nursing home with his former mother-in-law. Even though he'd known her most of his life.

Corby, who had settled back into his spot under the window, jumped up and once again trotted over to the front door. Thinking her little home was becoming more like a parade ground, Ricki didn't have to wait long before the door popped open again as Corby stood in front of it, his tail wagging frantically.

Clay gave the dog a good scratch under the chin before looking up and smiling at Ricki. "Morning. I hear there's a decent cup of coffee to be had here."

"You heard right." Marcie walked over with two large

steaming mugs in her hands. She set one down in front of Ricki and held the other one out to Clay. "Here, you take this, and I'll get two more for Cy and myself while you and Ricki talk shop."

The chief took the mug with a grateful smile and walked around Ricki to perch on one of the tall stools. "How much sleep did you get?"

"A couple of hours. How about you?" Ricki picked up the mug and took a long sip before sighing in appreciation.

"The same," Clay replied. He gestured toward Anchorman's belongings splayed across the counter. "Find anything interesting?"

Ricki set her mug down and studied the jumbled pile. "Haven't been through it yet."

"Looking for something in particular?" Clay asked, his gaze narrowing when she pushed aside a T-shirt and then a pair of jeans and reached for the thick leather belt.

She straightened the long strip of black leather out along the counter, smoothing it down with the fingertips of her good hand. She stopped at the D-link clamp attached to the belt, her gut tightening at the sight of smooth, curved metal, a firm clasp, and nothing else.

Clay's back went rigid as he stepped off the stool, staring at the empty D-link. "Is that where Anchorman kept his keys?" When Ricki silently nodded, the look in his eyes went fierce. "All of them?"

"Yeah," she said, her hand still resting on the belt. "All of them." She raised her gaze to his face. "To his place, his car, and the diner." She kept her eyes on his as she called out to the woman standing next to Cy, sipping a cup of coffee.

"Marcie, did you and Sam get into Anchorman's place last night?"

"Yes. We did," Marcie said. "Why?"

"Was anything missing?"

"Not that I could tell," Marcie said slowly.

"How about his car? Was it still parked out front?"

"Yes." Marcie's grip tightened on her cup, turning her knuckles white. "Why? What's the matter?"

"So, his place and car weren't touched." Clay's voice was flat and his expression hard.

Ricki's gaze narrowed in silent agreement with what she saw on his face. "No. But the diner caught on fire."

Chapter 37

"Roger said he'd be here around ten." Clay glanced at his watch. "That's in half an hour or so."

Ricki nodded. "Okay. Good." She took out her key to the Sunny Side Up's front door just in case she needed to use it, but she doubted the firemen had locked it behind them. If anyone was interested in looting, they wouldn't have had any trouble getting in. The back of the diner was completely open, with the door and long rectangular window missing. The part of the wooden wall that was still standing was completely charred, and everything beyond it in the kitchen reduced to either ash or useless hunks of metal. Since Clay had already warned her that nothing in the kitchen, or the front counter just beyond it, could be saved, she was already bracing herself for the emotional hit as she reached for the doorknob.

"Maybe we should wait until Roger gets here," Clay suggested.

"No need," Ricki said over her shoulder. While she was grateful that Clay had reached out to an arson investigator he'd met in Olympia to come and verify what she and the chief already suspected, this was still her place, and she needed to see the damage for herself.

Pushing the door open, she paused for a moment as the smell of smoke and burnt wood rolled out into the open air. Pulling out the bandanna she'd stuffed into the back pocket of her jeans before she'd left home, Ricky tied it around her face, covering her nose and mouth. It wouldn't keep all the smell out, but enough to let her walk around and make her own damage assessment.

When she stepped out of the sunlight into the dark interior, she entered a surreal world of long black fingers of charred wood, crawling along the ceiling and walls, leading to a cavern of darkness that was eerily backlit by the indirect light coming in through parts of the missing kitchen wall.

"Walk carefully," Clay warned. "I don't know how safe any of this is." He looked up. "The ceiling might come down at any moment."

Ricki barely acknowledged his concern with a quick jerk of her head as she slowly moved forward, the moisture gathering in her eyes not entirely due to the small whiffs of lingering smoke in the air. She'd worked so hard, put so much time and effort into the little diner to make a go of it.

Now the back counter was twisted and charred, the coffee machine and the line of pots were all smashed into pieces on the floor. And beyond it, the kitchen had simply disintegrated into an unrecognizable mass of charred wood and seared metal. Even in the main dining room, the pictures on the walls were covered in soot, and she was wading through a sea of black ash.

A strange, muffled groan came from over their heads as the roof made its wounds known. Clay immediately grabbed Ricki's arm and tugged backwards. "Okay. That's it. We're out of here."

She resisted for a moment. Leaving seemed like giving up, but when a second, louder groan followed the first, common sense won out, and she retreated through the front door until she was again standing on the sidewalk. She pulled off her bandanna and slowly stuffed it back into the rear pocket of her jeans, then stood straight as a board, her hands clenched at her sides.

"What do you think?" Clay asked, his voice close to her ear.

Taking a deep breath, and then another, Ricki finally shrugged. "That I should take my gun out and put the Sunny Side Up out of its misery." She heard him sigh, felt the weight of it.

"Yeah."

They stood together for long minutes, not saying anything. Ricki closed her eyes and could see her son, sitting at the counter, eating a burger and reading a book, while Marcie flew around the room, pouring out coffee and taking orders. Sam was there too, standing at the front hostess station, and then at the grill while Anchorman watched his every move with a critical eye.

Anchorman. Ricki fought back the tears. He needed her now. As far as she knew, his diner family was all he had, and she couldn't let him down.

The sound of a truck with a large engine rolled down the street. Ricki turned around just as a big red Ford pulled up next to the curb. A short man with a bald head and long mustache hopped out of the driver's side. Slamming the door, he trotted around the extended hood of the truck, his dark-brown eyes homing in on Clay.

"Chief Thomas." The man stuck his clipboard inside the helmet he was holding in his left hand and held out his right. "How are you?"

"I've been better. Thanks for coming on such short notice." Clay shook the man's hand then turned to Ricki. "Special Agent James, this is Roger Jones."

Ricki took the man's outstretched hand and gave it a quick shake. The top of his head barely reached her nose, and he was thin enough that a good gust of wind might topple him over. "Thanks for coming," she said, adding a miserly smile. "I appreciate it, Mr. Jones."

"Everyone calls me Jonesy, and it's nice to meet the famous Special Agent Ricki James." The genuine enthusiasm in the investigator's voice had Ricki sending a puzzled sideways glance at Clay, who shook his head in return.

"I was at Tacoma before taking the job in Olympia, and Captain Davis has raved about your investigating abilities for years," Roger went on, a grin splitting his face. "I can see for myself that he left out what a great package all those brains came in." He instantly shuffled his feet as color flashed across his cheeks. "I didn't mean any kind of insult by that. Really, I didn't. I hardly even noticed how attractive . . ." He trailed off again, looking desperately over at Clay.

The chief frowned back at him. "Just stop there, Jonesy. That hole you're standing in is too deep to climb out of."

"I would appreciate your honest assessment of what happened here," Ricki said, all business as she pointed at the diner. "And as fast as you can give it to us."

"Right. Right." Jonesy spun around, grabbed the clipboard with one hand and slapped his helmet on his head with the other. He finished off by pulling a flashlight out of the oversized pocket of his jacket before walking straight through the open front door. The beam of light bounced against the ceiling for less than five seconds before the investigator called out, "Don't come in here. It's too dangerous. I'll get my ladder out once I'm finished in here and take a look at the roof."

Clay yelled back, "No problem," before cupping a large hand around Ricki's shoulder. "I'm going to go see if Adele can spare a couple of cups of coffee." Adele Harris owned the candle shop two doors down and always had a pot of coffee brewing in her back room. Ricki knew that because she'd sat and enjoyed a cup with the friendly shopkeeper on many occasions when she'd first started renovating the Sunny Side Up from a New Age crystal and incense shop into a cozy diner. Mostly on her own, with some help from Bear and her uncle, because back then, she'd had the time to do it. *BTB, before the badge,* she thought, using a phrase Eddie had invented.

She waited on the sidewalk, politely acknowledging the greetings from an occasional passerby, ignoring the looks of pity from the ones who were locals. Vaguely surprised that she didn't see Pete or any of his cronies, she decided they'd probably gathered down by the small marina to discuss and mourn the loss in their own way.

At least that was what she preferred to think.

Clay returned with two steaming Styrofoam cups of coffee. He handed one to Ricki, then took up a space on the sidewalk right next to her. When her phone rang, she absently pulled it out and held it up to her ear. "Special Agent James."

"Well, you're certainly in full official mode this morning." TK's voice sounded even fuller of gravel than usual, a loud testament to his lack of sleep the night before. "I'm returning your call, which you made close to the crack of dawn this morning, according to my answering service. And I don't care what kind of special this-or-that title you have, it's a damn good thing you didn't claim it was an emergency and drag me out of my bed. I didn't see much of it last night as it is."

Ricki waited patiently through the expected scolding. Somehow the familiarity of TK being, well, TK settled her own nerves a bit. Once he'd wound down, she made the expected apology and then went silent.

"Not much change," TK finally said. "I know this is hard to believe, but that's a good thing. Fentanyl is a dangerous drug at best, and when given in too great a quantity, will kill you. Given that Anchorman is still breathing, it could have been a lot worse."

"When he pulls out of this," Ricki said firmly, refusing to use the word "if", "what kind of care will he need? I can get started arranging it."

There was the slightest hesitation before TK answered. "Anchorman's family should be in on that discussion, Ricki."

"I already have Dan researching that," Ricki said. The last call she'd made before crashing on the couch had been a voice mail to her assistant partner, telling him to do a search for any relative of one Norman Beal, aka Anchorman.

"He works for you, doesn't he?" TK barked out. "Don't you know who he put down as his emergency contact on those forms everyone has to fill out? You did ask for that information, didn't you?"

She didn't bother to point out that those forms had all been stored in a desk drawer in her closet-sized office located in the kitchen, so they were now a pile of ashes just like everything else in there. "I asked, and he filled it out."

"So, let's talk to that person," TK demanded.

"You *are* talking to that person," Ricki shot back. The whole thing with Anchorman, the diner, and everything that had gone on before making frustration bleed into her voice. "He put me down because he said if anything happened to him, he wanted to be sure I knew why he couldn't make it into work."

"Stubborn idiot," TK muttered.

"Always," Ricki confirmed. "Now, about those arrangements?"

The old doctor sighed. "Let's not get ahead of ourselves here. We need to wait and see what's going on once Anchorman wakes up. Then we can do an assessment and go from there."

Ricki's heart sank. If she were a betting woman, she'd put her money on TK not being optimistic about Anchorman's chances of coming out of this whole again. "Okay," she said quietly. "I'm going to be heading over there with Marcie and Sam later this afternoon. I know they have a family rule about information and visitors and all that, but could you let the hospital staff know that right now, we're all the family Anchorman has?"

"I can do that." TK's gruff voice dropped into a softer tone. "You watch your back, Special Agent Ricki James."

"I can do that," Ricki said, echoing his words before disconnecting. She relayed the conversation to Clay, who listened quietly.

"He'll pull through," he finally told her. "He'll never let a drug beat him. Pride alone will have him waking up, ready to beat the shit out of whoever did this to him."

She hoped so, really hoped so, as she watched Jonesy exit the building, his face and clothes smeared with soot. The investigator did his trademark trot over to them, his mouth pursed so tight that his lips all but disappeared.

"Amateur," he announced without any preamble. "The accelerant's path couldn't be clearer if he'd drawn a chalk mark around it." Jonesy pulled off his helmet and ran a hand over his bald head, leaving a wide streak of black in its wake. "Whoever did this just walked in and splashed it everywhere. If he threw a match in there, he's lucky he got out without being seriously burned himself."

"Just walked in?" Ricki asked. "What makes you think the guy just walked in?"

Jonesy didn't look up from busily writing notes on his clipboard, using the old-fashioned method of pen and paper. "I took a quick look at the back door. It's lying on the ground out back. The wood is in bad shape, but the metal lock is old and pretty sturdy. I didn't see any signs of it being scratched or beat up like someone had tried to force the lock open. Of course, they might have gone the simple route and just used a crowbar on the door or one of the windows." He paused in scribbling away and looked up at her. "You would be better at determining that than I am. It's more your area than mine, but it looks to me like he just walked in. Maybe the back door was unlocked?"

"Was it?" Ricki asked mildly. "Unlocked, I mean. Did you notice if the deadbolt was still engaged?"

At first Jonesy looked chagrined, and then he sent Ricki an admiring look. "Sometimes it's easy to overlook the simple stuff when it isn't in your wheelhouse, isn't it? No. That deadbolt wasn't engaged, as you put it. It was flush against the door." He frowned for a moment. "Of course, the firefighters might have done that, I guess."

When Anchorman's keys were missing? Not a chance in hell, but she smiled and politely agreed. "They could have."

Jonesy's brown eyes turned a shade darker, and his mustache drooped even more. "I hear someone was hurt in the fire."

"Not in the fire, but related to it," Clay said.

"Bad business, that is," Jonesy declared. "I'm going to poke around a bit more so I can give you a solid report. And I still want to take a look at that roof."

Ricki thanked him for his time and work. When she told him where to send a bill, since he wasn't on any official clock, he shook his head. "This one's on the house, Agent James. Your chief here is a friend, and I'm glad to be able to help."

While Clay hung back to have a few more words with the investigator, Ricki headed for his SUV and climbed into the passenger side. She buckled her seat belt and stared straight out the front window. It was bad business all right, and whoever had hurt Anchorman, caused Amanda Cannady's death, and then burned down her diner was going to find out just how bad it was.

Chapter 38

CLAY SHUT the door to his office and walked over to take his seat behind the desk. He leaned back and smiled at Ricki, starting out by asking her the question that had already become routine between them. "Okay. What do you think?"

Since she knew he'd ask, she'd already lined up her thoughts during the drive to headquarters. "It's centered around Graham. He's the key."

"Why?" Clay asked bluntly. "We still don't know what Hardy was looking for up at that lighthouse."

Curious, Ricki's brow furrowed. "What makes you think he was interested in something up there?"

"He was a big guy," Clay pointed out. "Too big for someone to haul up there, which means he made that climb up the hill under his own power."

She relaxed against the back of her chair and considered it. As a theory, it ran parallel to her own. "There's something about that lighthouse or the land it sits on." She let her thoughts flow out from the tight ball she'd been keeping them in. She reached for her phone and pulled up a document with a number on it. Punching it in, she waited through four rings before someone picked up on the other end. Identifying herself, she asked to speak to Barbara Metler. Several minutes later, she hung up, a satisfied smile on her lips.

"Well?" Clay prompted.

"Mrs. Metler said that the last conversation she had with her brother was the first time he ever brought up the land." Ricki stared out the window and considered it from the different angles. "So, we have two different versions of the same thing." She tapped a finger against one knee. "The friend, Christopher, says Graham had no interest in the land. He was even going to recommend to the foundation that it dump the holding. Then the sister says that Graham asked her to tell the foundation that he wanted to buy the land. Something she doesn't tell Hardy for decades, finally mentioning it just a few weeks ago."

"When he makes another trip to Washington, looks into it, and ends up getting shot, just like Graham, by the same gun, and dumped in the same place," Clay said, taking up the narrative. "But you don't think the land is at the center of all of this?"

Ricki shook her head. "Not directly. I think the *reason* Graham wanted the land is why he got killed, and trying to follow the breadcrumbs to find Graham, Hardy stumbled onto something that got him killed."

Clay leaned back in his office chair, laced his fingers behind his head, and looked up at the ceiling. "Great. Then all we have to do is figure out why someone has a fifty-year-old hard-on about a remote piece of land."

"And a very old Smith & Wesson .22 caliber gun," Ricki added. She sighed. "Piece of cake."

"At least we know what makes this asshole nervous." Clay glanced over at her. "The bodies being found and then you asking around about the land was followed by your tire being shot out. And when you interviewed Christopher Toner, the Sunny Side Up became an arson target."

"I'd argue that I was just a target of opportunity and the

real agenda was to shoot you, but then it wasn't your diner that was set on fire." Ricki frowned as she turned it over in her mind. "But then again, both of those things were a guaranteed way to keep us both occupied doing something besides investigating two murders."

Clay dropped his hands to the desktop and folded them there. "Then Maxwell Hardy would be at the center of this case, and we both agree it's Graham. Which is your case, not mine."

"Whether its fifty years ago or yesterday, why do men kill?" Ricki pointed at Clay before answering her own question. "Money, a woman, or revenge. Take your choice. "

There was a knock on the door before Dan stuck his head around the edge. "Okay if I join you?"

Clay beckoned him forward while Ricki's foot pushed on the empty chair next to her.

"I was about to call you," she said. "Did you get that information on Anchorman?"

Dan strode across the room and sat in the offered chair. He began to sift through the pile of notes he was carrying. "I did, but there's nothing to report."

Ricki sighed. She had a feeling that Anchorman might have gone off the grid. If he had, and knowing her cook, finding his family wouldn't be easy. "So you hit a dead end?"

The ranger lifted his head, looking insulted. "I found his family. There's just nothing to report about them. His closest living relative is a first cousin in Denver. I called, just to verify, and the man said he had a cousin named Norman Beal, but last he heard, Norman was in the military." Dan shook his head. "He didn't have any idea how to get hold of his cousin, and didn't throw out one question about why I was asking. Aside from that, there's only a smattering of second cousins and a couple more distant relations, mostly by marriage and not a bloodline."

Even though Dan's findings were no surprise, Ricki felt a

pang of sympathy for Anchorman, but it didn't last long. It wasn't as if the ex-sniper was all alone in this world. He had his Sunny Side Up family, and a couple of close military buddies he could call on at any time. But she'd have to get hold of TK and let him know that she was indeed Anchorman's next of kin. There simply weren't any others. She'd need the doctor to clear that with the hospital.

Putting that on the back burner for the time being, she nodded at Dan. "Anything on the land?"

Dan shuffled a few of his notes around. "Nothing to report there either. No mineral rights or any other claims filed. It was bought by the Lillian M. Young Foundation after World War II, and the title was transferred to Barbara Graham Metler forty-three years ago. After that, there's nothing, except the annual property tax bill."

"Then we have a couple of other things we need you to look into," Ricki said. "We were just talking about women and money."

Clay's lips curved into a rueful smile. "*You* were talking about women and money. I was just sitting, waiting to hear what you had to say."

Dan lowered his notes and stared at Ricki. "So what money trail, and what woman?"

She grinned. "You already answered the question about the money." She switched her gaze to Clay. "Remember what his sister said? Graham stated he wanted to hang around a little longer to take care of a personal debt."

"And the land would be a way to do that," Clay mused. "So maybe he was a gambler as well as a womanizer."

"Which brings us to the second reason, and what we need you to research," Ricki said to Dan. She had set an envelope on top of Clay's desk, and now she handed it to Dan. "You remember the photo of the ranger group? I want you to look into a couple of backgrounds." She pointed at the envelope he was holding. "I've taped a note with a couple of names on it to the photo." She waited while he pulled the picture out and removed the note, putting the photo into Clay's outstretched hand.

"Aren't these the names of other rangers?" Dan asked. "What am I looking for?"

"Spouses. Or former spouses, who once lived in the Bay, or maybe even grew up here." When Dan still looked puzzled, she filled in the blank. "We're looking for the other guy, or the OG in Benjamin Graham speak. The jealous boyfriend, or maybe even a husband. And since Graham was spending time in the Bay, she must have lived here back then."

"If this person even exists," Dan countered. "But okay. I'll take a look."

Clay tossed the picture back across the desk. "Not the sharpest image I've ever seen."

"Yeah," Dan agreed, replacing the photo in the envelope. "It's a lousy picture."

AN HOUR LATER, Ricki and Marcie were on their way up the shoreline, headed for the Edmonds–Kingston ferry that would take them across Puget Sound, just north of Seattle. With any luck, they would make it to the University Medical Center in two hours, just in time to get Marcie settled into her hotel room and then look in on Anchorman. Sam wouldn't be arriving until the early evening, but he was also going to stay over with his sister, so Ricki could get back home that night to her son. It was a juggling act, but with everyone helping out, they'd get it done.

Ricki smiled when Marcie reached into the large paper sack she'd placed between them on the front seat of the truck and pulled out a rice cake. "I know you like to keep all your meals in balance, and I'm sure you had pizza for lunch."

"How do you know that?"

Marcie took in a deep sniff of air. "I can still smell it. You must have eaten it in the truck."

"I did," Ricki laughed, "but I've suspended the balance rule for the time being. Sometimes you just need the carbs to keep going."

Her waitress patted a solid hip and sighed. "I'm the one who should adopt that balance rule. You're as thin as a snake." Marcie looked her boss over with a critical eye. "Thin but not skinny, and filled out in all the right places. Sometimes it just isn't fair."

"I'm also twenty years younger and have had five fewer kids than you have," Ricki pointed out.

"That's true. And you still have time to catch up on the kids." While Ricki laughed, Marcie reached into the bag again and pulled out a baggie filled with sugar cookies. "Here. You eat those. I'll have the rice cake." Ricki set the baggie on the dashboard and counted off to ten as the waitress bit into the rice cake and then made a face. "Ugh. Balance is overrated." She reached across and grabbed the baggie. "Give me one of those sugar cookies. You shouldn't eat all these anyway. It's bad for you."

"Uh-huh." Ricki grinned. "Why the sudden concern with an extra pound or two? Does it have anything to do with your new social life?"

Marcie's face beamed with a broad smile. "It's more than a pound or two, and yes, it does." She took a bite of cookie and slowly chewed as she eyed Ricki. "I like him. I really do. And I think he likes me."

"He'd be a fool not to."

The older woman let out the breath she'd been holding. "Do you think so? I mean, are you all right with the two of us, well, you know, being together?"

"I'm all right with the two of you dating," Ricki said firmly. "What you do on those dates is none of my business." She turned her head and gave Marcie a quick warning look before returning her gaze to the road. "And don't you make it my business either."

Marcie's laughter bounced around the cab of the truck and was infectious enough it had Ricki grinning too. "That's a good sound. I haven't heard it in a while."

"Not much to laugh about, I guess." Marcie set the baggie of cookies back on the dashboard where Ricki could easily reach it. "I appreciate you making this trip, but I wish it didn't take you away from everything." She paused. "I like Eddie, and the bot building session yesterday went pretty well. No one got hurt, nothing blew up, and your uncle seemed to enjoy himself."

"Uncle Cy always likes spending time with the guys," Ricki said. "No matter what age they are. He likes talking sports, which Eddie keeps up with, fortunately. It's the one thing my uncle misses about Bear."

"Cy has been a bachelor too long," Marcie pronounced. "We should work on finding him a wife."

Ricki made a choking sound partway between a laugh and a snort of disbelief. Now wouldn't her uncle just love her to get involved in something like that? "*You* find him a wife. Leave me out of it."

"I might just do that." She chuckled at Ricki's look of horror. "What are he and Eddie going to be doing tomorrow while I'm in Seattle and you're out doing your investigating?"

"Uncle Cy is going to take him over to Tacoma to see Mom." Ricki wished she could go with them, but just couldn't stretch her time to include a visit to Anchorman and to the Golden West Home where her mother was slowly slipping away to Alzheimer's. "I hope Mom recognizes Eddie. She seems to remember him more often than she does me."

Marcie reached over and gently patted Ricki's shoulder. "Don't take it personally, honey. Your mom wouldn't be this way if she had any choice in the matter."

"I know." Ricki forced her one fully functional hand that

was gripping the steering wheel way too tightly to relax. She wanted to talk about something else. Anything else, actually, so she dove into the subject that was guaranteed to set Marcie off and running on a one-woman talkathon. "How are your kids doing?"

The rest of the trip passed in a pleasant retelling of her six grown children's latest antics and traumas. Marcie was still talking when Ricki exited the interstate and headed down 5th Avenue. A few minutes later they pulled into the parking lot of the hotel on Roosevelt Way. "I'll go with you and pay for the hotel."

"You will not." Marcie grabbed her small overnight bag that was sitting on the floor, right next to her feet, and opened the truck door. "You stay put. I only need to check in, grab a couple of keys, then dump my stuff in the room. I'll be back in ten minutes. You pull up a map of that hospital and figure out where they're keeping Anchorman."

Ricki started to argue but found herself talking to thin air when Marcie hopped out and shut the heavy passenger side door behind her. Wondering how she'd come to be surrounded by so many stubborn, bossy people, she took out her phone and pulled up a map of the medical center. Marcie was as good as her word, and ten minutes later they were on their way. Since Ricki had the map on her phone, they had no trouble finding the right elevator. Having been in this same unit when her dad had passed away, Ricki knew the drill. She turned off her phone and had a paper with all her personal information on it so the nursing staff would have the contact number for what they called the family spokesperson. She hoped she wouldn't have to argue with them about it, since she wasn't a legal relation, but she was prepared to do just that if that was what it took to make sure Anchorman knew his family was there.

They had just made it to the nursing desk when TK exited a room directly across from it. Relieved to see the old curmudgeon, Ricki told the desk nurse she'd be back in a moment and turned to face TK.

"Glad to see you made it." He peered around her and looked at the nurse. "These are the people I was telling you about." He pointed at Ricki. "She's Special Agent James, and she'll be the spokesperson."

Ricki smiled her gratitude as she handed over the paper with her contact information on it. "Thanks, TK. I wasn't expecting to see you here."

"Heard you'd be headed out this way today, so thought I'd come and run a little interference and also look in on my patient." He narrowed his gaze on Ricki. "I thought it would be safe to leave town today. Since you wouldn't be around, I figured no one would be run over, shot, or filled with narcotics against their will."

Next to Ricki, Marcie snickered. "You might want to rush home since she isn't staying long, TK. She needs to get back to town."

"Of course she does," TK snapped back. "Someone has to catch the person putting people into hospitals." His voice dropped several levels and he peered at Ricki over the rim of his glasses. "Or the morgue. I haven't forgotten about that young girl, Ricki James, and I doubt if you have either."

Ricki's blue eyes went fierce as she stared back at him. "No. I haven't."

Chapter 39

Ricki tiptoed down the stairs to the kitchen below. Her hair was still damp from the shower, but she felt better after a thorough dousing under hot water. Getting her hair washed for the first time in two days—and being able to put on clean jeans and a fresh shirt after spending another night on the couch sleeping in the same clothes she'd worn all day—had been close to heaven. Not wanting to wake her uncle up by going into her bedroom to retrieve her hairdryer, she settled for a towel around her shoulders while her long fall of dark hair drip-dried into a slightly wavy column that hung down her back.

Corby had roused himself when she'd stood up and stretched her back before heading to the only bathroom in the cabin. Now he was sitting patiently by his food bowl, an expectant look in his liquid-brown eyes. Having no doubt he'd been waiting there since she'd first stirred that morning, she rewarded his patience by filling his bowl and giving him a pat on the head as he did his usual nosedive into his food.

The clock still hadn't reached 7 a.m., so it was too early to make her first call of the day. Flipping her wet hair back over her shoulder, Ricki padded her way to the stove and contemplated the coffeepot. She was feeling a little desperate for a morning hit of caffeine, but wasn't sure her empty stomach could take the result of her particular lack of skill in brewing it up.

"Don't touch that." Her uncle stood at the bottom of the stairs, clad only in a T-shirt, boxers, and a pair of tube socks. He looked like the caricature of a grouchy old man, which was also exactly how he sounded. "I'm pretty sure you making coffee has to be a crime somewhere."

She rolled her eyes to the ceiling. "Like wandering around the house in your socks and underwear?"

"For the time being, this is a bachelor pad, so it's appropriate attire. You're the lone female, so you're the one intruding." He walked over to the stove and tried to push her to one side. "There's a message on that machine in the corner." He looked over at her and frowned. "Why do you still have one of those things, anyway?"

The old-fashioned answering machine sat on the far corner of her desk, its red light blinking. Surprised she hadn't noticed it last night, Ricki abandoned her place by the stove and crossed the room in five long strides. "Mom's never liked cell phones, so I always keep a landline for her to call." Not that it mattered. She doubted her mom even knew how to dial a phone number anymore. But she wasn't ready to let go of the longtime habit of catering to one of Miriam McCormick's little quirks. "How did your visit go?"

Cy carried the coffeepot over to the kitchen sink and turned on the cold-water tap. "Good. She thought Eddie was your dad, but he didn't seem to mind it." There was an uncomfortable pause before he added quietly, "She didn't ask about anyone else. I'm sorry, Richelle. But she was happy to see Eddie and didn't bring up any more visits from dead people, so overall, it went pretty well."

Another small piece of Ricki's heart broke off and floated away, but when it came to coping with what was happening to her mom, she was used to it. Nodding, she reached over and pressed the play button on the answering machine, waiting through its first announcement that she had one new message.

"Hi, Ricki James. It's Wanda." Wanda's voice flowed out into the room. "I've had this landline number of yours for a while, and thought I'd leave a message on it instead of your cell phone. I know you're visiting Anchorman today, and Eddie is off to see his grandma, so didn't want to disturb any of you."

From behind her, Cy muttered, "How the hell did she know that?"

"Anyway," Wanda continued. "On the way home from visiting my friend, I swung by mama's place in that retirement home she's living in. I'd have brought her back to talk to you herself, but her arthritis has gotten so bad, she doesn't leave her apartment these days. But she's still as sharp as ever and had some things to say about those questions of yours. I'm home now, so you come by anytime and I'll fill you in on all the details. Just give me a call. I'll have the coffee waiting."

Ricki saved the message then walked over to the narrow table in front of the couch and picked up her phone.

"You aren't calling her now, are you?" her uncle asked. "It's not even seven thirty in the morning yet." He set the full pot on the stove and started measuring out coffee grounds from a can he'd taken out of the cupboard. "And since when is being the town gossip passed down from one generation to the next?"

"When you're a natural at it, I guess," Ricki said, quickly switching to a greeting when Wanda answered her phone. They agreed on an eight o'clock meetup at Wanda's place, which gave Ricki just enough time to finish drying her hair and get on her way. As she dashed from the room, her uncle's voice chased after her.

"I suppose this means you'll be skipping breakfast again?"

~

TRUE TO HER WORD, Wanda was sitting in a porch chair when Ricki pulled up exactly thirty-five minutes later. As she climbed the steps, she caught the heavenly smell of coffee, and smiled her thanks when Wanda picked up one of her unique, oversized ceramic mugs and handed it to her. Taking a seat, Ricki held up the mug in a silent toast before taking a long, slow sip.

"Thanks." Ricki set the mug on the table and twisted her upper body so she was facing Wanda. "What do you have?"

"I don't know for sure," Wanda said, but her eyes were bright with anticipation. "But I'm thinking you'll be able to make something of it. But first, I'd like to know how Anchorman is doing."

Tit for tat, Ricki thought as she nodded. "Fair enough. According to TK and the nurses on the intensive care unit, he's holding his own, which we're all taking as an encouraging sign."

"What can we do?"

The simplicity of the offer of help had the small knot that had taken up permanent residence in Ricki's stomach loosening a little. "I don't know yet, but when I do, I promise to give you a call."

"I'm holding you to that, Richelle James." Wanda settled more deeply in her chair. "Now, for Special Agent James, here's what I know. Mama doesn't remember any ranger going missing, and that goes back to her own childhood. She did say there was one hanging about town back then. He drove a fancy sports car."

Ricki's pulse sped up, but she kept a blank expression and held on to her patience, knowing she'd get more if she let Wanda tell the story in her own way. "The only local girl who Mama could think he might have been seeing is Glory

Rancup. Mama said she had the morals of an alley cat, and didn't care who she jumped into the sack with."

"Glory Rancup," Ricki repeated. She took out her phone and tapped the name into the notes function.

Wanda kept talking, even as she strained to see what Ricki was writing down. "According to Mama, Glory was the only girl in town who'd play fast and loose with some park ranger. Especially one with a fancy sports car. She ended up leaving town with some salesman who was passing through, and she's never been back. The only other girl to leave town around then was Jenny. But she came back a year later, after her husband was killed."

"That would be Ray Dunning's sister?" Ricki asked.

"Well, sister-in-law, I suspect. Jenny's maiden name was Norris. Since she married a Dunning, and Ray's last name is Dunning, then it follows that Jenny's husband was Ray's brother. Mama said it was a big surprise to everyone that Jenny just upped and ran off with a young sailor."

When Wanda paused, Ricki carefully asked, "Why was it a surprise?"

The older woman flashed a self-satisfied smile. "Now, I asked that very same thing. It was because Jenny had a boyfriend at the time. Mama said she and Jimmy Anders had been together practically since she was in diapers and he was a toddler. Her running off like that broke his heart."

"What happened when she came home after being away for a year?"

"Mama said she just moved back in with her parents and everything went back to the way it was, except, of course, that Jenny had a baby with her. After that, she couldn't say for sure. Mama stopped keeping track of things in the Bay right when Jenny's parents died in some kind of car accident. It happened about six months after their daughter and grandchild came home. Mama said that Jenny didn't last long after that, and they're all buried together in the family plot next to the church on Tucker Street. Do you know the one I'm talking about?"

"I know it." Ricki's gaze went blank as she silently fitted puzzle pieces together. She didn't like the way it was coming out, but that was how the picture was forming in her mind.

"I guess it wasn't long before John Dunning's uncle showed up to take over his upbringing. Mama wasn't sure about how all that happened, and let me tell you, that's a rare thing when my mama doesn't know all the details about something that went on in town back then. But anyway, it was a very unselfish thing for Ray to do, and we're all very proud to have a man like that living in the Bay." Wanda ended on a triumphant note, as though Ray's sacrifices for his infant nephew had been her idea.

"If Jenny didn't have any other relatives around to take care of her baby, who buried her?"

"Why, I imagine Ray did. That's just something a good man would do, I think."

When Ricki didn't say a word, Wanda gave her a considering look. "So, what do you make of it all, Special Agent James?"

"I'm not sure yet. But there's something I need you to do."

Wanda's eyebrows drew together. "What's that?"

"I need you to keep everything you've told me to yourself until I can check some things out." Ricki's stare hardened. "I need your promise on that, Wanda."

The older woman smoothed down the tight cloth of her yoga pants, then set her chair into a rocking motion. "I can do that, since I know once you figure out whatever it is you're trying to solve, I'll be the first one you call." She set her heel down hard on the ground and stopped the rocking motion. "Won't it?"

Deciding it was a bargain she could live with, Ricki held out a hand. "We have a deal."

~

THE SMALL CHURCH still shone under a fresh coat of white paint. The steeple rose above the tree line, and the bells housed there still announced a service every Sunday morning. Behind the back lawn, where social events where held throughout the summer months, was an old wrought-iron fence, separating the area used by the living from the space cleared out for the dead.

Generations of families who'd lived out their lives in the Bay were buried on the other side of that fence. Whenever more space was needed, a few more trees were sacrificed to make way for new grave sites.

Ricki's truck was the only one parked in the lot when she pushed open the back gate and started down the narrow gravel path that wound through the cemetery. It took her a good forty minutes of searching, but she finally came across the large plot for the Norris family. She read each marker, marching down through a hundred years before she came to a double headstone with the names Fred and Ethyl Norris, loving parents to Jenny. Ricki stared at it for several moments before moving on to the grave with an angel on top of the white-granite marker. Fresh flowers lay in front of it, right below the inscription: *Jennifer Anne Norris. Loving daughter and mother, taken from us far too soon.* Ricki stood there, her hands clasped in front of her, her head bowed as she thought of a young girl who had chosen a road she wasn't prepared for. She finally reached out a hand and laid it gently on top of the gravestone. "There never was a Dunning, was there Jenny? I'm sorry for what Benjamin Graham did to you, but I have to make all this right. I have a promise to keep. I hope you understand."

Chapter 40

"I CAN'T GO into it, but I'll have him over there as soon as I can arrange it. Thanks." Ricki pressed the button to end the call, cutting off any more questions from the other end. She knew she would pay for that later, but right now she didn't have the time to deal with any more on her plate than she already had. At least that was the last call she had to make in order to get the wheels into motion.

Stepping out of the truck, she headed for the front door of her cabin, stopping to wave at Eddie and Corby, who appeared in the open door of the bot-building garage. When they both vanished back inside, she pushed open the front door, startling her uncle, who was sitting at the kitchen counter, a cup of coffee in front of him and the morning paper in his hands.

She ignored him as she headed straight for her desk and scooped up a stack of blank index cards along with a black marker. She carried them over to the counter and started writing notes on them as her uncle snapped the paper shut and slowly set it aside.

"What are you doing?"

"Lining up the case." She leaned to the side and gave him

the once-over before straightening up and returning to her notes. "Glad to see you've got pants on. I need you to do something for me."

"Such as?" Cy asked, tilting his head as he read one of the cards she'd set to the side. "Who is Jennifer Norris?"

"I need you to take Eddie over to Bear's place and stay there with him," Ricki said, as if she hadn't heard his question. "I've already talked to Bear, and he's expecting you, Eddie, and Corby."

Cy slid off the stool and stood with his legs braced apart and his arms crossed over his chest. "Even the dog? You know something. What is it?"

Ricki paused in her writing and looked over at him. "I *think* I know something," she corrected. "And we might need to move fast."

"Who's we? And what are you going to be doing?" Cy demanded, not budging an inch.

"Clay and Dan are on their way over, and we'll make our plans from there."

"So is Hamilton."

Ricki blinked, then groaned. Her boss was on his way? What was he doing out of his Seattle office? She slowly turned to face her uncle, grimacing when he simply nodded. "Why is he here?"

Cy shrugged and stepped over to grab his jacket, which was draped over the back of the couch. "You'll have to ask him yourself. I've been told to run Eddie and the dog over to Bear's place." He thrust his arms through the jacket's sleeves and zipped the garment up before reaching for the knob, yanking open the front door, and closing it behind him with enough force to make his mood known.

Ricki sighed. Something else she'd have to deal with after this was all over and the dust had settled down. She watched out the window as Cy herded a reluctant Eddie, along with a willing Corby, into his truck and backed down the driveway far enough that he could make a three-point turn and point his vehicle in the right direction. A moment later they were gone in a swirl of dust and gravel.

Picking up the marker, Ricki went back to making notes on blank cards and then setting each aside. Once she'd filled in what she needed to, she started arranging them outward, starting with the card with Benjamin Graham's name on it. She was still fiddling with the order when there was a sharp knock on the door and Clay stepped inside.

"Okay. I'm officially out taking care of a minor noise complaint. Care to tell me why all the sneaking around?"

"Couldn't be helped," Ricki said. "Did you happen to see Dan leave?"

"Yeah. He was headed for the back door as I was going out the front. What's going on, Ricki?"

She sat on the closest tall stool and pointed at the cards laid out across the surface of the center island. "I know who killed Maxwell Hardy, and Benjamin Graham. Dan's bringing the final pieces of the puzzle with him." She picked up her uncle's unfinished cup of coffee and took a sip, wrinkling her nose at the lukewarm, overly sweet brew. Setting the cup back down, she watched as Clay studied the index cards.

"What am I looking at?"

"I'll go over it, but first, I need to know something. When Dan showed you that blown-up photograph yesterday, was that the first time you'd seen it?"

"Yeah. Why?"

"Do you keep aspirin in your office desk?"

Clay rolled his eyes. "Again, yeah. A big bottle of it. What cop doesn't?"

Ricki had thought so. She wished it had dawned on her a lot sooner, but it hadn't seemed like any more than passing conversation at the time.

Clay scowled. "Look. Explain the cards first, and then we'll get into the picture and aspirin thing." He pointed at the center card. "I know who Graham is, and Hardy, and Metler. You've got the lighthouse down here, but who are Jenny Norris and Jimmy Anders?"

"If I'm right, Jenny was the woman Graham was coming to see in Brewer, and Jimmy Anders was her longtime boyfriend." Ricki lifted her gaze to meet his. "But it isn't who they were then, Clay. It's who they are now. And I don't think any of us are going to like that answer much."

He looked down at the last two cards. "And you think Ray and his nephew are a part of that answer?" He took a step back and shook his head. "You've got to be kidding."

Wanting to ease some of the shock, Ricki kept her voice low and matter-of-fact. "Jenny Norris is John's mother." At Clay's puzzled look, she nodded. "Norris was her maiden name."

The chief went back to studying the cards. "Then since Ray and John share a name, that would also be John's father's name, so Jenny Norris would be Ray's sister-in-law."

"That's how someone wants it to look." Ricki glanced out the front window, silently wondering what was keeping Dan.

"I'm going to let that go for the moment," Clay said. He used his index finger to stab at the card in the center. "What does Graham have to do with all of this, besides chasing after Jenny Norris before breaking up with her?"

When Dan's car finally came into view, Ricki slid off her stool. "Hang on a minute. Dan's here." She strode over and opened the door, impatiently tapping one foot as she waited for the ranger to gather up a folder and an oversized book and exit the car.

He stopped in front of her and jerked his head backwards. "Your boss is right behind me."

Ricki looked past him just as Hamilton's Lexus pulled up behind Dan's SUV. "Go on inside," Ricki told her assistant partner. "I'll be there in a minute." She waited, her hands stuck in the pockets of her jeans, doing her best not to look irritated at seeing the ASAC striding up her driveway. She'd bet under that expensive coat was a perfectly tailored suit with a contrasting shirt and tie. Not exactly the kind of attire to track someone down in the backcountry, if it came to that.

"Special Agent James."

Hamilton's greeting was a bit formal, but not frigid, so she figured he wasn't too annoyed with her. "Sir. I'm surprised to see you here. Is something wrong?"

"Let's just say I get worried when I hear one of my agents had her place burned down, and it wasn't an accident. Not to mention that the guy who's her self-appointed bodyguard was also taken out and is in critical condition in a hospital."

Ricki kept her hands in her pockets and rocked back slightly on her heels. "I think I covered that in my reports."

"Barely," Hamilton said. "You were a little shy on details, so I thought I'd come check up on things myself." He peered through the door Dan had left open and nodded at Clay. "If you're having a briefing, I'd like to sit in." He paused. "That wasn't a request."

"Please. Go on in." Ricki stepped aside but didn't follow Hamilton into the cabin. Instead she waited on the porch as her uncle's truck came barreling up the driveway, coming to a quick, skidding halt within half a foot of the Lexus's back bumper.

Cy strode up the driveway, a scowl on his face and carrying a pair of boots in one hand. Before she could get a word out, he shook a finger at her. "Eddie's all settled at Bear's place, and the two of them are hunkered down playing video games. Whatever you all are up to, I'm in." When she started to shake her head, his scowl deepened. "Anchorman isn't here, Ricki. But I can shoot if it comes to that, and I'm pretty fair at tracking too. So, I'm in." He stomped past her, greeting Hamilton by holding up his hand and saying, "I've got your boots," as he crossed over the threshold.

Ricki greeted that pronouncement with a disgusted snort.

Her uncle had probably taken them out of the stock Bear kept to sell to anyone on a tour who didn't have the proper attire.

Feeling like she'd lost control of her own op, Ricki tamped down her exasperation and followed the men inside, closing the door before crossing the short distance to the kitchen. They were all gathered around the island, staring at her line of index cards. She pushed in between Clay and her uncle and picked up the marker.

"Okay, Dan. Tell us what you found out."

The ranger nodded and opened the manila folder he'd brought with him. "You asked me to track down a Jimmy Anders who grew up here in the Bay. I didn't find much. A James Raymond Anders showed up on the DMV records list with an address here in Brewer."

Clay's hands gripped the edge of the counter as he cleared his throat. "James Raymond? Did you say Jimmy Anders's middle name is Raymond?"

Dan nodded. "Is or was. I couldn't find anything on him after 1973, so he might have moved to another state, or died. I didn't have a chance to search the state's death certificates file. They also didn't scan DMV pictures back that far, so I can't produce one of those either. But I dug out all those yearbooks we confiscated from our last case and took a look through one of those. According to his birthdate, he should have graduated in 1958, and that's where I found him." Dan opened the yearbook lying underneath the folder and flipped to a page with a paper clip on top. He turned the book around so it was facing Clay. "Here he is. If he's still breathing, he'd be eighty."

Ricki leaned over and studied the black-and-white picture. It wasn't as sharp as the ones any phone could take today, but it was clear enough to show a much younger Ray Dunning smiling into the camera.

"Shit," Clay said under his breath. He rubbed a hand down one cheek as he shifted his gaze to meet Ricki's. "Jimmy

Anders. Jenny's long-term boyfriend. Which would make him the 'Other Guy,' if I'm following along here?"

"You are," Ricki said quietly. "He's changed his name, but yeah. He was Jenny's boyfriend, and according to Wanda's mama, the one the whole town expected her to marry. He was heartbroken when she ran off with a sailor no one even knew she was seeing, and then returned to town with a baby ten months later, after her new husband was killed."

"Convenient," Hamilton said. He looked over the cards. "Judging by the way you have this lined up, you're thinking Graham was the father, but how does Ray Dunning fit into all of this?" He glanced over at the chief and frowned. "I'm assuming we're talking about the older gentleman who sits at the lobby desk in our joint headquarters."

"I can't believe it," Cy stated flatly. "What are you saying here? That Ray killed Benjamin Graham fifty years ago in a jealous rage, and then his girlfriend ran off and married someone else because of it? I've known Ray for almost thirty years. He wouldn't do something like that, much less kill Hardy to keep it all a secret."

Ricki laid a hand on her uncle's arm. "He did kill Graham, but he didn't kill Hardy. The PI must have gotten too close to the truth about what had happened to Benjamin Graham, so John killed him in order to protect the man who raised him." She nodded at Dan. "What else did you find?"

As everyone's eyes turned toward the ranger, he shifted the papers in his folder. "You also asked me to look up the DMV record for John Dunning, and the corporate filing papers for MMG."

"What's MMG?" Hamilton asked.

"It stands for the Money Management Group," Ricki supplied. "John Dunning's company in Seattle."

"I didn't find any DMV record for a John Dunning, but I did find that MMG is listed with the state as a limited partnership, and the principal partner was identified as John B. Graham."

Ricki's gaze scanned the group crowded around her. "*B* as in Benjamin. Jenny might have come back to Brewer with a made-up husband and a fake name, but she named her son after his father. When she died and Ray decided to raise her child himself, he took on the name of Dunning, and time, along with faded memories, did the rest. People just started accepting Ray's story that he was John's uncle, and over time, no one remembered the truth." Wanda's voice talking about her mother echoed in Ricki's mind. "Well, anyone who's willing to talk about it."

"Why all the subterfuge?" Hamilton threw out to the room. "Why didn't Jenny just keep her own name of Norris, or call herself Graham?"

"I'd guess that she knew Jimmy pretty well, and what he might do if he ever found out that Graham got her pregnant and then deserted her," Ricki said. "And she'd need a married name to save face in the community. She was an unwed mother. Not exactly a way to keep your reputation in a small town. Especially back then."

Cy snorted and stuck his hands into the back pockets of his jeans. "That former ranger was a real prince of a guy."

"That means John Dunning knew who his father was all along," Clay said. A tic ran along his jaw and his eyes were flat. "And that Ray killed him all those years ago." He turned those cop eyes on Ricki. "Then John killed Hardy and started causing all those accidents whenever you got closer to the truth."

Ricki nodded her agreement, keeping a leash on her own growing anger. All this sorrow because of a crime committed half a century ago? Even if Hardy had been checking out the land and stumbled across Graham's skeleton, so what? That still wouldn't have told him who killed his client's brother. And if Ray had been caught, he wouldn't have been punished for long. He'd managed to live a normal life in spite of what he'd done. There was no reason for Amanda Cannady to be dead, or for Anchorman to be lying in a hospital bed.

"So where do we find Jimmy Anders and John Graham?" Hamilton asked.

"I've got Jules keeping an eye on Ray down at headquarters," Clay said. "If he tries to leave, Jules is under orders to stop him."

Hamilton nodded his approval, addressing his next question to Ricki. "What about John Graham? Do we pick him up in Seattle?"

"He's not there," Dan put in. "I called his office. He's out of town."

"He's here." Ricki was certain of it, and from the corner of her eye she saw Clay add his confirming nod. "He sees himself as Ray's protector, so he'll keep close. He's here in the Bay somewhere."

Cy's mouth pulled down at the corners. "There's a lot of ground out here. It's worse than looking for a needle in a haystack."

"Not quite." She looked at Hamilton. "Can you pull some strings and trace a ping off a cell tower?"

"I could if I had a number to go with it."

Ricki stood up and pulled a business card with a number inked on the back out of her shirt pocket. She held it out to her boss. "It just so happens that John Graham gave me his."

As Hamilton stepped outside to make his calls, Ricki went to a small closet tucked next to the even smaller kitchen pantry. It was the only part of the cabin she'd done any modifications to, enlisting the help of her uncle to reinforce the floor beneath it. It had been necessary for the extra weight of the tall, solid steel safe inside. She quickly entered the electronic code, then swung the heavy door open. Reaching inside, she removed her rifle and a box of ammunition before casting a questioning eye at the men watching her. When all three shook their heads, she glanced over at the cabin's front door.

"What about Hamilton?"

"He's armed," Cy said. "I already asked when he mentioned he might need some boots."

"And something to protect that expensive suit of his," Ricki said, shutting the safe's door, waiting for the beep that would indicate the lock had reengaged.

"He's a good agent, Ricki," her uncle insisted. "He'll hold up."

She stood and faced Cy. "I know he will. I just hadn't expected an army to chase down an eighty-year-old man and his fifty-year-old nephew."

"A gun is a gun," Clay said. "No matter whose finger is on the trigger."

The front door swung open and Hamilton strode in, holding up his phone. "Last ping was an hour ago off a cell tower north of here. The closest town is Massey."

Chapter 41

RICKI TURNED Clay's SUV onto the narrow street that served as the main thoroughfare for Massey. The small village was busy with late-morning anglers ducking into bait shops or scurrying along the sidewalk toward the dock. She maneuvered the big car through the narrow gap between the imaginary center line and the curb with cars parked all down its length, with Dan's vehicle, carrying everyone else, following close behind. Once they'd cleared the last shop, Ricki gently pressed down on the gas, gradually taking the speed up as she held out her right arm.

Clay finished unwinding the bandage and gently removed the splint before wrapping her wrist up again. He paused when Ricki made a face and drew in a sharp breath.

"It's going to have to be tight if you want it to hold up." When she nodded, he continued winding the cloth around her wrist.

"TK said it was a hairline fracture," Ricki said, her eyes glued to the winding road, slowing down as she came up to the turnoff for the dirt road leading up to the lighthouse. "It will hold."

Clay finished up by attaching the two small copper clasps to hold the end in place. "You're going to have some pain when you move those fingers."

Ricki wiggled two of them, the immediate pang moving up her arm, confirming Clay's warning. "I'll manage. I need my right hand."

"Copy that, James," Clay said. "You shouldn't be going out at all. I could leave you one of the radios, and you could monitor us from the car."

"Not a chance."

"Didn't think so," Clay muttered, a heavy dose of resignation in his voice. When his phone rang, Clay glanced at the screen. "It's Jules."

He put the phone to his ear. After a few seconds he was visibly gritting his teeth, telling Ricki without words that something was wrong.

"No. Take a drive by his house but don't stop or go in. Just check to see if his car is there, and send me a text letting me know one way or the other. A text, Jules. Have you got that?" He didn't say anything else but hung up on a heavy sigh. "Ray said he was going to the bathroom, then slipped out the back. Jules saw him drive off."

"Let him go. We'll deal with him later."

They rode along the last half mile in silence, wordlessly exiting the car when Ricki stopped just below the last curve before the small clearing that served as a parking area for the lighthouse. They waited as Dan pulled up behind them and the three men quietly joined them. Cy gave his niece's newly bandaged wrist a long look, but didn't say anything as she turned and headed up the road with Clay right behind her.

Once they reached the base of the switchback trail that climbed up to the top of the hill, Ricki stopped and held out the radio she was carrying to Dan. "You find a spot to hide here, where you can keep an eye on that." She pointed to the lone vehicle in the clearing. "Dunning grew up here, but he's been a city boy for thirty years. If he gets past us, he'll head for his car. Make sure he doesn't get away."

"I could let the air out of his tires," Dan said. "That would make it pretty tough to get down the hill."

Hamilton clapped a restraining hand on the ranger's shoulder. "Don't go near it. That's a new car he's driving, and it will have an alarm on it."

Looking chagrined, Dan nodded as Ricki continued. "Go back and move your car so it blocks the road and then take up a position near there." She gave Dan a hard look. "And not inside your vehicle. He'll spot you for sure." She turned her attention to the other three men. "We'll take the trail up. Single file. Keep low. Keep alert. He might have been warned we're coming."

Hamilton's head snapped around. "What? How?"

Ricki didn't look over at Clay as she said smoothly, "I was just informed myself. Small town, Hamilton, and we weren't exactly invisible driving through Massey. Like I said, he grew up here, and might still have some friends around to give him a warning. It was always a risk."

As Dan peeled away from the group, Ricki set off up the trail, keeping to a slight crouch as she quickly ate up the distance to the last turn. She hesitated, then signaled for the last two men to fan out to the sides as she and Clay kept going, dropping to one knee in tandem when they crested the top.

"What do you think?" Clay's voice was barely above a whisper.

Ricki squinted against the weak sunlight streaming from behind the cloud cover. "I think the door is wide open."

Clay shifted his position so he could get a better sight angle on the door and softly grunted. "A trap to lure us in, or a quick departure?"

"My vote's with a departure, but let's see." Ricki took a

small pair of binoculars out of her pocket while Clay produced a pair of his own. They both began a slow scan of the building. When Ricki lowered hers, she whispered. "I don't see any breaks in those boarded-up windows upstairs."

"And no movement downstairs," Clay responded. "I'll head to the fallen log, and you cover."

Since she was the better shot, Ricki nodded and lifted her rifle to her shoulder. She constantly moved the gun sight over the open door, to the upper deck, and then back around again as Clay broke away and made a dash for the log. There was no response from the lighthouse, and Ricki didn't see or sense any movement from the interior shadows beyond the open door.

When Clay looked back at her, she nodded, waiting until he'd raised his rifle before heading to the stone wall of the lighthouse at a dead run. Still nothing. She waited for Clay to join her, and both of them cautiously went through the door, their gazes darting around the empty space inside.

"Unless he's upstairs, he's gone," Clay said.

Ricki moved so she could look to the top of the curving stairs. "He's not up there, but we need to check."

"I'll do it while you call in the others." Clay moved toward the stairs while Ricki headed for the door.

When she waved her hand high over her head, her uncle and Hamilton stepped out from the trees and into the overgrown grass surrounding the lighthouse. Since she had no idea where Graham was, Ricki led both men inside before turning to her uncle.

"He's gone. Probably rabbited as soon as he got word, or spotted us. Maybe fifteen or twenty minutes ago."

Cy nodded. "Okay. I'll go take a look."

"I'll go with him and watch his back," Hamilton offered, following Cy out the door.

Ricki waited for Clay to make his way back down the

curving set of iron stairs. Once he'd joined her again, they walked outside then split up so they could cover the entire clearing around the lighthouse.

When Cy's fist shot into the air, Ricki and Clay both trotted over to where he was standing with Hamilton beside him, still watching the tree line. Clay took up a vigil on the other side as Ricki squatted down next to her uncle.

He pointed to the ground in front of him, where the grass was flattened. A boot print was outlined in the mud beyond it. "One nice thing about the rain in Washington. The ground is always soft." He added a nod. "Those are fresh." He rose to his feet and Ricki followed suit.

"Can you follow him?" Clay asked.

Cy's nose wrinkled with the insult. "I'm guessing he has no idea how to cover his tracks. A cub scout could follow him." His smile was grim. "Let's go."

Ricki motioned for Clay and Hamilton to fan out as she slowly walked beside her uncle, her gun raised and her eyes quartering the area through the trees as her feet tested out every step of the ground in front of her. The last thing she needed to do right now was to trip over some hidden rock or small log.

After ten minutes of moving through the trees, Cy stopped and leaned over to whisper in her ear. "You called it. He's headed back toward the cars."

Ricki lifted the radio to warn Dan, barely getting two words out before a volley of shots whizzed past them, pinging through the trees. Cy grunted and dropped like a stone, with Ricki sinking down beside him.

"Two o'clock," Hamilton called out, and Ricki swung her rifle in that direction.

"I need you over here," she answered back, listening to the heavy breathing coming from her uncle. Without glancing down, she scooted a few inches closer to him. "Where are you hit?"

"Leg," Cy panted. "Upper thigh. Bastard got lucky with a ricochet."

"How badly is it bleeding?"

"I'll check." Hamilton appeared behind her. There was a minute of Cy biting back a litany of swear words as Hamilton poked and prodded around the wound. "Not bleeding too badly, but I only see an entrance wound, no exit."

Clay took up a position beside Ricki. "If we don't move, he's going to get to the car."

"He's right," Cy said through gritted teeth. "He won't come back this way. I'll keep low and you all go get him."

There was good sense to that, but she didn't like the idea of leaving her uncle hurt and alone. But with Graham circling around to his car, the man in the group with the least field experience was the only one down there to stop him. She looked over her shoulder at Hamilton. "Stay here with Cy." She handed him the radio. "Dan's closest to the cell tower. Radio him to call for an ambulance to stand by at the bottom of the hill. We'll be back when it's all clear."

Hamilton didn't waste time arguing. He took the radio and nodded at Ricki. "Good hunting, Agent James. Don't get shot."

Her lips curved into a half-smile before she concentrated on studying the trees in front of her. Since Graham had fired from their two o'clock, she calculated the best angle to cut him off and headed in that direction.

She and Clay moved together, making swift, quiet work of getting around any obstacles in their path as they made their way back down the hill. About halfway to the spot where Dan was waiting, Ricki suddenly stopped. Ten feet to her side, Clay did the same, turning his head and raising a questioning brow. She pointed at one ear and then moved to tap her finger against her lips. They both stood motionless, listening.

She heard the faint crackle of twigs. The sound made when something or someone steps on them. It was coming through the trees, off to her left and not too far away. She motioned for Clay to circle more uphill and to the left, which would bring him up on the other side, while she kept to a parallel course, her breathing light as she listened.

Graham was close now, and making enough noise he was easy to follow. She stealthily kept pace, skirting around the random patches of sunlight and making her way from tree to tree as she caught flashes of color moving through the forest.

The dumbass didn't even wear dark clothing, she thought, even as she gauged the point she'd intercept him. There was a sudden spate of noise a good fifty yards away as a flock of grouse suddenly rose into the sky. Graham immediately swiveled around and aimed his gun in that direction, shooting off several rounds in quick succession.

Not knowing if their suspect had spotted Clay and had him in his crosshairs, Ricki took advantage of the noise, using it as cover to swiftly move up behind Graham, almost getting close enough to drop him. But somehow he sensed her presence and whirled around, aiming his gun at her chest.

Ricki looked down the center of her own rifle and deliberately smiled. The desperation in Graham's eyes told her the man was already teetering on the edge of a knife, and she wanted to push him even more off-balance. "I guess this is what they used to call a standoff in those old-time movies."

Graham wet his lips and tried to move sideways, stopping when Ricki matched him step for step. "Lower your gun. I'll let you walk off, and you let me do the same. How about that?"

"Not my first choice, Graham."

His face went red, and the hand holding the gun barrel started to shake. "Dunning. When I'm in this town, my name is Dunning. Just like my uncle. I don't recognize the pig who sired me. He took advantage of my mother, then just walked off as if she meant nothing to him. As if *I* meant nothing to him. He deserved what he got."

"And Maxwell Hardy? Did he deserve a bullet in his chest too?" Ricki watched his gun waver and a bead of sweat slowly trickle from his hairline down to his cheek. "What did Maxwell Hardy ever do to you, Graham?"

"Not me. He was asking about the land, about that dead ranger. He was making Uncle Ray nervous, so he had to be stopped."

Ricki spotted Clay slowly moving through the trees behind Graham, so she kept him talking while Clay moved into position. "And what about Amanda Cannady and Anchorman? They weren't asking any questions about anything."

"I don't know any Amanda. And it's your fault if that cook of yours dies. I wouldn't have had to come up with something to distract you if you hadn't been nosing around. Who cared about some guy killed fifty years ago? Why couldn't you just let it alone?"

Ricki's anger boiled up from the pit of her stomach. Two people. And he didn't give a second thought to either of them. "Amanda Cannady. The young woman who died in the car crash you caused."

"You caused, you mean," Graham insisted. "I wasn't driving. And I told you, you should have left everything alone, then no one would have been hurt. It couldn't be helped."

The wall she'd carefully constructed around her emotions broke down, sending a hot boiling wall of fury flooding through her system. Her eyes narrowed on her target, and she waited until his wavering gun drifted off to the right. Before he could jerk it back into place, Ricki took a quick step to the left while she dropped her barrel, putting off a shot right into his foot. He screamed in pain and his finger reflexively jerked against the trigger, sending a bullet in her direction. It screamed past her shoulder with an inch to spare as Ricki leaped over the remaining space and kicked Graham's gun well out of his reach before pivoting on one foot and bringing down her other right on top of his private parts, applying enough pressure that it forced him to go still, even as he kept whimpering with pain.

"I'm shot, I need help." He glared up at her through his tears, all color leaving his face when she deliberately set the end of her rifle right against the center of his chest.

"Couldn't be helped?" she repeated softly. "You robbed a twenty-year-old of the rest of her life, and you think it couldn't be helped?" She used more pressure to push the barrel harder against his chest. "You put someone who's like family to me into a hospital bed, fighting for his life, and you claim it couldn't be helped?" Her mouth pulled back and she bared her teeth at him. "What do you think can't be helped if you aim a weapon at a government agent?" She poked him again with the barrel of her gun. "Answer me that, Graham? What do you think happens then?"

"Ricki." Clay's quiet voice penetrated her haze. "He's down. You need to let up now."

She continued to stare at John Graham, holding his terrified gaze captive with her hardened one until her breathing began to slow.

"Ricki?"

Finally lifting her gun a couple of inches, she took a step back. "I heard you."

"Okay." Clay reached down and grabbed the back of Graham's belt, hauling him to his feet. "Up you go. Neither one of us are carrying you down that hill."

"Have you got hold of him?" Ricki asked mildly, setting her rifle down on the ground.

"Yeah," Clay said. "Just let me get some cuffs on him."

"You do that," Ricki said, before she reared back and put a fist right into Graham's whining face. Clay swore and let go, jumping back as Graham crumpled to the ground once more. This time he was out cold.

Pain shuddered its way from Ricki's wrist all the way up

her shoulder and into the back of her neck. She grinned at an exasperated Clay. She'd probably have to make another trip to the hospital, and sit through a lecture from TK, but it was definitely worth it.

Chapter 42

THE SKY WAS OVERCAST, barely allowing a soft gray light to thread its way through the trees. Ricki walked along the deserted trail with the solid rush of the river on one side and the sound of branches swaying in the wind on the other. She wasn't dawdling, but wasn't in any rush either. The forest was peaceful, going about its daily business without any concern for the worries of a two-legged visitor.

Forty minutes in, Ricki rounded a curve, but instead of continuing on the path, stepped off to the side, following the faint line of footprints in the patches of soft ground that veered off toward the river. Beyond a low set of rocks, she could barely make out the top of a head, covered in a light-blue wool cap with a burst of white from a pom-pom sprouting from its top. The lone figure was sitting on a long, flat rock, his back curved in a relaxed slump, the fingers of both hands curled around the end of a fishing pole.

"Used to be that I could hold on to this thing with one hand and eat a sandwich with the other." The raspy voice floated back to Ricki as she steadily closed the gap between herself and the edge of the water. When she stopped a few feet behind him, Ray turned his head and smiled. "Hello, Special Agent Ricki James."

Ricki didn't say anything, only watched as he slowly reeled in his line and shook his head at the empty hook.

"Fishing isn't what it used to be around here," Ray said. "But then, things have a tendency to change, don't they?"

As he set his pole aside, Ricki walked over and sat down next to him. Bending her legs and drawing her knees up to her chest, she folded her arms on top of them and waited, watching the water roll by as the silence dragged on.

Ray finally sighed, but he kept his gaze on the river. "This spot hasn't changed much. It looked exactly this way when I used to bring Jenny up here for a bit of fishing and maybe steal a kiss or two." He reached up and slid the wool cap off his head, holding it to his cheek for a moment before setting it down beside him. "Blue was her favorite color. She wore it all the time." He heaved another sigh and looked over at Ricki. "I loved her, you know. Still do, for that matter. I would have done anything to see her happy." He smiled. "Jenny wasn't my sister, but I'm sure you've already figured that out by now."

Ricki kept her gaze on the water flowing past. "There never was a husband named Dunning, was there?"

His expression took on a wistful look. "Nope. No Dunning. Her parents insisted on making up a husband to save face." A smile ghosted over his thin lips. "Most of our lives it was just Jimmy and Jenny. People always said it that way, almost like it was one word. We were supposed to be together forever."

Ricki shifted her gaze away from the river to Ray's face. He looked at peace, with none of the upset or anger she'd expected to see. "She would have been happy with you, Ray. Any woman would be," she said slowly, drawing a smile from him.

"Maybe. But she wanted that ranger. And I loved her enough to try to make that happen for her." Now a hint of the anger she'd been expecting crept into Ray's voice. "But he wanted nothing to do with her. Got her with child and then was just going to walk away like she and the baby were some kind of minor inconvenience." He barked out a short laugh that ended on a cough. "Hell's bells. To him, that's all she was. An inconvenience."

When he abruptly stopped, Ricki waited until his breathing slowed before quietly asking, "What happened, Ray? Why did you shoot him?"

"Because he deserved it," Ray said simply, then ran bony fingers through his thinning white hair. "He laughed, Ricki. When I met him outside of town that night and told him he needed to do right by her, he laughed." Ray's legs moved, his knee joints giving off slight creaks as he shifted them to a more comfortable position. "All that money, driving up in that fancy-schmancy car of his, talking to me as if I were a dim-witted servant. 'Don't be ridiculous,' he said. 'I'll make some provisions so she and her child can get by.'" Ray's chin quivered and his hands balled into fists. "Get by. That's what he said, as if barely managing to keep body and soul together was good enough for her. I don't even know why I brought along the gun. I guess I had a reason, but all I remember is that suddenly it was there in my hand and it was pointed at him. He was so sure of himself, so smug, that I don't even think he saw it." Ray's shoulders slumped over again. "He looked so surprised at first, I thought maybe I'd missed. And then I saw the blood coming out of his chest. He had on a white shirt, and it started to turn red. The blood just kept coming, and coming, and then he just fell to the ground."

Ray turned wide, haunted eyes on Ricki. "And that was it. That was all there was. He fell down and then there was silence. At first, I didn't know what to do. And then I just started doing things. I put him in the back of my truck and drove him up to that lighthouse. I knew he owned that land. He told me he was going to give it to Jenny and the baby, so I figured if I left him there, his people would eventually find him. But I hoped not too quick. Jenny would need some time to heal. So I took his uniform and drove that fancy car of his back through town and then out south. I knew someone would see me, think I was him, and tell anyone who came along asking that he'd left town, and his friends would look down that way for a while. I was buying Jenny that time she'd need. That's all. When I sent that car into the canal, I figured someone would find it eventually and keep on looking for him, and then they'd search his land and find him." He returned his gaze to the river. "At least, that's what I thought would happen. I didn't think it would take fifty years."

He reached into his pocket and withdrew an object that he held out to Ricki. It was a watch, with a heavy gold band and small diamonds encrusted around the dial. "I always meant to return this. He'd told me his grandfather had given it to him. I didn't have any problem putting that car of his into the canal, but I couldn't see leaving this behind. I guess I should have left it with him up at the lighthouse, but I always meant to return it. Maybe there was someone else in the family who should have it. Trouble was, no one ever came looking for him except another ranger. And he didn't look very long. Made me wonder if Graham had any family left until that private investigator came nosing around a few years ago."

"Maxwell Hardy. The one John killed?" Ricki asked softly.

A single tear escaped and rolled down Ray's cheek. "I told him not to do it. I told the boy it was all right if everything came out now. What can they do? Put an old man in jail? I've already been in jail for thirty years."

When Ricki raised an eyebrow, Ray nodded. "It's true. As soon as John was raised and went off to college, I started volunteering at the police department. I was there every day for ten hours, and I never missed out. Even on holidays I would sit outside in my car, or just walk around the building to stay warm." He straightened his back. "I was serving my time."

Ricki knew that Ray believed that, but it didn't change what was. He'd committed murder, and so had John Graham, no matter how justified they both thought they'd been, with Ray wanting to protect the love of his life, and John determined to protect Ray. It still made no difference, and others had suffered as well. The thought of Amanda Cannady and her parents, as well as Anchorman lying so still in a bed, flashed into her mind. No matter how much she liked Ray, and she really did, he had no right to take a life. And she had no forgiving thoughts at all for John.

With nothing else to be said, she got to her feet and held out a hand. "It's time, Ray. Chief Thomas is waiting for us. We need to go."

Epilogue

"Uh-oh, uh-oh!"

The crowd standing at the bottom of the wide, curving staircase gasped and took a collective jump backwards as the strange contraption with a sleek metal body and protruding arms teetered on the edge of the top step. Every eye was glued to the bot as it gently rocked back and forth before balancing on both arms and lowering itself down a level.

Ricki smiled when the manager of the St. Armand exhaled a huge breath. He was standing next to her, a handkerchief in his hand as he busily dabbed at the beads of sweat popping out on his forehead.

When they'd arrived an hour ago, he'd nervously explained to her that a large wedding had needed an emergency change of venue and been booked into the glittering ballroom for the next day. The grand staircase was the favorite spot for wedding party photos, and the last thing he needed was to have cracked steps or splintered wood. Given his wringing hands and apologetic tone, Ricki was sure he would have canceled this little test of the bot if Clay hadn't been standing next to her, giving the already jittery man that flat cop stare that plainly said he might arrest you at any moment.

Since the nervous man was back to wringing his hands, she gave him an encouraging smile before looking over at her son. Eddie's dark hair was flopped over his forehead as he bent over the controls for the bot, all his concentration centered on his precious machine and the instructions Nate and Anson were calling out to him. Ricki smiled. Actually, yelling out would be more accurate. But despite their agonized looks and the high pitch in their voices, it was obvious the boys were having the time of their lives. She just hoped the poor manager's heart survived it.

It took twenty more minutes to maneuver the bot down the last stretch of stairs, and when it finally made came off the bottom step and folded its arms inward before resting on the ballroom floor, a huge triumphant shout went up from the crowd, immediately followed by an enthusiastic and noisy round of applause. The boys all leaped into the air, then raced to the bot, hugging each other over the top of its squat metal body.

Ricki's heart burst with pride and tears floated in her eyes. Her father would have been so proud of his grandson. She lifted her watery gaze and looked over at Bear. He was staring back at her, a huge smile on his face. He nodded, then shot his arms up in the air in the traditional sign of a touchdown, making her laugh.

The crowd watching had grown as the bot came down the steps. Not only were all the parents surrounding the boys and clapping loudly, but so were all their family and friends, as well as a good portion of the hotel's staff.

"That's quite a kid you have there, James." Clay's breath slid softly over her cheek.

Content, she leaned back against his chest and nodded. "Yes, he is."

They stood together as Eddie rushed up, his face lit up with happiness. He gave Ricki a quick hug, and Clay a high-five along with a fist pump, before hurrying off after Anson to help Nate and his dad load their successful bot into their truck. The boys intended to ride in the back with it as they took a victory lap through town.

Ricki and Clay walked across the ballroom side by side, heading toward the hotel lobby, trailing along in the wake of the small parade escorting the conquering heroes and their creation to the parking lot.

"TK called this morning before the sun was even up," Ricki said. "Anchorman came around last night."

Clay grinned. "That's good."

"Uh huh," Ricki agreed, a bubble of happiness and sheer relief slowly expanding inside of her. "Since he started issuing orders the minute his eyes were open, TK thinks he's going to make a full recovery."

"That's even better news," Clay said.

"When you talk to him, maybe it will help his recovery along if you let him know that Ray and his nephew have been transferred over to the county jail in Port Jefferson. They'll stand trial there." Clay tilted his chin down and smiled at her. "And after talking to the District Attorney, it sounds like you'll be a star witness."

She gave him a light jab in the side with her elbow. "You too. You were there every step of the way." She grinned up at him. "We did this together."

"Yes, we did. So, how's Dr. Blake?" he asked with a roll of his eyes. "That *was* Blake who called when we were driving over here, in that lime-green piece of junk you bought, wasn't it?"

"Charlie assures me the car is sound, and that it's a jeep classic."

Clay rolled his eyes. "It's older than Eddie, and lime green to boot. There's nothing classic about it unless butt ugly counts. And you didn't answer my question about Blake."

"Yeah, it was him on the phone, and he's fine."

Clay stuck his hands into his jacket pockets as he waited a moment, then shot her a sideways glance. "Well?"

All innocence, Ricki looked up at him. "Well, what?"

"I was sitting right next to you, Ricki. I heard you tell him that you'd let him know if you came across any other cases that you might need his help on."

"And so?"

"And so, I'm glad you're giving him the deep freeze."

Now it was Ricki who rolled her eyes.

"Glad that meets with your approval. If we're done discussing Jonathan Blake, I also heard from Josh last night." That announcement effectively distracted Clay from asking anything else about the FBI profiler, which was exactly what she'd intended to do. "He's taking some time off to search for whoever killed that deputy marshal." She hesitated as she carefully chose her words. She didn't want to keep anything from Clay, but she didn't know how he'd react to her decision either. "He might need my help. If he does, I'll be taking some time off too."

Clay nodded. "Just let me know when so I can get my request in."

Stunned, Ricki blinked, not sure what to say. "Clay, you don't need to do that. This isn't your fight."

He lifted a finger and ran it down her cheek. "I'm going to pretend I didn't hear that."

She stared up at him for a long moment, then reached over and took his hand.

They walked out of the hotel and into the parking lot, where the celebration was still going on as Bear easily lifted the forty-pound bot into the bed of the truck. Ricki laughed and cheered along with everyone else. When the party finally drove off, she smiled up at Clay.

"Pizza and beer at my place?"

His smile was tinged with regret. "Unfortunately, I have to get back to work."

Ricki grinned. "Fine. Pizza and beer at headquarters, and you're buying."

~

The End

Thank You!

Thank you for reading One Last Scream. Ricki's next case involves a murder that is very close to her—the death of her partner, Marie. Ricki faces one of her toughest cases as she finally faces her past in One Life Gone. You can grab your copy today by clicking right here: http://mybook.to/OneLifeGone

If you'd like to be the first to hear about upcoming new releases, sales, or giveaways, then please subscribe to my newsletter. In addition to receiving first notification on new releases, as well as sneak peeks into future books, you'll also be able to download a **FREE** e-book, Backcountry Murder! It's one of Ricki's first cases, and not only involves a murder in Shenandoah National Park, but it also tells the story of the first time Ricki and Anchorman Met. You don't want top miss it! Here's where you can subscribe to my newsletter and receive your **FREE** copy of Backcountry Murder! Free eBook Here!

~

I'm always interested in hearing opinions and suggestions from readers. If you like a particular character, or book, plot, setting (or if there is one you really didn't like!), I'd love to hear your thoughts. Or—if there's a national park you'd like to see in a book, or more of a favorite character or storyline—let me know. Interacting with readers on a one-on-one basis is one of the better parts of my day. (I will admit, I am not very good on the larger social media sites since I'm a little on the introverted side on those kind of stages. . . but I'm working on it). Drop me a line: Send an Email to CR Chandler

I do have a Facebook page if you'd like to drop by there as well—and maybe remind me I should be posting to it on a regular basis: https://www.facebook.com/crchandlerauthor/

Author's Note

NOTE FROM THE AUTHOR:

Dear Readers,

Time is precious, and I really appreciate you spending time to read *One Final Breath*. It's my first book under a new pen name in a new genre that I've wanted to write in for some time.

I spent most of my younger adulthood with serial killers as a regular headline in the newspapers and the leading story on the television news. I went to college in California when the Zodiac Killer was terrorizing the San Francisco Bay area. Then I moved to Seattle at the same time Ted Bundy was snatching his victims in the same vicinity where I had an apartment. And when I landed in Los Angeles? Along came the Hillside Strangler. And then came the Golden State Killer. Gravitating toward writing about murder, and the determined men and women who hunt them down and put them behind bars, has always seemed like a natural fit for me.

But without readers, it's just a story. I love hearing from readers—on plot point, characters, suggestions, critiques, and I hope you'll feel free to drop me a line whenever you want to give any kind of feedback.!

One again—thank you very much
Sincerely,
C.R. Chandler

Made in the USA
Middletown, DE
18 October 2023

41020930R00197